EV 2,00

P9-DHP-737

Everyone dreams of a place in the sun. High-rolling developer Marty Liss has made millions packaging and merchandising that dream. But for the residents of Golden Sands condominium the dream is becoming a nightmare.

The surly manager has an appetite for women, no taste for work, and an ironclad contract. And the manicured exterior of Golden Sands conceals a tangle of restless marriages and unsatisfied hungers. . . .

CONDOMINIUM combines all those elements that have made MacDonald's books bestsellers over the years—crisp dialogue, compelling narrative, and suspense that keeps the reader turning pages ever more rapidly."
            —*King Features Syndicate*

"Travels very fast and furiously, violently, grippingly. What more can we ask of a ripping catastrophe tale?"
            —*Harper's Bookletter*

"An absolute joy to read . . . Superb."
            —*Philadelphia Bulletin*

Fawcett Crest and Gold Medal Books
by John D. MacDonald:

All These Condemned
April Evil
Area of Suspicion
Ballroom of the Skies
The Beach Girls
Border Town Girl
The Brass Cupcake
A Bullet for Cinderella
Cancel All Our Vows
Clemmie
Condominium
Contrary Pleasure
The Crossroads
Cry Hard, Cry Fast
The Damned
Dead Low Tide
Deadly Welcome
Death Trap
The Deceivers
The Drowner
The Empty Trap
The End of the Night
End of the Tiger and
   Other Stories

The Executioners
A Flash of Green
The Girl, the Gold
   Watch & Everything
The House Guests
Judge Me Not
A Key to the Suite
The Last One Left
A Man of Affairs
Murder for the Bride
Murder in the Wind
The Neon Jungle
On the Run
One Monday We Killed
   Them All
The Only Girl in the Game
Please Write for Details
The Price of Murder
S*E*V*E*N
Slam the Big Door
Soft Touch
Where Is Janice Gantry?
Wine of the Dreamers
You Live Once

The Travis McGee Series

The Deep Blue Good-by
Nightmare in Pink
A Purple Place for Dying
The Quick Red Fox
A Deadly Shade of Gold
Bright Orange for the
   Shroud
Darker Than Amber
One Fearful Yellow Eye

Pale Gray for Guilt
The Girl in the
   Plain Brown Wrapper
Dress Her in Indigo
The Long Lavender Look
A Tan and Sandy Silence
The Scarlet Ruse
The Turquoise Lament
The Dreadful Lemon Sky

CONDOMINIUM

John D. MacDonald

A FAWCETT CREST BOOK • NEW YORK

CONDOMINIUM

THIS BOOK CONTAINS THE COMPLETE TEXT OF
THE ORIGINAL HARDCOVER EDITION.

Published by Fawcett Crest Books, a unit of CBS
Publications, the Consumer Publishing Division of
CBS Inc., by arrangement with J. B. Lippincott Company

Copyright © 1977 by John D. MacDonald

ALL RIGHTS RESERVED

ISBN: 0-449-23525-4

All the characters in this book are fictitious, and any
resemblance to actual persons living or dead is purely
coincidental.

Selection of the Book-of-the-Month Club

Printed in the United States of America

10 9 8 7 6 5 4 3 2 1

*This book is dedicated to these people
who were part of the good years in Sarasota
and were washed away:*

Bill Adams ● Walter and Margo Anderson ● George and Nancy Albee
Chick Austin ● Fran Barley ● Bart Bartholomew ● Les Baylis
Cosby Bernard ● Glen Berry ● Karl Bickel ● Gertie Blassingame
Don Boomhower ● Rosemary Bouden ● Ross Boyer
Dave and Sally Boylston ● Smyth Brohard ● Mary Lawrence Brown
Charles Brundage ● Vic Butterfield ● Carl Carmer ● Tom Chamales
John Z. Clarke ● Gabe Cohn ● Jack Coldwell ● Roy Cook
Jon Corbino ● Tom and Betty Crisp ● Ben Currier ● Pelham Curtis
Oscar Delano ● Bill Dobson ● A. B. Edwards ● Lee Eggers
Janet Elvgren ● Ray Englert ● Roger Flory ● Sandy French
David Gray ● Martin Griffin ● Miss Charlie Hagerman ● Randy Hagerman
Phill Hall ● Bebe Hamel ● Pop Harbert ● Jack Hasson ● Alden Hatch
Larry Heller ● Edward Burlingame Hill ● T. Dana Hill ● Al Hirshberg
Russ Hollander ● Lew Hughes ● Kent Innes ● Iz Jenkins
Harold Johnstone ● Mack Kantor ● Carleton Kelsey ● Warren Kemp
Nick Kenny ● Jim Kicklighter ● Verman Kimbrough ● Bill Kip
Reggie Lacatta ● Larry LaCava ● Jack and Liz Lambie ● Ed Langer
Hilton Leech ● Larry Lenihan ● Ray Littrell ● John Logan
Jean Ludwig ● Jim McCague ● Les MacFarlane ● Eddie Marable
Richard A. A. Martin ● Walter Martin ● Joe Marx ● Murray Mathews
Nappy Matthews ● Mike Matusak ● Pat McClerkin ● Crete McCourtney
Johns McCulley ● Oliver McGowan ● Kent McKinley ● Bill Moise
Bert Montressor ● Herman Myers ● John Newell ● Wally Norton
Bruff Olin ● Gordon Palmer ● Emmy Pete ● Glenn Potter ● Mel Potter
Harris Powers ● Ted Pratt ● Jay and Helen Protas ● Ralph Putthoff
Frank Rampola ● Loring Raoul ● Felix Reisenberg ● Jack Rhoades
Willy Robarts ● Bill Rogers ● Harry Saddler ● Bill and Janet Scher
Dave Scobie ● Taylor Scott ● Ernie Sears ● Squire Sessler
Alvord Sheen ● Eddie Shields ● Karl Shrode ● Ned Skinner
Jean Spanos ● Warren Spurge ● Lois Steinmetz ● Becky Sterling
George Storm ● Elmer Sulzer ● Hank Taylor ● Lyle Thompson
Rosie Tombs ● Maximilliano Truzzi ● Bert Twitchell ● Louise Utz
Bill and Laura Van Cleef ● Ted Wacker ● Paul Waner ● David Ward
Bill Watkins ● Joyce West ● Dorsey Wittington ● Fred Woltman
● Ed Younker

"It's a very dangerous thing to go so long between hurricanes. It just causes a larger number of incredulous people —nonbelievers."

Dr. Robert H. Simpson, Former Director
National Hurricane Center
Miami, Florida

CONDOMINIUM

1

HOWARD ELBRIGHT finally found Julian Higbee, the condominium manager, lounging against a concrete column, staring toward the pool area where two young women were taking turns diving from the low board.

"Excuse me," Elbright said. "The girl in the office thought you were maybe by the tennis courts. That's where I looked first."

Higbee, the manager, did not respond in any way. He just stood there beside Elbright, big brown arms folded, thick brown ankles crossed. He was a large and meaty fellow, and on all areas not covered by his pale blue sports shirt and his dark blue shorts, his sun-darkened hide was fuzzed with sun-bleached white hairs. On his solid jowls the hair was pale stubble. Though obviously too young a fellow for a hairpiece, his auburn hair was so carefully coifed to sweep across his forehead just above eyebrow level, it looked glossy and wiglike.

Howard Elbright wondered if the fellow could be deaf and also lack peripheral vision. Alternatively, there was the possibility that Elbright himself had become invisible and inaudible, condemned forever to wander around this bright Florida island trying to join incomprehensible conversations, trying to get people to take his money in exchange for indestructible plastic merchandise. It seemed to him he had been having dreams like that lately.

"Excuse me!" he said.

Without turning toward him, Higbee said, "The so-called girl in the office is my wife. She is Mrs. Higbee. Lorrie Higbee." He spoke in a curiously loud voice, accenting every syllable, as if accustomed to speaking to the semi-deaf.

"I didn't mean any—"

"What it was about the tennis courts, it was Colonel Simmins that lives in One-G. It was Colonel Simmins telling me there are ripples in the west service court, in the second of our two tennis courts, and his serve bounces funny. He made me watch his serve bouncing funny. Okay, so it bounces funny. So, like I told him, everybody's serve bounces funny." He spun so suddenly that he startled Howard Elbright. "Fair for one, fair for all! Right?" Julian Higbee shouted.

"I'm not a tennis player myself."

"What he should do, I told him, like I tell everybody: Take it up with your Association. That's what they are there for. That's what you elected them for. Then if they want something done, they'll come to me and they'll ask me if I can get it done. Right?"

"I guess that's right."

The manager put his big brown hand out. "My name is Julian Higbee, sir. I am the manager here. If you are interested in purchasing, there are only two units left here at beautiful Golden Sands. Five-A and Six-E. Every apartment has a breathtaking view of the Gulf of Mexico. If you are interested in renting, I can show you a wide assortment of beautifully furnished—"

"We're in Four-C."

Higbee went blank and then grinned. "That's right! I knew I'd seen you before somewhere. Moved in day before yesterday, right?"

"No. Ten days ago. May third, exactly."

"Congratulations on finding a new and rewarding lifestyle, Mister. . . . Don't tell me. Please don't tell me." Higbee closed his eyes, bowed his head, made a fist and pressed the back of his fist to his lips. He made a barely audible humming sound. "Elmore!" he yelled. "I never fail."

"It's very close. Elmore. Elbright."

"It's close enough, Mr. Elmore. What's on your mind?"

"I've got a list."

"A list? A list of what?"

"A list of things that have to be fixed. In Four-C."

"Have to be fixed? That's very strong language. Are you making a threat of some kind, Mr. Elmore?"

"Elbright. No threats. I just mean that you move into a new place, little things are always wrong and sooner or later they have to be fixed to make the place livable. For example, the air conditioning is—"

"Let's go to my office and I'll get out your file."

Higbee led the way through the parking garage. Golden Sands was an eight-story building. The parking garage, the entrance foyer and the manager's office and apartment were on the ground floor. The floor above that was called the first floor. There were seven apartments on each floor, but, because of penthouse patios, only five apartments on the top floor. Forty-seven, plus the manager's efficiency It was a pale concrete building, one apartment thick, shaped like an angular boomerang. It stood on four cramped acres of land, its rear convexity backing upon an impenetrable jungle of water oak, palmetto, mangrove and miscellaneous vines and bushes. Its concave front faced the constant noisy traffic on two-lane Beach Drive and, at a greater distance, the space between two taller beach-front condominiums and, beyond them, the wide blue Gulf of Mexico.

Higbee stopped suddenly, turned and put a big hand on Howard Elbright's shoulder, and turned him to the left and said, "Look at that! Damn it to hell, will you look at that?"

Elbright stared in the indicated direction, saw only a silver gray Oldsmobile parked with its nose toward the concrete wall of one of the storage enclosures.

"Don't you see it?" Higbee demanded. He took a steel tape out of his pocket and went to the Oldsmobile. A rear wheel was on the orange dividing line. He measured the amount of overhang, then went to the front of the car and measured the distance from the bumper to the wall.

"This is Hascoll's car. Five-F. This time he's slopped fourteen inches over the side line, and he's eight inches short of the wall. You know what that does? When there's a car over there, nobody can get by to these next two spaces, right? Then what happens? I'm watching the television and somebody comes crying they can't park their damned car. I told him once, I told him thirty times, if his old lady doesn't know how to park a car, he should park it for her. Is it too much to ask? Keep it between the lines. Touch the wall with the front bumper. Is that too much to ask? I'm telling you, you people have just got to learn how to park your cars."

Howard Elbright stared up at the young man's angry face. Howard felt his ears heat up and felt his neck swell. He knew he was not supposed to let himself get angry.

"Did you say 'you people'? Was that your phrase, Higbee?"

"What am I supposed to call you people?"

"Residents. Owners. With respect rather than derision."

"Rather than what?"

"Derision, contempt. I help pay your salary, do I not?"

"You pay for management, Mr. Elmore."

"Elbright. Then shouldn't you make an effort to please the owners here?"

"Why should I? Oh, I see. Look, you got it wrong. I don't work for you people. I work for the Gulfway Management Corporation. And Gulfway has got a twenty-year contract to manage this place. Me and Lorrie work for Gulfway. That's the people I got to please. There's no use you getting uptight about me, Mr. Elmore. You people can't do anything about me. Maybe you're better off with me than the next guy they send over here. You want to know how it works, why don't you talk with Mr. McGinnity. Seven-B. Pete McGinnity. He's president of the board of directors of the Golden Sands Association. He doesn't like it any better than you do. But there it is. Come on, let's get this list business over with."

They went into the small office off the ground-floor foyer, opposite the two elevator doors. Lorrie Higbee stopped typing when they came in. She was a small woman with long dark hair that would have hampered her vision had her eyes not been set so close together on either side of the knife bridge of a long sharp nose. In profile all that showed was the end of the nose projecting from beyond a sheaf of shiny black hair. Head on, the visible items were the small dark eyes, the long nose and a ripe red bulge of underlip.

"Mrs. Fish has been calling you," she said.

"What about?"

"She wouldn't say."

"Get the file on Four-C."

Mrs. Higbee went over to a file cabinet. She wore pale faded jeans, tighter than anything except the very best skin. Howard Elbright tried not to stare at her breasts wobbling unrestrained under her yellow T-shirt.

She brought Higbee the file. Higbee sat at the larger desk and waved Elbright into the visitor's chair. "Got that list? He's got a list, Lorrie. How about that?"

Elbright took it out of his wallet and unfolded it and read aloud, slowly and carefully. "The water which comes out of the hot faucets is quite warm, but not hot. The rain comes in under the sliding glass doors in the living room and the front bedroom. There seem to be two refrigerator shelves missing. The compressor on the air conditioner makes a loud yelping noise. The shower door will not close completely. The hot and cold controls on the sink in the smaller bathroom are reversed. The bathtub in the larger bathroom is badly chipped. The interior of one closet was never painted. Two wall plugs seem to be dead. There is a sizable crack in the balcony railing outside the living room."

"Is that all?"

"Thus far."

"Thus far? Okay, now do you remember coming into this office the day you arrived?"

"I do."

"What happened?"

"Happened? You . . . gave me the keys and a stack of literature."

"You're leaving out the most important part. Right in front of me and Lorrie you signed this here. You'll find a copy of it in with the literature, right?"

Howard Elbright had difficulty with the fine print. He read it with a growing dismay. He had certified that the apartment was acceptable to him in all respects, that all work had been completed, and the builder and the developer were relieved of any responsibility whatsoever for incomplete or unsatisfactory work or equipment.

"You said it was a formality," he said accusingly.

"That's what it is. A formal binding agreement. You don't believe me, see a lawyer. What you should have done, you should have taken a day or two to check it out, right?"

"My furniture was here. In the truck."

"You could have put it in storage. Anyway, I'll tell you what I can do for you, Elmore. I think I can get you those missing shelves with no problem. I think I got some in storage we didn't know where they went. About the air conditioner, you got the warranty papers on it, and the address of where it come from, and you can handle it yourself. Matter of fact, you can handle any of this stuff on your list yourself, getting a plumber, an electrician, a painter, whatever. Or you can let me go ahead. You let me do it, and it will be Gulfway's cost plus ten percent. What my advice would be, you let me handle it because Gulfway can get some crew from the builder that put up this place, and you ought to do better even with the ten percent than when you go outside by yourself, not being acquainted locally. The way it works, you let me do it, it will come through on your monthly billing in addition to the management fee and the land lease and the recreation lease and so on."

"But either way, I have to pay for every one of these things?"

"There's no way I can give you any free gifts, Elmore."

"Elbright. Please. Mr. Elbright. Think up a word association to help you remember. I was not very bright to sign that damned agreement. Bright. Elbright."

"That's pretty good, Mr. Elbright. Isn't that pretty good, Lorrie?"

"Fan . . . tastic," she said in a dead voice.

"I won't forget it again ever," Higbee said. "I've got an almost perfect memory."

"Ha," said Lorrie.

"You want me to take care of the list?"

Howard folded it and put it back in his wallet. "I'll let you know."

"Suit yourself. To me it's just another nuisance, but that's what I'm here for, right?"

Howard thought he could hear Higbee laughing after the door was closed. As he walked toward the elevators his ears got warm again. He pushed the button. One came down from three, empty. He rode it up to four, got off and turned left, toward the north wing. Four-C was the second door he came to as he walked along the narrow exterior walkway, behind the chest-high concrete wall.

He took his key out, but before entering his own domain he leaned against the wall and looked out toward the east, across the jungly acres to the pale silvery blue of Palm Bay and the misty mainland beyond.

You are now a retired chemist, he told himself. You are a very happy retired chemist, because you live in your fifty-eight-thousand-dollar condominium right here in Golden Sands on Fiddler Key with your loving wife. Your kids are grown and doing well enough. You have the use of an easement to the beach (thirty feet wide, no vehicles permitted) and an easement to the bay shore (twenty feet wide, no vehicles permitted). You are in reasonably good health (one infarction, healed). Edith too (high blood pressure difficult to control). Repeat: You are very happy, Howard. This is the Great American Dream. Enjoy.

Edith was in the kitchen slicing a tomato. "You were so *long*," she said.

"We retired fellows take a long time over everything."

She looked at him. "Is everything okay, dear?"

"Everything is just fine."

"Will they start soon? Not having hot water is driving me up my new walls."

"I'll keep after them, never fear."

"There wasn't any trouble, was there, about anything?"

"What kind of trouble could anybody give me? I am immune," he said. He hugged her and went into the living room and knelt and tried to figure out how the rain could come under the sliding doors. As he knelt there he had the grotesque feeling that he was part of some mass ritual, that up and down this west coast of Florida, on all these narrow elongated offshore islands tucked close to the sub-tropic mainland and named Clearwater Beach and Anna Maria and Longboat, Siesta Key and Casey Key and Manasota Key and Seagrape Key and this one he was on, Fiddler Key, there were thousands of sixty-two-year-old retired chemists named Howard something, all living in these tall pale structures by the sea, all of them at this moment kneeling and facing their sliding glass doors and wondering how the rainwater managed to seep in and stain their pastel shags. Face west, all you plump old men, and ponder your tropic fates.

2

GUTHRIE GARVER, known as Gus, was a small, quiet, knotty man. He and Carolyn had been the first couple to move into Golden Sands. They had moved into 1-C two days after the building was given a certificate of occupancy, when the land around it was still raw, with no swimming pool, tennis courts, or surfaced parking areas behind the building. One year ago last month, April.

He was a sallow man with a white brush cut. He looked like a bleached Indian. When he swam in the pool, he revealed a spare, heavy-boned body, with nicks and slices and welts of scar tissue on tough hide which slid across the strings and slabs and lumps of lifelong muscle. He had spent his life on construction jobs, most of them very large and in very far places. He liked solid structure, well specified, well planned, competently built.

Consequently he despised Golden Sands, but having

spent six months looking at condominiums up and down Florida's southwest coastline, he admitted to himself that he had not yet seen one he could not learn to despise. Carolyn had loved her bright clean shiny apartment. To her it was the symbol of the end of travel, a place for roots without the ever-present fear Gus would be sent somewhere else.

After long deliberation Gus had told her one evening that if he couldn't put up a better building using only toad shit and wax paper, he'd resign from the profession. But this upset her so badly and so obviously, he convinced her he was only kidding and vowed to himself not to mention his doubts to her again.

They had their first Christmas together in the apartment, and a week later over at Beach Mall Shopping Plaza, only a quarter mile south, Carrie had slipped on a banana skin and broken her hip. That was the old comedy routine. Banana skin. She had been pushing the loaded cart as they walked toward their car. When she fell she shoved it out ahead into the path of a tourist Cadillac. Most of the groceries went up in the air and fell onto the hood and windshield. As Gus knelt by Carrie trying to figure out how badly she was hurt, he was bothered by the stout florid man from the Cadillac who was bending over Gus yammering about who would pay to have his car repaired. At last Gus lost patience and stood up and said, "Hush!" At the same time he pushed two rigid fingers into the fellow's belly, two inches above the belt buckle. The man bent over and lowered himself to the asphalt pavement and sat like a fat baby, gray-faced and quiet.

They operated on Carrie and pinned her hip. A week later she went into pneumonia, and they moved her into Intensive Care and then had to perform a tracheotomy. Just as she was finally recovering from the pneumonia, she had a stroke which paralyzed her whole right side. In mid-February he was able to move her into a nursing home. He had medical disaster insurance through an ASCE group policy, so his out-of-pocket expenses were 25 percent of her $9,000 hospital bill, less that portion covered by Medicare.

In early April the doctor told Gus Garver that he could make a reasonable guess as to the permanent disability to be expected. There was some return of function to the large muscles of the right side, but he doubted it would ever be possible for her even to sit up without help, much less walk. Regarding communication, the stroke had destroyed that part of the left lobe of the brain which deals with the comprehension of speech and writing.

"The condition is called aphasia. Sometimes, in younger patients, the right side of the brain can be trained to take over communication. But one could not hope for such a result in the case of your wife, sir. Yes, to a certain extent she is aware of her surroundings. And she would recognize you, yes. As you may have noted, she attempts to communicate on a subverbal level, to make simple wants known with . . . those sounds. Words are essential to the processes of thought, we now believe. Much of our thinking is in word forms. Deprived of the tools of words, the processes become more primitive and simplified: hot, cold, hungry, thirsty. No, I wouldn't say her life expectancy is seriously impaired. At sixty-three she is quite a healthy woman, aside from her traumatic infirmities."

By mid-April Gus Garver had adjusted his needs to his resources. There was Social Security, the pension, the savings, the investments, the insurance and Medicare. The logical thing to do would be sell the apartment and find something to rent near the nursing home. But that seemed, somehow, to be letting go of life, even though he knew Carrie would probably never come home again. She seemed to be more present, the Carrie of memories, in the bright clean apartment than in her small shadowy room in the home. He sensed that it was good for him to take care of the apartment, serve as a member of the five-man board of directors of the Association, cook for himself, go grocery shopping, take the laundry down to the bank of coin machines at ground level. It created the subconscious feeling that she would one day return unimpaired, and he could not sustain that myth were he to move out.

He saw Carrie for two hours each day, from three until five. He would sit at the left side of the bed, her good side, or at the left side of her chair and hold her hand and they would watch the small screen of the television set he had gotten for her. It did not matter to her whether the sound was off or on. She watched the movement and the color. He sat and thought back to a flood-control project in Assam, a highway in Peru, an airfield in Fiji, thought of dead friends and jungle mountains, village cantinas and village maidens, rock slides and typhoons, while in the silent room on the back street of this small city of Athens, Florida, he watched without comprehension the prancings and grimacings of the game-show masters.

Whenever he had any free time, he examined the structure of Golden Sands. It stood upon pilings which reached an unknown distance down into the native marl. He estimated there would have to be over three hundred of them. From the ones he could inspect he saw that they were set to a minimum of fourteen inches diameter. Reasonable safety factor would call for a working capacity of fifty tons each.

Sure, the architect and the project engineer could call for any specifics they wanted. Fifty tons apiece. Forty-foot depth. ASTM standards. Minimum compressive strength of four thousand psi after four weeks. You could call for independent testing lab reports. You could watch them like eagles.

But these were uncased auger-drilled poured pilings, with the grout in direct contact with the native materials. All concrete was supposed to be pumped into the hole under steady positive pressure as the auger was pulled. And the grout had to be first class. Good cement up to federal specs, commercial-grade fly ash, fresh clean water, some Pozzolith #8 retarder or equivalent, and fine aggregate, all measured and mixed in spanking clean equipment.

To do it right you had to have men who knew what they were doing and were committed to doing it according to the book. Gus Garver couldn't inspect the underground pilings, but he could inspect the visible cast-in-place concrete and make a judgment of the piling work from that.

Over a period of weeks he had made notes of the defects he had found. He found construction joints badly located, impairing the strength of the structure. He found one where the bond at the joint was faulty. Where one pour stops, after the concrete has set, it is necessary to sandblast the face of it, scouring away the cement down to the exposed coarse aggregate solidly embedded in mortar. Then, before the new pour is made against that face, all the debris and dried drippings have to be blown out by compressed air. He found a hairline crack in a joint, and when he found two places along the crack too deep for the blade of his penknife, he had returned with a two-foot length of stiff leader wire and satisfied himself that the joint had been carelessly prepared in addition to being badly located.

He found joint marks and fins, surface voids and stone pockets, irregularities and leakage stains. In a bearing surface area where he knew that the specifications had called for class-A concrete, he found a wall in the garage portion where the pour had been skimpy, where he estimated cement content at four sacks per yard instead of six. He could tell by the look of it, by the sandy feel, by the way he could scrape it away with his pocket knife. He found a stone pocket in that wall and stuck the blade of his knife into it and worked the stones loose easier than he should have been able to. In earthquake country, he thought, the damned wall would come down like a giant Nabisco.

All the finish work seemed to be good enough. He did not pay much attention to it. It was all cosmetics. He was concerned with stress, with the ability of the materials, as used, to withstand all anticipated stress. Put something up and you want it to stay.

He could not make as informative an inspection of the prestressed concrete work. He knew only that it was more complicated and there were thus more things which could be done badly or not at all. The forms could lack the rigidity to prevent displacement by an external vibrator. The inserts could be installed a little bit off. The hidden tubes, ducts, spacer bars, anchorages and so on could have been improperly secured in place before the pour. Some congenital damned fool could have attached imbedded inserts to the main stressed steel. They could have skimped on the shoring during construction and gotten too much deflection in the stressed members. Some could even have been repaired after chipping or cracking, rather than replaced. The wires, strands and bars could be under-specified in some instances, and random sampling couldn't hope to catch it all.

The structure seemed to Gus to have been properly designed and engineered. It had that look. The elements and components were of sufficient size and apparent sturdiness. And he knew that good engineering adds a sufficient safety factor to overcome the minor goofs and oversights during normal construction, the ones not caught by inspectors and specialists. But in genuinely sloppy concrete work, as this seemed to him to be, there comes a point where the accumulated goofs eat up all the safety factor, and then if there is enough stress on any portion, enough to crumble it or crack it, the deflection is transmitted to other portions of the structure. They in turn crack or twist or crumble, and the whole thing comes down.

He remembered—what year was it, 1957?—going into Mexico City from the south after the earthquake. Mike had parked the Rover on the east side of Insurgentes, and they had put on their hard hats and walked across to take a look at what was left of the apartment house which had come down two nights previously. It would be impossible to determine just where the first failure occurred, but once it started, all the slab floors came down, one atop the other, so that something almost a hundred feet high was transmuted into a rubbly pile about sixteen feet high. The slab floor had remained curiously intact, forming a horrid sandwich, ten slices of bread with thin dollops of meat between them. Mike had picked up a piece of concrete as big as a walnut and had kneaded it between his powerful fingers until it crumbled to dust. He slapped the dust off his hands and gestured toward the work crews and said, "The folks were in bed when the jolt brought it down. Some Mexican comedian owned it." They did not have to discuss the problems of mixing good structural concrete. Or the penalty for not doing it right.

But, of course, Florida is not earthquake country.

He kept wondering about the underground pilings, and finally he checked and found out that the piling contractor on the job had been Romez Foundations. He found out they were down on Riley Key, putting in pilings. In dark pants and white shirt, wearing an aluminum hard hat and carrying a clipboard, Gus Garver went onto the job and roamed, unimpeded. Once he was asked what he wanted, and he said he was with the State Bureau of Regulatory Services, and was told that if he wanted anything, just ask.

The equipment looked overworked and undermaintained. The crew was slow and slovenly. Gus tasted the water they were using. It was salty, brackish. He was there an hour. He saw two interrupted pours. In each case the reason was the same. The auger evidently bit into some underground cavity in the underlying limestone, and then the pour used more yards of concrete than was immediately available. So they stopped and, after ten minutes, resumed pouring into the same auger hole, brought it up to the surface form, shoved in the reinforcing bars and poured the cap.

Checking the foundation work stimulated his curiosity about how these narrow islands so close offshore had been formed. He made his guess and proved it correct at the Athens Public Library. A very long time ago Florida had been under the sea. As the seas receded and the land rose, great rivers had come roaring off the mainland into the Gulf of Mexico, fed by continuing cloudbursts. When the seas retreated farther and the rivers shrank, these offshore islands appeared, composed of the materials the rivers had carried down to the sea and deposited in their delta areas. Thus they were quite unlike the true Florida keys, from Key Largo down to Key West, a long huge dead reef, composed of the googols of skeletal remains of tiny dead sea creatures.

Googol was one of the words which pleased him. It was easier than trying to say the figure one followed by one hundred zeros. And it pleased him to be right about the geological history of these false keys, which were alluvial deposits, long windrows of marl, of shell washed down the rivers and deposited and compacted over the centuries, slowly acquiring the living plants and the top-soil and the white ribbons of seaward beach.

It accounted for the narrowness of the bays which separated these islands from the Florida west coast mainland, and their similarities in structure, elevation and flora.

At night, alone in Apartment 1-C, in the dark bedroom silence, Gus Garver could feel the tangible weight of the six stories over him. And he could see, quite vividly and specifically, one of the underground pilings at the Riley Key project where the pour had been interrupted. During the ten-minute wait, there had been water seepage from the rough sides of the augered hole, bringing down with it bits of shell and marl and soil to form a thin layer atop the wet concrete. The new pour had not displaced this debris. It remained, like a form of insulation, weakening the bond between the two pours, creating the future fracture line, the place where it would go in the event lateral stress was ever placed upon it.

Wouldn't have to be lateral, he thought. Assume the mix was heavy and during the ten-minute wait it set up at a fifteen-degree tilt from the horizontal. Then, if the native materials in the side wall are soft enough, sufficient vertical stress could force slippage. On the other hand, during the ten-minute wait, a couple of bushels of dry shell could have tumbled onto the old pour and there could be no damn bond at all between the bottom of the piling and the top of the piling. And they wouldn't know it.

Okay, smart-ass engineer, how would you handle it if you had to pour right in that spot, and for some reason you ran out of grout? Hmmm. Pull the auger and the pressure pipe and shine a good light down the hole and make visual inspection. Drop a length of number-six reinforcing bar down and see how much sticks up out of the first pour. Ideal would be a twelve-foot length, with six in and six up. Drop about five of them, and on the new pour make it a little wetter, less aggregate, so the bar would help make a solid joint. They might end up too close together or too close to the exterior of the piling, but it was a lot better answer than nothing at all.

Thinking of the bars made him think of all the reinforcing steel in the building around him, under him and over him. All the marginal bars with their dowels and splices, the deformed bars and the melded wire fabric, all the supports and spacers and mesh.

He made a mental list of the things which could go wrong with all the reinforcing steel. Too long a wait—over an hour—before the tension reinforcing of the pilings. Steel with grease on it, or too much rust, or with mill scale on it. Bad welds. Too few dowels from footings to walls. Undersized bars. Brittle tie wire. Unstaggered splices in adjoining bars. Bending and field cutting of bars around openings and sleeves. Fast sloppy pours that left voids under and around the reinforcing, or knocked the bars off the chairs, unnoticed.

No, this was not earthquake country, but it was waterfront, and this was a low island indeed, and there was a great warm shallow sea out there, where the big storms come a-roving in season.

At night he began to think of structure in relation to the sea and the tides, and he began to think of Sam Harrison, who, as a green tough kid, had worked for him not too many years ago. They come on the job and you size them up. There are three kinds. The first kind can't hack it, for all the reasons known to man, and so you ease them out before they kill themselves or, worse, kill somebody else who is worth their wages. The second type you look for, because you can keep them a long time. They are competent, loyal, diligent and quite happy to have somebody else take the career risks and the money risks. Sam Harrison was of the third variety. At first you think they belong in number-two class. But then you slowly learn that they are doing just a little bit more than you asked for, and doing it a little better than you thought possible. Then, feet on solid ground, they start coming to you with innovative ways of doing things more easily and quickly, and some you approve and some you don't. Then you know what you have on your hands. So you make an extra effort to keep them on the team as long as you can, knowing you are going to lose them. The Sam Harrisons always get restive. They have to run their own store. It is the only way for them. So, when the highway and the bridges were finished in the Peruvian mountains, Sam went his own way.

Sam had gone to follow his own most intense area of interest, man's efforts to tame the sea. In lonely places when work is done there is time for talk. Sam had said that you can't tame it, you can't overwhelm it by force. You have to comprehend the way the sea uses its power, and use its own strength to make it defeat itself. Gus had heard later how Sam Harrison, in his first job, had devised a new kind of dog-bone groin which, laid in rail-fence fashion and laced with cable, had rebuilt a Spanish beach without causing the usual deep erosion down-current from the groin.

This was the sort of problem Sam Harrison would like to tackle. Relate the remaining safety factor in the construction of Golden Sands to the possible and probable impact of hurricane tides this far from the actual beach front of Fiddler Key, and recommend measures to be taken. It would be no great feat finding him. But paying his fee would be. There are too few Sam Harrisons in the world at any one time, and they are in demand.

And so, thinking again about his list of defects, he drifted into sleep, where he stood on the lip of a deep river gorge in Peru watching his survey crew work out the precise dimensions of the span he had calculated from the aerials. . . .

3

MARTIN LISS STOOD on the blue pile carpeting by the big corner windows of his office on the mainland, in downtown Athens, and looked out across the roofs of smaller buildings toward the bay and toward the caramel and vanilla buildings along the beach front of Fiddler Key. It was a clear hot windy day, a breeze off the Gulf blowing the usual smutch inland. The big windows were tinted blue-gray. The north bridge over to Fiddler Key was open to let a small sailboat through, the stacked traffic glittering in the mid-morning sunlight. He could see the red markers of the Intracoastal Waterway spaced down the middle of broad Palm Bay, and he wondered how long it would be before he could get the *LissLess III* out of freshwater storage and go cruising.

He was a short plump man in his forty-third year. The lifts in his shoes brought him up to five foot six and a fraction. He was deeply, permanently tan. The entire front half of his head was bald. From that midpoint the hair was combed straight back, falling in dark ringlets over his collar. He wore a small goatee, black salted with gray, squared off. He had a third wife he mistrusted and two grown children he despised.

For a week he had experienced that familiar hollow breathless feeling which meant it was decision time. It was the high-roller feeling. After a series of straight passes, do you drag down, or do you try to make just one more pass?

From his windows on the twelfth floor of the Athens Bank and Trust Company, he could see the jungle-green fourteen acres of the Silverthorn tract on the bay side of Fiddler Key, with the familiar shape of Golden Sands just beyond it. Beyond Golden Sands, across Beach Drive, rose the higher towers of Azure Breeze and the Surf Club. Martin Liss did not see only the fourteen raw uncleared acres. His mind superimposed upon it the architect's rendering of the Harbour Pointe Club with its 168 units, tennis courts, pools, yacht basin and clubhouse.

The concept represented thirteen months of planning, negotiating and spending. Twenty-eight thousand for an option on the land, not recoverable no matter what, against the price of $1.28 million. One hundred thousand spent on architectural fees, legal fees and other service fees. Allocation to payroll and personal expenses of the Harbour Pointe Club project, say fifty thousand.

Now it could be started. No more roadblocks. Corps of Engineer approval, approvals from four departments of the State of Florida, from three regional commissions, from five Palm County governmental bodies, and even from the Fiddler Key Association. The contractors were lined up. An $11-million line of credit was all established. The feasibility study indicated that, after sellout, there would be a $2.8-million net before taxes. Or fold the whole tent right now and swallow the loss of the out-of-pocket hundred and seventy-eight thousand. It would be a legitimate business loss for the Marliss Corporation.

Arguments in favor of folding it: Seventy-five thousand unsold condominium units in Florida, either completed or being constructed. Brutal interest rates. Fantastic prices for materials. A whole world on the slide into depression. And right now you could cash in for how much? Three and a half mil? Cashing in is the wrong term, being as how most of it is already in Treasury notes. So right now, dummy, you could put it into those municipals that are guaranteed by the Fed and paying like six and a half almost tax free, make it a net two hundred thou tax free. Rent a damn palace at Acapulco. The best booze and the best broads. Big staff. Keep house parties going for weeks at a time.

And never have this feeling in the gut again? Never feel the queasy flutter of risk-taking, of high rolling, of doing things they said you'd never pull off?

Arguments in favor of going ahead: When things look the blackest, then is the time to make your move, because you get the jump on the ones holding back. The politicians can't risk big unemployment. They'll goose the economy. The government protects industrial pensions. Social Security will keep going up. They have to come to Florida. Where else can they go? They'll keep coming down and all you are betting, Marty, is that one hundred and sixty-eight of them will be able to spring for an average eighty-thousand-dollar apartment, sixty for the cheapest, a hundred for the tops. They'll be on the water with an easement to the beach. They'll keep coming until there's no more water to drink or air to breathe, and that is a long time off. Like five years? And I can be in and out in two—*if* I decide to go ahead. Jesus Christ, it *is* scary.

Miss Drusilla Bryne tapped upon his door and came in, a tall slender handsome girl, a blue-eyed brunette with delicate features and a strong Dublin accent. "It's the ones from Golden Sands, darlin'. Maggie says they're in reception a bit early."

"The who?"

"The delegation. Four, not five, so one is missing. And one is a Mr. McGinnity, their president."

He frowned. "Oh, shit! I forgot. Would you get me my confidential file on Golden Sands?"

"There on the corner of your desk where I put it not an hour ago, love."

"So what are the rest of the instructions?"

She laughed. "Oh, to tape it, in case there's any threats at all. And to stay at my desk and watch the little box, so if the blue light comes on I can come in and tell you you have something important to do. And . . . hmmm . . . tell Lew to stand by in case you should call him in for some legal matter."

"Almost perfect. The only other thing is give them the coffee routine, the first-class version."

"They're all that important now?"

"No. But they are going to be very pissed. Benji's arithmetic was way off."

"You'll tell me when to go bring them?"

"It'll be about five minutes."

She went out and he opened the folder. Two left unsold: 5-A at seventy-two five, and 6-E at seventy-five. And they had been transferred from the Marliss Corporation to Investment Equities, Inc., for a total of a hundred and ten thousand, severing the last direct connection between Golden Sands and Martin Liss. No, not quite the last direct connection to be severed. That severance happened early last month, in early April when they held the meeting of all the owners in the communal dayroom on the first floor at Golden Sands. Up until the meeting, the officers and directors of the Golden Sands Association had been Martin Liss, president; Lew Traff, vice-president; Benjie Wannover, treasurer; Drusilla Bryne, secretary; and Cole Kimber, director at large.

It made for a cozy relationship, to have a board composed of the developer; his secretary; his attorney, Lew Traff; his accountant, Benjamin Wannover; and the contractor who had built the place, Cole Kimber. It was the same team he had fielded on his other condominium projects on Fiddler Key: Captiva House, Azure Breeze and the Surf Club.

During the period they had held office, better than a year, they had operated the association according to the provisions of the Declaration of Condominium, as drawn up by Lew Traff. They had made the contracts, set up the Association obligations, devised the rules for the owners, amending the Declaration of Condominium whenever useful or convenient.

Prior to the April meeting, they had appointed a nominating committee, and at the meeting the owners accepted the resignations of the original five directors and voted the five new ones into office.

The names of the new directors were in his confidential folder. They were all retired. He remembered the meeting. Three of the ablest owners, when approached by the committee prior to the meeting, had refused to serve, saying they had had enough of responsibility before retirement. And that, Martin knew, was a mistake. If the Association was well run, it would be a good place to live. If the new officers were not qualified, it would go downhill quickly. They all had a substantial investment to protect.

He ran quickly through the names, trying to remember the faces. He had attended many of these meetings. Except for variations in size, they were all about the same. He had written the prior occupations opposite the names. McGinnity, VP and sales manager of an industrial belt company in Pennsylvania. Forrester, partner in a Cleveland ad agency. David Dow, CPA from Indianapolis. Wasniak, plant manager from Youngstown. Garver, civil engineer from Baltimore.

Very probably he would remember the faces when they walked in. He wondered how ugly they would come on, and how well organized they would be. They had come to let off steam. And that was all it would be. Steam. Hot wet air.

He leaned to the intercom and said, "Okay, Dru."

"Lew won't be available. He'd already left for the airport. He's meeting that man who's coming about the claim."

"It's okay. I probably won't need him."

He got up and opened his office door and stood in the doorway. Soon he saw Drusilla leading the four grim-faced men through her office. She was smiling back over her shoulder, chattering about how lovely it was indeed to see them again.

McGinnity had to be the big broad one with the red face, potato nose and shaven skull. So greet him warmly by name, shake his hand long enough to identify Wasniak as the one with the shoulders and the hair dyed rusty brown. Take a chance that Dow is the one with the glasses. Right! So the lanky and consumptive-looking one is either Forrester or Garver. Had to be Forrester. So look around and say, "Where is Mr. Garver? He couldn't make it?"

McGinnity was put off balance by the cordiality, trying to smile and trying not to smile. "Gus may be along later. He hasn't been . . . very active. Because his wife is so sick."

"Come on in, gentlemen. Miss Bryne, I think we would all like coffee. Come on in. Let's sit over here."

One corner of the large office was furnished like the corner of a lounge in a men's club—with a couch and three leather chairs arranged around a big slate coffee table. Martin Liss maneuvered himself onto the couch with McGinnity beside him and the CPA at his right. It broke up their formation. Forrester unzipped a leather portfolio and took a sheaf of papers out of it. He put the portfolio on the coffee table and placed the papers on top of it, saying, "We have been over the—"

"On my bathroom radio this morning I heard on the local news there's some red tide off the south end of the key," Martin said. "Can you notice anything where you are?"

Wasniak shrugged and said, "I jog every morning right about dawn to an hour after. This morning I got the old tickle in the throat and I didn't know what it was, and then I said oh-oh and I started looking for dead fish. In six miles, three down the beach and three back, I counted seven dead fish, not big, dead a long time, they looked."

Liss shook his head. "It's a terrible thing. I hope we're not in for a summer of it. Important scientists are working on it, but they seem to come up empty. Ah, our coffee wagon, gentlemen."

Dru Bryne wheeled her stainless steel cart in. She put the big hot coffee urn on the table and plugged it in. McGinnity said coffee was off his list. Drusilla, with a deepening accent, asked him if she might bring him a nice cup of Irish tea, and he beamed and said that would be nice. She filled the other four cups, large cups, bone white and delicate. She put out the sugar and cream and the dish of scones and the dish of ginger cookies and the spoons and the small linen napkins. In her serving she managed, in some mysterious way which Martin had never been able to dissect, to make each man feel she was treating him in a more special way, to make each man feel he and she had some unspoken secret between them.

As soon as she left to get McGinnity's tea, Martin Liss became very sincere and slightly oratorical. "Gentlemen, a piece of my life went into all the planning and the accomplishment of Golden Sands. I am proud of it. It is a unique life-style, a unique and distinctive place to live. I feel that when I can bring together the dream and the reality, then I am making my contribution to the society in which we live. Golden Sands was one of those dreams, and now it is a reality. I want to tell you that even though I no longer have any legal or financial connection with it whatsoever, I will always feel a responsibility to give my advice and counsel to the directors of the Association, whoever they may be. That is why my door is open to you today. Now please tell me how I can be of any help to you."

Hadley Forrester was the first to recover. He even managed to look amused. "First, to explain our position, Mr. Liss, at Pete McGinnity's direction Dave Dow and I have worked up a little presentation, which will show you the shape and size of the problem."

Martin smiled and nodded, and the little voice in the back of his skull said, Look out for this one, Marty.

Forrester said, "Though we have been over this many times, I think we should all be looking at the figures along with Mr. Liss." He handed out the sheets. "Every purchaser of an apartment made his decision to buy based upon average monthly charges of $81.50, or $978 a year. This was supposed to cover the management contract, the recreational lease, normal maintenance and incidentals. Now look at the next page. At the top are the fixed expenses, the contractural obligations of the Association, as made by the previous officers and directors. Following that total are the other, more flexible expenses: elevator maintenance, lawn and landscaping maintenance—which we had thought was covered in the management contract but isn't—pool service, outside lighting, and so on and so on and so on. At the end there you will find a reasonable amount as a provision for reserves for future maintenance problems. All the bills are in. Everything has been analyzed and investigated. The annual budget is $91,000. Divide that by forty-five apartments, and the average monthly tab comes to $168.50."

"That much!" Martin Liss said, with warmth and concern.

"In addition," Forrester continued, "we find that you left us a little over eighty dollars in the Association checking account as of April first. We collected the full assessment from all owners last month and this month: $3,667.50 each month. These monies have been expended. Because the assessments were too small, we have a two-month deficit of $7,830. That means the bills that go out on June first will have to be for the new average figure of $168.50, *plus* an emergency assessment of $174 to catch up: $342.50 for the average apartment. We have to make a total assessment of $15,412.50, and our chances of collecting it all are slim. Our first question is this: Why were the old assessments so far out of line?"

Drusilla brought McGinnity's steaming tea and was warmly thanked.

Marty Liss said, "Let me go way back. Let me give you the history of that $81.50 estimate. That figure was worked out when we were doing the original feasibility studies, over four years ago. Benjie worked it out. You all know Benjie Wannover. He has a very sharp pencil, usually. But in the beginning we were dealing with a density factor of twenty units per acre. Before we could lock everything up, the Planning Board recommended new densities to the County Commission and that whole area got reduced to twelve units per acre. It was originally planned for eighty units. That assessment was based on eighty units, and, I am frank to admit, we slipped up. We never revised it to apply to the forty-seven units we've got there. Let me tell you something else, my friends. I slipped up because I kept noticing that the cost of sales at Golden Sands was way too high, and I never got off my duff to check it out and find out why. You see, during that whole year the Marliss Corporation was picking up the slack between actual costs and assessments. And let me tell you, when there was only a dozen owners paying that $81.50 a month, the slack was very heavy. I should have gotten it boosted, but I was asleep at the switch."

David Dow cleared his throat and said, "And the lower assessment made it easier to sell the apartments, didn't it?"

Martin sipped his coffee and put the cup down, smiled, spread his hands and said, "Are we here to make childish accusations not based on fact, or are we here to solve problems?"

"I don't think David was making an accusation," Forrester said. "I think he was stating a fact. We've come to ask your help in getting the assessments and the budget back to a reasonable size."

"In these days and times, and considering the location and the advantages, maybe the new budget is about right."

"We have people who can't pay it," McGinnity said.

"Mister President McGinnity, the people *have* to pay it. It is that simple. In the Declaration you can read in black and white that failure to pay the assessment gives the Association a lien against the apartment in question. You four men have all got personal liability insurance at Association expense. You've got fidelity bonds likewise. So you are protected against suit. So what you have to do is move on the people who try to refuse to pay. Like my brother-in-law one time in Tenafly, a nice piece of property with a nice home and four great big beautiful elm trees. So all of a sudden the elm trees are dead of the Dutch elm disease and the town ordinance says they have to be removed and he has to pay. So it was twelve hundred dollars a tree, and a forty-eight-hundred-dollar lien against his house. He didn't have the money, but he found it. When he found out what they could do to him, he had to find the money."

"We have mostly retired people on fixed incomes," McGinnity said. "Some of them just can't swing it."

Martin made a sad face. "In this life people are always biting off more than they can chew. Businesses go under. Cars get repossessed. If a person buys an expensive apartment and then can't handle it because costs go up by eighty dollars more a month, than what kind of judgment did he use when he bought it? We all want to be our brother's keeper, and I say it's because too many times our brother needs a keeper. He needs somebody coming after him with a net."

"We're getting away from the point," Forrester said. "We want to question the morality, if not the legality, of the recreation lease agreement in the Declaration. The lease payments come to twelve thousand five hundred dollars a year, twenty-three dollars per apartment per month. It is a ninety-nine-year lease, with an escalator clause that ties the annual payments to the cost of living index. Over the life of the lease, that comes to one and a quarter million dollars. The lease covers the pool, the tennis courts and the dayroom. We want you to make it possible for the Association to buy those facilities. We have to maintain them as it is."

"Now how in the world could I do that?" asked Martin in blank astonishment. "I don't own that lease."

"We pay the money to Investment Equities. Isn't that one of your corporations?"

Martin looked incredulous. "One of *mine?* What kind of a weird idea is that? What I am there is a minority stockholder. I have a little bit of stock only because a friend of mine runs it, name of Frank West, and he let me buy a little, not much. It's an investment group, and it does okay. Developers get pinched, maybe oftener than other kinds of business. I'm willing to tell you that when Frank came to me to buy the recreation lease, I was glad to get the cash money to pay off against my bank loan. The interest was killing me. I'm not at liberty to tell you what Frank paid for the lease. I'd say it was a good deal for him and a good deal for me. To do what you say, I would have to go to Frank with the money in my hand and buy that lease back. That would be the first thing. Would he sell? I doubt it. Where would I get the money? From the Golden Sands Association? Why don't I tell you what he paid for it? Why not? It is like buying a bond that brings in twelve thousand five interest a year, with a little sweetening on account of the escalator. He paid a hundred and five thousand. If you can dig that much up, I promise I'll try to buy that lease back. Otherwise . . ." He shrugged.

After about twenty seconds of unhappy and thoughtful silence, Wasniak said, "Well, maybe you can do something about that management contract that runs for twenty years. We've got that clown Julian Higbee saddled on us who won't do a single damned thing anybody asks."

"The way I size up Julian, I think he is willing to learn. I think he is anxious to do a good job for you. Your previous directors gave a lot of thought to the problem before they placed the contract with Gulfway Management, and we made it a long contract in order to get the most favorable terms. I don't think you men realize what a good deal you have there. Because Julian and Lorrie also handle that thirty-unit Captiva House next to you there, it cuts the cost to Golden Sands. You want to bust the contract, throw the Higbees out and hire your own manager, right? You have no idea what you would be getting into. Julian is the sales agent and the rental agent. Lorrie keeps good books, clean and accurate. They make a good team. You hire people to do the same jobs, do you want to get into bonding, withholding, Social Security on them and the maids? You want to get into linen service, advertising, brochures: crap like that? I get the feeling there isn't one of you men hunting for a full-time job running that place, and that's what it is."

Hadley Forrester said, "The Higbees may be jewels beyond compare, and they may even be dirt cheap compared to some other arrangement, but it does make life difficult to have such an unresponsive slob listening to legitimate complaints. Though it is indirect, we *do* pay his salary, Mr. Liss. And he *is* a horse's ass. Pete and I visited Gulfway Management and finally were allowed to talk to a Mr. Sullivan. His attitude was that we had a twenty-year contract with his company, an unbreakable contract, and he could give us as much or as little service as he felt like, and if we pestered him he would make sure it was less. It made us feel that when you placed that contract you did not have our best interests in mind."

Martin said, frowning, "That is not right! I will have a talk with Mr. Sullivan and see if I can change his attitude. If I can, I think you will find that Julian will become more cooperative."

"We would appreciate it," Pete McGinnity said. "Let me get back to that fast shuffle you gave people who are going to be stung by that extra eighty-seven dollars a month. They're not some kind of clowns getting into something over their head. Retirement money hardly ever is more than anybody needs. A person has an apartment, he pays the mortgage payments, the county taxes, the phone, the electric, insurance, television cable. These are going up. As you know. Let's say John Doe, owner, is getting up there close to four hundred a month with everything he has to pay, and then we have to pop him with another eighty-seven on top of that. So all of a sudden he is paying fifty-five hundred a year for shelter, and if his retirement is nine or ten thousand, he is getting jammed pretty good."

"I can *understand* that," Martin said, "I really can. And

I can feel very sorry about John Doe getting mousetrapped by economic conditions. That's why the Social Security keeps going up, to help out with his problems. What I said before, I'm very very sorry Benjie made such a bad estimate on the monthly assessment. I have to take part of the blame, but . . . Wait a minute! Maybe I can help. Investment Equities bought those last two apartments from us as of April first. Do I miss my guess, or is Frank West getting a free ride, just holding those two with no assessment until they're sold?"

"Free ride," David Dow said. "I wrote two letters, but got no answer at all. My next move was going to be to hold back assessment money out of the recreation lease money."

"I'll tell you what I will do. I'll negotiate with Frank West, and I can practically guarantee I can get him to pick up that money he should be paying in all fairness. He owes me a favor. Won't that help the payments?'"

David Dow took a little calculator from his pocket. In a few moments he said, "If they will pick up their share of the accumulated deficit, average monthly payments will drop to $161.35, and the deficit payment drops to $166.60. So it will be $14.55 less per apartment on the June assessment. Not much."

"Anything at all is a help," McGinnity said. "What else can you do for us, Mr. Liss?"

Martin laughed. "Whoa! There's no guarantee I can even do that much. All I say is there's a pretty good chance. You have to understand, with Golden Sands I've got no more leverage. I'm all the way out of it. Being human, I want to have my projects turn out well. I want people to be happy living there. That's why I'm trying to help."

Forrester stood up so suddenly he startled Martin Liss. He said, "Thank you for your time and your help, Mr. Liss. We'll be leaving now. We know you're a busy man."

"Please be in touch if there's anything I can do to help."

The four supplicants rode slowly back out to Fiddler Key in Pete McGinnity's air-conditioned Cadillac.

"Well, couldn't he just be mister nice guy?" Wasniak asked. "You say he didn't have to see us at all."

"He didn't," Hadley Forrester said. "He took the money and ran. Golden Sands is ancient history to him. And I do not think Marty Liss goes around wasting his time advising strangers."

"So what's the answer?" Pete asked.

"He wants to calm us down. He wants us to live with our problem. We've got some kind of leverage we don't know about."

"A strike?" Wasniak asked.

Forrester thought a moment and gave a single harsh bark of laughter. "Jesus, Stan, maybe you hit it. What if we all, every owner, stopped paying the recreation lease and the management contract assessment? Could they dispossess everybody? Who would they sell the apartments to in this market? Think of the stink in the *Athens Times Record*. The wire services would pick it up."

"But what difference would that make to him?" Dave asked.

"Good question. It might somehow screw up his next project. These things need lots of permissions. If there was a stink, it might give him political problems somehow. My friends, we are going to have to find out what he's planning to do next."

"Nobody," said Pete, "but nobody is ever going to get all the damn owners to get together on anything, ever. So Marty Liss shouldn't worry."

Five minutes after the directors left, Martin Liss had Frank West on the phone.

"Frankie, I don't see you at the club anymore. You tired of giving me your money? Or maybe you got smart and give up the game."

"I've been having this soreness in my shoulder, like bursitis but it isn't that. Honest to God, I try to swing a club, it looks as funny as your swing, Marty. The doc told me to lay off awhile, and he's giving me shots. Don't worry about me. I'll be back and whip your ass good any day now."

"You should wait so long. Look, what I called about, you got a couple of letters from Golden Sands about paying assessments on Five-A and Six-E."

"Wait a minute. Let me think. Oh sure, from some joker there signs CPA after his name, like it is going to make me pay up. Don't worry about it, Marty. In the file I've got the letter from Benjie when he was a director there, saying the transfer to us is free of all assessments and so on and so on. Airtight. There's nothing they can do."

"Frank, I got a two-word message for you. Pay them."

"Am I hearing what you said? Pay? Look, I know it's peanuts, a few hundred bucks, but unless we sell those two, assessments go on and on, and what the hell is the point anyway, when we don't have to?"

"The only point you have to know is I told you to pay them."

"But it just doesn't—"

"Some days, honest to Christ, you got nothing between your ears but dog shit. What makes you think I got to stay on the phone and discuss things with you? What's this with wanting explanations? When I want something done, I tell you to do it, and all you have to do is go do it, you dumb fuck!"

"Now, Marty—"

"None of that either, West. All you do right now is you say to me, Yes, Mr. Liss, I'll pay it."

"Yes, Mr. Liss. I'll pay it."

"Frankie?"

"Yes, Mr. Liss."

"Take care of that shoulder, and give my best to Fran and the kids." Marty hung up and asked Drusilla to get hold of Sully. "And when you get him, hold him about three minutes before you put him through."

"I've got Mr. Sullivan on the line, sir."

"Well, well, well! What a real pleasure it is to me to talk to Mr. Sullivan the big shot in person! This is a real honor for me, such an important man."

"What's with you, Marty? What's this about?"

"Two executives came to visit you. One was a vice-president of a manufacturing company. One was a partner in an important firm. I know how your mind works, Sully. These two guys have got more style, more class, more smarts than you have. That's why you pissed on them."

"On who? Why would I do that? Who's been lying?"

"Why are you getting so excited?"

"My God, Marty, I'm excited because I don't know what you're talking about."

"I'm talking about two friends of mine, two successful men I respect. Do you know about respect, Sully?"

"Honest to God, this is some kind of terrible mistake! When is this supposed to have happened? What are their names?"

Drusilla Bryne came in with a letter for his signature, put it in front of him and waited there. He said, "Hold on a minute, Sully."

Drusilla said, "I'm going to lunch now if it's okay."

The office door was closed. That was the rule. Always close it. She was standing to the left of his chair. He winked up at her, switched the phone to his right hand, rolled his chair back a foot and reached his left arm around her. He pulled her close and bent forward and rested his left ear against the trim almost-flat belly, warm and soft beneath the summery skirt.

"The two gentlemen, Sully, were Mr. Peter McGinnity and Mr. Hadley Forrester."

She stubbed strong slender fingers into the shoulder muscles near the nape of his neck, pressing and stroking, massaging away the tensions. The internal she spoke into his left ear, a *querk* and gurgle, a small growl of midday hunger. Sullivan spoke into his right ear, his voice light with relief. "Hey, I get it! You're making a joke. Those guys are a total *nothing,* Marty. They're senior citizens. Retired. There's nothing they can do to anybody. No leverage. They came bothering me and I told them to shove it. What else?"

As he stroked and caressed Dru with his left hand, he said, "What you are going to have to do is kiss ass. You are going to have to tell them that you are going to take care of every complaint, because that is what you are going to do."

"Marty! I get it! They're in your office, right? They're hearing your end of it. A snow job."

"Wrong, Sully baby. I'm completely alone." As he said that he stopped listening to Drusilla with the other ear, leaning away from her to look up at her questioningly. She made a face at him and raised a fist in mock threat. He cowered back against the fragrant softness of her.

"Well . . . whatever you want me to do, I'll do. You know that. But can you give me a guideline?"

"Such as what?"

"One thing those old clowns want, they want Higbee taking orders from the Association instead of out of this office."

"Then you tell Julian that's the way it is."

"I just want to remind you that Julian is milking a nice return out of that situation, and if they give the orders it is going to stop fast. I'm not making an objection. I'm just reminding."

"What I want over there at Golden Sands is people thinking somebody gives a damn about making them happy."

"Okay. It isn't going to be easy turning Julian around. Lorrie will get the message with no problem. Julian is a mule."

"There's the joke about the mule trainer."

"I know. Sure. The guy hits him with a sledge and drops him in his tracks and says, 'Now I've got his attention.' Okay, Marty. Wilco. You never ask for anything without some kind of reason, and you're not going to tell me until you're ready."

"Sully?"

"Yeh, Marty?"

"Kid, you're doing a good job there. I've been over the statements. One word of advice. This will take the cream out of Golden Sands for a while. So don't try to look good by squeezing it back out of the other condos we're managing. Okay?"

"Got you."

"Take care," Martin Liss said and hung up. He released Drusilla Bryne. She turned and sat on the corner of his desk, one leg braced, one leg swinging, and looked down at him with a half smile. He noted that she was flushed and her eyes and lips looked heavy.

"So?" she said.

"On your way back from lunch stop in at Benedict's and get me a liverwurst on rye and a large ice tea."

Her smile disappeared and she stood up. "Is that all?"

"I'll be reviewing a lot of figures this afternoon. Maybe I'll have to ask you to stay over after five. Will you be able to?"

Thus reassured, her smile came back. "Ah, darlin', I was starting to wonder if you'd ever ask."

After she left he stood at the windows and looked out across the bay toward the Silverthorn tract, and then went into his private and personal washroom, relieved himself and, after washing, stared at his face in the mirror with the same remote and objective expression he had used at the windows.

GEORGE GOBBIN WAS a tall dark-complected man in his late fifties, slightly stooped, lean except for a watermelon bulge of belly. He had a craggy face, a gentle, likable manner. He smiled easily and he was interested in people. He enjoyed civic meetings and social events equally, and these virtues had helped him make a pleasant living as a longtime personnel manager at Porter-Gifford, Inc., an old-line manufacturer of industrial pumps, valves and controls located in a small Iowa city.

Throughout his executive career he had clung to the two-hundred-and-forty-acre farm on Bird Creek, twenty-five miles southeast of the city, the farm his great-grandfather had worked and had died on, kicked in the head at seventy-five while harnessing a team to the rock sledge. During hard times he had almost lost the farm, time and again. He had bad luck with tenant farmers. Elda had urged him time and again to sell, but in him there was a stubborn love of the rolling land, of the earth smells in springtime, of the watersong of Bird Creek.

And then, last year, several events changed the lives of George and Elda Gobbin. A new interstate link was rammed through the countryside within roaring distance of the farm, with a numbered exit a half mile from the dooryard. A remote and mighty conglomerate picked up Porter-Gifford as easily as a child buys a cookie, and soon some shaggy and intense young men had appeared and dismantled Gobbin's personnel records system and coded everything into the conglomerate computer systems. And a lifelong friend, Hap Sexton—insurance and real estate—said he would like a chance to see what he might be able to get for the farm, and George, dispirited by events, said go ahead, and Hap did, and George accepted the offer that left him with four hundred and twelve thousand dollars after taxes and commissions.

After thirty-seven years with Porter-Gifford, he was able to opt for premature retirement at fifty-eight, selecting that alternative which would pay him seven hundred and twenty dollars a month for life, with Elda to get three hundred and sixty for her lifetime if he predeceased her. Through his local bank he put his four hundred thousand into tax-frees at an average five percent, earning twenty thousand a year. With their savings and the proceeds from the sale of their home, Mr. and Mrs. George Gobbin, after a twenty-day search, found and bought Apartment 3-C in the Golden Sands Condominium in November, paying twenty-two thousand down and signing an eight-and-a-half-percent mortgage for the thirty-four-thousand-dollar balance.

On the six-month anniversary of moving into Golden Sands, on a Thursday, the sixteenth of May, George drove them down to the Beach Mall Shopping Plaza. While Elda did the grocery shopping, he wanted to pick up the new reel he had ordered at Fisherama. They had phoned to say it was in. When he picked it up, he decided he would not tell Elda what it had cost. He cashed a check at the Beach Bank, bought blades and corn plasters at Eckerd's, locked his purchases in the trunk of the Chrysler and went looking for his wife. He found her in one of the middle aisles of the supermarket, standing and staring mutely at a display of canned soups. She was a small gray-blond woman with a tendency to gain weight. Lately she had been dieting, keeping careful track of weight and dimension, and swimming an hour a day. She had lost inches around her waist and hips, though not very many pounds as yet. She had a round, worn, pretty face, small hands, large breasts, and eyes of an extraordinarily clear and vivid shade of green.

"What's the matter?"

"Oh, George! You startled me, dear. Nothing's the matter. Edie Simmins said she cooked the meat the other night in chicken broth. I was trying to remember how she said she did it."

"You can ask her."

"Oh, I don't want to ask her. I mean unless it comes up again. You know."

"Sure."

"Is anything wrong?"

"What should be wrong? How far have you gotten on your list?"

"About halfway. Don't look at your watch, huh? I'm doing the best I can. They keep moving things around here, all the time."

"They want you to have to look for stuff every time, so you'll see other stuff you didn't know you had to have."

"Why don't you go look at the magazines or something?

You make me nervous hanging over me. You've done your errands?"

"Okay, okay," he said and walked away. He walked slowly through the mall looking in the shop windows, and when he came back she was at the checkout line. He waited and then wheeled the cart out to the car. Three big bags. The white tape dangled out of a bag. He looked at the total: $48.41. "Where does it all go?" he asked.

"Into damn good meals, friend."

"Okay, okay. The question was rhetorical."

"Don't keep saying okay okay okay to me in that tired draggy voice as if you're being terribly patient with some kind of stupid tiresome person."

"I'm sorry if it sounds that way. I don't mean it to."

He walked away from her, wheeling the cart back to the walk in front of the supermarket. He gave it an extra push and watched it roll into the other carts. When he got back behind the wheel she said, "Thank you for apologizing so quickly, dear."

"What do you mean by that?"

"I mean it's all over before it got nasty, is all."

"Oh."

"Don't you want it to be over?"

"I guess so. Sure."

"That doesn't sound very definite."

"It is definite."

"Are you cross again today?"

"What makes you think I'm cross, for God's sake?"

"Look out for that girl on the bicycle!"

"I *see* her!"

"Why did I bother to warn you anyway? Of course you'd see her. You'd never miss a bare brown ass wobbling in the sunlight, would you?"

"If I start going after kids that age, they'll come after me with a net."

"I don't think she was really much younger than that Antonelli girl was."

"For Chrissake, that was twenty years ago!"

"Which makes it okay?"

"Nothing happened anyway."

"Those letters didn't sound like it to me."

"Let's drop this right now. Right now, Elda, and I mean it."

They were soon back at Golden Sands. The Gobbins had one of the twenty-four protected parking places under the building. George put the Chrysler into his slot with geometric precision. He took their folding cart out of the trunk and loaded the three bags of groceries into it, along with his purchases. They rode up to the third floor in silence. He placed the bags on the countertop in the kitchen and took the cart back down and put it into the trunk before checking the doors to be sure the car was locked.

Mr. Ames startled him by saying, close behind him, "Won't do a damned bit of good, George."

"Oh. Hi, Brooks. What won't do any good?"

"Locking it. A thief could open up that car in six seconds. Everybody should realize we've got no security here at all. We're alone here, George. If I was a hoodlum I could hit you on the head, take your wallet, roll you under your car and walk away and be miles from here before anybody could find you."

Brooks Ames was short and round and stood so very erect he seemed to lean backward. He had thick white hair, a heavy white mustache, a veined red face, bulging blue eyes and a high loud voice. He had owned a small printing company before his retirement.

"Or Peggy Brasser could come steaming in and run me down before I could hide behind a column."

"Don't make jokes about it, George. In the prospectus it clearly states that there is to be an armed security guard on patrol at all times. I'm demanding that we take legal action. People like you just don't understand the danger. The courts let people off with a slap on the wrist: Be a good boy. The police have stopped giving a damn. What's the use arresting people if nobody goes to jail? You got eyes in your head, George. Use them. Go up to Beach Village and look at the scum hanging around. Sick, dangerous persons. They always get money from somewhere. Now times are hard and getting harder. You think they're going to give up booze and hard drugs and gasoline when all they have to do is come swaggering in here and take our money? What's to stop them? The law? Don't make me laugh."

"Maybe it isn't as bad as you think."

Brooks Ames stepped close and clamped his thick red hand around George's arm just above the elbow. The painful force of the clasp surprised and disconcerted him. Brooks lowered his voice to a stage whisper. There was peppermint on his breath.

"You better wake up, George. I happen to know they've been casing this place. Everybody else is living in a fool's paradise. I've seen them on the stairways, loitering and watching. I found one getting off the elevator on four, on my floor."

"One what?"

"Oh, I confront them every time. I want them to know somebody is onto them. But they've all been briefed. They always have a cover story. It always sounds plausible. But they are sly. I can always tell them by the look in their eyes."

"What are they after?"

"Are you really all that innocent? Listen. A week ago I went into the office. It was unlocked. Julian wasn't there and Lorrie wasn't there. The key cabinet was closed but . . . get *this* . . . the key to the key cabinet was in the lock!"

"I don't know what—"

"Don't interrupt. Do you know what is inside that service room over there? You ought to be interested in these things. I'll tell you. Every single phone line comes down to a big unlocked circuit box in that room and then goes out of here in an underground cable. Suppose somebody hasn't got a key to the service room? What could be easier than just giving it a nudge with a corner of a front bumper. In seconds you are out of the car and in there with tin snips cutting that cable. Then you go from apartment to apartment, using the keys you've had made from the keys you took from the key cabinet and replaced. You've got chain cutters. Unlock a door, cut the safety chain, hit you and Elda over the head with a hunk of pipe and clean out everything you have of any value. Pack the stuff in your own suitcases and take them down to the waiting truck."

"That's a pretty wild notion, Brooks."

"You bet it is, and I can prove it."

"*Prove* it?"

"You bet I can. There's a place in New York City called Olympic Towers. It is a place with absolute total security. You never have to leave the building. Everything is right there for you. And do you know what they are selling nine-room condominium duplexes for, George? Six . . . hundred . . . and . . . fifty . . . thousand . . . dollars . . . per! And a monthly fee that would stagger you. What do you think of that?"

"What does it prove?"

"You're not thinking, Gobbin. Are any nine rooms in a tall building worth that much money? Hell no! What are they buying, anyway? Security! People with that much money to spend are smarter about predicting things than you and I are. That's why they have that much money. Why are they willing to spend it on total security? Because they know that the streets are going to be full of ravening mobs of hoodlums, smashing and stealing and killing, and they are going to be safe, while we go under."

Brooks gave George's arm an extra-powerful squeeze. He moved even closer and in that strange hoarse whisper said, "Are you willing to serve?"

For a few moments George Gobbin lost contact with reality. He stood amid concrete cubes and walls, amid metal machines in a shadowed place separated from the bright sun outside by a jungle of plantings. A short strong person stood at the wrong distance for his bifocals, too close for the distance lens, too far for the reading lens, blurred red face and blurred blue eyes, huffing warm peppermint smells at him, hurting his arm, making an incomprehensible request.

He wrenched his arm free and yelled, in fear and anger, "Serve what?" He massaged his numbed fingers.

Brooks Ames stepped warily back and said, "What's wrong with you, George?"

"Nobody is after us."

"You *yelled* at me."

"Serve what? How?"

"I ran it up the flagpole with Pete McGinnity, and he said he had no objection if I could get the gun permits. The way I see it, suppose we sign up twelve men. Four times twelve is forty-eight. Four hours of armed patrol duty once every two days. That wouldn't hurt anybody, would it?"

"Wander around here with a gun for four hours?"

"The patrol station would be right outside Higbee's office where you can watch the elevators. Actually, what we ought to have is closed circuit television so you can watch the stairways and outside walkways too."

"Brooks, I am not going to watch anything."

"That's your option, of course. Nobody can force you to do your civic duty."

"Are you going to be wandering around with a gun?"

"When I am, you can sleep sounder at night, neighbor."

"I don't think it will work exactly that way."

"I'm disappointed in you, George."

"I just don't happen to think the corridors of Golden Sands are going to be awash in blood any minute now."

Brooks Ames smiled sadly. "Go ahead. Make your jokes. Your innocence is really very very touching." He walked briskly away, whacking his metal-shod heels against the concrete, the sound bouncing off the hard walls and metal cars.

George rode back up to 3-C. As he got off the elevator two children about six or seven years old raced into it, shrieking, and pressed all the buttons from 7 to G.

"Hey!" George said. "Don't do that, kids! You're not supposed to push all . . ."

The door was closing. The browner of the two children, wearing only red swim pants, blond hair hiding most of its face, said with a painful clarity, "Fuck off, gramps!" The door closed and the indicator showed it was heading upward.

George went thoughtfully into his apartment.

"Where *were* you? What kept you?"

"Brooks Ames. He wants me to volunteer to be an armed guard. I think he's lost his wits."

"Audrey says he worries all the time about thieves coming in here. He wakes up in the night, she says, and paces around, worrying and hearing noises."

"Some children hopped on the elevator and pushed all the buttons."

"I thought I heard children screaming. Who are they visiting?"

"I wouldn't know."

"Did you check for the mail?"

"It won't be there yet."

"Why can't you just say you forgot to check?"

"I didn't check because it is too early to check."

"Instead of going three steps out of your way and looking in the box?"

When he made no reply, she went back into the kitchen, holding her shoulders high and rigid. He sat on the couch and opened the package with the reel in it and took out the little instruction pamphlet and began reading it. At the Fisherama he'd had the clerk fill the spool on the reel with eight-pound monofilament, and fill the extra spool with twelve-pound. He reviewed how to remove the spool and replace it and then did so, admiring the oily click with which the spool settled into position on the reel.

Elda leaned and spoke through the pass-through. "If you had any consideration at all, you'd go find out about the mail without my having to beg you."

"The children are using the elevators."

"Is that supposed to be humorous? You know it was nine months for Judy over a week ago."

"And you know she had the first two with about as much trouble as your average brown rabbit, and if there was any trouble, Hal could certainly phone."

"Maybe he phoned when we were marketing."

"If so, he'll try again."

She came out of the kitchen, marched past him and went out of the apartment, slamming the door behind her. He went into the utility room and got his fish box and spinning rod. By the time he had taken the old reel off and put the new one on and threaded the line through the guides, she was back. In her anger she had forgotten to take a key. The door locked automatically. He decided not to answer the first knock. After the second knocking he waited just long enough so that when he opened the door, she stood there with her fist upraised to start again.

"Couldn't you hear me?"

"Hear you what? You knocked and I came to the door and opened it."

"I knocked twice."

"Then evidently I did not hear the first knocking, or I would have opened the door."

He went and sat on the couch. She slung the mail at him from ten feet away. The corner of a small catalog stung the corner of his mouth and the rest of the mail fluttered down around him, on the couch and on the rug.

"There is all your terribly important mail," she said. "It ought to keep you busy the rest of the day."

He gathered it up. Ads, circulars, solicitations. "I'll try to make it last. We retireds have to spread things out."

"Hah! Retired!"

"Didn't you know?"

"*You* may be. *I'm* not. What the hell has changed for me? Cooking, cleaning, shopping, dusting, laundry, bed-making. Not only you don't have a job, you don't even have a yard to take care of anymore. Retirement is one hell of a laugh."

He faked astonishment as he looked up at her. "My God! I never realized you're working your fingers to the bone stacking dishes in the dishwasher and putting the washing in the washing machine. Wow! Here you are waiting on me hand and foot and—"

"You can be one ice-cold sarcastic son of a bitch. You are—"

"Exactly like my mother?" He jumped up from the couch. "I knew it was about time for that."

"She was a cold person, George. Through and through. And she had that terrible sense of . . . superiority, of being a little bit better than everyone around her, without any cause in the world that I could ever discover. You are exactly like she was."

"You know what you have? You have a compulsion to feel abused. Any idiot could run this apartment with one hand during the television commercials. But that would take away the kicks. You have to dawdle and futz around and fool around until you make every ten-minute job take an hour. Then you can blame me for keeping you in harness."

He saw the familiar tears well into her green eyes and spill and run. "That is *stinking!* That is a cruel stinking thing to say. I've worked hard and I've sacrificed having a life of my own just to—"

"Come here to this garden spot where you can swim in the pool and walk on the beach and enjoy the sunshine."

"As if you earned it all for me? Just for me? *Bull*shit, George. If we had to retire on your very own pension, we damned well wouldn't be retired yet, would we? And if we did hang around and retire on it, we wouldn't be living here. We live here because they put an interstate past the farm."

"You would have sold it years ago."

"And you hung onto it because you're so shrewd? Ha! It is to laugh, George Genius Gobbin. We did without a lot of things while the kids were growing up so you could hang onto that farm and go out there and pretend to be the big man bossing those thieving tenants around. You kept it for sentimental reasons, and if Hap hadn't gotten after you to sell, we'd still be up there, if they hadn't already fired you."

"So I'm a weak sentimental failure. Or I'm a cold superior person. And you haven't decided which."

"You are cold and indifferent and hateful. And if you'd done your job as well as I did mine, you'd have been running that company instead of just being some kind of clerk."

"A vice-president, damn it!"

"And you're proud of that? Gee! I remember you telling me when Vance made every salesman a vice-president so they could get in to see more purchasing agents."

"You are not happy unless you're pulling me down. What you are is an emasculator. Maybe I would have done better if you hadn't been all the time right behind me, destroying my confidence."

"Destroying! That's a wicked thing to say. I always tried to make you feel as if—"

"I couldn't do one damn thing right."

"Oh, you are so rotten and unfair. So-o-o unfair to me."

Elda stood there, facing him, her face crumpled with despair, and he knew that his next line was supposed to be an accusation about overacting, and then she would get back to his mother, and then transpose into his talent for spoiling things for everybody. Then he would go storming out in an enormous rage and come back later and they would comfort each other with a sexual solution.

But the little anger he had drummed up had dwindled. He felt tired and misplaced. Quarreling was an evening affair, or a weekend affair. Not here in the sunlight, like this. He couldn't storm out saying he was going to the office, or to the club. What he wanted to do, actually, was try the new reel.

The pain and drama ebbed from her small face and she looked at him with growing concern when he did not respond.

"What's the matter, dear?" she asked earnestly.

"I don't know. I feel confused, sort of."

"What about?"

"I stopped being angry. I don't think I could get sore no matter what you say."

"Is that some new kind of way of saying you don't . . ."

"No. No, Elda. We're here. How we got here is past history. You do what you do, and I do what I do. Maybe we'll live longer. Maybe, hell, it will seem longer."

"Why do you say a thing like that?"

"You're still wanting to fight. I'm trying to say I'd *like* to fight. Okay? It's something I'm used to. But I got to be angry or it's just saying lines I know by heart."

"George!"

"Look, I want to try out casting with the new reel,

okay? I'm going down to the bay side. Want to come along?"

"The bugs are fierce. Well . . . sure. Give me five minutes."

As she changed she kept worrying about George, and she kept telling herself it was probably a good thing if they could stop having these nasty fights every so often, saying terrible things. She told herself she had always wished they could stop fighting. Maybe they had, now. She wondered why she should feel frightened. No, not frightened. Threatened.

5

WHEN HIS SECRETARY told him Loretta Rosen was on the line, Greg McKay's heart gave a happy bound. Maybe, at long last, she had managed to rent one of those goddam apartments at Golden Sands to some off-season pigeon. To have at least one of the three rented would partially staunch a flowing wound.

"Hey, Loretta. What's the good word?"

"The good word, darling, is one you won't hear me saying over the phone. In fact, I don't want to say any of this over the phone."

"What's the matter? Didn't they like it?"

"They both thought the apartment was absolutely darling. They are a nice quiet couple, thinking in terms of a lease for one year before deciding whether or not to buy on the beach. I should have closed it right then and there, six hundred a month. But I always close in the office. How could I know? How could I guess?"

"Know what? Guess what?"

"A veritable plague of urchins, dearie. Little brown

foul-mouthed ones. They came charging around a corner by the elevators and knocked Mrs. Granlund right onto her patrician ass."

"But . . . the rules say no children!"

"I know. I know. That's what I'd already told the Granlunds. The kids didn't even stop to find out if they'd killed her. She claimed she wasn't hurt at all. But it gave her a nasty little limp. And it turned them both off Golden Sands but good. I tried to retrieve the situation by marching them down to the manager's office. Lorrie Higbee was very evasive at first. Finally she confessed that Julian rented an apartment on the sixth to two couples on vacation with small children, apparently for a nice fat figure."

"It's illegal!"

"Not really. The Declaration says no children under sixteen. But that's for the owners who live in their apartments. Not renting to anybody with little kids is more like an unwritten rule, you know? Greg, dear, I tried. I really tried, but it was no way."

"Did you rent them anything?"

"Elsewhere? As a matter of fact, I did. But, believe me, I am trying to fill yours first, God only knows why. You didn't buy them through me, darling."

"I bought them predevelopment, from Marty Liss."

"I know. I know. Two years ago. But if you'd had your wits about you, you would have come to Loretta first and said, Loretta dearest darling, if I buy those three, will you keep them full or sell them at a profit, and I would have said, Greg, honey, my crystal ball says that the days of investing in condominium apartments have just about ended, and it will be a good way to get bruised."

"Bruised? I'm getting lacerations you wouldn't believe."

"I can believe. There's something else I want to tell you. When can you get away from those torts and writs and things? It's important to you."

"You've had lunch? So've I. What say I stop by your office in . . . oh . . . forty minutes?"

McKay's secretary was watching her automatic typewriter clatter through line after line of boilerplate in a trust agreement, waiting for it to stop so that she could type in the specifics McKay had dictated.

"I've got two stops to make," he said. "I'll be back by three or a little after. Okay?"

"What about the admiral?"

"When is he set for?"

"Quarter of."

"Well, I'll try to hurry and you try to keep him from having a heart attack."

Ten minutes later, as he turned onto Fiddler Key and drove south toward Beach Village, he was wondering if he should have tried to get some other realtor to handle the renting of apartments 2-D, 2-E and 2-F. Having a realtor at all was an additional expense. According to the management contract, ten percent had to go to the manager no matter what. And another ten to Loretta took a good bite out of any rental. On the other hand, she had found that January through March rental for 2-F, three thousand gross, twenty-four hundred by the time they finished cutting it up.

He had been involved in several closings for clients where Loretta Rosen had been involved as a realtor. He had found her to be energetic, shrewd, handsome and funny. He guessed she might be even as much as ten years older than his thirty-four, but his guess was based on conversation clues, not on her looks. If she was that age, she worked very successfully to conceal it. She was a medium-tall slender lady with a long gleaming weight of dark blond hair. Her tanned face was very mobile and expressive, her pale gray eyes striking. She had a gravelly voice and salty turn of phrase, and a hundred small nervous mannerisms, forever folding and unfolding her sunglasses, lighting one cigarette from another, fingering her hair back, tapping her teeth with a pencil eraser. She knew everybody. Her advertising logo said, SEE LORETTA! She seemed to work twenty-six hours a day.

He parked beside her little building on the outskirts of the Village. The front-office girls knew him. Loretta was waiting in her small office in the back. She sprang up from behind her desk and shook his hand, and waved him into the big comfortable armchair across from her. She went to the door and said, "Hey, Bonny, no calls, okay?" She closed the door and went behind her desk, leaned back in her chair, shook a match out and grinned at him. "Big mystery, huh?"

"So far."

"Hmmm. The guard is up. Sweetie, relax. I'm going to try to do you some good, even though I shouldn't, I guess. It could be a question of ethics. But it is also a question of friendship. We're friends?"

He smiled. "So far."

"The thing is, maybe I'd be doing you too small a favor for it to matter too much to you. I mean you talked about being lacerated, but you could have been sort of kidding. You *are* a partner. Are you really hurting, or were you kidding?"

He asked for scratch paper. She slid a yellow pad over to him. "These are guesstimates, but close," he said. He worked it out. "Cash down on the three, eighteen thousand. Cash for furnishing the three apartments, about twenty-two thousand. Call it forty invested. Total outstanding mortgages at this time, about a hundred and twenty thousand. Annual interest charges, about ten thousand five hundred. Annual assessment about three thousand. Repairs and maintenance, call it fifteen hundred. So that means total carrying costs of about fifteen thousand, plus reduction of the principal amount of the mortgages."

He showed her the figures and said, "The legal fees I earn go into the kitty, and the partners split it all up each year according to a formula which favors the guys who've been aboard the longest. So it isn't exactly all that great. I'll admit it. The apartments are a real drain. I wake up in the middle of the night and wonder why I got into such a thing. It's going to make me old before my time. And some of the money was my wife's: ten thousand of the twenty-two we put into decorating. Nancy had fun doing the decorating and buying the furniture. But with no rentals, it isn't fun anymore. We've been jabbing at each other about it. Tales out of school. Sorry."

"You've told me just what I have to know. Really. All kidding aside, it wasn't a good investment, Greg."

"I bought one at Shoreline four years ago, paid forty

and sold it for fifty-eight. I guess it made me overconfident or something."

"Look, I was never very high on Golden Sands. It seemed to me there aren't enough apartments to support the facilities. I had a client seven months ago. Stan Wasniak. I tried to find the right place for him and his wife. He knew I was a little bit dubious about Golden Sands, but his wife flipped so badly over it, I had to close or lose it. Wasniak read me pretty good. I ran into him yesterday. He says that as of the first of June, it is *really* going to hit the fan. He's an officer of the Association. He told me they've been over all the financial records and there is just no way they can operate that thing without more than doubling the monthly assessment, *plus* a double assessment in June to take up the slack."

His mouth sagged. "Double? From three thousand to six thousand a year for those three of mine? God, that really kicks it in the head. I can't make out at all."

"The way rentals are going, no. You can't. Even without that extra, I don't think you can make out."

"Have you got some kind of answer?"

"Yes, but you aren't going to like it. It could be called biting the bullet. You are a young man with a good profession. I've been around a long time. I was divorced when I was twenty-two, and I've made out because I've got money sense. I manage a lot of property for a lot of people. I have seen too many guys go through too much agony trying to save things, only to lose them in the end. Sweetie, my old battle wounds tell me that Golden Sands is going sour. I've seen some of them go that way, and it isn't pretty. As your friend, and your volunteer financial manager, I think you ought to dump those three just as fast as you can. I think you ought to cut the price down to where I can take you out of them fast."

"How far down is that?"

"The present state of the market, I'd say that in order to get people to stand still for a hundred and sixty something a month assessment, you've got to get down under thirty-five thousand. Furnished."

He swallowed hard and fingered his throat. "God,

Loretta. It will add up to better than a sixty-thousand-dollar bath, counting everything in."

"You made a sixty-thousand-dollar mistake. You are entitled to one of those at your age. If you'd bought only one, you'd have made a twenty-thousand-dollar mistake. If you'd bought six, you'd have—"

"Please. I thought of buying six. And didn't."

"Praise the Lord for small blessings. Do you want me to go ahead and try to move them?"

"Probably yes. You are probably right. It would be such a wonderful sense of relief. But I've got to talk it over with Nancy first."

"Of course. But I think you should move pretty fast. I've got some pigeons I can work. Usually I let people . . . find their way out of their own swamps. But . . . I don't know. We've worked together and I like you, I guess."

"I really value your advice. It's hard to take, but it's good, I know."

They both got up and moved toward the door, smiling. He shook his head. "It's going to give Nance a migraine."

They both reached at the same instant for the door-knob. Their hands touched, and he took hold of her thin wrist, and then reached and captured the other wrist. Her pale gray glance was apprehensive, swift-moving, somehow ironic. With a quick lift of her head she threw her heavy hair back.

"Look," she said. "I'm not much for this kind of thing."

"Or me."

"I didn't think so. Greg, honey, it really isn't an area where I have any confidence at all. Okay? Unhand me, sir?"

He let go of her. They gave each other clumsy smiles. He said, "I don't know what the hell I had in mind. That was dumb. I'm not . . . one of those."

"I know. I know. It happens. I give a lot of people the wrong impression. I'm kind of a fake."

Their eyes met again. She looked away, uneasily, and then met his direct gaze again. He looked into pale gray, into the shiny black pupils. It was a specific physical impact, an electrical tingle of awareness. She said, hardly moving her lips, "I'm . . . really not any good at anything like this."

"I think because of the way you said you like me . . ."

"You are so damned unbelievably young, Greg. You were born way too late for me. I mean even if I wasn't so jumpy about . . . getting involved."

"I wasn't asking for anything to happen. I don't *really* want . . ."

"I know. Look. Turn around and go out the door. Okay, dear Greg? Just do that."

He took a deep breath and let it out, and turned and went. As he went blindly through her office and out to his car, he could not remember what she looked like. He could not remember what Loretta Rosen, Realtor, looked like though he had known her for several years. He could remember only what the new Loretta looked like. Before his eyes, she had changed into loveliness. Defects had now become the hallmarks of her authenticity.

He sat in his car and tried to yank his mind back out of fantasy, back to the realities of the waiting admiral, and the reality of taking a frightful bath on the three apartments. But nothing seemed as real or as important as her gray uneasy eyes.

On the way back to the office he had to drive past Golden Sands again. It looked, from Beach Drive, bigger than it was. It glowed orange and gold in the hot afternoon sunlight. In the occupied apartments the draperies were pulled across the tinted glass doors and tinted picture windows. From desperate habit he picked out the windows and balconies of apartments 2-D, 2-E and 2-F. Once again he heard himself telling Nancy what a great deal it would be. He slammed the heel of his hand against the steering wheel and groaned. Nancy would have to be told. He began to rehearse how best to tell her. But Loretta Rosen sat in the back of his mind, listening to the rehearsal, smiling and nodding when he devised a particularly apt phrase.

Loretta Rosen sat at her desk, alone, going through her list of prospects. But her attention kept wandering.

She leaned back, dug at her scalp, lighted a fresh cigarette, put the old cigarette out, scratched her thigh and thought with exasperation, Not again, goddam it: I don't *need* all that hassle.

All that sneaking around, full of crazy excitement, all that glowing, that breathless talking. Having someone to think about all day, and getting horny thinking about him. Little phone codes and signals, and all the frantic desperate screwing, at odd times in odd places. Somebody said the trouble with adultery was you have to do it mostly in the daytime when everybody looks dreadful. It had been . . . how long? . . . a year and a half since the last one broke up. Cole Kimber. Funny-coincidence department. Cole built Golden Sands for Marty Liss, had been building it when the affair began and was still building it when it ended. Mostly in that construction trailer of his, or out in the Gulf in his cabin cruiser, or way out in that crummy shack he called his hunting lodge.

No, woman. Not another one. Cole was the very last one forever, the last one this side of the grave. Not that there had been exactly a whole regiment or anything during the twenty-four years of divorce from rotten Rosen.

Not Greg. Not for me. Too young. Absolutely great shoulders and long dark lashes and a voice that makes me feel tingly. Be honest. You picked him out six months ago, dear, and you have been putting on all your little acts and games, and he finally lunged and you struck him good and sunk the hook. That's not quite honest either. It wasn't that definite, dear. It has just been a case of like. And people always show their best side to those they like, right?

No trick at all now, she thought, to move in for the kill. Greg has a set of keys. I have a set. Lorrie Higbee has a set on her key board. Call Greg up and tell him you'd like to check over the furnishings in 2-D, to be able to answer some questions from a potential buyer. Put on your pretties and meet him there. He's ready now. Too easy. Like that heavy old gal in the B.C. comic strip who is forever clubbing that poor snake. Snake has no chance.

Snake is sexual symbolism. Greg hard, like warm pink marble, blue curl of the great vein . . .

With great effort she stilled her visceral trembling. Erectile tissues softened. She firmed her mouth and lifted her chin and thought about money. That always brought it under control. Love affairs always cost money, one way or another. And the worst loss had been the commission on the Carstock Ranch. She would never never never forget that. Eighty thousand commission. All hers. And who got it? That goddam sneak bastard Marvin McGraw, that's who. Sneaked in and closed the deal when she was out on the *Leona III* with Cole Kimber, at anchor, napping and drowsing and banging the hot lazy October afternoon away.

Never again. And the time to stop it is before it starts. Once it starts you lose track of your priorities. The office goes to hell. Your people get sloppy. The bandits steal your clients and your properties, while you walk around in a silly buttery haze, alive from the waist down, simpering and sniggering. So the hell with it, Gregory. Find somewhere else to put that damned thing. The lady has had her last ride on snap-the-hip, had her final cotton candy day at the fair, won her last tin mandolin.

She looked up a number and dialed it on her unlisted line. Mrs. Neale answered on the second ring.

"Florence? This is Loretta."

"Who? Oh, yes, of course. For a minute I just—"

"I couldn't blame you for forgetting me entirely, dear. But you remember, I *did* promise that when I found something really exceptional, you'd be the first one I'd call."

"Yes, but—"

"This is a very dear little apartment in Golden Sands. You know. On the beach, on the bay side, across from Azure Breeze. Of course there's guaranteed access to the beach. Tennis courts, pool, resident manager. Everything, really. It is beautifully furnished. The owner is in serious financial trouble, and I *think* he's going to unload it at a fantastic bargain price. If he does, I'll have an exclusive. Meanwhile, if you wouldn't mind taking a chance on wasting your time, I could sneak you in to take a look at it."

"Well, I'm not really in the market, Loretta. Not the way I was when we talked before."

"You've decided on something else?"

"Well, practically. The bank says I *have* to get rid of this huge place. It is eating me up, you know? I wish Charles hadn't given those trust people so much authority over me. I'd rather stay right here than have to pack up all the stuff we accumulated in our lifetimes. Anyway, I think I would be happier in a house than in one of those little boxy things way up in the air, and I've almost decided on a sweet little house over on Domingo Terrace."

"Florence, whether I sell you anything or not, I couldn't let you move into that neighborhood."

"What's wrong? Why?"

"It's changing. I watch things like that. It's my business. You might be perfectly safe for a year. But after that? After that you better buy a gun and a big savage dog."

"You're kidding!"

"Florence, believe me, I think that the day when women alone like you and me could live alone in little houses in the city is almost over forever. We *have* to have the protection of high rise."

"I'm not really all that nervous about—"

"Will you let me show you the apartment at least? Actually I'd like any excuse to get out of this darn office for a little while."

"Right now?"

"Why not?"

"Well, okay. Shall I meet . . . ?"

"Sit tight, dear, and I'll come get you."

Loretta Rosen went into her small washroom off her private office and fixed her hair and her mouth. She turned from side to side, craning to see as much as possible of her slim figure in the small mirror. Not too bad, she thought, for a forty-six-year-old hag. And that's another good reason against getting into anything with Greg

McKay. It always makes me gain weight. And each time it is a little more hell taking it back off.

She took her purse and went out through the outer office, and smiled radiantly at her people and told them she would not be back.

VIC YORK HAD laughing eyes and a merry face. His brows were ridged with old scar tissue. One ear was a welted button. He was almost completely bald. He was a light-heavy from the waist up, a welter from the waist down. He'd had his last professional fight fourteen years ago. His waist was the same size as when he had been a perennial contender. He worked out every day of his life. His neck looked a little bigger than his head.

When Lorrie Higbee looked up, there was Vic York standing there beaming at her with extravagant approval. It startled her. He wore a beige knit sport shirt with a little alligator on the pocket, and tight fawn slacks. She could smell his male cologne from ten feet away.

"Hey, Gorgeous," he said. "Long time."

"What do *you* want around here, Vic?"

He had the fighter's voice box, a high-pitched raspy whisper. "That's no kind of friendly greeting to give your old buddy, Lorrie. Your old man around?"

"What do you want with him?"

"Hey, he got Mr. Sullivan pretty sore at him. You know that? Mr. Sullivan said to me, he said, Vic, you go over there and tell Julian he should show some respect. So here I am."

She bit her lip. Julian hadn't listened to her advice. So

here was Vic York. There was no way in the world to appeal to Vic. She remembered the terms from the anatomy course in nursing school. Civilized man has highly developed frontal lobes. In these lobes is the fine edge of coordination, along with mercy, restraint, imagination, self-control. The frontal lobes are snugged up against a sharp edge of the sphenoid bone, known as the sphenoidal ridge. And every time during his long career that Vic had been hit in the head, the ridge had damaged nerve tissue in the frontal lobes. Nerve cells are not replaced once they die.

She got up and took the file she was using over to a filing cabinet. She heard the grunt and looked over her shoulder in time to see Vic vault lightly over the dividing railing. He came up behind her when she opened the file drawer. She tried to ignore him. He put his arms around her and ran his hands up to cup her breasts. He pulled her against him.

"Lorrie, why you wanta all the time wear these T-shirts way too big for you. You got a nice body, huh? You got great little boobs and you hide them so nobody can see. Why?"

"Shall I phone Sully and ask him if he sent you over here to grope me?"

He let go and backed quickly away. "Now, that isn't friendly. That isn't friendly at all. You shouldn't say that."

"Why should I be friendly if you come over here to hurt Julian? Everybody knows that's what you do for Mr. Sullivan."

"Lorrie, Lorrie, that's *dumb*. I got to learn him a little is all. Which you rather have, sugar? He gets bounced a little by the old pro, or he gets his ass fired out of here? How are you two going to get anything this good, times like we're having? What you draw for unemployment isn't all that great, sweetie. Listen, I *like* Julian. And I like *you*. We're all traveling on the same team. You know he called Sully a name and hung up on him, and you knew right off it was going to be some kind of trouble."

"I told him," she said quietly. "Jesus, I told him, all right. How . . . how much do you have to hurt him?"

"No hospital, kid. Nothing like that. It isn't that big a deal. Just sort of refresh his memory of the way things have got to be, is all. So he'll have some respect."

He was smiling, speaking softly, moving toward her again. She sensed he wanted to touch her again, no more than that, and she thought that maybe if she let him, it might be easier for Julian somehow, but she could not bring herself to let Vic fondle her again. His touch had made her feel ill, in almost the same way Julian's touch was making her feel ill more often lately, ever since sneaking into 2-D that time and holding the water glass against the wall, her ear pressed to the base of it, listening to Julian and Mrs. Fish in the Fish apartment, all that snorting and thrashing and groaning.

She managed, without being too obvious about it, to put the desk between herself and Vic York, and sensed that he had given up his automatic pursuit of her.

"Where is Julian, anyway?" he asked.

"He's somewhere on the property, Vic. If you wait here, he'll come in sooner or later. Are you in a hurry?"

"Me? I got all the time there is. What I think I'll do, I'll go walking around the place, and if I don't find him I'll come back here again and talk to you some more."

"You do that, Vic."

Each weekday and Saturday morning at quarter to nine, after his four-minute egg and well-done sausage patty, Mr. C. Noble Winney kissed the soft folds of the right cheek of his wife, Sarah, went out to the rear parking area, got into his pale orange Gremlin, with his empty dispatch case on the seat beside him, and drove down to the main post office in downtown Athens. There he transferred the contents of his rental drawer to the dispatch case and then drove back to his day's work at Apartment 5-C, Golden Sands Condominium.

Mr. Winney had converted a bedroom into the kind of office which best suited his function. He had fashioned long tables of sawhorses and plywood. He had tall bins for vertical storage of his giant scrapbooks. A glass case held the looseleaf notebooks containing the thousands of pages of his daily workbook. He had a small efficient copier, an A. B. Dick 625. He had pots full of marker pens for his color coding system. He had razor-blade holders, spray adhesives, stacks of new pages for the scrapbooks and brilliant fluorescent lighting.

Sarah knew better than to allow anyone to interrupt her husband's work for the first two hours after he came back from downtown. That was when his need for total concentration was the greatest. That was when some seemingly innocent item might slip by him were his concentration flawed.

C. Noble Winney subscribed to fourteen daily papers, nine weekly newspapers and magazines, and twenty-one monthly publications. He had plotted this at 5,830 items per year, 309 visits to the box, for an average of 19.04 items per visit. The spastic rhythms of the Postal Service could provide five items or fifty on any given day, in addition to the correspondence.

On this day in May there were seventeen newspapers and five magazines, and no letters at all.

After he shut himself in the office-bedroom he separated the items into proper piles. And then he began reading. Years ago he had taken a speed-reading course, and since then had trained himself to the point where he could read a book as quickly as he could turn the pages.

There were two editions of the *New York Times*. That was always the most interesting because it was the most clever and devious. For fifteen years C. Noble Winney had been researching the progress of the conspiracy that ruled the world. Once you could comprehend it in all its devilish intricacy, then you could find the proper meaning of the items in the public press. Winney knew beyond any shade or shadow of doubt that the Rothschild–Zionist Axis determined the shape and direction of all history. Fools and dupes were taken in by the stage-managed drama of the menace of world communism. The Rothschild bloc was intent on maintaining such a balance of power between the democracies and the communist bloc nations that they could fatten themselves on the by-products of this everlasting tension. When you had learned to read between the lines you could not help knowing that the Jew Conspiracy controlled Wall Street, the public press, the television networks, the Congress, Parliament, the Kremlin, the Arab nations, the world's gold supply, all the universities of the world, the military and the Pope of Rome. It had become obvious to him that the United States of America had, for a time, posted a threat to that carefully maintained balance of power due to its dynamic strengths. But they had taken care of the problem by thrusting the world into depression, which gave them a chance to put President Franklin D. Rosenfeld into the White House. Rosenfeld had enlisted the help of a lot of so-called social scientists in tearing down the fabric of rational society and setting up the machinery for penalizing thrift, honesty and management skills, for rewarding the Africans for breeding faster than the white man by the device of child welfare payments to unmarried mothers, for destroying American education by adopting the anti-disciplinary theories of John Dewey, whose real name was Jon Dewaski, for corrupting the currency and resources of the nation by forcing America off the gold standard, for weakening social and sexual standards and thus taking the country into the era of rapes and riots, degenerate music, drugs, group sex orgies, muggings and murder.

It was all in the newspapers and magazines, all the sick and evil perversions of a once-great nation. Once you knew about it, it was remarkably easy to read the self-satisfied smirks on the faces of Cronkite, Chancellor and Reasoner. Sometimes a man in high office would guess at the dimensions of the conspiracy. And then the word would go out from Rothschild headquarters to destroy him, and destroy they would, even when it was Richard Nixon, the most popular president in American history. On other occasions some of their own creatures, who had been put in office by the power of the Rothschilds, would rebel against their masters, as did the Kennedy brothers. The death of Marilyn Monroe was a warning the brothers did not heed. And so it was very easy and very necessary to make the arrangements at Dallas, in California, at Chappaquiddick. And for a little while apparently George

Wallace had seemed dangerous to them. As had Willy Brandt, Allende and Krushchev.

Noble Winney could only guess what his own fate would be if one of their agents became aware of the depth and scope of his research and the damning detail of his scrapbook files.

He went through the *New York Times* and the rest of his incoming mail, clipping articles and using his Hilighter pens to color-code them in the margins, using combinations of colors: red for international, yellow for monetary, green for confirmation of prior facts on file, blue for new facts. He wrote the sources and dates in the margin and put the clips into the bin ready for filing.

As he clipped various stories, Winney kept looking for one which would help prove a point to Henry Churchbridge in 6-G. He had been bringing Henry along slowly and carefully, logical step by logical step. Henry was like most of mankind, strangely content to think the world a place of random happenings, completely unconscious of the monstrous conspiracy which ruled the world. Henry had a good mind, a good education and wonderful access to the workings of American diplomacy all over the world, and so it was astonishing to Winney that Churchbridge should be so reluctant to accept the proofs.

When Henry had begun to express astonishment and concern, and to read the photocopies of old clippings with mounting consternation, Noble Winney had become too confident of his pupil, and he had taken too big a step for Henry to accept and thus had nearly lost him.

He had explained to Henry how it was possible to decode portions of the Old Testament to understand the prophecies. In Ezekiel, chapters 38 and 39, instead of Israel, read Heartland of America wherever it says Israel. These chapters, he showed Henry, describe an attack on America by the Chinese and the Russians, called Gog and Magog, by means of paratroopers and airborne infantry coming over the North Pole and across Canada to land within the rough rectangle between Pittsburgh, Chicago, Omaha and Fargo. In fact, in chapter 39, Hamonah refers to Omaha. He had showed Henry how the twenty-eighth chapter of Deuteronomy is actually a concise and complete history of the United States, with verses 1 through 14 covering the period from 1607 to 1837. Starting with verse 15, by careful analysis one could see how, during the period from 1837 to 1861, the House of Rothschild had plotted and fomented the War between the States.

Suddenly he had seen the look on Henry Churchbridge's face, amusement and skepticism, and he stopped at once and changed the subject. But Henry had lost interest in the simpler aspects of the Conspiracy and was apparently quite anxious to get away from Noble Winney.

Why did they always resist the true knowledge? It took a long, careful, painful time to make each convert, and some escaped before they could be converted, preferring to live in a fog of ignorance, unaware of the world around them.

He found an item which would appeal to Henry. A coordinated national campaign by homosexual rights groups had been launched to limit or prevent the showing on ABC Television of a segment of *Marcus Welby, M.D.*, dealing with the molestation of a fourteen-year-old boy by a male teacher. The executive director of the National Gay Task Force had said that the television play would reinforce old myths and play upon the apprehensions of parents at a time when homosexual-rights legislation was pending in the Congress and about twenty major cities. He reported that the campaign had induced three ABC stations to reject it for broadcast, and that they had persuaded four regular advertisers to withdraw for that episode. These were Bayer Aspirin, Listerine, Gallo Wine and Ralston Purina.

Henry had seemed receptive to the proposition that the manners and morals and ethics of society could not possibly go downhill as fast as was happening without some hidden force at work. Now Henry could see from this clipping how the perverts were beginning to control network television, not only the programs but the advertisers as well. Henry could not help but be impressed.

He clipped it, coded it and ran off copies on the A. B.

Dick 625 Copier, taking pleasure from the way the carrier slid slowly across and then hastened back, dropping the duplicate in the tray, smelling pungently of toner.

He vowed to take it very slowly with Henry, to bring him along step by step until at last he was clear-eyed: conscious of the reasons for the porn manuals in the best bookstores, for the weakening of all religions, for the collapse of marriage, for the corruption of children through the hidden messages in the textbooks provided by corrupt and venal state governments.

When Sarah called him to lunch he took her a few of the more interesting photocopies to read, while he perused the most recent copy of the *American National News-Herald*. He was a soft, hulking, pallid man with gray hair, gray eyes and thin lips which were oddly, vividly red. His afflictions were severe dandruff, hemorrhoids, and abdominal walls of such fragility that after two hernia operations on each side he was able to avoid pain only by wearing a truss. He had worked as a civil servant, as an auditor for the State of Indiana, and during the final fourteen years before his retirement, his researches had become so engrossing and so time-consuming that his hours on the job seemed both unreal and pointless. Since retirement he was able to give his research program the full seventy to eighty hours a week that such intricate work required, if it were to be done well.

Sarah Winney finished one of the clippings he had given her and slapped it down and said, "Well! We certainly know Congress is corrupt. That's for sure."

"Eh? Oh, yes. That's right."

"You know what I think? I think it's the Jews in Washington. The president is too innocent about the Jews."

"Yes, dear," Noble Winney said.

"Is that a good book?"

"Yes, dear."

"Am I bothering you, talking?"

He stood up and wiped his mouth. "Well. Back to work."

"You ought to take longer for lunch, darling."

"Too much work, and too little time."

"You'll make yourself sick if you keep it up."

"Don't you worry about me, Sarah."

7

THE HIGH SUN blazed down through the screening into the pool and patio area at the rear of the Fiddler Key bay-front home of Justin D. Denniver, appliance dealer (Don't Miss the Deal at Denniver's) and one of the five county commissioners of Palm County. A thick high hedge of punk trees made the backyard area completely private, screening the yard and pool area from the houses on either side. From the pool and patio area one could see the bay shore, some mangrove islands, the misty mainland and, nearby, Commissioner Denniver's L-shaped dock and Commissioner Denniver's nineteen-foot Mako, tarped and snugged close to the blocks of the twin davits mounted on the dock.

In the silence of the early afternoon, a silence broken only by the *thup-thup-thup* of the lawn sprinkler system, the tiny drone of the pool filtration system and the distant bliss of a mockingbird three houses away, Lew Traff, Martin Liss's lawyer and minor partner in several ventures, was engaged in lengthy and dogged copulation with Molly Denniver, the plump, pretty, giggly, fortyish wife of the Commissioner, upon a faded blue sun pad beside a pool as still as lime Jell-O.

Mounted there upon her, he kept his eyes closed against the blinding glare of sun on white stone, glass and aluminum. Close at hand were the sounds of their effort, the moist lisping sounds of locked sweaty bodies, muffled thud of her hips against the sun pad, the whuffling, whinnying sound of her fevered breathing. Lew Traff felt like that man condemned for all eternity to roll a big boulder up a mountain. When they had made love the first time today, he had been too quick for her. She had not let enough time pass before manipulating him back to a sufficient stiffness to permit penetration. Now he felt engorged, swollen, irritated. His back ached. He wondered if he was going to get a bad sunburn on his white buttocks. There was little sense of pleasure in the frictive motion. From time to time she would grasp him convulsively, squeak, and snap like a bait shrimp. He felt glad somebody was having some fun. Not only was she having fun, she was also in the shade. His shade.

From far off, from way back, he felt his own reluctant climax approaching. It was quick, meager, constricted and painful. He was glad to collapse upon her, his labors finished. She held him tightly, purring her gratitude, then wormed out from under him and rolled into the pool, splashing water onto him. He followed her in, relishing the feel of the water on his overheated body. They swam a couple of lengths and then he stood, winded, in water up to his waist, and looked down and saw that he had been congested for so long, very little diminution had occurred, giving him a fallacious look of readiness. Were she to misunderstand, he did not think he could endure any more of it. He climbed out and hurried to the borrowed swim trunks and pulled them on, tucking himself into unobtrusiveness.

She got out of the pool and tugged herself into her yellow and white swim suit. They toweled and sat in big deck chairs under the shade of the roofed portion of the patio, each with a cigarette and a can of cold beer.

"I wasn't ever going to let it happen again, Lew."

"Well, I guess we got carried away, honey."

"Promise it won't ever happen again."

"I promise."

This was her charade. He humored her, knowing the dependence of everyone on his own rationalization. He would call Molly next time or she would call him, and it would be about some legal or business matter, and she would say, "Hey, whyn't you come over for a swim, hey?" This afternoon, or tomorrow morning, or tomorrow afternoon.

So he would go over to 88 Bayview Terrace and park in the drive and go into the long low blue cinder-block house with the white tile roof, and go into the guest room and put on the borrowed trunks and pad out onto the patio and have a little swim. There would be some giggly little games of splash and tickle and chase, until finally he would peel her out of her suit in the shallow end, slip out of his trunks, hoist her out onto the sun pad and have at her. There was something to be said for her rationalization. In case of interruption, it was a lot quicker and easier to slip into swim togs and start swimming than to get entirely dressed and go out a side door. Also it gave her the chance to say to herself that it had not really been intentional. It had just sort of snuck up on them, in spite of promising each other it would never happen again.

She had dark red curls, round green eyes and a fatty little mouth. Though she looked chubby, she was solid meat and hard heavy bone. She enjoyed golf, tennis, waterskiing, swimming, jogging, bicycling and lovemaking. She combined superb health, excellent reflexes and a tireless enthusiasm for all energetic pursuits. Lew Traff was thirty-four, lean, swarthy, languid, hairy and sardonic.

Molly chugged her beer, beamed upon him and said, "It was pretty fabulous, huh? You like to have ruined me, lover."

"It was really great."

"But we've got to give it up, right? It just isn't fair to Jus. He ever finds out, he'd kill us both, and you better believe it."

"How would he find out, Molly? One of the two of us would have to tell him, and it won't be me."

"Golly, it wouldn't be me either. Anyway, it's never going to happen again, so we shouldn't worry. From now on it's just a memory we share between us, a very sweet memory."

He drew an icy line across the lower part of his chest

with the bottom edge of his beer can and stared gloomily at his toes, his knobby ankles and his scrawny shins.

"You bring it?" she asked.

"Eh? Sure I brought it."

"Look, I didn't have any lunch or anything, and I got a tennis lesson at the club at two thirty, and . . ."

"And get off the dime. Sure, honey."

Lew Traff got up and sauntered wearily to the guest room. After he had dressed in his pale gray slacks and light green shirt-jacket, he went into the bathroom and hung the wet trunks over the shower rail. He looked at himself in the mirror with customary distaste and combed his black hair over the places where it was thinning badly. The whites of his eyes looked yellow. His tongue was caked with white. He sighed and went back into the bedroom and put his dispatch case on the bed, clicked it open and took the Denniver envelope out of the file flap on the case lid.

With envelope in hand he went in search of her. She was in the master bedroom, all dressed in her little white tennis outfit, sitting at the dressing table, leaning toward the mirror, painting bigger lips onto her small fat mouth.

Looking at him in the mirror she said, "I got time I could make us fried egg sandwiches, okay?"

"Sure. Great."

He put the envelope on the dressing table and backed away. She finished her mouth, inspected it, then picked up the envelope and ran her stubby thumb under the flap and ripped it open. She riffled the stack of bills and looked at him.

"Something wrong? One hundred hundreds equals ten big ones."

"Well . . . Jus and I were talking about it last night. Like he says, he's dedicating a part of his life to public service and all. But what Marty Liss wants to do is a lot bigger than before, you know? And it isn't like there wasn't expense coming out of it. Well, we thought it ought to be more."

"How much more?"

"Justin thought maybe double?"

She had swiveled around on the bench. He walked a slow thoughtful circle and then sat on the foot of the king-size bed and looked at her and shook his head sadly. "You disappoint me, honey. You really do."

"What's the matter with you?"

"You are the brains, baby. Justin D. Denniver can't use a urinal without an instruction book. You are supposed to be smarter than this kind of shit you pull on us. I won't go into arguments, like telling you this time we don't need any zoning exceptions so there won't be any public hearing, or telling you that interest charges and construction costs are so high, maybe Marty shouldn't be taking the risk at all, or reminding you that the building industry in Palm County is so flat on its ass, out of the five commissioners we could probably get three in favor without any help from Justin at all. What you're trying to pull isn't worth argumentation. What you should know, and what you know already, is there are wheels within wheels within wheels. Harbour Pointe is twelve million to fifteen million, and the visible part of it is the Marliss Corporation. You two are taking. And you know what Marty wants in return, right? That minor work permit for the so-called scouring of the channel, and an extension of the time limit on the permit on the land clearing."

"I *know* that. But Justin said . . ."

"Down, girl." He sighed, smiled, shook his head sadly. "I wouldn't want anything to happen to you."

Her mouth tightened. "What the hell kind of—"

"Shush, honey. Just listen. Marty and Benjie and Cole Kimber and me, we are not syndicate-type people. Take Azure Breeze, for example. A big project like that, it has to be a miracle of timing, not only getting all the permissions and certifications and so on, but getting it up on time. Big delays mean big losses. What happened there was bathroom fixtures. The crews were all ready to put them in, and the main supplier is struck, and also there is a trucking strike. Marty had found out that if he could steer the maintenance and service and supply contracts to local subsidiaries of a Miami corporation, they could solve problems for him, they said. He got in touch, and all the bathroom stuff came right through, because of some kind of arrangement with the unions. It's a permanent relationship on all the projects now. It's all clean legal business, you understand, but the money behind it could have come out of Mafia links."

She looked uncertain. "Just what are you trying to tell me?"

"Marty gets excited and does things on impulse. All the costs have been cranked into the formula on this Harbour Pointe project. I can't guarantee that if I go back to him for another ten, he won't complain that he's being held up for more money by a local county honcho, and then there would be the danger somebody might overreact."

She moistened her lips. "Like how?"

"There was that situation over in Hallandale, where a subcontractor was stalling a big project for more money, and persons unknown went in one night and rapped him and his wife on the skull, put them in the trunk of their Chrysler, drove it out into the boonies and lit it like a big gasoline lantern."

She swallowed with obvious effort, tried to smile and said, "Come on, Lew, really!"

"Maybe he won't get excited. Maybe he will think it's worthwhile to pay you, but he certainly will find somebody else in the future, to do little favors. Nobody likes a gun in their ribs."

"Well . . . maybe you better forget I said it."

"The east coast people who take care of little problems for Marty do so as a way of cementing goodwill. From what I've observed, they seem to react badly to situations where people want to change an existing agreement."

"All *right,* Lew," she said angrily. "Just forget it. It was a rotten idea anyway. I won't push that way again. Justin thought it was worth a try, that's all. He needs money. He says business is terrible."

"As a friend of both you nice people, I felt I had to speak up, just as long as there was any outside chance anything might . . ."

"You scared hell out of me, just as you wanted to do. Don't worry about Jus. I'll quiet him down."

She got up and went to the long wardrobe and racked one of the sliding doors back, revealing a rainbow array of Justin Denniver's sports jackets and slacks. She pushed them apart, sliding the clothes along the bar, revealing the little barrel safe cemented into the cinder-block wall behind the clothes at waist level. She bent over to see the combination as she turned the dial. She kept her legs straight. Her little tennis skirt hiked up in the back, revealing the white panties and the full round buttocks. He smiled, knowing that if she'd been alone she would most probably have squatted or knelt to work the combination. And he was reassured by a stirring tingle in his groin. He was glad to know that he might come back to life some day. She chunked the safe closed and spun the dial, backed out and stood up and rearranged the hangers.

He stood up as she turned, looking at her watch.

"I think we talked right through fried-egg time," she said. "I'm sorry. I'm really starving. What we're down to is peanut-butter-sandwiches time."

They went to the kitchen. He leaned against the counter and sipped a tall glass of milk as she assembled the two thick sandwiches.

"I bet I made forty-five thousand of these before the kids went off to school," she said.

"What are they going to do this summer?"

"God knows. I think Midge wants to work at Disney World again if they'll take her. Brud is looking for something that'll grow meat and muscle." She gave him his sandwich and said, "Do you ever think about getting married again, Lew?"

"If I can find a lady as smart as you I'll get married and run for governor."

"You always keep saying I'm so smart. Mostly all I'm good at is games. And what . . . we do. I mean what we used to do. We swore off. Right?"

He toasted the thought with a lift of his milk glass. "Absolutely right. Never again."

"Lew? You know the money from my mother's estate, that I put into certificates of deposit? Remember, over a year ago it was, I told you if Marty went ahead with

Harbour Pointe, I wanted a predevelopment price on a real nice one?"

"I remember."

"Well, if anybody counted me in, you better tell them to count me out."

"You're probably on some kind of list of people to be contacted, but no obligation was set up. Just say no thanks."

"Would you buy one yourself?"

"No thanks."

"That's what I thought."

It was time to go. He wiped away the crumbs with a paper napkin and kissed her on the temple. "I didn't mean to frighten you, honey."

"I guess I'm glad you did. Look, some hot day when you want a swim, you call me up, hear?"

Her face was earnest, her round green eyes without guile. "I'll just do that," he said. "Thanks, Molly girl."

He backed out and drove around the circle and west on Bayview Terrace to the stop sign at the corner of Beach Drive. In his rear vision mirror he saw Molly Denniver right behind him in the Lincoln, wearing her big mirrored shades. He waved and she honked and they turned in opposite directions on Beach Drive.

When Lew Traff stepped off the elevator at the twelfth floor, the receptionist told him that Mr. Wannover, the Marliss accountant, wanted him to come to his office as soon as he got in.

Benjie Wannover was behind his desk, going over large work sheets, his fingers dancing across the keys of his big desk-top electronic calculator. Benjie was about fifty. He looked to be in the final stages of some wasting disease, gray, frail and transparent. In actuality he had ten children and a very contented wife. He ate like a timber wolf, played scratch golf and had never been sick a day in his life.

Benjie nodded Lew Traff into a chair, finished his calculations, tore the tape off, leaned back and studied the figures, then crumpled the tape and missed the waste-basket with it.

"I had Cole Kimber in here, funning me," Benjie said. "He priced out the architect's working drawings for Harbour Pointe twenty months ago, and he just priced them out again. Make a guess."

"Hummm. Up twenty percent?"

"Twenty-one. Very damned good for a horseback guess. Okay. Take total costs and translate that into per-square-foot costs of the hundred and sixty-eight apartments. Total costs work out to $37.80 per square foot, and at an average 2,265 square feet per apartment, you've got $14,383,656. So I worked it backwards. We'll have to see three million net before taxes. That means an average sale price of $103,474 per apartment. Call it from $85,000 to $125,000."

Lew whistled. "Rich for the neighborhood. Gulf front-age, yes. But the Silverthorn tract is on the bay."

"I know. I know. With the eleven-mil line of credit, we'll have to take in three and a half million in advance payments on the units before completion."

Lew said, "I think we ought to cut back. Different materials. Smaller units. Cut out one pool. Shrink the marina."

"That's what *you* think. And that's what *I* think. But do you know what *he* says? He says we won't compromise. He says we'll go first class. And that decision could send the whole group right down the tube."

"He's got an instinct. He's a winner."

"So far. We had some other winners around Athens. And they're in bankruptcy Chapter Eleven."

"You are a pessimist, Benjie."

"Me? I'm a very cheery guy. All I've got here is the figures. And they look terrible. Anyway, your problem is with Cole Kimber. He says the only way he'll touch it is on straight cost plus. No upset price. He says that shortages could kill him, and he isn't going to try to out-guess them. He says he can make a nice little living with a shrunken crew, making repairs on the stuff he's put up over the last ten years, and there's no need for him to take a fat risk. So you have to draft a contract he'll sign that won't send Marty up the walls."

"Maybe some kind of sliding scale on cost plus, the longer the delay the lower the percentage. I'll talk to Cole first, then take a formula to Marty."

"Sure. Oh, and he said to tell you to set up a closing on the Silverthorn tract. One million two hundred and fifty-two thousand. That'll be the first draw on the established line downstairs. You should take the note down when you get a date for the closing, and make a transfer into Marliss Special Account, then you and Marty will both sign the check to the Silverthorn Trust."

Lew Traff went down the corridor to his own office. His secretary was out sick. He punched an outside line and phoned Cole Kimber. They said he was expected back a little after four. He left his number. He got out the Silverthorn file, but he could not keep his mind on the clauses of the option agreement. He closed his eyes and leaned back into one of his favorite fantasies, the one about the nuns and the haystack. But it wouldn't come off. Their squeals and gigglings were on mylar tape. The straw was dynel. Up under the habits, the smooth young bodies were plastic, warmed with clever wires. It was trite, boring and mechanical, like a play which started as a hit but now, after two years, was about to fold.

He had hoped to avoid getting into the inventory. But he slid into it, helplessly. It happened too often lately. A portfolio of—hah!—stocks worth twenty-one thousand, and they had cost him a hundred and eighty. Maybe they'd come back. Before the century changed. Working off three notes at the bank. Working off a compromise settlement with the IRS. Forty thousand a year from Marty, plus maybe another forty in little side things that opened up on account of working with Marty. Where in Christ's name did it all go? Taxes, and alimony to that pig, Adele. And eating out. And drinking out. And three fairly steady women: Margo, who was elegant and expensive and sexy and quarrelsome, and Ruthie, who was a lot handier, cheaper, rounder and more loving, and Molly Denniver, the water girl. And a rented apartment.

And an ulcer, small. And some root-canal work needed. And an eye exam. And new glasses. Nothing at all in the whole wide world seemed worth a shit, but oh, God, the thought of losing it turned his belly to ice. Weird Martin Liss was going to blow the whole thing. He could feel it. Right down the tube. Marty and everybody close to him. Where the hell could he go? Could anybody use a shrewd-stupid shyster name of Lew Traff? Not after the disaster that was called Harbour Pointe.

He worked his way back to the nuns, snuggling into their haystack world, accepting the fact it was all plastic. Hell, anything was better than the inventory.

ROBERTA FISH, R.N., and her husband, Gilbert, a young administrator with the Palm County public school system, had rented Apartment 2-C for one year from a Mr. Horuck of Cincinnati, beginning February first when Mr. Horuck despaired of finding a seasonal tenant for a high weekly rent. Mr. Horuck was due to retire in three years and had been persuaded to buy an apartment at Golden Sands on the theory it could carry itself.

Bobbie Fish worked the 11 P.M. to 7 A.M. shift at Athens Memorial, on emergency-room duty. She was twenty-nine, five foot ten, a big-boned woman who tried, usually without success, to keep her weight under one fifty-five. She had glossy cropped black hair, deep blue eyes and black brows which met over the bridge of her nose, giving her a look of wearing a small perpetual scowl. She had pale flawless skin, endless energies and a full classic figure. With less jaw she could have been beautiful.

She got home in time to have coffee with Gil while he had his breakfast. She was asleep by eight thirty and slept until three thirty when the bedside phone awakened her. Julian Higbee said, "You alone?"

"Yes."

"Be right there." He hung up before she could ask him to give her a few minutes to get organized. The phone had hauled her up out of nightmare depths. Nightmare seemed ever more frequent. People did such damned awful things to themselves and to each other. They were brought in during the long stained hours of the night, ripped and bloodied, smashed and slashed, charred and scalded, making monkey sounds and crow sounds and kitten sounds. Lately when she heard the rapid oncoming *weep-weep-weep* of the siren, racing toward the hospital, there was no quickening of mind and reflex, no challenge to save someone from dirty death. A sick weariness instead, a resignation, a distaste. They would all die anyway, soon enough. So wheel in your burden of agony and let Doctor Tucker and Nurse Fish dab away, exercising small skills and traditional remedies. "You and I," Tucker said, his odd thin mouth with its little doll-teeth shaped into the imitation of a smile, "you and I, Bobbie baby, we get the absolute worst, the ones who won't make it up to the O.R. unless we do our magic act first. The penalty of excellence, eh? Goddammit, nurse, find me a vein somewhere! How does that foot look?"

She yawned and stretched, knuckled her scratchy eyes, put on her blue robe and trudged to the door. She opened it and looked through the crack until she saw Julian approaching rapidly. She let it swing wide and turned and walked away. He thumped the door shut, caught up with her, stopped her with both arms around her middle, worked the shoulder of her robe aside with his blunt bristled chin and kissed the top of her shoulder.

He turned her around and looked at her. "Hey, you all right?"

"Fan-damn-tastic."

"What's wrong with you, Bobbie, huh?"

"I was sound asleep when the phone rang. I think it would be very nice, very touching, if you sometime said you'd be along in fifteen minutes, so maybe I could pee and brush my teeth."

"So go ahead, for God's sake. You're in a bad mood, huh?"

She looked at him, at the auburn hair carefully arranged and sprayed to cover the evidence of the receding hairline, at the heavy, dull, sensual features. He was such a towering hunk of solid meat and bone, of sun-crisped hair on massive arms and legs, he made her feel fragile and feminine. When she came out of the bathroom he had stripped down and lay supine on her unmade bed, thick fingers laced behind his head, afternoon sunlight filling the room. She saw that he was becoming tumescent in anticipation of her, the brute weapon lolling across his thigh, inching upward to each beat of his muscular heart.

She put her robe on the chair and got in with him. He folded her close and small in his big arms and said, "I thought you wasn't going to phone down there anymore like yesterday, Bobs."

"I know. I'm sorry. I had a couple of drinks and then I thought, Well, why not?"

"You shouldn't get on the sauce so much."

"I guess not. But what difference?"

"You've got a really great body, you know? A woman goes on the sauce, she goes down the road pretty fast. Look at Peggy Brasser."

"I've got a long way to go before *that*."

"Calling the office, you can get me jammed up, you know? When Lorrie says your name, she's got that funny way of doing it already, like it hurts her mouth. She don't play by any rules. She could go to your school-teacher husband and tell him about us."

"She wouldn't!"

"Hey. Lay down again. It's no sweat. She won't if you stop calling down there all the time."

"Oh, great," she said. "I'm just supposed to keep my

mouth shut. What I am, I'm just available ass. Anytime you've got a minute or two in between renting an apartment or fixing somebody's john, you can trot up to Two-C and get fixed up. Bam, bam, thank you ma'am."

"Oh, shut up, Bobbie. Jesus! If you didn't want it too, there wouldn't have been a first time, right?"

"I was drinking."

"I didn't notice it slowed you down any. Then or since."

"You're a way of taking my mind off things, like drinks are."

"What things?"

"I don't want to talk anymore. Okay?"

"But that's . . ."

"Shut up, Julian."

For long minutes after she heard the discreet closing of the door as Julian let himself out, she could feel the fast bumping of her heart, slowing as her breath slowed. This time, as had happened several times recently, she had thought to remain a bystander, to help him along with apparent enthusiasm, but actually feel very little. Sometimes it had worked, but more often it did not. He seemed to have a strange knack of lasting just a little bit too long, and once she felt it beginning to happen, no matter how faint and far away, there was no stopping place for her. She felt that if she could learn the knack of deadness, learn in the midst of sweaty and energetic copulation to think of other things and to feel nothing at all, then she could start to be rid of him.

She showered, dressed, made the bed and fixed coffee. Each time she crossed the small kitchen she was aware of the hidden bottle under the sink, behind the two rolls of paper towels. Finally, she squatted and took it out. Without looking at it, she unscrewed the top, poured an unmeasured, unwatched amount into a water glass and drank it down. The tepid vodka bounced back up into her throat. She leaned against the sink and coughed shallowly, mouth wide, shuddered, swallowed several times. She put the bottle away and rinsed the glass. She looked out the window at the tropic jungle between the parking area and the bay. Fingers of heat felt their way through the narrow places of her body. Heat and softness, blurring the edges, melting the hard spaces.

"Nothing is wrong with me," she said aloud.

It had been on account of the Avery kid. Hell, you are supposed to be on the lookout for things like that. The leg was definitely broken and there were a lot of bruises, but the bruises were all the same age and color, and X-ray found no old healed breaks. And after all, a fall down a flight of stairs will cause a lot of damage. A very silent little girl. It could talk but wouldn't talk about the fall. That should have tipped her off. Nervous little big-eyed mother. You hesitate, wonder, and finally decide to leave it alone. The kid goes home. Two months later it is back. With a broken finger, arm, shoulder, pelvis and skull, with internal bleeding and with pressure building inside the skull. A dying blonde named Anne. Come home then and start having a couple of off-duty drinks daytimes, and one day get big Julian up to fix the leaking faucet and start kidding around, and all of a sudden as you are beginning to get annoyed and beginning to get ready to turn him off, he has you perched on the edge of the bathroom countertop next to Gil's toothbrush and towel and aftershave, and he has somehow slid that big purply thing up into you, and he is grunting and thudding away, and you are clinging to him and sobbing and gobbling with shock, fright, guilt, consternation and shame.

"Nothing is wrong with me," she said again, knowing that some terrible thing she could not define was happening and had been happening for a long time, starting well before the Avery child was brought in, long before the affair with Julian Higbee began or the drinking began. It made her think of the summer days of her Florida childhood in Tangerine, where her father owned small groves. A storm could climb the sky behind you while the sun shone brightly all around you. And before the day began to darken, before you could hear the thunder, there would be a change you could not define. Perhaps it was the way the wind turned the leaves or moved the grasses. These are the little winds plowing across my heart, she thought. A blond child and Smirnoff and Julian. The sad little winds have names. The storm is so close behind me now that if I looked straight up, I could probably see the leading edge of it. Soon I will hear the rumble of the thunder.

"I am all right," she said, and the tears ran down her face, tickling the pale fuzz at the corner of her mouth.

She sat on the kitchen stool and folded her arms on the countertop and laid her cheek against the cool Formica in the circle of her arms. She shut her teeth so tightly her ears rang and then she whispered, "Whatever is becoming of me now?"

When Julian Higbee sauntered into the office, elaborately casual, Vic York stood up from where he had been half sitting on the corner of Lorraine's desk, one leg dangling, and said, in his raspy, rusty high-pitched voice, "Well, here he is finally at last. Mister Julian Higbee himself. Kid, I was about to give up and come back tomorrow, maybe first making an appointment through your beautiful little wife and better half and helpmate here."

"Hi, Vic," Julian said. He looked at Lorrie. She was pale and her eyes looked wide and frightened. He felt a chill in the pit of his stomach. "What you want, Vic?"

"Hey, I found a place where we can have a little talk, you and me. Come on, kid."

Lorrie got up quickly when they left, and closed and locked the office door behind her. She hurried after them as they went across the basement parking area, between the support columns, to one of the service rooms. She got there just as Vic closed the door behind them. She tried the latch. Vic had apparently bolted it on the inside.

She leaned her ear against the utility door and covered her other ear. One of the residents, a Mrs. Dawdy, had just gotten out of her car. She stared at Lorrie and came over, brows raised in query, and said, "Is something wrong, dear?"

"Get the hell away from here!"

The woman backed off. "Well, parm me, I'm sure. You don't have to be shitty to me, you little slut."

Apologize later, Lorrie told herself. She could hear voices in the service room, Julian's loud and angry and blustering, Vic's much fainter. Then there were other sounds. Faint gasps and grunts of effort. Thudding thumping sounds. She squeezed her eyes shut. She wanted to stop listening, and could not. There was a sour taste in the back of her throat. In an eerie way, it was much like listening that time to Julian and Mrs. Fish, the big nurse. There was the same sense of both fascination and personal loss. It had been evil to keep on listening and then say nothing to him, nothing to stop him doing it with her. Nurse Fish was freeing her from Julian. Now Vic was doing the same thing, somehow. It frightened her. She could hear no further sounds. She hammered on the locked door, hurting both fists.

The door opened a few inches and Vic filled the opening, looking out at her with disapproval. "What are you banging on the door for? What are you yelling about? This is dumb, Lorrie sugar."

"Let me in. Let me see him or I'll call the police."

"Go ahead."

"Let me in!"

"Go ahead. Call the cops. Then neither one of you has a job and everything you own gets thrown out in the street. I thought you were the one with sense. Go turn his bed down. I'll walk him in through that back door in about five minutes."

He shut the door in her face and she turned and did as he had told her. She left their back door open.

It was closer to ten minutes before they arrived, Julian with gray slack face, leaning heavily on Vic, scuffing, dragging the heels of his sandals. There were tear tracks on Julian's face.

Vic grinned merrily at Lorrie and swung Julian around and sat him on the side of the bed. Julian sighed heavily several times as Lorrie helped him undress. He rolled to face the wall, knees pulled up. She covered him over and left him, quietly closing the bedroom door.

Vic was waiting in the tiny kitchen. "What I wanted to say was he took it good, like I figured he would. You noticed I didn't mark him none. I didn't think you'd like that. There is some cartilage sprung between his ribs that will hurt him for breathing for a couple weeks probably. And if he should piss some blood, not to worry. He is going to be too sore all over to get out of bed tomorrow. Better he should rest up. He understands if it ever happens again, it's a hospital case, like a week maybe." He held out his lumpy broken fists, with the dimpled knuckles where the bone had been compressed in combat long ago. He winked at her. "Better me with these than he sends some punk kid with a pipe wrapped in a towel to scramble his head. Always hire a pro. Look after him, Lorrie. See you around, huh?"

LeGrande Messenger eased himself to a more comfortable position in his big black leather lounge chair in Apartment 7-A and told himself the pain would soon go away. And he wished that this Mr. Stanley Wasniak would go away.

"We believe," Wasniak was saying, "that everybody here in Golden Sands is entitled to a personal explanation from one of us that got elected to be officers of the Association. You could say that everybody turns out to be a patsy, some kind of pigeon for the group that set this whole thing up. Everybody thought an average eighty-one fifty would cover it, but it has got to be more than twice . . ."

"Mr. Wasniak."

". . . more than twice what we counted on. What I

want to assure you, we've been over the contracts and charges and all with a fine-tooth comb and—"

"Mr. Wasniak! Please!"

"What? What's the matter?"

"I am trying to tell you that I am not particularly interested in what the monthly charges might be. Whether they are eighty dollars or eight hundred dollars is a matter of indifference to me."

Wasniak stared at him, mouth hanging open for several seconds. "Well, excuse me all to hell, Mr. Messenger. I din't know I was talking to some kind of millionaire-type person."

"I am sorry if I was rude. I'm in pain."

"Is there anything I can do?"

"No. It comes and goes. When I hurt I am likely to be irritable, as Mrs. Messenger will doubtless confirm."

"I didn't mean to bug you when you're . . ."

"Sit down, sit down again, please, Mr. Wasniak. You may have to run through it again, as my attention was . . . less than perfect the first time. Let me ask some questions to clarify my own thinking on this. Would you say that it was or should have been obvious to the developers that the monthly maintenance would not cover the costs?"

"Oh, hell yes. What Liss says, he says the original figures were worked out for a lot more units, but then the project got cut back by a regulation on density, and they never changed the figures. Look at me. I'm supposed to be retired. I'm supposed to be fishing, playing golf and all that. What am I doing? I am running around like a damn fool asking people to understand it isn't my fault they pay double from now on. How I got sucked into this I'll never know. I wanted to be Mr. Popularity maybe. Some popularity!" He checked his list. "You go from a hundred and five to two oh two. One of the things I'm supposed to tell you, you can inspect the books. Hadley Forrester has all the books and records in his apartment, in Seven-D, right here on the top floor. It averages out—"

"I'm sure that the accounts are in good order, and I

am sure that there is absolutely nothing any of us can do about it."

"I'm telling you, that's a lot better attitude than I've been running into most places, Mr. Messenger."

"I appreciate your stopping by. And you'll forgive me for not seeing you to the door, Mr. Wasniak?"

"No, don't you trouble yourself. A real pleasure talking to you, sir. The new billing will be along first of the month."

Just as Wasniak opened the door, Barbara Messenger was reaching to put her key in the lock. She gave him a brilliant smile as he stood aside to let her in. "Hi, Mr. Wasniak. I thought I'd be back here before you arrived."

"Well, it was going faster than I figured, so I was early."

She wore an open robe over her blue and white swimsuit, and carried an orange beach bag by its nylon cord. Her raw tawny brown-blond hair was as casual as noonday lions. She was a honey-tanned, long-limbed creature, handsome and graceful and totally assured. There was a very tangible force about her, almost a flavor of violence under control. Without conscious effort she received special attention from everyone and accepted it without surprise.

"And?" she said expectantly.

"What? Oh, I was just leaving. Good-bye, sir. Good-bye, Mrs. Messenger."

She looked thoughtfully at her husband after Wasniak had gone. "He looked sort of concerned and shaken, darling."

"I think I got impatient with the fellow."

She went to him quickly and sat on the footstool and took his hand. "A bad one?"

"No. It's fading now. Grade Three plus."

She knew his grading system. Three was a dull red color like fireplace coals. The pain was like an expanding pocket of gas trapped in a coil of bowel, shortening the breath. Grade Two was a flickering, pulsating, evil yellow. Grade One was glaring white, and hissed and made sweat and sometimes made him yell.

"Want a shot?"

"There were a few minutes there when I would have said yes. But I'm really all right now, thanks."

"Where's Mrs. Schmidt?"

"She asked if she could leave early. She got a call from her daughter. Some kind of trouble. I gather it isn't very serious. How was your walk?"

"Four miles long. And hot. I went two miles south down the beach and turned around. Starting a mile south I began to come upon dead fish washed up, and fewer people. Very long-dead fish. Down where the motels are, the stench would knock a goat down. People say it's a new outbreak of red tide."

"And the seas shall rot, the animals die, the birds vanish, and all the people flee."

"What's that from?"

"The instant inventions of LeGrande Messenger."

"When I think it's you, it turns out to be a quotation."

"Child, you came along after they stopped educating people."

"I know, I know, I know," she said, getting up. "I was born on your fortieth birthday, and the world has been going to hell in a handbasket for a long time. I better go change."

After she left the room, Messenger leaned forward, braced the heels of his hands against the leather arms of his chair and with a brisk effort levered himself to his feet. He swayed, caught his balance and walked slowly over to the window wall and looked out across their roof patio to the bright afternoon dance of the Gulf, seen between the pale stiff shoulders of the Azure Breeze and the Surf Club.

Be grateful it was Grade Three and didn't last, he thought. And be grateful that age slows the growth of the inoperable invader cells. You old bastard, you want to get so old the growth will stop. You want a remission. Mother had an aunt who lived to a hundred and six and kept her wits until the end. Lost her teeth, hearing, eyesight and mobility. But kept her wits. Heredity? Or is it all the vitamins Barbara keeps shoving into your ancient carcass? The wretched part is in looking so damned old. Part of that is the disease, of course. Eats you out. What the young never realize, can never comprehend, is that inside this husk there is a baffled man aged thirty. Barbara's age. A man who feels hope and fear, love and lust, anger and greed, pride and despair. The young man wonders how this creeping, dismaying, destroying thing called age ever happened to him. He wonders how the years were all so short.

Given a choice, he thought, of being old and sick and poor, and old and sick and rich, rich is better. A life-long exercise of wits, weighing with great care the risk-reward ratios in all things. Dim little men try to conserve, and so they have to be right fifty-one percent of the time to hope to stay even with the board. Deepen and broaden the risk areas, and eventually you can reach a point where being right ten percent of the time will pile money atop money. Big money expands the choices, multiplies the options.

He stretched with care, clicking an elbow, creaking a shoulder, checked for the last morsel of pain and found it entirely gone. He went over to his desk in the corner of the room, eased himself into the chair and played back the tape of the morning phone call from Zurich, listening to it for the third time, listening with care for each nuance in Muller's heavy voice, his eyes closed. When he felt Barbara's hand on his shoulder he said, "I don't think we gave him enough to show to his people upstairs. Tomorrow I'll dictate a new clause and put in a three or four year reversion."

"But that won't really mean anything, will it?"

"It will to Muller, I think. He has to bring the stick back, wagging his tail."

"Okay, I know you are a very clever man, and I'll re-type the damned thing and mail it, but you should be saying, My, what a pretty dress and how nice you look, darling."

He opened his eyes and smiled ruefully. "My, what a pretty dress and how nice you look, darling."

"How sweet of you to notice, Lee!"

She sat in the chair beside the desk. He rewound the tape and ejected the cassette and put it aside for her to file. "While you walked did you think about what I asked you?"

She nodded, head atilt, her smile small and solemn. "Of course. I think it is really a good place for us to live. Like you say, this is a very gaudy and vulgar building. But the climate is good, and this penthouse apartment is pleasant and roomy enough for us, dear. There's good medical attention handy. I *know* we could live anywhere in the world. With a staff of dozens. And no privacy. These people don't know who you really are. They've never heard of you. We don't have to have any social or political or business involvements here. I know, I know. Don't say it, please. You worry too much about me, about what I might want. My God, Lee, I love the sun and the water. I'm no little kid aching to go to parties. This place is *fine,* really. And if I ever start to get sick of it, I will let you know immediately."

"Promise?"

"Of course."

"Tomorrow maybe we could go over those inventory lists and see what we'd like to have with us. The bank can arrange it all. I don't want to clutter the place with too much stuff. Some of the small bronzes, maybe."

"One of the Chinese horses maybe?"

"If you'd like."

"And the Miro with the balloons?"

"On that wall?"

"Oh, yes. Why are you frowning, Lee?"

"Wondering if it is enough of a life for you, Barbara."

"I had all that other stuff."

"And I've made you a rich lady."

"Which really bugs those three prune-mouthed sons of yours, dear."

"They take after their sainted, long-departed mother. There'll be enough to go around. You just got yours earlier."

"When I think of it, I want to laugh."

"It's funny?"

"Lee, when I worked in your office for four hundred dollars a week, I formed my lifelong opinions about money. I can be terribly solemn about fifty thousand. I can be awestruck by one million. But the amount you stuck in trust for me is so grotesque, it makes me laugh. It's like a little kid at the Macy parade seeing a duck twice the size of an elephant float by. It is beyond belief. It is a delight. And it is absurd. I look at it from the outside. You know? Office girl fleeces tycoon. Premarital contract sets record."

"What if I *had* to buy you?"

"No way. The lady is not for sale."

"I would cheerfully have paid that just to have you near me while, as they say in the song, the days grow short."

"Shall I whistle for the violins?"

"I just have to reassure myself that you are here and want to be here. I have to hear it now and then."

"Where else would I be but with you? I had all that other stuff, Lee. I had the house, the husband, the babies. I don't ever want to be that vulnerable again. The fates mess around with the people who have the most to lose. Ever notice that?"

"A couple of times a day."

"Hey, I'm sorry."

"It was a joke, Barbara. Slightly sick, but a joke nonetheless."

"It isn't going to have me laughing helplessly."

After the worst of the heat had gone from the sun, she went out onto the private terrace with him. She brought him his small carafe of red wine and put it and the glass he liked on the tiled table beside the arm of his chair. Eight pelicans in single file glided by, heading home after the day's work out on the broad Gulf. She sat in the deck chair beside his, drifting back and forth across the edge of sleep, made drowsy by the walk along the beach.

He held her hand and talked to her. She could tell that the old man wanted her and was trying to hide it. He was as shy and strange about that as he was about almost everything. He seemed to feel that she should be sickened by the needs of a frail, dying man. He had come to despise his own body to the point where he could not comprehend how she could caress him or endure his caresses. Love made her take pleasure in giving him pleasure. After the first time he had told her he had not intended that to be part of their bargain. She had said she did not think in terms of bargains and agreements. Frailty made them gentle. Each time might be the last time. There was sweetness and there was gratitude.

The angry fire had burned up the grinning happy husband and the fat adorable babies and the white house with the Tory chimney. It had burned up all their letters and their music and their yearbooks, their photographs of one another, her diaries and his tennis cups. It had burned her heart to a black cinder. The strange old man had waited long enough and then had sent people to bring her back to her desk, no excuses acceptable. She had been thinking then of sleeping pills and deep fast rivers, of high high places and razor blades, of gas ovens and kitchen knives. But that weird old Mr. Messenger had piled work upon her as if to crush her under the weight of it. She had dived down into work and had lived there for over a year. When she had raised her head and looked around she found she was as mended as she would ever be, could ever be. She raised her head to hear Lee telling her that he was phasing out the office, that he had cancer, that, as an arrangement, and in order to be fair to her, he would marry her. He needed someone around him who was attractive, who'd had some nurse training, who was a superb secretary and who had no one else close to her. He said he might live six months or a year and would expect her in attendance to the end. But it had been two and a half years now, and though he looked more wasted than ever, the pains were not as frequent or as harsh.

He had offered her places to live. Corfu, Madeira, Saint Thomas, Crete. Islands in the sun. Agents had brought pictures and floor plans of the houses they could have. But one could not run a big house and manage to make the end of a long life graceful and easy at the same time.

So it would end here. The day after tomorrow or the year after today. She yawned and sighed and pulled the grave-marked hand to her mouth and kissed it, then went in to fix the sparse evening meal. She thought of the money. She did not think of it often. It was up there in the Chase, growing and growing in a fetid mushroom darkness, feeding its own tax-free income back to itself in the form of more tax-free municipals. Lee selected them. All from the South and Southwest and the West. General obligations, whatever they might be. Oh, there was enough to go around without that. She had seen all the trusts he had set up for the disapproving sons, with their long lists of holdings. She had seen how carefully he was liquidating, consolidating, minimizing the estate taxes. There was lots to go around. Without the trust fund he had settled on her, there had to be ten millions left per son, at least. And it could be twice that. Beyond a certain point money ceased to have any meaning. One could ride in but one car at a time, eat one meal at a time, sleep in one bed at a time.

Beyond that certain point, yes, quantity ceased to have any meaning, but up to that certain point it represented a pattern of living so at odds with her background she did not believe she could ever accept it without a sense of wonder and unreality.

The leased car was down there in the parking space underneath the building. If it developed any odd noise, or ceased to run perfectly in any way, one phoned and they came and took it and brought another. And there was always the limousine service, of course. If you bought a suit which did not really please you after one or two wearings, you gave it to Goodwill and bought another. When Lee ordered your birthday ring by telephone, a courier brought it down from New York. Mrs. Schmidt, that competent Swiss, did all the buying, cleaning, and almost all the cooking. Lee's bank received all their mail, paid all bills, accepted all income and forwarded the personal mail. They never had to stand in lines, wait in waiting rooms, bicker with bureaucrats, or suffer the attentions of fools and boors. Best of all was never having to think about money at all, about how much or how little for this or for that. It was there, and this life-style could not use it all as fast as it accumulated, so you never thought of what anything cost anymore.

COMMISSIONER JUSTIN DENNIVER SAUNTERED into Billy Scherbel's office in the east wing of the Palm County Courthouse, closed the door behind him, beamed at Billy, who was on the phone, and settled into one of the chairs facing the desk.

Billy was saying, ". . . there's a set procedure everybody has to go through, Mrs. Johnson. I'm not saying it's actually required, but I do think you'd be better off having an attorney check into this for you. No, there wouldn't be any point in talking to the County Manager at this stage of the game. Right. Thanks for calling."

Scherbel hung up and grimaced and said, "She wants a platted road vacated. Right now. Kids riding trail bikes up and down it, and she and her neighbors want to fence it off."

"How's Bets?"

"She's coming along fine. They got her walking up and down the hall already."

"That fast! Glad to hear it."

"I'll tell her tonight you asked about her, Justin."

"Lew Traff get hold of you?"

"Sure did."

"What did he have in mind, anyway?"

"You sure you don't know, Commissioner?"

"Now why the hell would I be asking you if I knew?"

"Well, don't get in an uproar. I just thought he'd maybe mentioned the two items to you before he came to me. What it is, both items are on that Silverthorn Tract on Fiddler Key, on the bay behind Golden Sands. Both come from Al Borne over at Palm Coast National Bank, in the trust department, the bank being executor for the estate of Becky Silverthorn. First, to extend the permit to clear the land for another year, it running out the end of this month, and second, a minor work permit they want to do some dredge and fill. Those permits would go along with the property in case of transfer, and it's obvious Marty Liss would be the one to follow through on it, him having the option to buy."

"Billy, friend, you seem defensive."

"Well, it's on account of about nine thousand people jumping the hell all over me if I ramrod these things, Justin. Now damn it all anyway."

"Listen, now. What I want you should do, Billy, is come in with a whole list of stuff for the meeting next Thursday, and you have those two buried in the middle. You make Palm Coast National the applicant, and you give the government lot line numbers and parcel numbers. I don't want to hear the name Silverthorn in any part of it, hear?"

"Yes, but—"

"I know, I know. You got those environment freaks all poised to jump all over you for recommending it and us commissioners for passing on it. What I'll do, I'll question you first. I'll ask you is there any big deals and you say it's a lot of small stuff, and I'll move we let you go down the list and we'll vote them all to once to save time. Jack Dorsey will give me a quick second, and we got me, Jack and Steve Corbin for the three aye votes. All you got to do is drone through the list in that go-to-sleep voice of yours and turn in just the one copy for the record."

"What if Mick picks up on it?"

"On the agenda, we've got the extension on the Crestway sewage disposal plant coming up before we get to you, Billy, so that newspaper son of a bitch, Mick

Rhoades, is going to be over at the press table so busy writing that story in his head, he'll never pick up on those two little things you'll have stuck in the middle of a long list."

"Jesus, it makes me pretty nervous. It really does. I get this indigestion all the time lately. Honest to God, Justin, the favors we do Martin Liss, I'd like to see a little gratitude."

"Figure it this way. We're doing a job for the community. The odds are that Marty won't go ahead with his project anyway. Times are too rough, costs too high. Would we want to be responsible, you and me, for loading on the straw that breaks his back and makes him give up on it? The building trades here are really hurting, Billy."

"I know. I know. But what they want to do isn't any minor work permit. They aren't scouring any little channel, Justin. They're building a goddam yacht harbor. You want to see the drawings?"

"No. And don't bring them to the meeting. Hold on to them. If anybody thinks to ask for them for the record, say you'll submit them later and apologize for forgetting."

"For what I do for you, I could go to jail."

Justin Denniver stood up and grinned at Billy Scherbel and shook his head. "Hell, we could all get put in the slammer for a lot of things, Billy. Take that Conference on County Administration over in Orlando in January. That little piece you hustled in the bar and took to the room, she hadn't even turned sixteen."

Billy paled and wiped his mouth with the back of his hand. "Go on! She had to be twenty or twenty-one."

Wearing the same merry smile, Denniver said, "It would be some kind of laugh, wouldn't it, if someday somebody showed up with a certified copy of her birth certificate and a signed and notarized statement from that kid."

"What are you trying to tell me?"

"I'm not trying to tell you a thing, Billy. I'm just saying this is no time in our lives we ought to worry about jail."

"She was at least twenty."

"If you say so."

"Justin, you weren't even there!"

Denniver winked at him. "Her name was Cindy Martinez and she was born and raised in Ybor City, and she was wearing yella jeans and a white top, and you took her to Room Thirty-eight in the Tropic Winds Motel, baby."

"Jesus Christ! What are you trying to *do* to me?"

"Do? Nothing. What's the matter with you, Scherbel? We've always got along in the past and we'll keep getting along in the future, as far as I can tell. I don't fault a man for chasing tail when he's out of town on business. You take care, hear. And give my best wishes to Bets. She's one wonderful woman."

"How do you know about Cindy Martinez?"

"Cindy? Cindy? Who you talking about, boy? I never heard of her. See you Thursday."

Frank Branhammer sat in his living room, clenching and unclenching his big red fists. He had a white crew cut a quarter inch long, broken veins in his broad red face, faded tattoos on his forearms, and a belly that rested in his lap like a semi-inflated beach ball tucked under his white T-shirt. His wife, Annabelle, sat beside him on the couch. She was a spare bony woman with a long sallow face, frightened eyes behind gold-wire glasses, sucked-in lips, and hair dyed sulfur yellow.

David Dow, representing the Condominium Association, sat facing them across a marble coffee table, wishing that Stan Wasniak had been assigned Apartment 3-G. With an inward sigh he tried once again to slip past the man's uncompromising hostility.

"Please, Mr. Branhammer. The five of us accepted the responsibility of running the Association."

"You can run it up your ass, fellow."

"Frank!" the wife said.

"Keep out of this, Annie," Frank said.

"I will put the facts in the simplest possible way, Branhammer. You *will* make up the hundred and sixty-six sixty deficit just like everybody else has to, and you *will* pay monthly maintenance of a hundred and sixty-eight fifty from now on, like everybody else."

"It's like you don't hear me, fellow. I do no such goddam thing. No little prick spent his whole life in an office is going to walk in here and tell Frank Branhammer the rules is changed. From the time I was seventeen, I worked hard all day every day. All my life I sweated. Mother and me raised three kids. One boy got killed in the army. The other boy got drowned surfing in California. The girl got killed when the car she was riding in went off the road and hit a tree. Killed her and three other girls, bam. There's nobody left to leave anything to except Annie's brother I wouldn't give house room to. A drunk. I decided we'd both worked hard all our lives, lost our kids, we'd live nice the time we got left. On the pension and the Social Security. I bought this goddam place in good faith, fellow. I figured it up how we can afford eighty-one fifty a month maintenance, and that's what it was, and that is what it is going to be, and not one dime more, and I'll pay it on time."

Dow said in exasperation, "I'm not your landlord, for God's sake. I represent *you*. Read your Declaration of Condominium, for God's sake. In black and white it says that when the costs go up, the assessment goes up, and you either pay it or we go to court and get a lien against your apartment."

"In a rat's ass *you* represent *me! I* represent me. All my life there's been little lightweight pricks like you coming around with big words, trying to screw me out of anything they could get. Go get your fucking lien, and then see if you can figure out what to do next. Anybody comes around here making to throw us out of our home we paid for, I throw them through that fucking glass there and over the fucking railing, and that goes for you too if you come back here with more of this shit, fellow."

Dow stood up, shrugged, and said, "Well . . . I tried."

Branhammer stood up. "Need any help getting out through that door?"

Dow took two quick steps and then his pride slowed him down. He turned and nodded at the couple before he closed the door behind him. He leaned against the wall and took out his notebook. He put a check mark beside the name and apartment number. He hesitated until he found the right words to express Branhammer's decision. *No way,* he wrote. He told himself he ought to resign. The thought came to him six times a day. But if he resigned, who would step in? And if Golden Sands went down the drain, what would the rest of retirement be like?

Annie Branhammer was huddled over. She saw Frank's big slippers standing in front of her.

"Stop bawling!" he said.

"We . . . we . . . we're going to lose this place."

"Don't you never believe stuff like that!"

"All I wanted I told you I wanted some little place on an acre of land so I could grow stuff and have an orange tree. I told you."

"Jesus Christ. Here we got every kind of convenience, Mother. And tennis and the community room and the pool and the beach."

"All my life I been scared of water and you know it. It could have been any kind of shacky little place long as there was garden land around it. And we could have brung Duke down with us instead of you have him put away. He was only ten. He had good years left. Everything I ever love keeps dying off."

"Shut up, Mother."

"We're going to lose it. I'm telling you. That's a nice man came here. You talked so ugly to him. So ugly."

"Stop your bawling, will you?"

"Nothing has ever turned out good for me and I shouldn't get so foolish as to hope anything ever will, not in my whole life, not ever."

"Oh, for God's sake!"

"You wouldn't listen to a word I said and you just don't care what I want, ever. It's always what Frank Branhammer wants. I got no rights at all. Where are you going?"

"I'm going to put on some shoes and go walk on the beach. You get on my nerves lately something terrible."

"If you walk south, Frank, we need a loaf of bread and a half-dozen eggs."

"Okay, okay, okay!"

11

The Sand Dollar Bar was on the southern outskirts of Beach Village, beyond the Beach Mall Shopping Plaza, on the left-hand side of Beach Drive for anyone heading south down Fiddler Key. It had been a private residence, one of the oldest structures on the key, a high-shouldered frame building made of hard pine and cypress. Road widening had brought Beach Drive to within a sidewalk's width of the front of the building. The front was boarded up and curtained and beer signs flicked on and off in the shallow space between the glass of the unused windows and the plywood interior. There was a small modern annex adjacent to it, and opening into it, called the Sand Dollar Discount Package Store.

Inside the bar structure the ceiling was hung with nets, with glass and cork floats. Harpoons were chained to the walls. The low-power wall sconces held orange bulbs with orange shades. Overhead prisms shone puddles of white light down upon the black Formica bar. The front edge of the bar and the barstools were upholstered in red Naugahyde, spotted with cigarette burns and old stains.

On that afternoon in late May, Peggy Brasser was the only customer. Though a relatively recent arrival on Fiddler Key, she had quickly become a regular bar customer.

Tom Shawn, the owner, and bartender most afternoons, saw her put down her empty glass, and in a little while he drifted closer to her and said, "Try another one on for size, Miz Brasser?"

"Honest to God, how'm I going to get you to ever call me Peggy? How many times have I asked you to?"

"I forgot, Peggy. I'm sorry."

"Okay, you forgot. I forgive you, Tom. Sure, you can hit me again. I'm ready."

She liked Beam on the rocks, doubles, which came to two fifty a pop, two sixty with the tax. She would come in about two, have three or four doubles, usually three, and drop a ten on him and leave the change.

It had taken him quite a while to figure out a good safe way to work any kind of leverage on her. If she'd been a gin drinker, it would have been easy to short her. Beam was fairly heavy, and so it was easy for her to watch the color, drinking it on the rocks as she did. He couldn't give her strong tea, certainly, Darleen Moseby's safe and sane habit when she was hustling. It tantalized him until finally, with water and vegetable coloring and about thirty percent of the cheapest bar whiskey he carried, so the taste would be there, he had mixed up the first of many quarts of what he called, privately, Brasser Blend. When she came in sober, indicated by a slow and slightly unsteady walk and an almost inaudible voice and no desire to chat, he would give her a legitimate double Beam to start her off and Brasser Blend from then on. If she came in stepping quickly, confidently, with good coordination and a sunny smile, then she was already bagged and he could go right to the Brasser bottle, with which he could make her the two-dollar-and-sixty-cent drink for an estimated raw-material cost of eleven cents.

He put the glass in front of her and she smiled wistfully and said, "I just can't get my husband off my mind today."

"That's the way it goes sometimes."

"What his real name was, it was Newcomb Carlyle Brasser," she was saying, "but everybody called him Charley. Honest to Christ, he must have had ten thousand friends all over everywhere. What he did for a living, he sold heavy equipment, stuff for construction. Euclids and draglines and cranes and big cats and stuff like that. I ever tell you how I come to be down here in the apartment?"

Only about fifty times, Tom thought. "You and him visited down here?"

"No, no, no. It was a *sales* trip he made down here and he brought me along. Those last years of his life Charley took me along with him, which he never done before, you know, when the kids were growing up and so on. All those years I never did get to go, I know for sure Charley had girls everyplace he went. Girls always liked Charley. It was a way he had, laughing and kidding around. He was some hundred-and-ten-percent man, you better believe it. I knew about the girls, even though he wouldn't never confess it, but he'd still come home and make me a very happy woman. . . . Wanna hit me again, Tom? Right on this old ice is okay. . . . Whoa! You trine get me drunk or something? There was a time no som-bitch on earth could get me drunk, or Charley neither, but nowadays it really hits me after a while, and Charley got to where two drinks and he mumbled so bad you couldn't tell what he was saying hardly. . . . Be that as it may, he'd had some bad luck selling for a half a year, and we come down here and stayed in Fort Myers and worked out from there, and maybe you won't believe this, but he made one sale to a big developer opening up raw land, Charley's commission was damn near a quarter million dollars! My Charley made good money his whole life, and the som-bitch spent good money too. Hell, I helped him spend it. Anyway, we saw that Golden Sands place and they had a model apartment there to look at, and Charley says to me, Peggy, he says, we grab one of these, then we'll have a place to go when I retire. So we signed up for Four-A and paid cash. Just like that. And he was sixty years old the day we got back home, and he was dead a month later. He had terrible varicose veins in his legs and the doctor kept telling him he ought to have them stripped because he could get clots in there, and that's what he got. You wouldn't believe how his left leg swole up, enough to make you sick looking at it. I was in the hospital with him the afternoon before they were going to operate on him the next morning, and I went home and come back in the evening and went right in and went to his room and it was empty! I went storming around wanting to know what they'd done to my Charley, and finally I found a nurse knew he was dead. A clot come loose and went to the heart. They'd tried to phone me, but they missed me at the house. . . . Where was I? Oh, when the kids come home for the funeral bringing their wives and the grandbabies, we had long talks and the boys figured out the best thing I should do is sell the big house and come down here into Four-A, which I did. Cheers, Tom."

He had been listening with one tenth of his attention, picking stemware from the slotted rack overhead, dusting and polishing it, replacing it at the other end of the rack, pushing the glasses along. He liked to have the stemware gleaming and perfect, picking up a sparkle from the overhead lights.

As the voice went on and on, and as he made small sounds of sympathy in the right places, he wondered what ironies of fate had brought him right to this point in the forty-first year of his life. He was five ten and weighed two sixty-five. He had glossy curly black hair, bright blue eyes, boyish red lips, pink cheeks and a flawless complexion. Once upon a time he had been a very fast running back up in Georgia, but he had crossed up the gambling interests on a point spread in a bowl game and so they had broken his knees with a ball bat. After that he had driven stock cars and then worked on a drilling rig in the Gulf, in an emerald mine in Brazil and on a shrimp boat out of Key West. Finally he had gone into partnership with a Cuban, smuggling hash from Jamaica into Miami. After their most successful trip, the Cuban suddenly shot Tom Shawn in the stomach. Tom drowned him in the pool of a motel near where they were staying, hid the total profits in a safe place and collapsed just inside the doorway of a hospital emergency room. After he was out of surgery and out of danger he repeated his story of having been shot while waiting on a street corner for the light to change, repeated it until they bought it. He had come across the state to Athens with the money, at thirty-seven years of age, and after tending bar for a year he had bought his own place. He thought of it as refuge and a kind of retirement. The world out there had begun to make him too jumpy. Each year you had less chance of guessing what people would do to you next. He was making out well. He overlooked no possible source of income. He was not bored. He watched and waited. He had a hunch that someday there would appear to him the chance to make a truly big score with absolutely no risk at all. He did not know what, how, or when. Enough to keep waiting and score in small ways off customers like Brasser here.

He had learned how to tell about them. This lady was well down the tube. If you couldn't tell by listening to her, you could tell by looking at her. Once upon a time she could have been a very special piece, he thought. But what booze does to these old ladies, they all begin to look like twins of each other. They all get the weird lumps and creases on their face. Their arms and legs get thin as sticks, and they get a big bloated belly. Stary eyes and scaly skin, dead-looking hair, hoarse loud voice telling the same old stories over and over and over.

Two village businessmen came in and sat at the two barstools farthest from Peggy Brasser. He moved down, greeted them by first names, took the order for two Schlitz, served quickly and deftly, plucked up the five, banged the register, slipped the bills and change in front of them.

"Ross been in?"

"Not today, Henry."

"You see him, tell him the order he gave Wendy came in. Wait a minute. You go off at six?"

"Not today. Lou's got the flu so I'm working through. So I see Ross, I'll tell him."

Tom Shawn had backed off to that carefully calculated distance which let the conversation go either way. If the two men wanted a private talk, they had only to lower their voices and he would move away. But if they wanted to include him in the conversation by speaking up, he could move closer. The two men lowered their voices. He had to move to where Peggy could rope him with her voice.

"Hey, Tom, you want to hear what was one of Charley's favorite bartender jokes? Charley had a million jokes, and nobody could tell them like my Charley. You hear the one about the guy that was always unlucky?"

Not more than twenty-eight times, he thought. "Unlucky?"

"This guy liked to go in the bar and bet. Ball games, pinball, matching coins, whatever, always this unlucky bum would lose. He brooded about it, see. One day he finds something weird going on about himself and he goes to the doc and the doc examines him and says, 'It's nothing to worry about, Willy. What you had all the time was a third testicle and it just now descended. It's very unusual.' So this Willy, he thought and thought and thought, and he come up with a great idea. He waits until the bar is full of all the guys that had been taking him for years, and he hangs on the bar for attention and he puts down two hundred bucks and says, 'Listen, you guys, I'm betting even money that between me and Joe the bartender, we got five balls.' Just about the time they are covering the last of the two hunnerd, Joe leans across the bar to Willy, and he is looking nervous, and he says, 'I don't know what you're up to, pal, but you better have four.' "

She hooted and slapped the bar and laughed and laughed. Tom laughed. She had raised her voice to bring in the other two customers, but they had kept their attention on their conversation.

The bell on the package store door dingled, and he went through the doorway behind his bar to the brightness of the store and sold a pint of blended to a yard man, and a bottle of Smirnoff to the tourist who came in right after the yard man. As the tourist left, Francine arrived. She was a tall girl with narrow shoulders and heavy hips. She wore a brick-colored slack suit over a low-cut yellow blouse. She took the coat of the suit off and hung it in the back room, while he told her Lou wasn't coming in. She punched the cash drawer open on the package goods register and said, "Want to watch me count it?"

He looked at the tape. "As of right now you got eighty-eight sixty-four, so go with that or count it and tell me if it's over. It sure God won't be under."

"Not enough pennies and nickels."

"I got a roll of each for you in the other machine. Come buy them when you got to have them."

"I think I'm coming down with what Lou's got. Honest to God, Tom, there was almost too much table business last night for one girl to handle. It gets like that, can we close bottle sales down earlier?"

"Eight?"

"Okay, thanks."

"But only if you got full tables and booths."

When he walked back through to the bar, the businessmen were gone. An old tourist couple were just settling themselves on the barstools, and Darleen Moseby had come in and was sitting two places away from Peggy Brasser. Tom made straight-up extra-dry House of Lords martinis with lemon twist for the old couple and took Darleen her no-cal cola. Peggy put her ten on the bar and slipped from the stool and steadied herself by grabbing the edge of the bar.

"Girl can't spend her life in this snake pit," she said. "See you around, hey, Tom?"

"You take care, Peggy."

"Surely will," she said, wheeled about, swayed, then strode directly to the heavy door, pushed it open and went out into the blinding glare of sunlight as the door hissed shut behind her.

"I couldn't stand listening to her as much as you do," Darleen said. "She'd drive me up the wall."

She was a small girl with a warm golden tan. With her face scrubbed clean of makeup, with colorless brows and lashes, with her swim-damp hair hanging darkened and lank, she looked hardly more than high-school age. Her short terry beach coat was parted, showing her flawless figure in an orange string bikini. She was barefoot. From instep and arch to earlobe and hairline she was exquisitely fashioned in every small texture and detail, as if of finer materials than most of the race of man.

"You weren't swimming in the Gulf, were you?"

"With those yucky dead fish floating around? You got to be kidding, sweetie. I asked Bernie could I swim in the motel pool, and all the business we steer, what could he say but yes?"

"Darleen, I told you before, I wisht you wouldn't walk around the sidewalks barefoot. It's all spit and dogshit out there."

"My God, Tommy, I'm about to take a big hot bath and I watch where I walk, okay?"

He left her and made another round for the tourist couple and came back, leaning on the bar to keep the conversation private.

"I didn't hear you come in," he said.

"It was like six thirty."

"Go okay?"

She had dug a cigarette out of her beach basket. She did not answer until she lighted it and took a deep drag. "Sure. Why not?" she said listlessly.

"Why not? I talked to Lou on the phone when he called to tell me he's not coming in. He said the one you took off with, he said it was about ten o'clock, he looked hard case."

"He was okay. I got an instinct, Tommy. Five minutes talking and I knew he was okay. I'm not taking any dumb chance of getting beat up on again. Look, he's out of Tampa, selling and servicing some kind of machines they use in banks. He was going to drive back, but what he did was phone his old lady and say he was staying over. Say, I almost forgot, I see Dusty coming out of the Suprex and she said Louise was feeling enough better maybe both of them would come in tonight. It's the kind of flu doesn't last long, I guess. Louise will be in anyway, and maybe the both of them."

"What are you going to do?"

She yawned, pink tongue curling. "Geez, I don't know. I'm kind of beat. I'm going to get me a hot bath and go to bed and if I wake up in time, okay, I'll come in and see if there's any action. Hey, you didn't line me up, did you?"

"No, I didn't set up a thing."

"You decide anything about Francine yet?"

"I don't know. I think maybe it's a bad idea."

"Look, she needs the extra money bad. She's got the kid and she's got her old mother. If you don't run her, she'll free-lance and get jammed up."

"I mean, Darleen, she's a kind of weird-looking girl."

"Don't kid yourself. There are plenty guys like that kind. I talked to her, you know, and she gets chances enough. The thing is, she's scared. She needs somebody to screen out the freaks, and some muscle if she needs it, and no trouble from the deputies, and an okay from Bernie at the motel. Look, if you can run three of us, you can run four hookers, Tommy."

"I want to stay small and quiet. You know that."

"Francine Hryka won't be any trouble. I'll kind of help out. The way she wants to do it, she stays on waitress nights like now, and works in some afternoon business. If she can clear three tricks a week it's about what she needs extra, after your cut."

"Let me think about it, okay?"

"You don't help her out pretty soon, friend, she'll quit you and go work massage."

He smiled at her and put his big hand over hers and squeezed her small hand into a fist, watching her mouth go loose and her color change with the pain. "What you do, honey, you keep on hustling your ass and you leave management to me."

"Tommy, please . . ."

"I want you back here on this barstool at no later than eight thirty."

"Sure, sure. Okay." She slid off the stool and went out through the back to Tom Shawn's little frame house, her eyes stinging as she blinked the tears back.

Peggy Brasser had stopped at her second bar, her usual spot, and after the bartender had served her, she realized she had lost track of time. She didn't want to gulp her drink, and she didn't want to miss her television program. She asked Teddy if she could carry the drink out, and he found a big paper cup and dumped it in. She tipped him a dollar and walked back to her car, parked diagonally in front of the lounge. She got in and pulled her skirt up a little and tucked the paper cup between her thighs. She waited until she thought nothing was coming and then backed smartly into Beach Drive. There was the yap of a horn, a yelp of brakes, and a pickup truck swerved around her, the passenger leaning out the window to yell, "Crazy old bitch!"

"He'll kill somebody going so fast," she said righteously.

She drove north up Fiddler Key toward home, driving at a sedate fifteen miles an hour, stacking the irritated traffic up behind her. She always remembered lately to drive with care. That damned prissy young judge had told her with such obvious relish that she'd had her last chance, that one more DWI and he would not only give her a one year suspension, but he would guarantee she would spend a full thirty days in the county stockade. Nobody seemed to understand that it had been an accident which could have happened to anyone. It was night and the oncoming lights were bright, and so instead of turning in at Golden Sands she had gone one driveway too far and turned in at Captiva House, and then, because she had expected the driveway to be straight she had not anticipated the sudden curve of the road and so had driven through the fence and into the shallow end of the Captiva House swimming pool, and that old fart who'd been swimming at the time was only faking a heart attack in hopes he could get well on somebody's insurance.

From time to time she took a quick neat little sip of her drink and put it back between her thighs. Once she made the turn into the Golden Sands drive, the sun was behind her. She drove around to the back of the building and into the vehicle entrance for the ground-floor parking facilities. She had to make a curve around the laundry room to get to her assigned slot. As she approached the curve she was heading west, and a shaft of sunlight came through the pillars and momentarily blinded her. She stabbed the brake, and the bourbon and ice sloshed out of the paper cup into her crotch. She looked down, and when she looked up again she was inches from that goddam skinny blue bicycle that some goddam old fool had gotten permission to keep padlocked to a goddam ring bolt that had been set into the wall for that very goddam purpose. She wrenched the wheel but it was not in time. The front right corner of her bumper wedged into the bike somewhere in the pedal area, between the wheels, and wrenched it free of chain and ring bolt, and scraped it along the wall for twenty feet before it seemed to come apart and sag down under her front wheel, then bump against the underside of the car as she finally stopped.

A brown skinny old man with curly white hair came running toward her, his mouth open and his eyes bugging. He wore a khaki shirt and shorts, and he had a bright orange pack on his back.

"What are you *doing?* What are you *doing?*" he cried.

She got out as he got down on hands and knees and peered under her car. "What I am doing is running over some goddam bicycle chained right in my way."

He straightened up, still on his knees. "My machine has been parked there for over three months and it is not in *anybody's* way."

"Your machine, hah? Who the hell are you?"

He reached under and tugged and pulled out a warped skinny wheel with a random tangle of bent spokes aiming in all directions, a limp tire sagging off the rim, a jumble of bent gears fastened to the hub.

"Ruined," he said in a dragging voice. "Absolutely ruined."

"I'll pay for your toy, dads."

He hopped spryly to his feet, tossing the wheel aside. "Toy? Toy! Madam, I have done three centuries on that machine."

"That's some long time."

"A century is a hundred miles done in one day."

"You kidding? You? A hundred miles in one day?"

"In six hours and seven minutes, to be precise. That was my best time."

She looked him over. "Recently?"

"Last month. It was a splendid machine, and I couldn't guess how many hours of work I've put in on it. It fitted me perfectly. It weighed just under twenty-six pounds. I just changed from Shimano to SunTour derailleur and installed an elliptical sprocket and . . . But why am I standing here like an idiot talking to you? You are obviously so drunk you can hardly stand. And you have . . . uh . . . apparently had some kind of personal mishap there."

"Right. I spilled my drink."

"You were drinking while driving? I know who you are, of course. You are the notorious Mrs. Brasser in Four-A. I think you are a menace. I shall now place a call to the authorities."

"Now wait a *minute!* Who are you?"

"I am Roger Jeffrey. From Five-B."

"You rent it?"

"What possible difference could that make to you? We own it, Mrs. Brasser. We moved in during January. Your car is blocking the way if anyone wants to get in or out. Perhaps you should move it. Or shall I?"

She realized she had the paper cup in her hand. She finished the dregs of her drink, handed him the cup, got in, started the engine and backed smartly away. He began hollering and waving his arms. The bike made a long scraping sound. She stopped, shifted, darted forward. He leaped out of the way. She had thought he would go the other way. She had turned in the direction of his leap. She nearly got him. The scraping noise stopped and the back wheel bumped over something. She looked in her side-view mirror and saw a squashed mess of blue tubing and shiny metal bits back there. She drove another thirty feet and put her car in its slot. She locked it and turned and found Roger Jeffrey standing there.

"What's the matter with you, Roger?"

"Did . . . did you try to run me down?"

"For God's sake! You're trembling like a leaf. Hey, you want a drink?"

"I do not want a drink. I am going to report you for drunken, reckless, insane driving, destroying personal property, leaving the scene of an accident and—"

"I am going to buy you a brand-new bike. Right? And we are going to forget all this police talk. Right?"

"Wrong."

"Now be a nice guy, will you? I've got *enough* problems already. I'm a widow. You shouldn't go around yelling at widows. Come on, Roger. You call the cops, and you won't get dime one out of me, and the insurance company I've got, you'll get a check for half what that thing was worth in like 1980. Know what I'll do for you? I'll buy you one with a motor! How's that."

"Please. I don't want anything with a motor."

"Okay. One better than the one you had, then."

"But . . ."

"Come on. I got the money up in my place. Come on."

"I can't just leave it there like that," he said and he went and picked up the mashed machine. He hesitated, and then carried the various pieces back to the ring bolt. The chain and lock had fallen to the cement floor. He wove the chain through the two wheels, the broken front fork, the drive chain. He stuffed the twisted drop handlebars into the mess, and balanced the broken carrier on top of it. He unstrapped his small tool kit, selected a wrench and took the black leather seat out of the ruins, freeing it from the support. He slipped his knapsack off and put the seat and tool kit into it and shouldered it back on. "Have to put the same seat on the new machine," he explained. "I've put twenty-five hundred miles on this one. It's just nicely broken in."

At the open door to the elevator he hesitated. "I really ought to take steps to get you off the highway, Mrs. Brasser, before you kill some innocent person."

"Look, you. I am a careful driver. You want a new bike or don't you?"

They rode up to the fourth floor and walked down the exterior walkway to 4-A. After considerable fumbling she discovered she was trying to open her door with her car key. She found the right key and opened the door and said, "Excuse, it's kind of a mess."

He stood in the doorway and stared at the apartment. "What happened in here?"

"Nothing happened in here. All that happened is, that the girl that comes and picks up, Leanella, she's had flu for two weeks, is all. Pick any chair, Roger, and dump the stuff off it and have a seat. Sure you don't want a drink to steady your nerves? Now, what does it cost to get you a better bike. Hundred? Hundred and a half?"

"My dear woman! That machine cost me two hundred and seventy-five dollars fourteen months ago. I have put a minimum of seventy dollars into custom improvements, and that does not allow anything for my time. Had someone on the street offered me four hundred dollars for that machine, I would have said no."

"Listen. Are you trying some kind of rip-off?"

"I assure you—"

"Those skinny bikes where you got to ride all bent over, they cost that much? Really?"

"That was a Schwinn Voyageur, ten-speed, opaque blue, with a lugged frame, center pull brakes, rat-trap pedals—"

"Okay, okay. Jesus! Settle for four hundred?"

"I just told you no. There is a factor of mental anguish involved here. And my sense of duty, about phoning the authorities. I think I would now like to buy myself an eight-hundred-dollar machine."

"You have *got* to be kidding."

"Where's your phone?"

"Right over there. Well, it *was* right over there. What the hell? Oh, here it is, under this pair of slacks."

"I suppose I just dial operator and ask for the police."

"There's a number in the front of the book, I think, but I looked for the book the other day for an hour and never did find it. I did find a shoe that had been missing. Woops!"

"Careful! You are very drunk, madam."

"Not for this time of day, Roger. Go ahead and call."

"Thank you. I will."

"Hold it! You would, wouldn't you?"

"Of course."

"Six hundred?"

"No, and not seven hundred or seven hundred and fifty. In fact, in a very short time it is going up to eight hundred and twenty-five."

"You are trying to take advantage of a widow, you rotten stringy curly-haired old son of a bitch."

"Now it is eight twenty-five!"

"All right! *All right!* Put the phone down. I'll get my checkbook. Jesus! If I can find it."

She came out with her checkbook. She looked back through the stubs. It had been a long time since she had balanced it, but there should be at least three thousand left. She asked how he spelled his last name. She handed the check to him. He examined it, folded it once, put it in his shirt pocket and thanked her, gravely.

"You know, Roger, you are one hard-nose old bassard. You are mean, you know that? What did you do for a living, sell orphans to the circus?"

"College professor. I spent thirty years at Syracuse University."

"Teaching what? Blackmail?"

"Comparative religion, madam."

"Sure you don't want a drink?"

"I must be off. Thank you for the generous settlement. Good day, Mrs. Brasser."

"Good day to you, professor. Don't let the door bump you in the ass on the way out."

After he left she said, "Peggy, you've just been taken by that leathery old son of a bitch. It depressed you. What you need is a drink. A nice drink to cheer you up." She went into the kitchen and opened the cabinet. No glasses. She selected one out of the sink and rinsed it out. She opened the refrigerator and found she had forgotten to make ice again. Have to remember the ice, dammit. The case of booze was on the floor by the liquor cabinet. The first two she started to lift were empties. The third was full. She cracked the seal, poured the tumbler half full, hesitated, filled it to within a half inch of the rim. She drank, leaning against the counter. She wobbled into the bedroom and sat on the side of her unmade bed. She hoisted the glass. "To you, Charley baby." She drank. She put the glass on the bedside stand, an inch of liquor left in it. She lay back and closed her eyes and in ten seconds she began snoring.

12

AFTER LEW TRAFF REPORTED BACK, saying that Fred Hildebert had personally put a freeze on the Marliss Corporation's line of credit, Martin Liss forced a smile and said there had to be some mistake, that Fred would have had the courtesy to contact him first before doing a thing like that, and he would get hold of Fred right away and clear it up. Hell, Marliss and the Athens Bank and Trust Company had a special long-term relationship.

Two days passed before Liss could get together with Hildebert. Neutral ground was selected, a corner table for two for lunch at the University Club on the top floor of the Palm Coast National Bank building, three blocks south of the Athens Bank and Trust Company. Hildebert was a tall, bald, thick-bodied man with a soft husky voice and glasses with lenses which made his blue eyes look huge and misted.

"I don't blame you for being sore, but let me give you some background on this, Marty. Things have changed very damned fast. The fat rosy ass has fallen off the economy. You have no idea the fits the FDIC examiners have been giving me. You have no idea the loans they have classified. You have no idea how deep we will have to dip into loan loss reserves. Off the record, I see a very bad statement coming out the end of the year. Frankly, we got too deep into resort construction, and we've got some very sorry loans we're going to have to do something about. The reason—"

"Fred, I am not interrupting you in any way. I am just reminding you right here in the middle of your speech that you made some nice interest money on the Marliss Corporation, and the last two projects, Golden Sands and Captiva House, they paid out right on time, and you picked up very nice sound mortgage paper on both of them, on good-value apartments."

"Marty, believe me, I am aware of that, and I wish all the developers had your ability and good sense. What I am trying to tell you, the examiners say we are too heavy on development loans. We're not a giant bank. We're a one-hundred-and-twenty-million-dollar bank. We were all set to go into a holding company situation when this construction collapse killed it."

"All the background is nice, Fred, and I'm glad you're telling me, but in my office safe there is a piece of paper with your name on it, and it says I have an eleven-million line of credit."

"Some things take precedence."

"So what does that mean? I planned on the basis of that. I am one hundred and seventy-eight thousand dollars out of pocket so far, counting on that money. You want to make my loss up to me?"

"Marty, Marty. Don't get in an uproar. Believe me, I understand your problem as if it was my own. Can I do something the examiners tell me not to do? And believe me, even if I could, the very best I could do for you would be nine point seven five percent. But there's another reason why I can't. You'd be over the bank limit for an individual borrower."

"The borrower is the Marliss Corporation!"

"Which is you, Marty. You are the major stockholder. But what would take us over the limit is money owed the bank by two other businesses: Gulfway Management and Investment Equities. We're holding their paper."

"But I have a very small interest in them. A few shares. Hell, I can sell those shares tomorrow and be out of both of them."

"Am I some kind of dummy, Marty?"

"What do you mean?"

"Give me credit for knowing my own line of work. On account of the loans, I asked for and got a list of the shareholders in Gulfway Management and Investment

Equities. So you are on the list for a few shares. And there is a corporation on the list with enough shares for control, in both companies. Right? A Miami-based outfit called Services Management Group, Incorporated. I have to follow through in my line of work. I had to ask a couple of favors of a couple of friends, but I came up with the shareholders in that Miami outfit, and what do I find?"

"Okay, Fred. Okay."

"I find that the Marliss Corporation owns a large equity in Services Management Group."

"I said okay, didn't I? What you should understand is that there are some other people in SMG with me, and they have the leverage to make sure I don't get hung up by my suppliers and I don't get hung up by any construction union. It's like insurance to have them in there."

"Marty, it is one of the reasons I can't honor that line of credit for eleven million. And I may be doing you a favor."

"Thanks."

"I mean this is a very bad time to get into anything that big. I went over the figures with Lew. With the empty condominium apartments, can you sell a hundred and sixty-eight of them at prices from eighty-five to a hundred and twenty-five on today's market?"

"Right this minute, no. But remember, if I move now, I'll be selling them two years down the road, and I am betting things will be a lot better by then."

"Do you really want to go ahead with it?"

"What do you think? Hell, yes!"

"Well, there's a way. I don't know if you'll go for the conditions. All I can do is get you and the other man together."

"I make it a rule never to give away pieces of my action."

"I know that."

"And I do not put myself personally on any paper I have to sign. I am on there only as an officer of a corporation."

"I know that, Marty. Let me put it this way. This friend of mine has certain problems and you have certain problems, and I think they fit together in a way that will help you both out."

"Explain to me."

"I'd rather he sketched it all in for you."

"Can I know his name, at least?"

"Why not? His name is Sherman Grome and he is C.E.O. and Chairman of the Board of Equity Mortgage Management Shares, with headquarters in Atlanta."

"On the big board? The REIT?"

"One and the same."

"A fellow who does some of my personal stuff, he says the REITs are heading into big trouble."

Fred Hildebert shrugged his big soft shoulders. "The ones without good management, certainly. Sherm is a very smart young man. He made a good record running a group of mutual funds, fantastic capital appreciation. When the Atlanta group put EMMS together they went shopping for the best talent they could find. Besides, Marty, why should you sweat about the future of the real estate investment trusts? What you want is their money."

"What makes you think this Sherm buddy of yours will want to loan money to build Harbour Pointe?"

"I was talking to him about other matters and I brought up this problem of financing you and he seemed receptive. I told him the good record you have with us."

"What do I have to do? Go to Atlanta?"

"Sherm has the use of a leased Lear. I'll check with him and get back to you and make sure the time is okay with you."

"I'll make myself available anytime, Fred. As a favor to you."

Sherman Grome was tall. He was very tan. He had a hard protruding shelf of brow above deep-set eyes. His hairdo was spray-shaped to cover his ears and most of his forehead. His nose was imperial. He wore a brushed denim leisure suit and a blue work shirt open at the throat. His manner was one of total indolent assurance and half-concealed amusement. He wore oval sunglasses with blue lenses. To get to the Athens Airport lounge they had to pass the car rental desks. The rental girls glanced at him, came to attention and stared. Sherm had the celebrity look.

He said, "Thanks for the invitation, Mr. Liss, but I'm running on so tight a schedule, if we can find a quiet corner right here, we can see if there's any way we can do business."

Mr. Grome was accompanied by a slight man in his middle years, plump, neat and expressionless, carrying a black dispatch case. Grome had not attempted to introduce him. There was a room beyond the lounge, roped off. "In there, Dud," Grome said to his man. Dud intercepted the waitress. Marty saw her object, then accept what Dud gave her, and hurry to unhook the rope and let them in. She rehooked it and made no attempt to take an order, so evidently Dud had told her they would not need service. They sat at a round table by a big window. From his chair Martin Liss could look over toward the private plane area and see the white droop-nosed Lear parked near the end of the taxi strip.

Without preamble Sherman Grome said, "Fred briefed me on your project, Mr. Liss. Since then I have verified his estimate of your ability with other persons and confirmed your track record. Is that the feasibility study there? Good. Dud, put it away and give it to me to look at on the way to Houston. I'll use it as a basis for board approval, Mr. Liss, but that's only a formality, you understand."

"Sure, but   "

"Let me lay this out for you in its entirety. You estimated an eleven-million line of credit needed for your upcoming project, and you have related your needs to the construction loans and the unit sales as you go along. I suggest that EMMS loan you twelve million dollars immediately. At ten percent. Out of that twelve million you immediately pay us one million two hundred thousand dollars as prepaid interest for one year. We do not want any part of the loan amortized until after the second anniversary of the loan."

"But that gives me one hell of a—"

"Not as bad an interest expense as it might look. You can estimate your cash requirements over your construction period and use the overage in the early stages to buy certificates of deposit for appropriate periods."

"In the Athens Bank and Trust?"

"I have to put that kind of a string on it. However . . ."

"I see what you mean. It still increases my cost of doing business."

"There's something else I would like you to do."

"Such as?"

"You are acquainted, of course, with Tropic Towers?"

"South of the village. Who isn't? A bad plan, bad design, bad construction, rotten administration, lousy sales job. Less than half sold, less than thirty percent occupancy. A disaster, Mr. Grome. The jerk who put that package together is bad news. Jerry Stalbo. From what I hear, he's ready to jump off the top of it."

"He's in default on a loan to us, a first-mortgage loan."

"How did you get suckered?"

"Let's say I had bad local advice. And I did not handle it personally. The amount outstanding is one point two million, plus a hundred thousand back interest. We've talked to Stalbo. He'll sell out his equity for a hundred thousand cash."

"I should think so!"

"He wanted more, but some associates have had discussions with him."

"What has this got to do with me?"

"You have a competent team, Mr. Liss, and a good track record. If you would form a new corporation to take over Tropic Towers and assume the existing first mortgage at the very favorable eight-percent rate, we would loan you an additional five hundred thousand at ten percent. You would use that money to buy out Stalbo, pay up the back interest and have some left as working capital."

"It's a dog. I don't see how you can even give away those empty condominiums."

"I think you could price them to move."

Martin Liss thought it over. He did not like the sound

of it. It would be a joyless distraction. He shook his head slowly. "There would have to be some sweetening."

Sherman Grome looked at Dud and nodded. Dud got up and left, ducking under the rope with an unexpected agility. Grome had a disconcerting habit of looking directly at Martin Liss, unwaveringly, expressionlessly, motionlessly.

Martin Liss knew he should wait Grome out. But the stillness and the silence of the large man unnerved him. "Some kind of sweetening," he said unsteadily. "The deal narrows my margin and increases my risk."

"Who holds title to the option on the bayfront tract you plan to build on, Mr. Liss?"

"What do you mean?"

"In what legal entity does the option reside?"

"Oh. I own it. Me, personally. Martin Liss, citizen."

"Then you are setting up a personal capital gain?"

"Nothing greedy. I paid twenty-eight thousand for the option twenty months ago. To buy for $1,252,000 more, from a bank as executor for an estate. The value is there. Even without the permissions, the zoning is okay so the value is there. With the land clearing and the boat-basin permissions going along with the deed, I am perfectly in the clear selling my option to the Marliss Corporation for *two hundred* and twenty-eight thousand, and let the corporation close."

"Or a *million* and twenty-eight?"

"You've got to be kidding! A million capital gain on a twenty-eight-thousand-dollar option?"

"You brought up sweetening, Liss."

"But not the kind of sweetening where Uncle comes back on me for fraud. No thanks. Taxwise, I am a very cowardly person."

"Fourteen waterfront acres? Let me see. That would bring a per-acre total to a hundred and sixty-two thousand. I can't see that as excessive. In fact, I could mention the opportunity to a couple of large developers on the East Coast—incidentally, people with whom I have no business relationship at the present time—and I am quite sure they would make appropriate offers. In writing."

Martin Liss thought it over. "And of course I would take the offer from the company in which I own stock. But at an established fair-market value. Mmm. I would have to talk that over with my associates."

"All it means really is that we loan thirteen million instead of twelve, to cover your profit on selling your option to Marliss."

"Can't you loan it to me as I need it?"

"We have to have our money out and working," said Sherman Grome.

"So what's your security?"

"Oh, the certificates of deposit you'll buy from Fred Hildebert. They can't be cashed in without EMMS approval."

"So it's my money but it's your money?"

"I look forward to a productive working relationship."

"How soon will all this happen?"

"I'll set it in motion when I get back from Houston tomorrow. You'll be contacted. You can fly up with your attorneys, and all the requisite documents can be signed at our headquarters."

"I don't like taking over Tropic Towers."

"I beg your pardon?"

"I said I don't like taking over Tropic Towers!"

Sherman Grome stood up. He smiled. He did not offer his hand. "We're through negotiating, Mr. Liss. And I am not very interested in your likes and dislikes."

"What's the percentage in being snotty, Grome?"

Grome smiled again. "It saves a lot of time, Mr. Liss."

Martin Liss watched from the observation deck when the small white jet took off. It slanted up at a very steep angle, dwindled to a glittering speck and was soon invisible. If it doesn't fall out of the sky, he thought, I pack away one million private and personal money. If it does fall out of the sky, I don't have to worry about taking over that damned dog project Tropic Towers, and I don't have to worry about most of the profit being skimmed off Harbour Pointe. So should it fall or shouldn't it? He looks like some kind of cowboy. Those goddam blue glasses. He is making me old before my time.

Martin had called Lew Traff and Benjie Wannover into his office and had told Drusilla no interruptions except for class A emergencies. At one point during the discussions Benjie made a call to a stock broker whose opinions he respected.

After he hung up he said, "The way the real estate investment trusts like Equity Mortgage Management Shares work, of course, is that they have to distribute almost all income quarterly to the shareholders or lose their tax status. EMMS has three and a half million shares of common stock outstanding. Last year they paid dividends of two dollars and forty cents, which was eight percent of the market value of the stock, which was thirty dollars. Management, meaning Sherman Grome, has predicted the same or better this year. But because all the REITs took a beating in the market, EMMS shares are down to twenty bucks, nineteen and five eights as of today's close. The first quarter they paid a dividend of sixty-two cents. That annualizes at close to two dollars and a half which would be . . . a return of twelve and a half percent. Now what we've got is, we've got this Grome character running around making funny deals to clean up his own books so he can hold the dividend rate high enough to keep the stock in some kind of reasonable range. I'd say that what he is doing is like a fellow taking timbers off his foundations to patch his leaky roof. After he takes away enough support, the whole thing comes down. He has a reputation for smart. So he knows what he is doing. If he is going to make himself look like a dummy, there has to be compensations. If he can give away a million dollars to you, Marty, then he has to have a way of giving a lot more than that to himself."

"How is it given away if it gets paid back?"

"How can *he* be as sure as *you* are, as we are, that it can be paid back? The way the industry looks, any new project now is going to run into trouble. And right here let me say that I am not so damn sure it is going to be paid back. That is one hell of an interest load."

"Like always, Benjie, I value your advice. And yours too, Lew. But I want to go ahead with this."

"Regardless?" Lew Traff asked.

"But I want to limit the risk."

"Oh?" said Lew.

"It's something Grome can't object to. He was the one suggested a new corporation to take over Tropic Towers and try to sell it out and pay it off. So what I want to do is stuff the Harbour Pointe project into the new corporation too. We've got too many goodies tucked into the Marliss Corporation to take a chance of it going down the tube. How soon can you set one up?"

Lew Traff scowled at the ceiling for a moment. "We've got a shell we can use. I was going to close it out and then I thought, What the hell, it might come in handy. It's the one you had me set up three or four years ago on that fried chicken franchise that didn't work out. The charter is broad enough. Let me see now. You've got five hundred and two shares, Marty, and Benjie and I've got two hundred and forty-nine each, and there's a thousand unissued."

"Can we transfer all the rights and permissions we've acquired?"

"Why not? They go with the parcel. Except for the building permit, and we haven't gone after that yet."

"What's the name of the shell?"

"The Letra Corporation."

"What the hell does that mean?"

"Marty, you're hurting me. This one you said I could name after me. Like Marliss, Le from Lew, and Tra from Traff. Maybe that's why I didn't let it die."

Marty said, "Benjie, if it doesn't work out, if Harbour Pointe doesn't work out out, Letra files bankruptcy."

"There would be a stink."

"But we'd be out of reach. Right, Lew?"

"Out of reach. Except it won't be easy to get back into any size operation no matter what name you use, not for a while."

"Lew? Benjie? Let's take a vote. If Harbour Pointe goes under, things are going to be so bad all over we don't have to worry about new projects anyway. And I will make sure you two don't get hurt in any way, no matter what. Affirmative? Good. And we are going to have a couple of months of work ahead like you've never seen before. So let's——"

"Martin?" Benjie said. "There's something we shouldn't overlook. This Sherman Grome is playing little games to hold up the quote on EMMS shares, like a man holding up a tent while he can crawl out under the flap. Maybe through some kind of dummy setup, or friends, or some fund, he is easing out of a position in EMMS, selling off from five hundred to two thousand shares a day whenever there's a little strength in the stock market."

"So?" said Martin Liss, frowning.

"So if it is a good bet the smart money is selling, then it is time to sell. We should sell short. It would cost six hundred thousand to take a thirty-thousand-share short position, if you can find a house that can borrow that size block under present conditions. If he goes sour all the way, which something tells me it might, it's a nice double."

Marty looked at Lew Traff. "Is that insider information?"

"Who is inside? Nothing is on paper. But if you're going to do it, you ought to take the position in it before you become a borrower."

"Benjie, can your pal in Miami handle that size?"

"Whyn't I ask him how much he could swing and get back to you with a figure?"

"Tomorrow."

"Sure. I think if I want to come in for some, or Lew does, it's better we make our own arrangement elsewhere. It would be smaller and not so hard to arrange."

"Good thinking."

"That's what you're supposed to be paying us for."

After Traff and Wannover had left, he sat in silent thought for ten minutes and then punched out his home phone number on his private line. The maid answered and said that Miz Liss was in her baff. Martin said that he was certain his wife was the cleanest woman in Palm County and would she please take the phone in to her. The woman giggled and said yessa.

"Marty? I've been expecting you any minute! You should *be* here, darling."

"That's why I called. You go ahead, will you? And I'll join you there later on."

"How much later on? I hate taking two cars."

"As soon as I get a few more details cleaned up, I'll shower and change and go right to the party from here. I've got lots of good news to tell you."

"Just don't be too damned late. And if this is one of those times when you never *do* show up, I swear, I'll . . ."

"See you there, honey. 'Bye."

Drusilla Bryne brought in two checks for his signature. She adjusted the thermostat, warming the large office to a temperature more comfortable for her. She sat naked on the black Naugahyde of his big judge's chair. The round red sun was sitting on the rim of the gray sea, filling the office with furnace light when she straddled his lap, facing him, her long legs threaded through the opening of the padded arms of the big chair. The sun was gone when they had finished, the room full of shadows. When she stirred to leave him, he held her close and stroked her long back, silk-smooth and moist with her exertions. Her dark hair tickled his cheek and temple. He kissed the side of her throat and inhaled the scent of her. She was beginning to feel uncomfortably heavy. He stirred and she lifted away from him with easy agility.

"You go ahead first," she said. "You're late enough already."

"Francie won't be lonely. She always makes friends."

"And you're always suspicious of the poor woman, now, aren't you?"

"With cause, Irish. With good cause." He went off and took his shower. He shaved while she showered. She had laid out fresh clothing for him, suitable for an informal cocktail party. He was ready to leave when she finished her shower. He kissed her and patted her wet behind and told her to be sure to check the lock when she left.

When she was dry she put her office clothes back on, brushed her hair, fixed her mouth and went in and turned on the office lights and sat in Mr. Liss's chair and dialed a local number.

When he answered she said, "Dean? Dean, darlin', this is Dru here, who else? That nice little bit of money that you've been keeping at work for me there in the Tampa Electric stock, tomorrow I should like you to take me out of it and go short on Equity Mortgage Management Shares. Pardon? Oh, for as much as the sale will afford me. That's a dear fellow. Forgive me for phoning you at home, love, but I might not have the chance in the morning. Give my best to your lovely Clara. What? Ah, don't you remember our rules? No questions and no explanations. Yes, of course I have been lucky on these little things, and as I told you before, it does not matter to me at all if you decide to do as I do. Right. Good night, darlin'."

13

THE HEAVY-SET WOMAN was having her hair done at Connie Lee's House of Hair by one of the older operators. The customer had long since been classified as BTLT (big talk, little tip) and thus did not have any steady operator but was assigned by Connie Lee, who out of a sense of fairness and good employee relations did not give Mrs. Cleveland too many times to the same girl.

"All your life," Mrs. Cleveland was saying, "you think about retirement and what it will be like, but it sure isn't anything like I imagined. The first few months at Golden Sands were kind of fun, getting the apartment fixed up the way we want it. Of course we brought too much stuff down. You pay a fortune to have some slobby men smelling of beer throw your furniture around, but when it gets down here in the tropics, it doesn't look the way it did in Warren, Ohio. The light is brighter, or something. It looks all shabby and tacky. We sold a lot of it. I don't really know why I say sold, because we practically gave it away. When the man made that offer, I actually broke down and cried. But Jack said we better take it, so we took it. The new things were very costly, and they're not made as well as the old things were, but I must say they look a lot nicer in the apartment.

"The thing that is driving me out of my skull is having Jack around every living minute of the day. I am even coming here and getting my hair done oftener than I should because it is the only way I can get away from him, and even now I'm not really away from him because he is right out there roaming around in the parking lot, or roaming around in the drugstore or the hardware store, or he is sitting in the Buick rattling his fingernails on the horn ring. The thing about my husband, everybody knew him up in Warren. It isn't really a very big place. Jack had the lumberyard his father started way back, and the building supply business. He was in the Rotary and the Kiwanis and the VFW. He was on the board of directors of Ohio Federal Savings and Loan, and he was chairman of the Community Chest a lot of times. And he was on the hospital committee. And he was on the house committee at the country club. He'd walk down the street, and about half the people he met would know him by name and he'd know their names. He isn't used to people not knowing who he is.

"But it's more than that, I think. He had a lot of things going all the time. He had to keep track of an awful lot of things going on all the time, and make decisions and so on. It was the way he lived for years and years and years, and all of a sudden there isn't enough going on to use up all that energy, so he is just about to drive me crazy. I could do the grocery shopping for the two of us in certainly no more than twenty minutes, but he comes along every time, and it takes an hour and a half, because he has one of those little electronic adding machines with the batteries, and he has to read the number of ounces on a package and get the price per ounce and compare with three or four other kinds and pick out the one that's the best value. He makes lists and charts and so on. He keeps putting things in the shopping cart and taking them out until I don't know where I am and I get so confused I get all shaky, I really do. He's got another thing about the Buick that is driving me crazy too. He keeps track of every single mile, and he keeps getting the tank filled to the top every time we go by a gas station, so that he can figure out how many miles we are getting to a gallon. Two weeks ago he had the tires blown up to thirty-five pounds of air, and he says they will last longer and we are getting better mileage than before, but you can feel every little crack in the pavement and the car goes *bang-bang-bang*, hard enough to jar the fillings out of your teeth. He's started keeping a chart on the temperature and the cost of the electric too. And if I touch the thermostat, he flies into a rage, yelling and cursing. I wish he could get some kind of a hobby. He doesn't like fishing very much. He never cared for boats. And you know how it is with shelling. If a shell washes up anywhere on the beach there are five old ladies ready to pounce on it and run home with it.

"At first Jack was willing to wear resort clothes, you know, bright pretty shirts and walking shorts and so on, but I think he's decided that somehow he'll get treated with more respect if he wears a suit and tie. Over a month ago we were over in downtown Athens because he was looking for a kind of clock thermostat you can set so that —oh, I don't know what it does, but it is supposed to save money, and he said to the clerk that he used to have a building supply business and the clerk gave him a fish-eye look for about three seconds and then said, 'So?' He needs to feel that he accounts for something in the world. He needs to be Jack Cleveland that people would go to when they had personal problems because they wanted his advice. He feels like he is absolutely nothing down here, and so he just fusses and fusses about everything under the sun. Now he is grumping around because when they were looking for people to be directors and officers of the Golden Sands Condominium Association, Jack said he was retired and he'd had enough of that stuff to last him forever, and now we understand the directors are going to make us all pay a lot more money every month, and more money to catch up on some kind of a deficit. Jack looked up the Florida law and it says that the administration of any condominium cannot have a meeting and decide anything unless they post a notice of the time and place of that meeting in some place where the owners will see it at least forty-eight hours before the meeting, so he is going to declare that the new assessment is not valid and nobody has to pay it until they do it right. Maybe if he makes enough fuss they will make him a director, and then he can spread himself out a little bit and drive a lot of other people crazy along with me."

Harlin Barker stood by the counter in the manager's office waiting for Mrs. Higbee to notice him and come over. She was engaged in inaudible animated conversation with a tall dark-haired sturdy young woman who looked familiar to Barker. After a few moments he remembered where he had seen her. She had been on duty in the emergency room at the Athens Memorial Hospital when he had taken Connie Mae in at two in the morning a month ago with her coronary. He could remember everything so vividly from that night that he was able to close his eyes and visualize her in uniform and even read once again the gold and white name tag on her blouse. Roberta Fish, R.N. She had been very swift, competent and reassuring. He was tempted to interrupt, but there was an intensity about the muted conversation which made him reluctant. Mrs. Higbee's eyes seemed to be glistening with tears. With an almost awkward abruptness the two young women embraced, and then the nurse left swiftly, head down, never glancing toward him. He had hoped for a chance to prove he remembered her.

Mrs. Higbee blew her nose and came over to the counter. He could see that she was trying to remember who he was.

"I'm Harlin Barker. Four-G."

"Oh sure, Mr. Barker. Can I help you?"

"I don't know. Maybe. Connie Mae, my wife, had a heart attack a month ago and . . ."

"How is she doing?"

"Well, she'll have to take it easy for quite a long time. It was a massive coronary occlusion. She's doing real well, considering. The problem is that I've got to get some help for her. I was talking to Dr. Keebler yesterday. He says I can bring her home next week, if she continues to improve the way she has. But she'll have to stay in bed for two weeks or maybe three, and then she can be up half days for the next month. There was quite a lot of . . . damage. I was wondering if you could suggest how I should go about finding somebody to come in and, you know, do housework and cook and sort of look after her. We're new down here, and I don't even know how much I'd have to pay to get a person like that."

"What would the hours be?"

"I think if she came in about ten o'clock in the morning six days a week and left . . . oh, about six?"

"Well, Mr. Barker, I'd say you could figure on about thirty dollars a day, say about two hundred a week to get someone experienced in that kind of thing."

"My God! That much?"

She shrugged. "That's the way it is."

"Excuse me. I just recently heard how high our monthly charges are going. And even with the Medicare there are a lot of things that aren't covered. You know how it is."

"Mr. Barker, I didn't say you could even find a person at that money."

"How should I go about it?"

"Well, you can try Florida State Employment, and you can put an ad in the paper."

"Do you know anyone?"

She peered over his left shoulder for so many seconds he had to turn and see if there was anyone behind him. Her small ripe mouth was sucked tight, and there were frown lines between her eyebrows. She leaned forward and lowered her voice. "Look, Mr. Barker, this is none of my business, okay? A lot of people in this building are having it rough on account of the prices of everything going up. I think maybe you could work out something with one of the women in the building."

"What do you mean?"

"You know the Twiggs? They're on four too. Four-E."

"Do you think she . . . ?"

"I don't think anything. You lay this on Mrs. Twigg she could maybe hit you in the mouth. I don't know."

"I know them to say hello to. That's about all. We didn't have a lot of chance to get very well acquainted here before Connie Mae . . . got sick. And since then I've been spending a lot of time at—"

"You don't know where the idea came from. Okay? How you should handle it, start talking about how the fee is doubling. My God, everybody in the building is willing to talk about that."

"Okay. I'll try that. And . . . thanks."

"Don't mention it."

"By the way, wasn't that a nurse who just left? Her name is Fish?"

"Yes."

"She was in the emergency room when I had to take my wife there."

"So?" She looked at him without expression.

"I just happened to recognize her. That's all."

"Excuse me. I've got things to do. You try what I said."

Harlin Barker wandered out of the office, looked at his watch, sighed, wandered out toward the tennis courts. He was a smallish man, pyramidal, with a long narrow head, sloping shoulders, wide hips and thick, muscular, hairless legs. He wore brown shorts and a pale tan cowboy shirt with pearl buttons, snaps and elaborate stitching. His fringe of gray hair reached from ear to ear, around the back of his head. His habitual expression was one of mild puzzlement, and people tended to speak loudly when dealing with him, though his hearing was perfect. He had spent forty years in municipal civil service in Buffalo, New York,

138

moving slowly up from payroll clerk to his final slot as assistant to the city executive.

Colonel Simmins was playing tennis with his daughter, the mysterious thirtyish slender blonde who was reputed to have been in an Arizona jail and released in her father's custody. Father and daughter were spry tanned people in proper tennis whites, with agile feet, gasps and grunts of explosive energy, shiny metal rackets, head bands, wrist bands, orange tennis balls.

Harlin Barker stood and watched the long rally. They both hit the ball with great force, skimming it low over the net. The daughter had lovely legs. The colonel angled a shot across court and the daughter came scrambling and reaching to hit it back. She could not quite make it, but she swung at it. The rim hit the ball and the ball flew over and hit Harlin Barker before he could either dodge or catch it. It stung him high on the chest and glanced upward and hit him under the chin before falling to the grass at his feet.

He smiled broadly to show her it hadn't hurt him. He bent down and picked it up, and having bent over too quickly, he came up slightly dizzy. He wanted to seem forceful and athletic, so he threw the ball toward the woman. He was dizzy and it slipped from his fingers and went over her head, at least fifteen feet over her head, and across the next court and out into the grass beyond.

The woman put her fist on her hip and said, with a pale-eyed glare, "That's very funny. That's really very very funny."

To the total helpless astonishment of Harlin Barker, he began to weep. Tears burst into his eyes and bleared the world and ran down his face while his throat made a gravelly crowing sound.

The woman came running to him and dropped her racket on the grass. He tried to turn and flee, but she caught him by the wrists. "Hey," she said. *"Hey* now. It's *okay!"*

"Get away from him, Lynn!" the colonel ordered.

"Oh, shut up, Simmy. Hey, mister. Don't! Please."

"Are you going to play tennis or aren't you?"

The woman ignored her father. She gently steered Harlin Barker to a cement bench twenty feet away and sat beside him and gave him some tissue from the pocket of her brief white skirt. Barker wiped his eyes and blew his nose and, with a great effort, managed to still the rough sound of sobbing. "I . . . just don't know what . . . got into . . ." He was aware of her narrow tanned face, her light-gray questing eyes, her mouth pursed with concern.

"When you get close to the edge," she said, "any little thing can set it off. I thought it was a dumb joke, throwing the ball like that. That's all."

"I've been doing everything that has to be done. I thought I was okay."

"Nobody is ever really okay. Anything I can do to help?"

"No. No. Thanks for being . . . I'm ashamed of myself."

"You're a person. Like anybody. You just held in too long. It had to come out." She touched his cheek with her fingertips. "Look. You take care of yourself. Okay? You *do* that."

He nodded and she went back to her game, jaw clenched. She seemed to be hitting the ball harder than before. Both the colonel and his daughter looked over at Barker from time to time. When he felt quite calm he got up and waved at the woman shyly, and went off to find Mrs. Twigg.

14

THELMA MENSENKOTT HAD BEGUN to spend most of her afternoons in the jungle. That was what she called the acres of tangled natural growth which began at the rear boundary of Golden Sands and stretched to the shore of Palm Bay.

She and Jack had moved into 6-F last August. They were among the early settlers. She was a tall big-boned woman of thirty-two. She moved slowly and shyly, shoulders hunched and head slowly bowed. Jack Mensenkott was sixty-one. He had retired last June. He had been an executive in network television, concerned primarily with the operation of network-owned facilities. His first wife, Janice, had died with shocking abruptness of a brain tumor in his, and her, fiftieth year. One morning at breakfast she had been talking about a man in the neighborhood and called him "she." A day later she confused "you" and "me," "mine" and "yours," "his" and "hers," laughing, but with an expression of alarm in her eyes, at her own confusions. Three days later she had the first myelogram; ten days later she had no speech left at all; five weeks later she was dead.

A year later Jack married Thelma Borgren, then twenty-two, a researcher on the network news staff, a large, gentle, understated girl who listened well, talked little, and surprised and flattered him with her responsive sexuality. He had four children, one her age, the other three older, all married. They alarmed her. They and their wives and husbands had so much grinning, vibrating vitality. They gave their blessing. Better for old Dad to be married. She wanted a family. Jack wanted a second family. Through five years, four doctors and three clinics, they tried to reproduce. When she became pregnant it was a tube pregnancy, and she was a little too good at standing pain. It went on so long that when the surgeons went in there, they left her with no chance of another try. By then Jack was fifty-seven, and seemed relieved that he had to give up hopes of a second family, but saddened for her sake.

At sixty-one Jack Mensenkott looked a little under or a little over fifty, depending on the light and the time of day. He had, out of vanity, always taken splendid care of himself. At Princeton he had wrestled at five nine, a hundred and fifty pounds. At sixty-one he was five eight and a half (the discs all become thinner and harder) and weighed a hundred and forty-five. He was a very physical man. He had played hard fast games all his life. He owned three five-hundred-dollar hairpieces. He wore soft contact lenses and boiled them every night. He'd had one face lift and was thinking about another (they last but seven to nine years, depending). He had been tan all his life. He was never ill. Each morning he did fifty pushups in fast cadence, ran in place for three hundred steps and turned his shower to cold before he got out of it. And most mornings of every month he made love to Thelma, as deliberately as he embarked upon other exercises, because he believed that it kept him young.

The relationship troubled her in ways she could not define. It had been a love affair, intimate and intense, and they had revealed to each other all the secret dreams and fears, held each other close in the fearful night. They had become lovers and friends and then, somehow, lovers and acquaintances. There were no more revelations. She was stroked and patted with a casual affection, and when they talked it was a surface thing, involving things they had read in the newspaper, people who had moved into Golden Sands, changes in the weather and in the TV schedules.

Jack kept a twenty-foot Cobia at the in-and-out marina near the north bridge and had quickly become a dedicated and deadly hunter of fish. She sunburned quickly and painfully and, as Jack had observed, could become seasick on a wet lawn, and so she was glad when Jack ceased asking her to go out with him.

Were it not for the sexual part of their marriage they could, she thought, have been amiable and courteous strangers who lived together, sharing the chores of housework and shopping, enjoying similar books, magazines and television programs. For a time, after they had settled into the routines of Golden Sands, she had begun to feel a reluctance about lovemaking. She had felt a need to diminish her own participation in this obligatory rite, to avoid climax. But he was a patient and observant man. Afterward she would tell herself that she had been given pleasure, but she could not escape the feeling she had been used. It was one with the affable pats he might give a valued dog or horse. He had spurred her into performance, lifting her over the jumps, depositing her in a drowsy exhaustion at the end of the circuit. Somehow he was demeaning her, and there was no way for her to tell how. Or why. The books told her she was an extraordinarily lucky woman. But she felt like a refugee from her own life, living in the comfortable exile of the well-to-do, waiting for word to go home, knowing it would never come.

She had been at her peak of puzzled discontent when she had discovered the jungle. She had been a city child, used to the gritty air, the asphalt playgrounds, the truck stink and motor roar. Over three years the vital noisy grinning father who would lift her and gently bump her head against the ceiling and sing his loud songs to her had dwindled and shrunk and faded and died. From cane to crutches to wheelchair to bed and to the grave. She had become then, at ten, the solemn and shy and studious person she would be all her life. Her full scholarship to the university had been awarded when she was seventeen. She had lived at home, with her mother and her aunt and her grandmother, in the apartment where her father had died, and she got her degree in three years and went to work at the network, where a professor had given her a strong recommendation. She liked the work and she was good at it. Her mind was quick, retentive, imaginative. Within a year they were bucking the special problems to her. Give this one to Borgren. The Mouth wants some retrospective on Murmansk during convoy days. A twenty-second fill, but meaty. Give it to Borgren. And then she was on loan to Jack Mensenkott to help with a speech concerned with government interference with freedom of expression on television news and news specials. She and a writer named Hatch worked on the project. The network brass thought it important.

She knew Mensenkott's wife had died just three months before she was assigned. She had expected sighs and silences. The man was so full of vitality, energy, anticipations and good cheer that she wondered if he had loved her, even though everybody said they were close.

Because there was a possibility of last-minute changes, she and Hatch flew out to Chicago with Mensenkott in an executive aircraft. Approval of the final draft of the speech came through, so no changes were needed. He spoke to fifteen hundred people. He did beautifully. Applause was thunderous. He had told her to come up to his suite and listen to the eleven o'clock news. She had thought Hatch would be there. And other people. But Mensenkott was alone. He gave her wine. She sat and he paced as they watched the news. He was given good local coverage and fair coverage on the other networks. He kept darting to the set to change stations, hunting for the sound of his name.

Finally he turned the set off and laughed and went to her and plucked her up out of the chair and kissed her for quite a long time, stroking her back and flanks and rear. Then he told her to go on into the other room and go to bed. He had a long-distance call to make. She thought of all the things she should tell him: that she had never been this far away from the place of her birth before, that she had slept with a boy once but it had not been very successful, that her body felt bulky, clumsy and unlovable, that she had never thought of him in that way, that she was frightened. . . .

But he had seemed so totally confident that she would do just as he asked. . . . And she had come to the suite on his invitation, and he had not really said anybody else would be there, so he must think that she . . . She found herself, a-tremble with anxiety, taking off her clothing in the semidarkness and putting it on a chair, neatly folded. She slid nude between cool sheets, and worried about whether being so nervous would make her breath bad, and she tried not to think at all about the hardness that had pressed against her during the long kiss.

He came in humming, undressed swiftly, slipped into bed and gathered her into his arms. She was gasping and shaking, and he soon realized it was terror. He comforted her. They were married less than a year later. By then she had seen him in the total collapse of grief, had seen him in pain and anger and in need. And she had become so passionately infatuated with him she thought only of him when they were apart. He moved her into the big house in

Larchmont. It was alive with all the ghosts of Janice. She wanted to change the decor, but was not sure enough of her own taste in such matters. Two of his married children lived nearby. They threw her into the community. Club events, charity drives, teas, bridge, dinner parties. All in all, Jack Mensenkott found himself in a younger social group than when Janice was alive. It pleased him. He could keep up. Thelma tried to make herself look older, in hair style and clothing. It seemed to average out. There was a certain transient flavor to the community. In a few years she was welcoming newcomers, and they looked on her as a part of the community they had moved into. She tried hard to be the successful wife of a successful man, and she tried to have his children. She became accustomed to the life, and it shocked her when Jack retired at sixty. She was astonished at her reluctance to leave Larchmont. But he had made his plans long ago, had invested wisely, and grew irritated at her hesitations.

So there were a dozen farewell parties and, after the house was sold, an enormous garage sale. When they drove out of town, heading for the Jersey Turnpike and I-95, she felt old insecurities return. She could not express what she felt. She was being yanked away from the place where her protective coloration worked. And Jack always drove much too fast.

She had become interested in the jungle because of what she had learned on the beach. While walking one day she had come upon two young women taking photographs and making notes, seemingly involved with a scrubby-looking vine crawling across the sand above the high-water line. She asked what they were doing and they said they were taking a census of the grasses which aided beach stabilization along this particular mile of Gulf frontage. They said they were with the University of South Florida. They were pleasant and outgoing and told her the names of many varieties of grass, vines and shrubs in that area. Thelma was astonished at the variety.

A few days later she went to the Athens Public Library and looked into their reference works on the botanical profusion of the southwest Florida coast. Next she purchased appropriate handbooks from Athens' largest bookstore. Soon she could identify the finger grass, the spurge, the purslane, the salt grass and others, and with the typical determination and tenacity of the intellectual she memorized the scientific names: *Sesuvium, Distichlis, Chloris glauca, Chamaesyce*. She matched the leaves to the careful line drawings in her handbooks. It was satisfying to get back to intricate research and investigation. Yet at the same time she was amused at herself in a sardonic way. Man superimposed his compulsive patterns on nature, forever devising categories and subgroupings, seeking relationship in shapes and life patterns. It was a dry arrogance to look at the finger grass, moving in the sea wind, making its delicate rounded calligraphy in the soft sand, and say to it, "Ah, you are *Chloris glauca!* Of course!" No living thing on the planet except man knows its own name. It cannot possibly matter to plant, bird, fish or tree what man, fancying himself superior, agrees to call it.

One day a wind came off the Gulf out of the northwest so cold and strong it drove her off the beach after less than a half hour, chilled through. But around in back of Golden Sands it was warm in the sun, and so she went for the first time to the jungle and found a winding path into the dense growth.

It took her three weeks to determine that she very probably would not live long enough to identify every kind of growth in those fourteen thickety acres. There were century plants, black mangrove, white mangrove, Australian pines, sea grape, punk trees, Brazilian pepper, bay cedar, grape, bayonets, cabbage palm, saw palmetto, wild coffee, greenbriar vines, marsh elder. There were varieties of live oak, a stand of them deep in the middle of the wild place, some of them huge, with low outspread limbs bigger around than her body. In the oaks were air plants in bewildering variety, some of them as big as bushel baskets. There were wild orchids, trailing strands of Spanish moss, strangler fig. Parts of the tract were too dense for her to penetrate, even with the help of the heavy pruning shears she bought and with which she made herself new paths winding through her private kingdom, trying always to cause a minimum of destruction and disturbance. There were saltwater pools, brackish pools, rainwater pools. After a rain there was a deafening shrill of tree toads. Each morning and evening there was the sad moaning of the doves. Day and night in season there was the showoff repertoire of mockingbirds, one near, two others far, the area being big enough to provide territorial rights for three pairs. Big gray squirrels lived there. You had to move swiftly on one path or get bitten by furious red ants. The shafts of sun came down and illuminated high webs of great gaudy banana spiders.

She was happily busy, filling notebooks, taking leaf samples. She traced a map of the fourteen acres, marked in her paths, and devised a number and letter code keyed to her identifications and wrote the code in at the proper coordinates on her map. Several times she tried to talk to Jack about her special kingdom and the challenges it provided. But he listened with that alert and interested expression, that polite intensity which she at last realized was exactly the same way she listened to his endless tales of the cleverness of the yard-long snook, the noble fury of the bonito, the single run and thrashing leap of the barracuda, the merits of a particular reel, the crucial choice of what test line to use, the experiments with the proper depth and speed for trolling. She had listened to him with the same glazed intensity, losing the sense of the words, her mind wandering as she made the sounds and nods of the good listener. So, out of mercy, she stopped talking to him about *Schinus terebinthifolius, Melaleuca leucadendron, Coccoloba uvifera* and *Laguncularia racemosa*.

One steamy day in early July her infatuation with sorting and classifying and identifying, with imposing her own order on the disorder of nature, turned to something astonishingly different.

She had gone back to the biggest stand of oaks and had stepped on a fallen branch and turned her ankle. She hobbled to where a giant limb had sagged almost to the ground and sat on it and bent and massaged her ankle. Mosquitoes gathered, and she took the repellant from her canvas shoulder bag and greased the exposed skin of arms, legs, throat and face and forehead.

For a little while she looked frowningly at the growth nearby, identifying each plant. But then she relaxed and in the next few magical minutes she became part of what she saw and heard and smelled. She sat amid a complex unity, an exquisitely balanced pattern of interwoven, interdependent life forms. Around her was a veritable furnace of birthing and dying, a soft roaring of consumption, consummation, growth and contest, the heats of decay, the ripeness of blossoming. At first she was only a witness to the life around her, and then she became aware of herself, of her body, as part of it too. Within her was a ferment of microorganisms, dreadful combat, birthing of cells, and the gases and stinks of decay. She was a miniature of the miniature world around her, caught up in life rhythms independent of thought and mood. She was a furnace within a furnace, another strand in the complexity, a growing churning dying part of all wildness. The sense of unity was a revelation which shook her. She knew she had never felt at home in her body because she had never clearly identified herself with all the processes of life and death. She was a life form supporting within herself billions of smaller life forms dependent upon her for food and shelter just as the live oak under her rump was haven for spiders and moths and bugs under its skin of bark. She would die as would the tree, and their substance would fuel and provision other life forms in a chain too complex to ever comprehend.

She was dazed and dazzled by this realization of herself as a part of what she had been measuring and cataloguing. When she stood up, a squirrel yelled a sentry's warning. A dragonfly, the color of blue oiled steel, paused on high in an angle of sunlight. A breeze moved by, stirring the leaves far overhead. A brown beetle lumbered across the path. Far far away she heard a boat horn demanding that the bridge be raised.

From that day on she pursued her botanical tables with just as much discipline, but less fervor.

She did not know she had very little time left on those fourteen acres.

15

HOWARD D. ELBRIGHT, the retired chemist in 4-C, was perhaps the first occupant of Golden Sands to learn that unwelcome change was coming. During the couple of months they had lived in the apartment, Howard had become a fisherman. He had acquired a light spinning rod, with a reel that held a hundred and fifty yards of six-pound monofilament.

He was a methodical man. He had asked a lot of people a great many questions, and had ended up fishing with live shrimp from the bay-shore frontage of the Silverthorn tract behind Golden Sands. There was a narrow shell path which led from the rear parking area of Golden Sands, along the north boundary of the Silverthorn tract, down to Palm Bay. There was an oyster bar, exposed at lowest tides, which curved out into the bay. Howard Elbright, carrying his bucket of one dozen live shrimp, his rod, his little plastic box of gear, dressed in old khaki pants, white T-shirt, long-billed baseball cap on which was written *Athens Aggies,* would walk to the bay and immerse the perforated inner container of the shrimp bucket in a place next to the oyster bar where the water was deep enough, would carefully thread a shrimp onto the long-shanked hook, wade out along the bar until the water was halfway to his knees, and then cast his bait out toward the edge of the grass flats beyond a channel that ran close to the end of the bar.

He had learned to make up his own rigs, using brass swivels and twenty-pound leader material and threading the end of his line through a barrel sinker, half-ounce weight, before tying it to the swivel. He had learned that he did best when he retrieved the shrimp in an erratic manner, when the tide was coming in.

He used a newsstand manual to identify what he caught. He had become familiar with the look and escape efforts of trout, redfish, mangrove snapper, crevalle jack, catfish, grunt, blue runners, ladyfish, sand perch, blowfish and other common varieties.

There was a pleasant tingle of excitement in making each cast, awaiting the swift knock or the furtive tugging. But at the same time there was an uneasiness in the back of his mind, born of self-knowledge, that his interest would one day fade. And then what? All the attics and cellars and backs of closets of his mind were full of abandoned adult toys: Heathkits, rock tumblers, photo enlargers, tape decks.

He kept thinking that if he could but go back in time and cancel those purchases and put the money to work in good places, retirement would be a lot less worrisome. It had cost the Elbrights $1,181.40 for that necessary work on the apartment which he had detailed to Higbee soon after they had arrived. And the increased charges had come as a bitter blow. He had thought it was yet another rip-off until he had gone over it carefully with David Dow, the treasurer of the Association, and David had explained exactly how it had all come about and told Howard his options, the most attractive of which was to pay the extra money. It changed their retirement budget. He had thought he might get a small boat. Forget it. The golden years had become, he thought, a little bit brassy.

But, hell, a lot of people were worse off. This was very pleasant, standing and fishing in the summer heat, with a breeze to keep the bugs away. To the northeast, across the broad part of the bay, he could see the tall banks in the downtown business area of Athens, and see traffic glinting across the north bridge onto Fiddler Key. His fishing place was reasonably private. He suspected that if he told his acquaintances about it, soon the oyster bar would be lined shoulder to shoulder with other fishermen. And, he decided, they would look like him. An oldster uniform. The SocSec Army, in funny hats and ragged sneakers. When a

Y SATURDAY GUS Garver spent an hour and a
his wife, Carolyn, in Room B-4 of the Crestwood
Home. She was in her chair when he arrived, and
eemed displeased. He was beginning to be able to
pret the erratic gestures of her left arm, and detect
ances in the damp croaking sounds she was able to
ake.

He realized that she was tired of sitting up in the chair
and wanted to be back in bed, and so he helped her, adjusted the pillows so she would be comfortable, and
turned her little television set on. There were things he
wanted to tell her, the little day-by-day things that he had
seen and done and heard about. Though he knew she
would not understand anything he might say, he found
himself organizing the little bits of information, adding,
editing, discarding, a process much like that he had followed in writing to her, during the years when he had

Mr. Garver, it says very clearly on the ̶ ̶ ̶
ments that personal objects of value should no ̶

"Hold it!"

The size and the command timbre of Gus ̶
startled Castor. "I beg your pardon?"

"It's obvious your staff does the stealing. A lot ̶
goes on here. It's obvious your staff neglects patients ̶
Mrs. Garver. She can't demand attention. I found ̶
twice when she'd messed her bed. I found her once wi ̶
her good arm caught in the sleeve of her jacket. I was told ̶
she'd get therapy here, and I assume she must be getting
some, but I can't find out anything about it, so maybe she
isn't."

Castor stared at Garver. Gus guessed the man was about
forty years old. He had a nervous twitch at the corner of
his mouth. His thick glasses looked as if smeared by
thumbprints.

"I . . . am . . . doing . . . the . . . best . . . I . . . can," the
man said, voice quivering on the edge of control.

"Which isn't one hell of a lot," Garver said.

boat went by in the channel, if he had a fish on, he tried to look as if he didn't. Privacy was an ever more valuable commodity. It seemed to him that he was, in some obscure manner, *imitating* a retired person. He was the same Howard Elbright he had always been. But now indignities had been wished upon him. The years of gravity had tugged his flesh downward and it no longer fit his bones as well. He was an imposter, hiding inside this old-man body.

The bay shore of the Silverthorn tract was very irregular, with deep notches into the dense stands of mangrove. In the beginning, when trying to find the best fishing place, he had moved back and forth along that irregular shoreline, all the way to the south end of it where the channel curved well away from the bay shore. Once he had heard, over the lapping of the water, a sound he could not identify, and as he waded around a projecting point of mangrove he came upon an open white runabout tied to the mangrove in a place of a considerable privacy, and had seen a fat brown bald man with a black beard fornicating most vigorously with a fat young woman with short blond hair, both of them naked upon the upholstered bench that ran across the rear of the boat. He backed cautiously away from their thumpety striving and, one ladyfish and one snapper later, he had been startled by the sudden roar of the big outboard motor as the pair took off, heading south, dwindling down the long, narrowing bay, the boat kicking up a rooster tail that blurred his view of them. He made mental notes that this was the third and perhaps last time in his adult life that he had caught a glimpse of the sex act in progress, each time accidentally; that the episodes had averaged fifteen years apart; that the first time it had seemed to him to be deliciously wicked, the second time banal, and this last time wistful.

And so when he heard a male voice raised in laughter, he wondered if the hefty lovers had returned. There were thrashing sounds and chopping sounds, and then a man yelled, "Over here, Harry. I got it." There was more chopping, more thrashing, and a little while later two muscular men in sweat-soaked khakis came walking into view up the shoreline, towing a skiff.

"Morning," Howard said.

"Hi. Mister, that there path go on through to the west side of this here piece?"

"Right through to Golden Sands. What are you looking for?"

"Metes and bounds on this here parcel. Corners was socked in a long time back, but hell finding them."

"Is it sold or something?"

"I surely don't know, mister. We're out of Davis' office, just surveying. Keep an eye on the stuff in the boat a minute? Thanks."

He got three keepers that morning and let the rest go, and then ran out of shrimp. Edith didn't like him to clean them in the kitchen sink. He carried a sharp fillet knife and used a driftwood board, washed the fillets in the bay current and dropped them into the shrimp bucket. Make a nice lunch, if she hadn't maybe already started fixing something else.

He told her about the surveyors and she looked troubled. "Having other condominiums on the three sides of us is enough, Howie."

"I don't think it's anything like that, honey. I keep reading how the sale of condominiums is beginning to fall off so badly the banks and the construction industry are getting worried. God knows there's enough of them for sale up and down the key. I don't think anybody will be starting new ones. I heard they are going to stop working on some of the ones that are partway built."

"You know something? The compressor on the air conditioner is starting that noise again."

"Oh, Jesus, Edith!"

"It isn't my fault, is it?"

"I know, I know."

"It isn't really as *bad* as it was, not as loud maybe, and it doesn't go on constantly. Just a little yip every once in—"

"So I'll call that thieving son of a bitch and see if he can figure out how to void the guarantee this time too."

"Howard!"

"We're pigeons. You know that? We're a big field of old pigeons, too pooped to fly away, and those service sons of bitches roam among us, grazing, for Christ sake!"

"Howard!"

"We should never never never have been suckered into buying this rotten . . ." But then he saw that she was about to cry, and so he hugged her and comforted her and said he didn't mean it. She loved the rotten apartment and the rotten view and the rotten neighbors and every part of the whole rotten retirement.

16

ON A JULY SATURDAY GUS Garver spent an hour and a half with his wife, Carolyn, in Room B-4 of the Crestwood Nursing Home. She was in her chair when he arrived, and she seemed displeased. He was beginning to be able to interpret the erratic gestures of her left arm, and detect nuances in the damp croaking sounds she was able to make.

He realized that she was tired of sitting up in the chair and wanted to be back in bed, and so he helped her, adjusted the pillows so she would be comfortable, and turned her little television set on. There were things he wanted to tell her, the little day-by-day things that he had seen and done and heard about. Though he knew she would not understand anything he might say, he found himself organizing the little bits of information, adding, editing, discarding, a process much like that he had followed in writing to her, during the years when he had been in construction camps, apart from her. It was a reflex based on long habit.

When she began making her bathroom sounds and gestures he went and found one of the attendants to help her, waited until she was back in her bed and said goodbye to her, knowing she had no comprehension of any word he could use.

As he reached the foot of the stairs leading down into the front foyer, Mr. Castor came out of the office door, a large, plump, pasty man with a harried manner.

Garver stopped him and said, "Got a minute?"

"Not much more than that."

"My name is Garver. My wife is in B-four. Stroke and aphasia."

"Oh, yes, yes. If you have questions about finances, I can't help you. Mrs. Holly doesn't work Saturdays. She knows all the regulations and so forth."

"I wanted to know about her rings and so on."

"Rings?"

"They were stolen the third day she was here."

"Mr. Garver, it says very clearly on the admission documents that personal objects of value should not be—"

"Hold it!"

The size and the command timbre of Gus's voice startled Castor. "I beg your pardon?"

"It's obvious your staff does the stealing. A lot of it goes on here. It's obvious your staff neglects patients like Mrs. Garver. She can't demand attention. I found her twice when she'd messed her bed. I found her once with her good arm caught in the sleeve of her jacket. I was told she'd get therapy here, and I assume she must be getting some, but I can't find out anything about it, so maybe she isn't."

Castor stared at Garver. Gus guessed the man was about forty years old. He had a nervous twitch at the corner of his mouth. His thick glasses looked as if smeared by thumbprints.

"I . . . am . . . doing . . . the . . . best . . . I . . . can," the man said, voice quivering on the edge of control.

"Which isn't one hell of a lot," Garver said.

The control snapped. Eyes bulged behind the glasses. In a feverish half whisper Castor said, "God, how I hate you people. You goddam old lizards, acting like the world was made just for you. You come charging down here by the millions and take over everything and all you want is handouts. Complain, complain, complain. Jesus, I am sick of all you so-called senior citizens."

As he started away, Gus caught the man by the plump arm and swung him back and said, "You sure you really belong in this line of work, Castor?"

Even that small evidence of any kind of personal interest and concern made Castor's eyes fill. "I'm sorry. I'm sorry. None of you have any idea of the kind of shit I have to take. I'm supposed to clear nine percent on the gross. I can't pay staff enough to keep anybody good. I've got a turnover you wouldn't believe. People don't know the hassle we go through processing Medicare and Medicaid and those insurance policies. I can't keep nurses because they get sick of being bad-mouthed by vicious old ladies and cleaning up after dirty old men. They get shoved in here by their goddam relatives and then they come and spend ten minutes a week with Granny and want . . . want . . . expect . . ."

Garver patted the man's quivering shoulder. "Take it easy. Take it easy, fellow."

"I'm just about at the end of . . . I need . . ."

"You do something for me and I'll do something for you."

"What do you mean?"

"I've run some big jobs on small money. When we've gone over budget and were on penalty, I've had to keep things moving. Sometimes the answers are simple, but it takes somebody coming in from outside to see them."

"There aren't any answers."

Gus shrugged. "Take stealing. Had a job in India, where stealing is a way of life. Small tools started evaporating by the hundreds. So everybody on the payroll put in a voluntary contribution, which I asked for in a loud voice, and when something was missing, we paid for it out of the kitty, bought a new one. So everybody started policing everybody."

"State and local regulations wouldn't permit me to . . ."

"Maybe you haven't tapped all the sources for voluntary help around here. Is there a vocational training center? Maybe you could get them to send some people here for on-the-job training, for course credits."

Castor frowned, tilted his head. "Just possibly . . ."

"And you've been so busy you really haven't had time to see how much of the stuff your people do is really necessary. People tend to do the things they like to do at the expense of more important things which should be done."

"I can't really give the degree of supervision . . ."

"I *know* that. Why don't you just let me come around Monday and nose around your operation here and look at your records, and maybe I can come up with some recommendations to make things a little easier for you and give a little better service to the patients."

"I can't budget anything at all for that."

Garver smiled upon him. "Just as a favor. And all I want from you, Mr. Castor, is your assurance that Mrs. Garver will be tended to with . . . just a little more diligence?"

"Well, I . . ."

Gus found the man's soft plump hand and shook it strongly, and said, "It's a deal, then!"

As Garver walked to the parking area he was trying to remember the name of the man who had come up with the idea that every man is sooner or later elevated to that job which he is not competent to handle. Castor was the perfect example. Probably trained in nursing home and rest home administration. A competent and admirable second banana, but a disaster when put in charge. A hostile man, generating hostility in his staff, failure prone, riding the nursing home downhill to disaster. A nitpicker, pausing to pick his nit in the middle of the whirlwind. That was the kind you had to be able to identify and hold back, hold them in that ultimate slot they could manage.

Other men, and he remembered Sam Harrison once more, could never be content with second place.

Speak for yourself, Gus, he thought, as he unlocked his

car. Another one like Sam Harrison. Perfectly willing to tell Mr. Castor how to run his nursing home. Tell the mayor how to run the city. Correct the management defects of God's administration of the universe.

Garver is an old goat, he decided. Or an old horse out to pasture, rather, aching for the weight of the rock sled.

It will get better attention for Carolyn, but that is a rationalization. You itch to run something, administer something, manage something, because you did it all your life and you are better at it right now than in your so-called peak years. Retirement is a strange irony. A curious waste of training and talent.

And that, perhaps, accounts for some of the irritability of these old retired men. They are patronized, ridiculed and shoved around by self-important clerks, by men they would never have hired back in the real world.

But *this* is the real world, isn't it?

Never, said a loud voice in the back of his skull.

He got into his gray Toyota wagon and drove slowly back out onto Fiddler Key, through the late bright afternoon of July. Between the gulf-side condominiums and apartment houses he could squint into the sunlight and see the sun-brown throngs on the broad white beach, with kites and lotion, towels and Frisbees, with kids and koolers, blisters and beer, tubular chairs and sunglasses. Small waves lifted from the glassy flat, humping as they neared the beach, then curling and slapping at the broken shells and the swift-legged shore birds.

The tall buildings made oblongs of shade across Beach Drive. Traffic was heavy and slow. The several years of heavy construction of the high-rise buildings had broken the road up. The shoulders were crumbled, and the holes had been patched with asphalt over and over again. It was becoming increasingly difficult to turn left from one of the parking areas onto Beach Drive, or to turn left off Beach Drive into an apartment entrance. Bikers with their high red flags pedaled past the clogged traffic as a car waited a chance to turn, blocking all those behind it.

Backwards, he thought. Full speed ahead backwards. Things used to be delivered: milk, butter, eggs. Milkman made a hundred and fifty stops. Now a hundred and fifty cars have to chug to the convenience stores. Trouble with the engineering mind is an infatuation with simple logic. And you, Guthrie Harmon Garver, are just another old fart, yearning for the past, deploring the present.

He wished he could find a time warp, so handy for the writers of science fiction. A permeable membrane, a momentary resistance, then penetration into one of the places of his past. Toyota transformed to one of those noisy durable old trucks on the mountain roads of Peru, the Garver body transformed to the elastic, tireless toughness of those years. He would be driving to that grass strip where Al would use all of it before yanking the little airplane over the treetops, and then it would be all downhill to the coast, catch Pan Am's tin goose, and be home forty hours and a lot of stops later, to the soft perfumed haven of Carolyn's happy arms.

He drove past Golden Sands and went on to the mall, where he would buy the groceries and supplies written on the list in his shirt pocket. And he wondered, for the hundredth time, if it would be possible to bring Carrie back to the apartment, possible for him to give her the nursing care she required. And if he should do it, even if he could. As the doctor had said, she was a healthy woman. That servitude, once begun, would last through whatever years he had left. And then what would become of her?

17

On a Sunday morning Martin Liss sat with Lew Traff, Benjie Wannover, Cole Kimber and Drusilla Bryne in the small conference room off Lew Traff's office on the top floor of the Athens Bank and Trust Company building.

Because it was Sunday the computer had cut the air conditioning back to eighty. The men were in short sleeves. Drusilla wore a pale blue tennis dress. All the overhead fluorescence was on, shining down through the plastic honeycomb. The tabletop was stacked with piles of papers. It was a little after eleven. They had been going since eight.

Marty said, "Okay. I am not going to thank you for breaking your asses getting this all set up this last two months because in the first place it is going to make you a lot of money and in the second place I have been going at it as hard as any one of you. But what I do not care to see at this point in time is any kind of goof that is going to wreck the timing, so let's hit the high spots one more time. Benjie?"

"Okay, I set up the books on the Letra Corporation. Hoo, boy, some strange books! We got in—I mean Letra got in—a $13,550,000 loan from Equity Mortgage Management Shares at ten percent. Equity prepaid interest back to EMMS, $1,355,000. The $550,000 less $55,000 interest, equaling $495,000, went into the Tropic Towers Division of Letra. It got dispersed as follows: $100,000 to Jerry Stalbo for his interest, $119,300 to West Federated Savings and Loan to pay up the back interest, $22,000 legal fees, title and so on. That leaves Letra with title to Tropic Towers, with $253,700 cash working capital in the Tropic Towers Division, and owing $550,000 on a ten percent note to EMMS, interest paid for eleven months in advance, and owing West Federated one point two million at eight percent, and we negotiated a one-year moratorium on principal and interest payments on that one when we took up the back interest. I haven't done the feasibility on it, but when we multiply out the seventy-two unsold apartments by $24,300 we get the $1,750,000 owed. That's $6,250 below the average price he's had on them. And—"

"Work out the feasibility with the idea I want to be out of that project in the next twenty minutes, if possible. Get to the big one."

"Right. After paving one year interest in advance, the Harbour Pointe Division of Letra had $11,700,000 left.

Out of that Letra bought from Marliss Corporation all the plans, documents, permissions, plus a very small allowance for overhead for $131,000. From you personally, Marty, Letra bought the option on the Silverthorn tract for $1,028,000 then closed on the tract for the additional $1,252,000, for total land acquisition price of $2,280,-000 for the land, almost $163,000 an acre."

Marty glanced at Lew in question, and Lew Traff said, "Yes, we've got the arm's-length offers for the land on file, from important people you don't know personally and never met. The price is in line—or used to be—for land on the water zoned for high rise. But that price cuts into the expected profits according to the old feasibility studies Benjie and Cole worked out."

"So does that interest rate," Benjie said darkly. "Anyway, after I advanced half a million to Cole here, of which he had to advance two hundred thousand to Marine Projects on the dredging—"

"I didn't advance it. I escrowed it," Cole said.

"Whatever. Anyway, I had enough left to buy eight and a half million in certificates of deposit from Fred Hildebert downstairs. I staggered them according to Cole's estimates of when he'd need advances against construction, on percentage of completion. We'll make back about four hundred thousand dollars in interest on those CDs this first year. The second year will be the zinger, when we have to pay one point three million in interest to Sherman Grome and make back only about two hundred thousand on the remaining CDs. And so, down the road, we better be selling apartments like wild cakes or we are in deep trouble."

"Will Fred take the mortgages on the apartments?"

"Yes, and apply the proceeds directly to the EMMS loan, with the usual discounts. That is, if we sell any apartments."

"You're very funny today," Marty said, mopping the front and naked half of his skull. "Now you can be funny, Cole. Where do you stand?"

Kimber grinned and laced big fingers behind his neck. "What I have to do is cut back to an average cost of fifty-one thousand an apartment, that cost to cover everything: pools, roads, drainage, yacht basin, tennis and so on. I've taken out two million in costs without changing it enough so we have to go back for new permits. I cut back on the specs everywhere I could. It isn't first class anymore, Marty. I don't think they'll move at the price structure you've got to have. So I am now playing hard ball with my old buddies. Every week I lay the bills onto Benjie and he draws my check and the check is good and it includes my cost plus percent, or I pull my crews that same day and walk. If I was dealing with the Marliss Corporation it might be a little different. But, in these times, not a lot different." He shrugged, popped a match with his thumbnail and relighted his skinny cigar. He was rangy, leathery, sun-baked and virile, like a rodeo performer in a cigarette ad. "No hard feelings?" he said.

"No, no," Marty said impatiently. "Who blames you? Now, once again, Lew, what I want from you is a rundown on all the permissions and I want your assurance nobody can put a stick in the wheels."

"Don't get the idea there isn't going to be some screaming. There is. Lots of it. But everything was properly done. I'll go to court on any of it, and I'll successfully fight any injunction to shut us down. I went over it all last night with Denniver. The big thing on our side is that construction is falling off so bad, nobody really wants to kill this kind of big new project."

"The ecology freaks?" Kimber asked.

"They'll be the loudest," Traff said. "When does Herb move in?"

"He'll hit there with all his big yellow machines next Saturday morning. Saturday because the government is all closed down for the weekend. Mike's outfit, Marine Projects, should have the dredge, barges and draglines in place about the same time."

Marty nodded and closed his eyes and pursed his lips. Everything seemed to be all right, but it didn't feel quite right. There was less excitement than he had anticipated. A lot of the risk had gone out of it. And a lot of the fun. He had his personal million in capital gains. By hard scrambling he had managed to short three blocks of EMMS shares, eight thousand, five thousand and three thousand. Sixteen thousand shares. He had dumped three hundred and twenty thousand into his margin account to finance that short position. His brokers hadn't been able to find any more to borrow. It had faded to eighteen dollars on the big board, giving him a thirty-thousand paper profit so far. He was dimly amused to be playing Sherman Grome with that strange man's money.

"Marty?" Benjie asked.

"Yes?"

"I got to start repricing this whole thing with Cole here and his purchasing guy, and I ought to start today."

"Meeting adjourned."

Marty walked slowly back to his office with Drusilla. He had her bring her book into his office. "It's getting hotter," he said.

She pulled her dress away from her body. "Horrible."

"Look, I won't keep you. What you should do, I want you to write that up as if it was a meeting of the officers of Letra. Lewis Traff, C.E.O., presiding. Put in the reports and make up the motions and all that shit, and then have Lew sign it and you sign it and put it in the minutes book, okay?"

"Surely."

"Do I have to tell you what to put in and what to leave out?"

"I wouldn't think so, love. I'll run you a copy just in case."

"What have you got planned for today?"

"Well . . . a light lunch and then I've got a tennis lesson."

"You shouldn't try to play tennis in heat like this, Dru. I'm not kidding. People fall over dead."

She slapped herself on the haunch. "I do love the heat. It melts this off ever so much faster. What are you going to do?"

"Float around in my pool. Then she's got people coming in for drinks and we go out to the club for dinner."

She lifted her notebook, raised one eyebrow in question.

"Oh, yes," he said. "You don't have to do these now. It'll give you something to start on tomorrow morning. This is to Stalbo, Penthouse A, Tropic Towers. Dear Jerry. Reference our conversation Friday morning, I want to confirm what I told you at that time. I was given an information copy of the termination agreement between your company and Equity Mortgage Management Shares, as signed by you and Mr. Sherman Grome, duly notarized and recorded and so on. I need not remind you that this severed any relationship between you and the Tropic Towers project. I realize we have known each other a long time, but that does not mean that I can provide you with gratis housing at Tropic Towers. If it were up to me, Jerry, certainly I would do you the favor. But I am advised that to avoid clouding the agreement, you must vacate Penthouse A no later than the last day of this month. Naturally, if you wish to buy that condominium penthouse as a private person, that would be fine with me. I notice that on your last sales list it is down at ninety-five five. I also note that it is the display apartment and was furnished by Epic Interiors out of Tampa. A search of the records indicates that they still own the furnishings, and a suitable arrangement will be made with them to either remove the items or purchase them for a mutually agreeable figure. I will expect you to phone me after you receive this letter and tell me if you will vacate as requested, or if you will purchase. If you will purchase, I must have the necessary documents signed and in hand by the last day of this month. Make it cordially yours, I guess. Put it in paragraphs. Dru, I think what happened to that son of a bitch, he tried to be some kind of Hefner."

"What do you mean?"

"As soon as it looked like he was in real trouble and would maybe lose his ass, that second wife of his, that Irene with the big boobs, that barracuda about one year older than his oldest kid, she gets a smart lawyer and moves fast and puts a lock on liquid assets before he can dump them into the company to try to save it. He has to move out of the house, so he moves into Tropic Towers. So he turns that penthouse into a permanent house party. Booze all day and food brought in and stereo rock and some of those tough little teenage hookers that hang around the beach. It seems as if a man starts getting bad ideas, they gradually get worse instead of better. Maybe he's trying not to think about how he can't sell those apartments and can't pay the interest on the loans. Finally he gets a dose. What did he expect from those hustlers? He gets it cured with antibiotics. When he tries again, he can't get it up. Anxiety, I guess. Plus being pretty well burnt out with all the games and fun. When the food and booze stops, all the young boys and girls go elsewhere, but a housewife he has hired to sell apartments moves in with him and puts him on grass to cure the anxiety, and pretty soon he can make out with her, but then he has what he thinks is a heart attack while he's in the saddle and that turns him off again and she moves out."

"Love, who *told* you all this?"

"Who told me? Jerry Stalbo told me when I went up there to see him Friday. He wouldn't meet me anywhere. He had big draperies drawn across the windows. He looked like hell. He kept crying every once in a while. He looked like a dead man. What he wanted me to do was talk Grome into letting him come back into Tropic Towers for a piece of the action. A piece of nothing. I can't fool with Jerry. He's going down the tube so fast you wouldn't believe it. It is a terrible job of design and construction and planning, but the penthouse looks okay, what I could see of it. Look, honey, you want the penthouse? Same terms as when you were living in Seven-E in Golden Sands."

"Is there a pool? I know there is, but is it usable?"

"It was in use Friday when I was there looking around. And the tennis courts look okay."

"As soon as you get that dreary little man out, I'll move in. Thank you! Were there more letters?"

"There were, but the hell with it. I got to get out of here. Look at this shirt. Like I'd been under water. Get out of here, kid. And don't work too hard in the hot sun."

18

IN THE FIRST GRAY LIGHT of an early Saturday morning, George Gobbin drifted in and out of light sleep. Neither he nor Elda liked to sleep in the false chill of air conditioning, even in this torrid month of July, when, as George liked to tell his new neighbors, it was "almost as hot as July in Iowa."

By experimentation they had found it best to close off the bedroom, leave the rest of Apartment J-C air-conditioned, with the thermostat set at 75 degrees, and open the windows which faced toward the jungle behind Golden Sands. A small rubber-bladed soundless fan on the low chest of drawers against the foot of her bed kept the warm moist air moving. The early bird-sounds slid him back into a dream of the Iowa farm. He was small. He was crawling through the tall corn on black earth that muddied his hands and knees. It was cool and shadowed under the corn leaves, below a breeze that rattled their broad green curves. He heard a roaring grinding sound and in a sudden sweat of fear he crawled through the corn to the edge of a slope and looked up a slope to where a stone road crested the hill. With a louder roaring the lead tank of the column came over the ridge, black cross on the turret that turned slowly from side to side, the slender deadly 88 searching, searching. . . .

He came awake with a gasp, yanked back out of the hedgerows of that deadly war now fading so swiftly back into the myths of history and dropped into the new bed in the new bedroom. Elda was right over there in her bed, spread-eagled, face down. (How in hell could she

165

breathe with her face stuffed in the goddam pillow?)
The sheet was pushed down below her bare behind, down
to mid-thigh. As he looked over at her, he suddenly realized that the roaring grinding noise had not stopped when
the dream had stopped. He got out of bed, creaked as
he stretched, and went over to the windows. By pressing
his cheek against the screen and looking north, he saw
two big yellow bulldozers move along the edge of the
parking area toward the jungle. The trucks and flatbed
trailers which had brought them there were parked in the
Golden Sands lot.

It puzzled him. Were they going to widen the path,
clear the easement? He pulled on his trousers and shirt
and sneakers, made sure he had his keys and let himself
out of the apartment. As the fire door swung shut behind
him and he started down the concrete stairs in semidarkness, a voice above and behind him said, too loudly,
"Identify yourself, mister."

He stopped and looked up into a bright flashlight beam,
and the now-familiar voice said, "Oh, good morning,
George."

"Brooks? Brooks Ames? You startled hell out of me."

Ames came down the stairs. He wore a straw ranch
hat, khaki shirt and shorts, and a red armband with the
letters G.S.P. embroidered in white, and had a white ID
tag pinned to his shirt pocket which said CAPTAIN
B. G. AMES. The grip of a handgun protruded from his
black leather holster. Around his neck he had a red
woven cord with a black whistle at the end.

"Up early, eh?" Brooks said.

"I see you got your armbands and whistles."

"You say that as if it was some kind of a joke, right?
There are fourteen of us, George, volunteers, working
our shifts, keeping this place safe and secure. We should
be getting your thanks, not a lot of cheap sarcasm."

"We all sleep sounder knowing you brave boys are on
duty."

"There's no point in our trying to talk to each other.
We can't communicate. You have absolutely no idea of

what is going on in the world. None at all. You are naïve. That's it. Naïve."

"I'm a bleeding heart, Brooks. I'm a pinko crime coddler. And while you're standing here educating me, there are big trucks illegally parked in our lot. Go blow your whistle at them."

"The hell you say!"

"I saw them out my bedroom window."

Ames went plunging down the stairs, and George Gobbin had the vision of Ames bursting out the rear door, blowing his whistle and firing into the air.

By the time he reached the lot there were two more trucks there, and a pickup truck turning in. There were men in yellow hard hats. There were brush hooks and chain saws. The sky was turning pink in the east, beyond the bayside thickets. Some other early-rising residents had gathered. George saw Stanley Wasniak, the secretary of the Association, and went over to him and said good morning and asked him what was going on.

"Hi, George. I just talked to the foreman. They're going to clear off everything between here and the bay. He said he guessed somebody maybe is going to build something on it, but he doesn't know what."

"I guess you fellows will take steps to find out?"

Wasniak had to raise his voice to be heard over the sudden staccato of chain saws. It sounded like people warming up for a motorcycle race. "You people want your noses blowed or your backs scrubbed, just get hold of your Association officers."

"What the hell is everybody so touchy about?"

Wasniak leaned closer. "I am goddam sick of being held responsible for every goddam thing that happens around here. I came down here to retire, not be driven up the goddam walls by all you goddam people."

George stared at him for a moment and turned silently away and began walking back toward the rear entrance to Golden Sands. After a dozen steps Wasniak caught him by the arm.

"Look, I'm sorry. It's just one thing after another. It's

not you, George. It's nothing about you. You should know how many times every day somebody is at me about something."

"It's okay, Stan."

"I got snookered into this. What I want to do is sell and move out and get some peace and quiet. Sure, I'll try to find out what's going on, and I'll let you know."

"What's going on is land clearing," Gus Garver said as he approached them. "The whole fourteen acres between here and the bay shore."

"Are you sure?" Wasniak asked.

"I talked with a guy driving one of those little cats."

"*Little!*" said George Gobbin.

"Well, comparatively speaking. They're big enough for this job. Pretty good outfit, I'd say. That equipment has seen a lot of hard use, but somebody is keeping a close watch on maintenance."

"Clearing all of it?" Wasniak asked, wonderingly. "All those nice old trees and stuff?"

Garver said, "The land is so low it will need some fill, and if you put a couple feet of fill around the trees, it kills them. You can wall the fill away from the trunks, but that takes a lot of time and money. So the efficient thing to do is topple all that stuff, scrape it into big piles, douse it with oil and light it."

"But, dammit, we bought here on account of all that green out there," Wasniak said.

"Say good-bye to it," Garver said with a tight smile. "All the courts and lawyers are out of business on Saturday, and they got enough people here to do it fast. Anyway, what does it say in your deed about the scenery? Is it guaranteed?"

Wasniak shook his head slowly. "I hate to face my wife," he said, and walked slowly toward the rear entrance to Golden Sands. In a few moments George nodded silently at Garver and then headed back to his apartment.

When he let himself in, Elda was still asleep and still in the same position. He wondered that the chain saws didn't wake her up. He cranked the awning windows shut, muffling the sharp edge of the sound, turned off the fan and cracked the air-conditioning outlets, feeling coolness against his sweaty face. He fixed instant coffee and sat at the breakfast bar with the seven o'clock news whispering over the transistor radio as he looked at the paper. The thing about condominium living, he thought, was the difference between the brochures and the reality. In the brochures there were smiling friendly people in groups, having swimming parties and steak roasts and making shell ashtrays together, happy as clams, always smiling and hugging. And they all looked about forty. Move in and you were in the middle of a batch of suspicious, testy, cantankerous old folks, their faces pursed into permanent expressions of distaste, anxiety and hidden alarm.

What we should have done, he thought, was hang onto ten of those two hundred and forty acres, a piece on the back corner the farthest from the interstate link, that piece that fronted on Birch Road and had the foundation of the old farm that had burned before I was born, near the survivors of the orchard gone wild, near the oak grove, and with a stretch of Birch Creek cutting across the corner.

What we should have done was use some of the money and built a snug place tucked under the hill away from the north winds. We could have built a wing on it for a couple to look after the place. Then we could have driven into the city every now and again, and we could have had dinner with old friends and had them out to the place. Could have kept the same doctors and dentist and bank, and traded at the same places where we've been known all our lives. Could have gone down the street in the summertime and people would have said hi and asked about the kids and grand-kids. We would have been near where her folks are buried, and mine.

That's what we should have done.

What made us come down here? Nobody knows us, really. Nobody knows who we are. Nobody gives one fart in a whirlwind about George and Elda Gobbin. We mill around here with a couple million old foops who came down to take up room and die in the sunshine. For the sake of some hot watery sunshine full of gasoline stink, we became like refugees. It's as if we were driven out of our own home place, off our own land, to wander in strange places among strangers, treated with indifference and disrespect, and the only way to go home again is to die here and be shipped back. He was surprised to feel the sting in his eyes and the catch in his breathing.

19

NANCY McKAY WAS BADLY BLOATED as a result of her allergic reaction to most kinds of insect bites. In spite of all her precautions she had been bitten three days ago, apparently by some kind of a spider. At least after having been sat upon, the tan smear looked as if it could have been a spider. They always had the house sprayed heavily and frequently, but somehow a spider had gotten into Nancy's bathroom and had been sitting upon, or crossing, the closed lid of the toilet when she got out of her shower, toweled herself and then sat down to dry her feet. She felt the sting and had called to Greg in alarm and he had come through from his bath to examine the body and to look at the underside of her buttock where a small red welt was already forming. He made certain that the hypo and the digitalis were ready and waiting, and then phoned the office and said he would be late coming in. When it became apparent she would not get an extreme reaction this time, he went to work.

Now, three days later, she was at the peak of this particular incident. She was mildly bloated from head to toe, had a rash across breasts and belly, and had red puffy eyes and a runny nose. Ordinarily she was a slender pretty woman with good bones, dark hair and quick-moving grace. Now she looked, Greg guessed, as she had looked at three or four years old, her face round, petulant and sad. She had her elbows on the breakfast table, the fat fingers of both hands wrapped around her teacup.

"Today we close on Two-E," he told her.

"You say it as if we ought to buy champagne or something. What it does to me, it breaks my heart. That's what it does."

"Come on, honey."

"Come on and what? You took a twenty-thousand-dollar loss on Two-D when that Mrs. Neale bought it, and now it's the same thing again with this old couple. We're really getting rich, right?"

"Nancy, honey, I've been through it—"

"A hundred times and I'm too stupid to understand? All I know is that a big piece of our security is going right down the drain. I can't see why we couldn't hang on and wait. My God, there will be plenty of people moving to Florida and they'll have to have housing, won't they?"

"Eighteen thousand a year interest and maintenance and carrying charges? And damn few rentals? Look, we agreed. Both of us. Not just me. I talked it over with you when we went in, and I talked it over with you about cutting our losses. You agreed both times."

She sighed and tried to smile. "I know. I get to thinking about things and I can't turn my brain off, and I guess I work myself up. I'm sorry. I shouldn't worry. You're a lawyer. So we made a mistake. Some day we'll laugh about it. Maybe."

"Sure we will."

"I want to ask you if we couldn't keep just one of them, the last one left. But I guess that would be dumb, huh? It would be, you know, as if *my* money, the part I put in, wasn't really gone."

"We could probably handle one, if Mrs. Rosen can rent it often enough."

"No. Let's not. Let's get out of all three of them. How come you call her Mrs. Rosen now? Why not Loretta?"

"Gee, honey, I don't really know. I didn't realize I was

doing it. Maybe I don't feel as friendly as I used to, on account of the beating we're taking. Maybe that's it."

She walked him to the door to the carport and he gingerly enfolded her in his arms, the unfamiliar softness and bulk of her, and patted her and told her everything would work out just fine for them. Just fine and dandy.

As he held her he felt a great consuming tenderness toward her, an empathy so achingly sweet it brought tears to his eyes as he looked beyond her dark hair to the kitchen bulletin board. It seemed incredible to him that after three short weeks of the affair with Loretta, his mind could be so filled with the ten thousand erotic images of her, some of them frozen, some in a frantic motion. He could see her eye so close to him he could just manage to focus upon it, an eye swollen and staring, emptied by sensation. He saw her on hands and knees, saw the planes of her brown back and the fragile narrowness of her waist as she craned her head to look back over her shoulder at him, eyes narrowed almost shut, mouth a-twist in a fixed grimace. Gregory tenderly held his swollen wife and told her in his love voice that he did indeed love her, and everything would be just fine. Just dandy, old girl.

Loretta phoned Greg McKay at his office at ten o'clock.

"Bad, bad news, darling," she said in her gritty, resonant voice. "Brace yourself."

"Such as?"

"The dear little old Duckworth couple went over there to Golden Sands to admire the property they were going to close on today. So now they don't want it. They don't want it so badly they are perfectly willing to forfeit the five-hundred binder sitting in my escrow. They don't want it no how, no way, dearest."

"Why? What happened?"

"I thought they were exaggerating. I just drove up the key and took a look. They're clearing that Silverthorn tract behind Golden Sands. It's Herb Major's outfit and he's got just about every piece of equipment he owns out there. They've been working all weekend, and it is beginning to look mighty baldheaded out behind there. Also, Marine Projects has barged a couple of draglines in and off-loaded them on the bay shore. They've been shoving all the greenery into about ten gigantic piles and pretty soon now they are going to pour on the oil and start burning. The people there are really terribly upset and I can't blame them. All I've been able to find out so far is that something called the Letra Corporation, a Florida corporation, contracted for the work, has all the necessary permits in hand, apparently, and it's full steam ahead to build, so help me, a condominium project. Somebody must be out of their tree on this one. Sweetie, we lost the Duckworths. And it is going to play hell finding anyone else while that project is going on. It really diminishes your values there. I'm sorry. We moved as fast as we could."

"Why can't I get as worried as I should be, Loretta?"

"Because you are in a wonderful, wonderful stupor. Just like me. I missed you so. You know that."

"I know it."

"I was so damned horny all weekend, I could hardly stand it. I have about fifteen marvelous things I've thought up to do to you. Do you mind?"

"Lunch hour?"

"In good old Two-F. F for frolicking. Twelve thirtyish, eh?"

"Yes ma'am."

"I'm feeling fantastically oral," she said and hung up. She took a deep breath and held it, sighed a long sigh, picked up her private line again and phoned Cole Kimber's office. The girl put her right through.

"Hey, there, Loretta baby," said Cole. "Long time. I was thinking about you just the other day, about the great times we had, you and me. And I was wondering if—"

"No way."

"You don't mind I keep asking?"

"Hell, it flatters a lady. What I called about, I figured you would know if anybody would. What is . . . I mean who is the Letra Corporation? It couldn't be that damn Marty Liss, could it? I know he had an option on that tract once upon a time, but I thought perhaps it fell through."

"What would the information be worth to you?"

"Not what you'd like it to be worth."

"It figures. Well, for old times' sake, I'll tell you that Marliss, Marty's corporation, sold out all its rights and permissions to Letra, and Marty, as an individual, sold his rights in the option to Letra. And the president of Letra is Lew Traff."

"So Marty made a deal with himself and got rich?"

"He didn't do bad. He didn't do bad at all."

"But Cole, really, has Marty got holes in his head? A big project in these times? We've all fallen off the mountain, and it will be a long slow climb back. Who'll build the damn thing?"

"Me."

"You're crazy too?"

"For cash, baby, not for credit and not for any piece of any action. And on cost plus, money in front all the way."

"Make sure Marty isn't printing the money in his back room."

"It's nice clean green money, out of Atlanta."

"So a bank has gone crazy?"

"Maybe a couple of them. They're making a nice interest. So far."

"It really seems unreal," she said slowly, frowning. "How do you read the whole condominium situation? You know, you are really a very shrewd person."

"Little old me? I didn't know that was why you liked me."

"Come off it, dear. Really. Seriously. I'm in the real estate business. I would like to keep eating. And I would like to know which way to jump."

When he spoke his voice was heavier, more thoughtful. "Don't ever say ol' Cole Kimber told you this. The Chamber of Commerce would cancel my birth certificate. The way I read it, we slid over the edge, and a little ways down we grasped onto a little bush. Now the roots are slowly pulling loose and the only way we can go is down, a lot farther than you could guess, honey girl."

"Are you serious?"

"I have been turning every little thing I've got into cash. I've been selling my equipment and leasing it back, even. And I am right on the edge of selling Kimber Construction and taking on a consultant contract until I get this Harbour Pointe thing built or they stop construction. I've sold my boat."

"Somebody said they thought you had."

"And my three tracts of piney woods and pasturelands, including that one with the lodge on it."

"What are you doing with the money?"

"I'm shipping it out of state, honey girl. No Florida banks for me. I'm putting it in certificates of deposit and spreading them around, even. I've been bracing myself to jump for a long time. The bubble was getting too big. It took some bankruptcies to cut the ass off'n everything. That's when I started making my moves. How do the books look on that business of yours?"

"Still pretty good."

"Sell it if you can. Right now."

"Serious?"

"In a couple or four years you can buy it back for a dime on the dollar."

"What did you call that project?"

"Harbour with a U, and Pointe with an E on the end. One hundred and sixty-eight units. From eighty-five to a hundred and twenty-five thousand."

"On the bay? Not on the Gulf even?"

"High, eh?"

"I thought Marty was a very smart businessman."

"I can't give you the details. He was going to take the risk, and it was a very bad risk, but who could steer him off it? Not me. Not anybody. But then the bank put on the brakes, and he had to go elsewhere for the money, and they put strings on it. Now Marty is playing both ends against the middle, and there is no way he can take a loss. I don't even think there's any way he can keep from making a very nice package. He lucked into a nice arrangement."

"How about permissions, Cole?"

"In perfect order, even to permits to burn what they clear off the land."

"Jesus God. I can guess how they rigged it. A sleepy afternoon and a long list, and that little jerk droning on and on, and things get by, don't they?"

"It's the same the whole world over."

"Who are they paying off? Justin Denniver or Troy Abel?"

"Question time, is it? Okay, what young promising attorney is humping what sexy real estate broker?"

She thought of denial, rejected it, sighed and said, "You bastard! How many thousand other people have the same news?"

"Maybe two or three people. And I won't take out any ads."

"Thanks. And thanks for the advice. And the information."

"You just run for the storm cellar. Once it gets bad enough, you and I are going to have a lot of extra time on our hands."

"So?"

"I'll get back to you one of these years."

"Sure you will, Cole. 'Bye."

She sat slumped at her desk. She nibbled her lip, drew dollar signs on her scratch pad, rubbed her eye, dug at her scalp and thought of disaster. Cole had been right other times. He could feel the direction of every small breeze. Could it really get worse than this? She answered her own question out of her own knowledge. Yes, indeed. Much, much worse.

The telephone rang and she picked it up at once. "This is Loretta."

"Mrs. Rosen, this is Mrs. Neale."

"Mrs. . . . Oh, Florence. Sorry, dear. For a minute there my brain was turned off. How are things, dear?"

Florence Neale's voice was calm and icy. "You did arrange a very attractive price on this second-floor apartment in Golden Sands, Mrs. Rosen."

"Yes? Yes, it was a fabulous bargain."

"At the closing, Mrs. Rosen, I got the strong impression that the previous owner, young Mr. McKay, is a good and close friend."

"I've known Greg for years. Being a realtor, I know most of the attorneys in—"

"You frightened me off that dear little house on Domingo Terrace, talking about muggings and guard dogs. I would have been very happy there. *Very* happy."

"I don't know what—"

"You stood beside me at the bedroom window and we looked out at that lovely green tropical jungle beyond the parking area, looking east from my window, and I said I enjoyed being able to see trees and vines, and I distinctly remember your saying that it was all tied up in some kind of estate. I forget the name."

"Silverthorn."

"That's it. I have been trying to reach you on the phone all weekend. Right at this moment, Mrs. Rosen, all that lovely greenery has been scraped and pushed into huge piles and they have been lighted, and dirty, greasy, oily smoke is covering this whole part of the key."

"Oh, dear."

"And I am told that an enormous project is going up there, and it will be under construction for two years. Mrs. Rosen, I do not know how many years I have left, but I do know that two years of noise, dust, dirt and confusion is too big a percentage of that time."

"I'm really sorry about—"

"I am not going to put up with it. I expect that you will tell me that you had no idea this was going to happen. It really does not matter whether you are telling the truth or not. You advertise that you are an expert on Fiddler Key properties. You sold me an apartment at an oddly low figure. It was owned by a friend of yours. You assured me of peace and quiet and—"

"Nobody can be absolutely certain of—"

"I am giving you fair warning, Mrs. Rosen, that I intend to take this matter to court. I am suing to have the sale set aside on the grounds of misrepresentation, and my money returned, including my moving costs."

"But you have no basis for any such—"

"I wrote you a long note after we inspected the apartment, Mrs. Rosen. It was only two months ago, so I imagine you remember it. As it was a business matter, I typed it on my departed husband's old machine, and I did as he always told me to do, and as he did himself. I saved a carbon. May I read you the last line?"

"You better do that."

"It says, 'If I have misunderstood anything you have told me, please let me know before the closing. I have tried to write down all our understandings in this letter.' "

"Are you sure I got it?"

"Oh, yes. You made reference to it in the little memo you sent me telling me I was mistaken about the covered parking, that there were less spaces than apartments."

"That's great, Florence. That's really great."

"I believe I would be more comfortable if you were to call me Mrs. Neale."

"What are you trying to *do* to me?"

"If you did *not* know that a big development was going to be put in behind this building, then you *should* have known. I depended on you to know, you see. I had been told you were competent. I thought it only fair to let you know what I plan to do, so that you can ask your lawyer friend to make restitution and avoid any ugliness and publicity. Good-bye, Mrs. Rosen."

Loretta went directly from the phone to the dead file of recent closings. She found the letter and read it through, made a face, and folded it and put it in her shoulder bag. She looked at her watch. Time to head for 2-F. She smiled bitterly. Now there were two pressing problems for the attorney to take care of.

CARLOTTA CHURCHBRIDGE CAME OUT of the master bedroom of 6-G into the living room, carrying a bag of laundry. She was a tiny tidy woman in her sixties, sun-brown and brisk, with deep weather wrinkles around her eyes and mouth. She kept her long hair carefully dyed horsetail black, and today, as she often did, she had braided it to keep it out of her way as she did the housework. She could have disappeared into the midst of any Central American village marketplace.

Henry was still sitting with his morning coffee, reading a badly printed newspaper of tabloid size.

She stopped and looked over his shoulder. "More junk from your personal madman?"

"From the one and only C. Noble Winney."

"And he forced it on you. Read this, he said?"

"That's right."

"Getting easier to force things on you, isn't it, dear?"

He turned and looked up at her, frowning. "What am I supposed to infer from that? That I'm getting hooked on his point of view?"

"Infer that if you sit around here reading junk all day you are going to end up looking like Mr. Winney, all gray and soft and fat and wheezy, with little red eyes and little blue lips."

He had started to be angry but he had to laugh. She had always delighted him, ever since he had met her when he had been in London as a young man posted to the United States embassy and she had been the smallest and the prettiest of the three daughters of the Guatemalan ambassador. They had been posted all over the world, and now there was a son in Anchorage, a son with two children in Melbourne, a son with one child in Guadalajara. Henry Churchbridge had never risen to top rank in the diplomatic service. He had read once about the two kinds of racing greyhounds which are automatically destroyed: those too stupid too chase the rabbit and those too bright to chase it. It had lodged in a back cupboard of his mind. He knew the quality of his own mind. He had watched too many men who were more highly regarded than he, fumble for the answer, the information, the insight which he could supply at once. They had not destroyed him. They had merely conditioned him to chase the rabbit, and because he did not really believe in the rabbit, he did not run as fast as he could.

The retirement was comfortable, with its cost-of-living adjustments. And there was the inheritance from his mother, not large, but solidly invested. And Carlotta's income, from a Zurich bank.

"This is a new one," he said. "It requires a great effort to achieve a suspension of disbelief." He showed her a picture of three men in the newspaper and read aloud to her: " ' "Baron" Edmond de Rothschild, center, is shown with Charles Bartel and Finance Minister Pinhas Sapir. Occasion was dedication of the second oil refinery to be operated by the Tel Aviv government. The Rothschilds financed both the Russian Revolution and the establishment of the Khazar colonies in Palestine which led to the present Mid-East conflict. Their close kinsman, "Lord Bearsted" (real name: Mr. Samuels), owns most of Shell Oil Company, and the Shell tankers which fueled North Vietnamese Communists.' "

She made a horrid face. "How can you stand reading that slime? My God, darling, there is enough hate in the world—"

"Whoa!" he said, smiling. "Down, girl."

"Don't 'girl' me, you damn chauvinist. But really, Henry dear. Why read that terrible stuff?"

"I find that I am getting very interested in fear."

"Fear?"

She sank into the nearby chair as he got up and began pacing back and forth, brow furrowed, as he searched for words. This man was very dear to her, and this was a familiar scene during the long years of marriage. He had a hungry, roving intellect which sought to take apart the mechanisms of his culture to find out how and why they worked. He was a tall man, too thin, with a fleshy, predatory nose, small pale blue eyes, a sallow complexion, a few remaining wisps of sandy-gray hair. But there had always been, and was now, a subtle elegance about him. It was in the way he held himself, in his gestures, in the timbre of his voice, in the swift change of facial expression.

"I am becoming aware that Golden Sands and all of Fiddler Key stinks of fear. All the literature on these condominiums talks about the security measures. Look at Brooks Ames and his silly little platoon of vigilantes saving us night and day from unknown perils. Ames, and a lot of these good people, thinks that without the guard force, drug addicts and blacks and rapists and hoodlums and psychopaths will come skulking in here and break down the doors."

"But—"

"Let me work my way through the whole thesis, dear. On the local level they are terrified of predatory tax increases, drunken drivers, purse snatchers, muggers, power failure, water shortages, inflation and the high cost of being sick. Nationally they are afraid of big government, welfare, crime in the streets, corruption, busing, and industrial, political and fiscal conspiracy. Internationally they are afraid of the Arabs, the blacks, the Cubans, the Communists, the Chinese, the multinational corporations, the oil cartels, pollution of the sea and the air, atomic bombs, pestilence, poisons and additives in food . . ."

"Some of those things are certainly frightening."

"I know. I know. But it is the vast and wicked complex of interwoven fears, from the personal and the specific to the vast misty and uncharted, that gives all these people a feeling of helplessness when it comes to comprehending their total environment. A world of almost four billion people is so incredibly complex nobody can comprehend the causes and the trends and the nuances."

"So?"

"But these people think they have a God-given right to understand. They are educated Americans. They think that if anybody can understand the world and the times, it is an educated American." He hastened on before she could interrupt. "C. Noble Winney was an auditor, an accountant. Both sides of the sheet must balance. He could not cope with a nonsense world. He had to find a reason why he could not understand events. His only other choice was a permanent condition of confusion and terror. So one day he came across something which hinted at a vast conspiracy. He read further in that area. God knows, there is a very wide choice of fictional conspiracies to accept. The Rothschild anti-Semitic world-control mishmash made some kind of weird sense to C. Noble, and so now he documents it. He is still afraid, but he thinks he is doing something constructive to thwart the conspirators by exposing them to people who will join him in his work. Poor old Fred Dawdy in Three-E has been sold on it. He was ready to be sold. There are, of course, C. Noble Winneys on the far far left, too, blaming all world turmoil on the military-industrial complex of the right. The John Birch Society blames it all on a Communist conspiracy. Winney thinks that is simplistic. He sees conspiracies of both left and right, engineered by the Rothschilds. The Transcendental Meditators, the Jesus freaks, the diet faddists, the drunks, the bedroom athletes, the body builders, the spiritualists, every one of them has made their fear more controllable through having found the Real Answer. And every person with the real answer is savagely intolerant of anybody else's answer, because he does not dare risk weakening his own. The fabric is too fragile to start with. They are all true believers and—"

"What are you afraid of?" she asked him.

It stopped him in mid-stride and he turned and looked at her. Then his mouth curved downward in a mocking, ironic smile. "The green ripper, I suppose."

When the middle son was small he had overheard some adult comment about the grim reaper, and the next morning at breakfast he said he'd had a bad dream about the green ripper. It took some deduction to find out what he meant. From then on the family had called death the green ripper. It seemed a far finer name than any other.

"Like in any special form?" she asked.

"Mostly that he doesn't take you and leave me alone, or take me and leave you alone. And doesn't take either of us in any especially ugly way, long and painful, and so forth."

"Like you always say, we're way ahead. We beat the game."

"We've beaten it, yes." He moved to the windows and looked out at the wide slice of Gulf visible between the Azure Breeze and the Surf Club. Small figures strolled along the white sand in the bright dazzle of noon sunshine. Small waves crested white and whacked soundlessly against the beach. Gulls teetered and dipped around a woman throwing bread. Far out he could see a coastal vessel dragging a dingy plume of smoke northward.

"Maybe," he said, "people are always afraid of the wrong things. Maybe Winney should be thinking about hurricanes and tidal waves."

"Now can you smell the smoke? You couldn't before."

He lifted his head and snuffed. "I think so."

"I should hope you could. It really stinks. As if they were burning garbage instead of all those lovely trees. Five absolute mountains of garbage. I'll go put this wash in, if there's nobody down there I want to talk to, I'll be back right away and start lunch."

"A walk after lunch?"

"And then a swim. Fine."

He sat down and picked up the paper again after she left. On a back page he found a small headline, and the story had neither date nor source.

New York—The late Senator Herbert Lehman of
New York was the chief sponsor and protector of
Alger Hiss. Lehman's niece was a lawyer for Hiss,
and Lehman himself tried to hide Hiss in his New
York apartment. At the time of the Kennedy as-
sassination, Lehman was the most powerful leader
of the Left in America. He died—possibly an act of
counterassassination—only a few days after the
Dallas shooting.

Henry Churchbridge closed the paper and tossed it
aside. He could imagine poor old Fred Dawdy reading
that item avidly. It linked Jack Kennedy and Alger Hiss,
boiling and bubbling with the ferment of conspiracy and
corruption. And old Governor Lehman could not bring
libel suits from the grave. Hell, they could have stated
that Herbert Lehman had been proven to be the real
father of Marilyn Monroe, alias Rebecca Finestein, and
all the old Fred Dawdys would nod wisely and buttonhole
their neighbors and say that they, by God, had seen it in
print, and They wouldn't let them print it if it wasn't so,
would They?

Buy gold. Store food. Arm yourselves. All the trite and
timeworn warnings. C. Noble Winney was really afraid of
the green ripper. That was the fear behind the fear. Everybody's fear. And so now everybody could be too easily
sold on conspiracy theories. The junk merchants rushed
into print with their junk books. Supply and demand. If
the People demand conspiracies, give them some. Give
them some marksman prone behind the green knoll. Give
them the mysterious group that hustled King's killer into
Canada. Give the Northeastern Media Establishment credit
for enough sly trickery to bring down noble Richard.
Make all the goofs nod and mutter and feel that they are
really and truly on the track of the inside story. They
could not believe the stark and terrible simplicity of
events: that a weak, sexually warped little misfit in Dallas
could combine a lot of luck with Marine Corps skills to

l joke about what to say about a new
d, "Now *those* are *letters!*"
ee their importance, Henry. Can you
n group tomorrow night?"
ink so."
'The Plot Against Nixon.' "

The time you did come, you contributed

er time."
had been enough. Six men: Brooks Ames
olunteer guards, Fred Dawdy, Winney and
guided the discussion and supplied "facts"
out of a most impressive memory. Brooks
sion technique was to outshout anyone.
obbing his head, agreeing with everyone.
supplied coffee and cookies. Winney handed
ackets of material relating to the discussion

nothing more to be learned from Winney.
e theories of vast conspiracies came in con-
story. And when they did, Winney bent his-
orm to the theories. At times it was an almost
rformance, with Winney radiating such a con-
ncerity one wondered, after all, if perhaps he
ight in part of it. But some of it contradicted
ent history of which Henry Churchbridge had
fic knowledge, knowledge never published. So
the structure is that far from the truth, then all
t be intricate fabrication.
uld go further with his new insight without any
n Winney. The specter was fear. Fear was the
of age. The green ripper stalked the golden
filling all too much space in the *Athens Times*
filling all too many fresh-dug holes in the marl
d of what Hernando DeSoto had called a barren
t unfit for human habitation. With bifocaled stare
thritic finger they ran down the newspaper columns
ng the ages: 81, 74, 57, 68, 68, 60, 95, 84, 63,
. . The golden years had the mortality rate of a

kill the belove~~~
Arabian kitche~~~
a pistol to wor~~~
revenge and fat~~~
young man with ~~~
and cripple a gov~~~
from a demandin~~~
about reality he sh~~~
ciety by killing a b~~~
can be true, then an~~~
the beasts in the stree~~~
And with just a little ~~~
be made to appear lik~~~
conceived and well hidd~~~
in the consistency of t~~~
creature in the bottom o~~~

Conspiracy theories se~~~
difficult to merchandise. ~~~
and eager to manufacture ~~~
matter how meretricious.

He decided he was just ~~~
Noble Winney phenomenon. ~~~
had been given a guided to~~~
workroom, with its giant scrap~~~
ence files and intricate cross-~~~
drudgery involved in accumulat~~~
a clue to the strength of the com~~~

He had even been given a lo~~~
spondence. It was kept in the safe ~~~
velopes in a leather three-ring no~~~
locked. Letters to and from the leg~~~
Robert Welsh, Senator Joe McCart~~~
Ronald Reagan.

Stilted letters of praise from Wi~~~
acknowledgments from the recipients~~~
them to him, standing beside him, dam~~~
excitement, sour of breath, turning the ~~~
Henry could read them. He did not know~~~

remembered the ol~~~
baby, and so he sa~~~
"I knew you'd ~~~
make the discussi~~~
"I don't really t~~~
"The subject is~~~
"Sorry, Noble."~~~
"I'm sorry too.~~~
a great deal."
"Maybe anoth~~~
One meeting ~~~
and two of his ~~~
himself. Winne~~~
when needed, ~~~
Ames's discus~~~
Dawdy kept ~~~
Mrs. Winney ~~~
out little file ~~~
as they left.
There was ~~~
His grotesqu~~~
flict with hi~~~
tory to conf~~~
hypnotic pe~~~
cern and s~~~
might be ~~~
bits of re~~~
very spec~~~
if part of~~~
of it mus~~~
He co~~~
help fro~~~
product ~~~
beaches~~~
Record~~~
and sa~~~
sandsp~~~
and a~~~
check~~~
71. .

Cuban infantry battalion. Jamming the elderly together emphasized that epidemic of the incurable disease, age. And as more caught the disease, they came hurrying down to join the already afflicted, the years bending them closer to the ever-receptive earth.

Yet the culture has labeled death unthinkable and unspeakable. One is forbidden even to think about it. It could come out of nowhere with its first horrid warning: a lump here or there, black stool in pink toilet water, a raspiness of voice, sudden weakness of a leg, lights flashing behind the eyes. Don't think about it. Don't do anything about it. It will go away.

And that is, of course, the perfect promise of the green ripper, because it will, indeed, go away, taking you with it as it goes.

Unable to turn inward, all fear turns outward, hence all the weird sects, massive door locks, electronic alarm systems, rejection of bond issues, religious fever, pinched, bitter, ugly, suspicious faces in Florida, California, Arizona—wherever the old ones gather for dying.

Fear is resonant, he realized. It bounces around the condominium walls, growing stronger rather than fading. We reinforce each other's terrors. By guarding against assault, Brooks Ames creates the fear of assault. By speaking always of conspiracies, C. Noble Winney creates more fear of conspiracies.

We are not leavened by the generations we've sired. All the children would dilute fear by not believing in it. For the first time in the history of the world, millions of the elderly are isolated from the rest of life, and somehow it brings out the worst in us.

I will write it all down, he thought, and felt a little tingle of excitement. Maybe it is an insight familiar to lots of sociologists, but by God it is brand new to me, and I am in the middle of it, and I have had a grand total of five articles published, all on aspects of foreign service, and working hard at this one may help delay the rotting process that seems to have started in my head. I find it increasingly difficult to remember, each morning, whether or not I have taken my pills.

BENJIE SAID to Lew Traff, "Maybe you are remembering I've got ten kids to think about?"

"I know, I know. Ages one to thirteen."

"Two to fourteen."

They were riding down the sixth fairway of the Gator Hole Golf Club in a white cart with a yellow canopy. Benjie Wannover was at the tiller. It was eleven fifteen on a thick hot Saturday in July. Cole Kimber and a dermatologist named Francis Frake were in another cart on the far side of the fairway. Lew Traff got out and decided he would try to reach the green with his five wood. Frake was away. He swung. Neither Benjie nor Lew saw the flight of the ball.

"Don't sway," Benjie said.

"Sure, sure," Lew said, and hit the five well, almost too well. It rose and sailed and came down on the far side of the green and just trickled over, out of sight. He got back into the cart and said, "Because I don't have ten kids, I would enjoy being convicted of a felony?"

Cole hit next, dropping a towering iron into the trap at the right of the green. Frail-looking Benjie had outdriven them all. His eight iron hit beyond the pin, bit and rolled back to within a foot of the hole.

"You sorry little bastard!" Kimber yelled.

They all took their try, to rule out a miracle, and then Benjie dropped his short putt. As they whirred toward the seventh tee, they all heard the grumbling in the east and glanced at the huge thunderheads reaching halfway up from the horizon, and agreed that they might finish the first nine, but that would probably be it for the day.

They decided to have lunch and see if it would clear, but by the time they had finished the lightning and thunder had stopped and rain was coming down so hard and so steadily Cole called it an old-time frog strangler. They changed in the locker room and Lew had one of the boys from the pro shop go bring his car around near the side door of the clubhouse. He drove Francis to his car and Cole to his, and then parked beside Benjie's Olds station wagon.

"I don't want to scare you," Benjie said. "Shit, I don't want to scare myself either. These two guys are FBI out of Tampa."

"How does that work anyway? Who blows the whistle?"

"What happened was that Mister Sherman Grome, of Equity Mortgage Management Shares, Incorporated, has been borrowing his money to loan out from two banks, maybe more than two, in the Atlanta area. So during the normal course of events along came the bank examiners from the Federal Deposit Insurance Corporation and they went through the loan files. Usually they would not bother checking out a loan where the payments are up to date. But these are different times. A lot of development loans have gone sour, and a lot of real estate investment trusts have taken a dive. So, because EMMS was into this bank for a bundle, the examiners decided to check the books of the borrower. They have that right. They fine-honed it down to two months ago and related the last big bite to the money loaned to the Letra Corporation. Then they got a quick reading on the land cost, the Silverthorn tract, and made a report to the FDIC office in Atlanta, the regional office. After the boss man up there read the report, he bucked it to the U.S. Attorney in Tampa, saying there might be a little panky and a bit of hanky adding up to some kind of indictment somewhere down the road, and so the U.S. Attorney turned the file over to the Special Agent in Charge of the Tampa office of the FBI with a request to look into the Letra Corporation with particular regard to the expenditures made so far out of the big loan from Sherman Grome's outfit, because, you see, if the loan to Letra is sour, then the loan from the Atlanta bank to Grome is just as bad."

"Oh, dear Jesus Christ on a raft!"

"The FBI likes to hire lawyers and they like to hire accountants. These two guys are old hands: Barber and Grosscup. Like I explained in the office, it is no use making them go get subpoenas."

"I know that."

"I heard about how those aborigines in the Australian deserts, those jokers can be walking across a sandy waste and they can all of a sudden stop and kneel down and stick a straw down into the dry sand about eight or ten inches and suck up fresh sweet water. They know exactly where to start sucking. So do Barber and Grosscup."

"But how bad off are we? Level with me."

"What we did, when Letra took over the project, when the Marliss Corporation transferred everything to Letra, the plans and drawings and permissions and what all, then I had Letra reimburse Marliss for all the predevelopment expenses." Suddenly the rain was heavier and a gusty wind rocked the car. "Tucked in there, labeled 'Fees and miscellaneous,' was fifteen thousand for which I don't have a scrap of backup. Five thousand went out one time and ten thousand another time."

"You mean that out of the millions for the construction loan they pick a lousy—"

"They didn't *pick* it. They came across it, is all."

"You heard Marty tell me: 'Don't worry, Lew. Don't worry.' "

"The same thing Sherman Grome is probably telling his people in Atlanta: 'Don't worry your little heads.' Let me tell you something, my friend. Guys like Martin Liss, like Sherman Grome, they are programmed for boom times. They cut a lot of corners, and it works. They get fat. But when things pinch down, they turn out to be spread too thin. You can't reach out on the table and pull all your bets back because you've covered too many numbers. Lew?"

"What, Benj? What?"

"When they go down, people go down with them."

They looked at each other. The rain was bouncing high off the hood of Lew's car, seen dimly through the mist on the windshield caused by their body heat and exhalations. Lew sighed and thumped his fist against his thigh.

"Where are we, then?"

Benjie shrugged. "I'm not saying it's time to cut and run, even if we knew which direction or how far. Here's where it is. They got these two dates and they came up with the two canceled checks. Both checks on the separate account we set up for Harbour Pointe. I was careful with that account. Even the prorated charge for overhead, I would write a check back from that account to Marliss, so when the time came we could substantiate capitalizing everything they would let us capitalize, so we'd look better taxwise. Anything on that special account for one thousand and over takes two out of any three signatures, you, me and Marty being the three. So the five was last February, signed by Marty and me, and the ten was in May, signed by you and me. The checks were cashed. My books show miscellaneous fees and cash expenses. That is fine for nineteen dollars and fifty-seven cents. It is not too great for fifteen thousand. They want better identification."

"Like I should go get a receipt from Justin Denniver and his wife? What are you going to do?"

"Stall around. I don't know where they stand legally on this. But that doesn't make much difference. I've seen it happen too many times. These agencies, they've got all the muscle. You do like they say, or they get Justice to hit you with an indictment. Then you are under a cloud for eighteen months and maybe it is dropped or maybe it goes to trial. Either way, you are fucked. If it goes to trial and you come out innocent, you are twenty to forty thousand poorer because of the cost of defending yourself, and people say you hired an expensive lawyer and got yourself off. Hell, there is no middle ground between a public defender and an expensive lawyer. There is no bargain-price defense."

"Can we fake some backup for that fifteen thousand?"

"Sometimes, Lew, you really surprise me, you turn so

stupid. I told you, these are pros. The way we play it, we just can't remember. We run a busy shop. We're short-handed. Somebody should have made a memo. We deal with a lot of cash from time to time. We've plain forgotten. If something comes up that reminds us, we'll let them know right away."

"What do they suspect?"

"My guess is they suspect it is okay. They know how these things work. A little money has to be passed under the table, or nobody would ever get anything started or built or finished. They just like to have it look plausible, instead of half-ass careless. They seem to be more interested right now in the price Letra paid Marty for that fourteen acres. That's why I wanted a chance to talk to you. I had an old feasibility study stapled to my work sheets on the Harbour Pointe project. In that study I put down the land cost at $1,480,000, with $1,252,000 going to the Silverthorn estate, and $228,000 going to Marty personally for his option, which he held for twenty months before he sold it to Letra. It comes to $105,700 an acre. Yet on our books it shows $1,228,000 to Marty for his option, and $1,252,000 to the estate for the land, or $177,000 an acre. Barber and Grosscup got that same figure from Atlanta, from whoever looked at the EMMS books.

"Anyway, Grosscup comes to me and says it looks like a sudden change, a million more in May than it seemed to be worth in March, and I told him land prices tended to move quickly, especially waterfront. He's got a funny smile. He smiled and said that they certainly did move quickly, and lately they seemed to be mostly moving down. I pointed out that the land had moved for more than that an acre in this area, and when you have a fourteen-acre tract, it is so hard usually to put a waterfront piece together that size, it ups the price. Then I went and got those two letters that came in from those two big outfits on the East Coast, to Marty personally, offering just about the same. He looked at the letters and smiled his funny smile and said, 'This one is under investigation by the SEC for fraudulent sale of unregistered securities, and this other one is within a couple of weeks of filing in bankruptcy. Very interesting, Mr. Wannover. Very very interesting.' And he walked out of my office, back to that little conference room they're working in."

"I saw those offers. They look legitimate. They look good. And I would bet that there's no good way to prove that Sherman Grome asked those people to make those offers. It would be tough to take it to court, even to tax court, to try to deny him long-term capital gain status to that one million dollars."

"You take the extra million loaded onto Harbour Pointe and you take the debt service Grome stuck us with, and there isn't any way at all to make it work out, Lew. No way."

"Can that be proven?"

"I think so."

"Then, Benjie, maybe we all get named as part of a conspiracy to defraud. You and me, Grome and Marty, God only knows who else."

"Especially if they subpoena brokerage account records."

"You know, you could have gone all afternoon without saying that."

"Did you make out?"

"Not too bad. I shorted fifteen hundred shares at an average eighteen bucks a share. It went down to five two weeks ago and when it started to move up, I covered and got out. After commissions it was eleven dollars a share net. Ordinary income, of course. I made about sixteen thousand five."

"It's down to three and five eighths on yesterday's close."

"You still in?"

"I got out of some. But I'm still short on four hundred shares. Monday I cover. Lew, look. We're in kind of a funny position. We've known each other long enough and well enough, we know better than to trust each other too much."

"Right."

"I think things are going to move along pretty fast. I

think they are going to close down Sherman Grome and put in a receiver, and I think they'll put in somebody with good footwork, and he'll come down here and cut Harbour Pointe off right now and pull back that eight million sitting in certificates of deposit in the Athens Bank and Trust. That is going to leave Letra with our equity in Stalbo's Tropic Towers and the fourteen acres behind Golden Sands and about eleven cents in cash, against . . . call it five and a half million owed. So Letra goes bankrupt, and Harbour Pointe is dead. Don't ask me how I happen to know, but I do know that Marty has been putting money into Swiss francs. And the other day I walked in on Irish and she was reading brochures on the Greek islands. What would Marty hang around for? What would he need offices and staff for? He's got Frank West and Sully running the two money machines here, with the money flowing into the Services Management Group in Miami and coming back to him as dividends. We are going to be unemployed, Lew."

"How soon?"

"One month. Two. Right after Grome comes tumbling down."

"What's with him?"

"I think Sherm is plain old-fashioned nuts. In the pictures he looks like a kid. But he has to be close to fifty. Dietitians, face lifts, sunlamps, a gym in the office. I saw a thing about him in *Forbes* a year ago, saying he wanted to buy his own studio and make some movies about his life and star in them himself. He is nuts, but he has been in a line of work where it is very difficult to tell crazy guys from sane guys."

"Until too late."

"Everybody used to think Howard Hughes was nuts. Two billion dollars' worth of crazy. But Sherm is crazy in a different way. I don't think he really believes anything could ever go wrong. I've never met him, of course. I could be way off."

The rain was easing. "Benjie . . . I keep wondering if there is any way we could get some nice . . . terminal bonuses out of Marty."

"Like how much?"

"Like you and I split half of that extra mil he got."

"Like we mousetrap him somehow?"

"Something like that. You know, though, he always hints about the hard-nose people in Miami. What is it he calls them?"

"The firemen. They come and put out fires for you."

"Is he kidding?"

"I don't know. That outfit, that Services Management Group, it stands to reason they'd have troubleshooters. In construction there are always people trying to make trouble."

"Did he ever use them for anything?"

"I don't know. I've been with him nine years, a couple years longer than you, Lew. People have tried to make trouble and they've had bad luck. They have had bad falls and they have fallen asleep smoking in bed, and they have gotten cramps and drowned."

"Oh."

"It could be coincidence, but I don't want to run any test. Do you?"

"I don't think so. It's funny. I've used those people as a threat when somebody got out of line, but I never believed. Not until now. I'm not even sure I believe it all the way now."

"Maybe Marty just has natural luck."

"I don't want to test it. Oh, God damn it all, Benjie, what am I going to do?"

"You are a single guy with a law degree. You asking a guy with ten kids what you should do? Let's talk again about all this. I got to go now. You hear anything, let me know. I'll do the same." He rolled the side window down and held his hand out. "It's almost stopped." He got out and leaned back down to the window. "Maybe we can pick up some scraps while the big dogs fight, old buddy. Cheer up." In another minute he had backed the station wagon out and driven away.

Lew Traff drove back to his apartment, parked in back and hurried through the rain. His head ached. He poured a glass of milk and sat and sipped it, easing the dull pain of the ulcer.

Inventory time again. Stocks worth not quite twenty thousand, or one ninth of what they'd cost in the go-go days The money from the short sale of EMMS had gone to clean up two of the three demand notes at the bank and pay off the compromise settlement with the IRS. But that gain was ordinary income and the tax would be heavy.

And if the three thousand a month from Marliss stops coming in? Who needs Lewis Traff, specialist in real estate options, transfers, deeds, titles, metes and bounds? The times had suddenly rendered him obsolete.

His back teeth on the upper right side ached. He put his thumb tip back there and gently wiggled the molars. They seemed to be quite loose. He looked across the living room at the digital clock atop the television set. He closed his left eye and then his right eye. When he had his right eye closed the orange numerals of the clock were misty and blurred. He could sharpen them by squinting. The goddam teeth and eyes and ulcer and constipation and the goddam premature ventricular beats waking him up in the middle of the night, scared and sweaty.

If only Adele would get married. Without the alimony payments maybe he could get a little bit ahead. Enough to have breathing space.

Maybe the Jerry Stalbo solution wasn't all bad. It had really made Marty jumpy, the way Stalbo had done it. From the way the police had reconstructed it, Jerry had siphoned a two-quart milk container of gasoline out of his about-to-be repossessed Continental, gone up to the penthouse, stripped, put on his silk pajamas, stood on his rear wall, drenched himself, lit himself, and jumped flaring and screaming down through the soft black night, landing with sodden bursting impact upon the curbing of an auxiliary parking area. Dru said that when Marty heard how it happened, he had barely made it to his executive washroom. They had been close at one time, years ago, she said, back when they had both been married to their first wives, back when they had both been building small homes in an orange grove they had purchased jointly.

Marty had said to Lew, "It wasn't me, you know. Nobody forced him to build that big pile of crap and paint it brown and yellow to match. He had to be a big man. Live in the suite. Have a lot of broads. He thinks he could stay in the suite forever? If it wasn't us trying to move him out, it would have been somebody else. He was a bankrupt. Besides, he was nuts. Absolutely. I swear it. You should have seen how he was the last time I saw him, like he'd shrunk down to half his size. And he kept crying. My God, he used to have a laugh, that man, you could hear him a block away. In a restaurant, everybody would jump, like a lion was roaring."

Lew stretched out on his couch, wadding a pillow behind his neck. The hiss of the air conditioning shut out all sounds of the world, of rain and wet tires and music in the other apartments.

The Stalbo solution did not have to be in the Stalbo manner. The thought of burning made his flesh crawl. A nice glass of warm milk to wash down a handful of sleeping pills, and then crawl, yawning, into the downy bed and fade off into sleep, smiling, thinking of all the grasping bastards who would have to stop taking chunks of his hide and flesh. Disappear down the rat hole of dark sweet sleep.

He reached back beyond his head and picked up the phone and placed it on his chest. Margo's phone did not answer. Nor did Ruthie's. He hesitated, then looked up the Denniver number and exhaled his tensions when Molly answered.

"Hey!" she said with obvious delight. "This is a coincidence. I phoned you a couple times. Noon, I think. And one thirty."

"I was playing out at Gator Hole and we got rained out after nine. Whyn't you come on over here, honey. I've got some good wine cooled and—"

"Now you *know* I won't come there, Lew, not ever. You've asked me often enough. What would people think if anybody sees me going in or out of your place? I wouldn't want to start up any idle gossip about you and me. Besides, we promised it wouldn't happen again ever."

"I'm sorry. It was just an idea. Where's Justin?"

"He's staying over at that meeting at Kansas City. He left here a day early and he's not anxious to get back, and it isn't hard to figure out why, the way every fool in the county has been badgering him about the land-clearing on the Silverthorn property. What I called you about, my tennis tournament got called off, and I wondered if you'd like to come over here and have a nice swim."

"In the rain?"

"It's nice, Lew. It really is. The rain really comes down through the screen. Anyway, I want to prove to us that we can behave for once. Okay?"

"Okay, honey. Why not?"

JULIAN HIGBEE FOUND the service cart parked in the hall outside 4-B, and he went in and found Leanella in the kitchen, washing up. She was a six-foot black girl in a brief white uniform. Her skin tones were gold and ivory, and her hairdo was an enormous carrot-colored natural. She wore sandals with high cork soles. With the additions she was almost seven feet tall.

She beamed at him, eye to eye. Her little radio was on the countertop, turned so high the rock was hissing and frying. She was moving her shapely hips to the beat. Her belt was pulled tight around the slenderness of waist.

He turned the radio down to a whisper.

"They left?"

"What do you think, man? They sure God did. When the rent got raised, they took off like they were saying they would."

"How much longer'll you be here?"

"Nuther hour."

"I'll go down and get the owner's list. You can help me with the inventory."

"No way, Mr. Julian."

"What's the matter?"

"Get you Coreen. That woman *likes* counting up stuff and marking them off. It drives me weird. What I'm paid for is cleaning. No counting."

"See much damage?"

"Maybe more than usual. These Sappers spilt and dropped."

"Sapphiere."

"That's right. Sapper. Go look where that little throw rug got moved in front of the couch. God only knows what they spilt there. Hot tar, maybe. It's got a hard shine on it like a parking lot."

He went and looked and shouted to her—she had turned her radio up again—"Good thing we've got a security deposit."

She turned it down. "What?"

He came to the kitchen door. "We're holding four hundred dollars' security deposit."

Leanella leaned against the sink, long arms folded. She shook her head and said, "Folks sure change."

"What's that mean?"

"You run around working your white ass down to the bone these days. Anybody wants their nose blowed, you come on the run holding out the hanky."

"What the hell is it to you?"

"Now that sounds like you used to be. Want to fire me? I got nine better jobs I can go to. God knows why I stay in this rotten place. Force of habit. Get to know where everything is and get to know what's going on here and there. Like, you know, me and Coreen were talking about it, how the big nurse lady in Two-C, Nurse Fish, after she and Miss Lorrie got friendly, she won't let you run in and love her up no more."

"Now God damn it, Leanella!"

"And unless you keep on the run all day long, Mr.

Sullivan will maybe send somebody over to whip your ass again."

He reached her in two strides, drawing his hand back.

"Let it go," she whispered. "Pop me just one time, honky, and my man will have you talking soprano all the rest of your short life."

He sighed and slumped and let his hand fall. He studied her. "Will you please help me do the inventory on this apartment for the Coopers?"

She thought and then nodded. "I surely will. See? Anything you want, when you ask nice and polite, you might just get it."

"I don't need any—"

"You watch it, now!"

He turned away and hurried down to the office. Pete McGinnity, president of the Condominium Association, was just asking Lorrie where he could find Julian.

"Can I help you, sir?" Julian asked.

"It's just a suggestion, Higbee. I think we're going to get a very big turnout for the meeting tomorrow, and I was wondering how we could get hold of some extra chairs."

"I can get some from the company, Mr. McGinnity. It costs forty dollars for a hundred folding chairs, twenty to deliver and twenty to pick up."

"About thirty more chairs ought to do it. Can't you go get that many in the pickup? The Association can't afford forty cents."

"I've got a crew digging up that drain off the parking area to get it—"

"Before one thirty tomorrow?"

"Well . . . I guess so. Okay."

"Good man!"

As soon as he left Julian said to his wife, "Dig out the inventory on Four-B. The Coopers in Youngstown own it. Honest to God, these people are going to drive me crazy. They are going to drive me right up the wall. The more I do for them, the more they want. And we're not turning a dime out of this place anymore."

"Here's your inventory."

He flipped the sheets. "Jesus! They listed everything."

"Who'll help you?"

"Leanella said she would. Maybe she can do it. Maybe not. She's got a big mouth. You know that? She had something to say about your friend, the nurse."

"I was damned close to being a nurse when I met you."

"You tell your sad story to Leanella?"

"I wouldn't have to. Those two know everything that goes on in this building. I don't know how they know, but they know, every time. It's like the old story, you know, about the wife being the last to know."

"Isn't it about time you let up on me?"

"You haven't even earned the right to ask. You are a rotten bastard, Julie. Bobbie was going through a bad emotional time in her life and you came upon her when she was drinking and forced yourself on her and then blackmailed her into keeping on doing it with you."

"That's her version?"

"It's what happened."

"Then why was she phoning down here all the time, making you suspicious and making me nervous? Who was blackmailing who?"

"When she was drinking she . . . wanted to."

"For God's sake, Lorrie! I slipped once, okay? She called me up there to fix a leaky faucet and she was half dressed and ready, and you got to admit she is stacked. She was asking for it."

Lorrie stood with folded arms, glowering at him between the dark shining wings of her hair. "If it wasn't for that little number on the top floor over in the Captiva House, and if it wasn't for that pretty old lady over in—"

"Now, honey, please. I got too much on my mind to handle all this fighting too. Can't you just forgive and forget? Please?"

"I don't know whether I'll forgive you, but I know I won't ever forget. Not that it really means that much more anyway."

"Lorrie!" he cried, stung by the indifference in her tone.

"Go count things," she said, turning away.

"It would really rack me up, honey, if you ever . . ."

Her small smile was bitter. "Have no fear. It's never been all that great, lover."

LeGrande Messenger lay in restless sleep in the master bedroom of penthouse apartment 7-A. He stirred and wakened enough to hear the distant rapid ticking of the Selectric II as Barbara typed the corrections on the final reports which would wind up the last of the Mexican involvements. He could hear afternoon thunder bumbling across the horizon.

It was tidy, he thought, to be able to dismantle the interwoven, intertangled business affairs of a lifetime instead of leaving it up to the platoons of bankers, attorneys, trustees and executors. It was tidy to be able to steal the time in which to do it, time achieved at the cost of pain which was sometimes bearable, sometimes ghastly. The clumsy folk who entered the scene after death could yank out the wrong part first, toppling other parts in delicate balance. But he knew what had to come down first, and he could send the right people up into the superstructure and tell them which bolts and fastenings must first be loosened.

Corporations and companies, partnerships and syndications, fractional interests and majority interests. In each case you could take it apart most profitably if you knew just how it had been assembled in the first place.

. . . He was spending the weekend at his ranch north of Harlingen, renegotiating the overriding royalties on the oil leases with the Austin group and losing just enough to them in the Saturday-night poker game to keep them feeling expansive. He had showered and shaved on Monday morning and was just stepping into his pants when he heard the bray of the loud horn of Larry's white Cadillac convertible, playing the first five notes of "Home on the Range." The Austin group had left Sunday afternoon in the Bonanza. Larry would want to know how he'd made out.

He looked through the screen and saw that Bill and Ted were in the back seat, leaving the seat beside Larry, the driver, for him. Larry had turned around in the big area by the porch and was headed out. He shouted to them that he was coming, and when he had put his hat on, he gathered up the papers he had studied after going to bed and slipped them into the zipper case.

He hurried through the house to the front door, pausing to tell Lopez he'd be back in two weeks. He went out onto the porch and stopped at the top of the steps.

His three oldest and best friends were looking up at him expectantly. The top was down. They sat in the rusted ruin of a convertible nearly forty years old. Shreds of rubber dangled from the wheel rims. Parched grass grew tall under the car and beside it. His three best friends were stained and yellowed bone, clad in dry shreds of skin and the rotted fabric of ranch clothes. With lips gone, their broad toothy smiles were a deadly welcome.

That ruined car had not moved in years. Yet he knew they were waiting for him and had been waiting a long time. He knew that he was meant to go around and get into that car beside the driver, and knew that if he did, it would start up and they would roar away. He backed away from the porch steps, yelling "No! Oh, no, please!"

He burst up out of the dream, sweaty and panting. He wondered if he had yelled aloud and he waited and, when Barbara did not come to him, knew that the yelling had been only in the dream.

He waited for the dream to fade, but it remained vivid in his mind. Larry, the rancher. Bill, the geologist. Ted, the banker. They had come up out of the ground, into his sleep, to take him on another of those trips they made, to look at something "interesting."

Larry had been the first one to go. Predictably. A man of high blood pressure, vast appetites, great intensity. A noisy, red-faced, fat man, who all his life did a superb job of concealing a superior intelligence. After the coronary occlusion he lasted eight days under the oxygen tent. Bill went next. They took out his left lung at Ochsner in New Orleans, hoping to give him two or three years more, but all they gave him was six months of slow suffocation. Ted lasted until . . . my God, it was fifteen years ago he died. That long! Hit head on in Oklahoma by a drunken Indian in a pickup who came across the median. Three dead, one banker, one chauffeur and one Indian. Big funeral, but not as big as Bill's, whose was not as big as Larry's. And mine will be the smallest of all four. Messenger's equation: Funerals are small if you outlive the people who would have attended.

So what does the dream mean? Come join us? No way to avoid it, men. Except temporarily, as I have been avoiding it, with three little operations and chemotherapy and a few series of cobalt.

He wished there was someone he could tell the dream to, who would appreciate it, who would have known all four of them well. But the only people who could have appreciated it, really and truly, were Larry and Bill and Ted, appreciated the ghastly humor of it.

Larry especially. He could almost hear Larry's voice. "You mean the three of us was sitting there in that old car, in that gawdforsaken old white Cad I had that time, with the steer horns on the front and the calfskin upholstery with the hair side up? Jesus, I loved that dang car. Stomp it to the floor, it'd go like whistlin' piss. But that thang been crunched up into a little bale and recycled four or five times since those days. Me and Ted and Bill here, raised up from the daid to come grab you? That must have spoiled your undershorts for sure, Lee."

What the world does, Lee thought, it pulls out your plugs. You sat there with a big switchboard and you could talk to them all and they could talk to each other—about you, if they happened to feel like it. The little ruby lights go out and you have to manually yank out the plugs and let them snap down into their secret places where the cobwebs grow on them. You can plug in and talk to strangers. But nobody knows what all the past was like for you, and nobody cares. And, if the truth be known, you do not really give a God damn what their lives were like either, if you were not a part of them. Comparing pasts is the most tedious conversational exercise known to mankind. Everybody was a cute baby, once upon a time.

We are all in the path of a slow-moving avalanche, a gray, rolling clutter of unidentifiable, unimaginable junk. We can stroll on ahead of it, uneasy, but in no specific danger. If we look back and see some bright treasured object left behind, there is no time to dart back and rescue it. The avalanche rolls over it, grinding it down and out of sight forever. One day we tire or trip, we fall, and in moments we are covered, lost and forgotten.

Long ago, serving as a War Department consultant, he had stood in the light of a hot dawn in Calcutta in front of a hotel, waiting for a friend to come by in a jeep and take him out to Dum Dum airfield, where he hoped to hitch a ride on a C-88 headed for China. There were perhaps fifty people asleep on the broad sidewalk in front of the hotel, arrayed at random, ragged robes drawn up to cover most of the sleeping faces.

Soon three hotel porters in wine-colored uniforms came out carrying a fire hose. They clamped the brass fitting of the hose into the water outlet on the front of the hotel. Two porters handled the long brass nozzle while the third turned the water on with a large key. The flattened hose sprang to fatness, and the hard gout began to spray the sleeping people. Many of them sprang up with loud cries of rage and danced away from the stream of water, making ugly gestures and ugly faces at the impassive porters. Others got up more slowly, too weakened by the Great Famine of Bengal and by disease to escape being soaked and battered by the water. A very few crawled out of range. He counted eleven who did not move. The porters moved the hose to proper positions where, by directing the stream of water, they could roll the bundles of rags over and over, into the gutter. He wished the jeep would come. The still morning air smelled of rancid goat butter, charcoal fires, urine, sickness and hot wet sidewalk. But before the jeep came, a lorry came slowly down the street and men walked beside it, picking up bodies by wrists and ankles, and with a practiced and muscular swing, heaving them over the high sideboards of the truck onto the bodies already collected. The hose had been rolled up and taken back inside. The eleven were thrown into the truck.

He was frightened by the utter inconsequence of the eleven deaths. If they had names, only they knew them. The bodies were not worth searching because there was no chance there was anything of value on any of them. They were not even worth inspecting to determine if they were dead or merely nearly so. They were dead who left no echoes, no resonance, no mourners. In that one instant when they passed from awareness to nothingness, they became one with all the nameless dead from all the pestilences of mankind from the very beginning.

His friend from the embassy came in the jeep. He told him about the hose. His friend said it happened all over the city every morning. He said they did not count how many were taken to the municipal burning ghats, but merely estimated them by the number of truckloads.

With sudden insight he realized that only a very few years need pass before he was one of the anonymous billions of the unknown dead. Postmortem identifications were brief and faded quickly. Perhaps by the time of the death of his youngest grandchild he would be utterly gone. Name, pictures, letters, marker. He would become a statistical micron. The great Bengal famine killed X million. In 19— X retired persons in Florida died.

The accumulated wealth would provide a spurious kind of immortality. Out of an odd mix of vanity, irony and idealism, he had set up the Lee Messenger Foundation with objectives so carefully tooled to his own beliefs, the trustees of the future could not freely ride off in all directions. There was the Foundation, the bequests to the sons, the many trust accounts for the grandchildren, and of course the large gift to Barbara, predeath, no business of any executor or tax collector in the future.

But Lee Messenger the man will be as thoroughly gone as all the others without that special knack of attracting money. And when the man was gone and the century was gone, those now being born would perhaps look back and see the people of that prior century and see them as quaint, or innocent, or touching.

Not so, he thought. Each year on earth involves vast confusions for those living through it. There are shrill cries, confusing shapes, clouds of dust, and people running and pointing in all possible directions, most of them wrong.

You up there in the future, you can look back and feel that we should have *known* exactly what was happening. While you scramble around in your own clouds of dust, yearning for some less perilous niche where you can escape the crushing impact of your own history, remember that it was like that here too. And everywhere. Always.

He saw the door open a cautious crack, then swing wide as Barbara walked in.

"Saw your eyes open," she said. "How are you?"

"About to get up."

"Feel okay?"

"Feel good. I had a very funny dream."

"Hey, tell me!"

"I wish I could. All I can remember is how I laughed."

As he swung his legs over the side of the bed, she went and got his robe from the nearby chair to hold it for him.

GUS GARVER HAD TO WAIT over an hour at the Athens Airport for the Eastern flight out of Atlanta to come in. He recognized Sam Harrison at a considerable distance, taller than the other passengers, sun-bronzed, wearing a faded khaki bush jacket and a white canvas hat, carrying a disreputable flight bag and walking toward the terminal with that limber swinging stride he could keep up all day long in all kinds of terrain.

When he spotted Garver he smiled, teeth white in his tan face. He dropped the bag and shook hands. "How you, Mr. Garver?"

"Making it, Mr. Harrison."

Sam Harrison took off his hat, wiped his forehead with a heavy forearm and laughed and said, "Meaning I get to call you Gus?"

"Now you aren't working for me anymore, Sam."

"I thought that's what I came down for."

"It's a long story. You don't have any other luggage?"

"Just this thing is all."

"Car's over this way."

On the way through the city and on out to the key, Gus explained the situation. "When they scraped that acreage behind Golden Sands bare it began to make me uneasy. Now they're doing the dredging and draglining on the yacht basin. Hell, I couldn't afford you. I'm retired. There is an old joker named Messenger on the top floor. Seven-A. He looks next door to dead and probably is. But where most of the other people in the building have fried mush for brains, this Messenger has got very good machinery between the ears. He can talk my language and yours, and probably languages we never heard of, and he is big rich. All the signs are there. I told him why I was worried and what I was worried about, and he said, Let's get the best."

"Very nice that you should think—"

"Don't scuff any shy foot with me, Sam. I'm just glad you've got some time between jobs. What was this last one?"

"A new tower design for deep offshore drilling, up to two thousand feet. My end of it was how to guy the tower for security in all kinds of wave action. Not enough background information to run good computer models. And as I don't have to tell you, Gus, the scale-model approach is no good when you are dealing with forty-foot waves versus structural steel. It's some help, but not much. The oil company wants to give it too much mass and strength. My approach is that it has to give. It has to sway and bob and weave. I made my final report and got paid off, and God only knows what they'll decide to build."

"Where next, after here?"

"New Zealand. Tasman coast of the South Island. Breakwater for a harbor for a mining project. They've put in two and lost both. One wild son of a bitch of a sea comes slamming in there. You know, I can't think of you as retired. Don't you get the itch?"

"Never," he said firmly.

"Sorry to hear about your wife."

"One of those things."

"Should I stop in and see her, maybe?"

"Thanks for suggesting it, Sam. She always liked you. But there's no point in it. I don't even know if she knows who I am. I think she does, but I can't be real sure. About all I can do is make sure she's comfortable and treated nice. And I make sure."

"Where'll I be staying?"

"Right at Golden Sands. I might even feed you."

"The rate just went up."

"For five hundred a day and expenses, you can choke it down."

"Want to tell me what's bothering you?"

"You're the big marine civil engineer. You're the wave-action specialist and hydrologist and what-the-hell not. What I'll tell you is that Golden Sands is a marginal structure on questionable footings. Do your own investigating. I don't want to slant you in the wrong direction."

"Even to save time?"

"I'm not paying for your time."

"The maximum time I can spend here is two weeks."

"Which is seven thousand, plus travel and miscellaneous."

"When do I check in with the man who's paying me?"

"Soon as we can arrange it."

Sam Harrison shrugged. At the next traffic light, as they waited for the change, Gus looked sidelong at him, noting the small changes. Sam's hat was off, and his hairline had receded at least a full inch and the brown hair had turned gray at the temples. He looked thicker through chest and shoulders, but just as lean around the middle. He had the blunt features and the wind and weather wrinkles of the outdoor laborer. His hands were huge and looked clumsy, but Gus remembered the precision and delicacy of the drawings Sam would make to illustrate a point in argument. There was a new scar, a dimpled pinkness in the side of his cheek.

"Some husband shoot you in the face, Sam?"

Harrison grinned and put his fingertips to the spot. "Piece of reinforcing rod slid out of a bundle on a sling, bounced once and popped me. Went in here and smashed three teeth and knocked me cold. Very lucky. It could have hit three inches higher or three inches lower, and I am a dead engineer."

"Or it could have missed you."

"Why? Nothing ever does."

"Where are the guys lately? I know Dirty Eddie and Fix are in Alaska. How about Stover?"

"Iraq. Buster retired on disability. His back finally quit for good. Lindy is working a big one in Canada, good for three years at least. Those are the only ones I know about. I've been out of touch." They went across the bridge and turned south on Fiddler Key. Sam Harrison sat straighter and peered at the high-rise condominiums. "Jesus God, Gus. They are built practically *in* the water."

"I know, I know."

"Have they figured the hundred-year crest here?"

"Thirteen feet above high tide. That's the government stipulation of the floor level of dwellings to be eligible for high-water insurance protection. But most builders go after exceptions and get them."

"And the builders don't have to live in the houses with the exceptions."

"Right. But Golden Sands is pretty much okay on that thirteen-foot elevation. The violation is the manager's apartment on the ground level, where the parking is, plus some utility rooms and storage rooms and the laundry room."

"But it would knock out your heating and air conditioning and electric and phone?"

"Probably. But here we are. See, it's on the bay side, and those two structures there would probably break down the wave action, so by the time it got to us it would have lost its punch."

Gus Garver drove around and parked in back. They got out of the car and looked toward the bay, broad and clearly visible across the scraped marl where the jungle had been.

Sam Harrison shaded his eyes and looked at the tethered shabby blue-and-yellow dredge. The jointed pipe, attached to floats, came ashore off to the right, spilling mud, sand, weed, shell and small marine creatures into an area where the bulldozer had pushed berms into position to retain the solid matter and let the bay water run off. A yellow dragline was walking its way out from shore, building up sandbars and oyster bars into a broad curve of filled land which would encircle one side of the yacht basin.

"Eight-inch dredge?" Sam asked.

"I think so."

"All the approvals in order? Environmental impact, Corps of Engineers, Coast Guard, and all the others?"

"Don't need them."

"The *hell* you say!" Sam said, incredulous.

"You see, it's a minor work permit. They are just scouring an existing channel and repairing erosion damage."

"Bullshit!" said Sam Harrison.

"I know. But the plans were submitted as a minor work permit, and the commissioners approved it as a minor work permit, and some county clown comes out every day and inspects it to make sure it is proceeding as a minor job of scouring and repairing. See the markers out there in the bay? That's the Inland Waterway. They are going to scour out an existing channel out to that channel, with a five-foot depth at low tide."

Harrison strolled north to a point where he could see beyond the shoulder of Golden Sands, out toward the open Gulf. He turned and looked toward the bay. He sat on his heels and stared first east and then west. He poked a stick into the sandy soil and stood up and sighed and shrugged.

After they left Harrison's gear off in 1-C, they went up to LeGrande Messenger's apartment on the seventh floor. Barbara Messenger opened the door and came out into the hallway, leaving the door barely ajar.

She said, "I'm sorry, Mr. Garver, but he started to have quite a bit of pain about an hour ago and finally he had to give in and let me give him a shot. He was very anxious to meet Mr. Harrison."

"I'll be around for a while. I can talk to your father when he feels better."

She tilted her head and looked at him, and he detected her mild amusement. He realized what a handsome creature she was, beach-brown and glowing. "He's my husband, Mr. Harrison."

"I have this hoof-in-mouth disease. I thought Mr. Garver introduced you as Miss."

"It's perfectly all right. Actually he has a granddaughter not too much younger than I am. Neither of us is sensitive about age. If I were to guess about when would be a good time to see him, I would suggest about six this evening, but do call me first, to make sure."

"I've got the unlisted number," Gus said. "Are you coming to the big meeting today, Mrs. Messenger?"

"Lee asked me to attend and take notes. Mrs. Schmidt will stay here with him."

As they walked toward the elevators, Harrison said, "Pretty lady."

"Sure is. I did a con job on them, sort of. If there was any real trouble here, it could play hell getting Messenger out safely, especially if he was sedated. He's a big old boy, not fat. Just pretty big even if he has dwindled a lot, which you can see he has. And I could guess he's got money he can lay out whenever his self-interest is involved. So I went a little way into what's troubling me, and he said yes as fast as I thought he would. A lot easier than trying to take up a collection. You know, a lot of these people are really hurting. The monthly assessment on this place more than doubled a couple of months ago.

That, plus inflation, and the little expenses you didn't count on."

"You making it okay?"

"Sure, sure. What's your program, Sam?"

As they got off at the first floor and walked toward Gus's small apartment, Sam said, "Rent a car. Go make friends at the courthouse. Find out where I can find aerials and depth charts and surveys."

"The state university system has started a Sea Grant Program. They've published a few studies on coastal problems. Have you given any thought to some kind of cover story? If it looks as if you're out to bring Marty Liss's new project to a screaming stop, you won't get access to anything. He's pretty well connected politically, and with the banks and the Chamber of Commerce. Also, the construction people are making a big public outcry about the way new permits have fallen off."

"Maybe I better look as if I'm bird-dogging for some big outfit. Which means I better not stay here. You don't know me, Gus."

"Down the key below the village is a place where a rich bird dog would stay. The Islander. Ask for a beach cabana. You can get your car delivered there. I'll drive you down."

"How far is it?"

"Mile and a half."

"I'll walk it, down the beach. Learn more. This thing has a shoulder strap."

At high noon Sam Harrison walked down the broad white beach of Fiddler Key. He had stuffed his bush jacket into his carry-on bag. He wore his big oval sunglasses, with his white canvas hat tipped well forward to shade them. He walked slowly, sweating mildly in the noon heat of July, walking on the hard white sand exposed by the outgoing tide. The beach was very broad, and above the high-tide line were the small signs indicating that the uplands sand, with its foot-dimpled patterns, its groupings of folding chairs, its thatched sun shelters, was for the exclusive use of the condominium owners and their guests, owners of apartments in the Port Belleview, Imperial Beach, Seville, Tahitian, Brightwaters, Azure Breeze, Captiva, Surf House, Enchanted Shores, Patrician Sands, Regency Beach, Mariner Towers, Martinique Manor, Gulf Way, Silvery Sands, Beachcomber Reef Club, Polynesian Breezes, Regal Shores, Tropic Towers, Vista del Sol, Casita del Mar, Buccaneer Bay, Aloha Shores, Sea Grape Estates, Sand Dollar Dunes, Magic Horizons, Serenity House. . . .

Children and sandpipers and terns played at the edge of the water. The dumpy little swells came in off the Gulf, lifting in a lazy sheen to about an eight-inch height before slapping the wet sand and making a six-foot run of foam through the crab holes and broken shells. The sunbrowners lay like death under the hard weight of the hazed sun, their bodies shining and frying in oil.

Sam Harrison marveled at the unending column of high-rise buildings standing at attention at the edge of the water. Most of them had some supposed protection against high water, berms or seawalls or a slant of riprap. Far ahead they marched on, following the gentle contours of the sandspit island.

The unreality of the situation made Sam Harrison feel slightly dazed. Surely there were people here who knew what was happening. They had seen it happening. Didn't they give a damn?

The predicted maximum-wave uprush was, according to Gus Garver, thirteen feet above the mean high-water line. There was no dune protection here. The vegetation line was nil. Sweet, dumb, innocent people were living in these things, with all their worldly goods. They were encased in solid concrete, so they felt safe. "Good God, mister, the real estate agent wouldn't have sold it to me and the bank wouldn't have taken the mortgage if it wasn't safe as a church, right?"

Here were the big buildings, with their toes practically in the water, and out there was the benign and smiling sea.

With practiced eye he could see that the longshore current and littoral drift was from north to south. He could tell that from the visible erosion. The wave action far out gave him a clue as to the bottom contour, probably shelving off very gradually. Historically, this broad beach would have disappeared and reappeared many times, eroded and replenished over and over.

He went up to what he estimated to be the mean high-tide line and, with his eye, estimated a thirteen-foot crest against the nearby condominium. Of course, that thirteen foot was just the storm surge. Take storm surge and add to it all the factors to make a maximum-wave setup, and you could be looking at twenty or twenty-five feet, right here. Wave surge plus a coordinating high tide plus a wind increased by the velocity of the main body of the storm itself, plus recent heavy rainfall, plus a very low barometric pressure and, he thought, you could get those big gray bastards marching in and breaking against the third story and hurling spray up onto the roof.

He walked on. With sudden insight he realized that it was like the emotional anesthesia of combat. These condominium dwellers were absolutely positive that if something terrible did happen, it would happen at Sarasota, or Fort Myers, or Venice, or Naples, or St. Pete Beach. It would never happen here, at Athens, at Fiddler Key. And if it did, then it would knock down somebody else's building. And if it knocked down their building, they would be evacuated in time and the insurance would cover everything.

Near the village the beach dwindled due to erosion, and after climbing over a couple of new groins which were supposed to help, and hadn't, he went up to the road and walked through the village and then back out onto the beach, and through a public beach area. A couple of dozen cars twinkled and baked in the large parking lot. Lifeguards drowsed on their towers, shaded by fringed and faded canvas. A young girl was screening coquinas at the water's edge. Two hefty old women were slowly shelling their way along the high-tide windrow of shell and weed, dropping their treasures into string bags. He happened to be staring seaward when a big ray leaped high, going eight or ten feet in the air. It had at least a six-foot wingspread. It came down and whacked the water with its wings, sounding to Harrison like a distant pistol shot. One ichthyologist had told him the ray does that to rid itself of parasites that fasten onto it as it swims near the bottom, through the weeds. A second believed it does that to stun schools of minnows and then feed at leisure. Sam held to the private belief that they do it for the hell of it, because it feels good and makes a nice noise.

He noticed that the small waves had begun to break on a bar about two hundred yards offshore. He could see the pallor of the bar under the very blue water. He guessed that it was almost dead low tide. Say the waves were a foot high coming onto the bar, they would break when the water was 1.3 times as deep as the wave was high. So, sixteen inches of depth at low tide, and not much of a tide in the Gulf, call it three feet of depth over the bar at high tide. It could be a little protection this far down the key, depending on how broad the bar might be, and how broad it might become in the winter tides.

After a time he saw the Islander in the distance. It was imitation Samoan, a lot of beehive structures of various sizes, linked by sheltered walkways. He found his way through the maze to the front desk where the male desk clerk, all beads, tan and hairdo, forgave him at once for not having a reservation and rented him a cabana between the pool and the beach for forty-one sixty a day, including tax, a special bargain in the off season.

"That unit rents for a hundred and fifteen double in February," he said. "A hundred and nineteen sixty with tax."

"I'll remember to think about that," Sam said, retrieving his credit card and stowing it away.

"If you want to know about the action . . ."

"Not particularly."

". . . there isn't hardly any. There isn't hardly any in all of Palm County. It's conservative. You know."

"I know."

"On vacation, Mr. Harrison?"

"Yes and no."

"Well . . . anything you want to know about Fiddler Key, we'll be glad to try to help. Can you find it yourself? I can call . . ."

"I'll find it."

It was Cabana 3. It was air conditioned into the low sixties. He found the control and moved it up to eighty. He found that he had two double beds, a glass-enclosed shower, a lot of white furniture, an aqua shag rug, an ice maker, a closed circuit movie channel and a room-service menu for drinks and food.

He stretched out for a few moments to plan the rest of his day, and, as always when in a new place, he wondered if he was living as well as his ex-wife. He had seen a needlepoint framed on the wall of a restaurant once. It said, "Living well is the best revenge." He had never quite understood what it meant. Stel had to be living well, or she wasn't trying. She had fallen in love with a chubby, jolly little man from Shreveport who had a natural gas flow of half a trillion feet a day. It had turned out to be Sam's fault for being away so much. What do you expect? Anyway?

THE SPECIAL MEETING of the Golden Sands Condominium Association was called for one thirty, with notification posted beside the elevators on every floor forty-eight hours ahead of time.

The meeting was in the dayroom on the first floor, situated almost directly over the office and the manager's apartment. It was a room thirty feet by sixty feet, with windows looking west. There were minuscule toilet facilities at one end, and at the other end, behind folding doors kept locked by Julian Higbee, rudimentary kitchen facilities. This public space had been made available by limiting the size of the first-floor apartments.

During the period of intense sales effort to show and sell the Golden Sands apartments, the dayroom had been most attractively furnished, with Naugahyde, imitation slate, decorator lamps and inlaid game tables. It was pointed out to all prospects that this lounge area, along with the tennis courts and swimming pool, were for the use of the residents, with a small monthly charge for lease and maintenance. In late February when most of the apartments had been sold, two men in a moving van leased by Investment Equities had pulled up and offloaded a considerable quantity of cheap new wicker furniture, folding card tables and gooseneck floor lamps with flower-pattern paper shades. They had taken away all the attractive furniture.

There were roars of outrage from the owners. Julian Higbee, at that time not subject to restraint, roared back at them. It was only out of the goodness of their hearts, he said, that Investment Equities put in any furniture at all. The owners were leasing the space. Nobody had ever said that the furniture was permanent. If the Association wanted better furniture they could go buy it and put it in there and Investment Equities would gladly take back this fine wicker furniture and put it somewhere else. In a few weeks the fevered objections faded as new impositions took priority. And in a few months the wicker furniture looked as if it had had a generation of use, and the card tables tended to collapse without warning.

As was customary at such meetings, several card tables had been aligned in front of the folding doors to the kitchen, and the directors sat behind them. Pete McGinnity, the president, in the middle, with Hadley Forrester, the vice-president, on his left and David Dow, the treasurer, on his right. Beyond David was the secretary, Stanley Wasniak, and on the other end, beyond Forrester, was Gus Garver, the director at large. Wasniak was nearest the windows. Seated at right angles to him, her back to the windows, was Francine Gregg from Apartment I-A, an intensely affable little woman who was a wizard at shorthand and typing. Her husband, Rolph, spent most of his time soldering wire AB to terminal CD. He had become such an expert that when the Heathkit manual said the remote control color television set could be built in forty evenings, Rolph could manage it in less than forty-five. In addition to the electric organ, the high-fidelity components and a CB radio, Rolph had built the public-address system used at Association meetings. The mike stood on the table in front of McGinnity, and the speaker stood under the table, aimed at the audience, with the controls atop the speaker cabinet. Francine and Rolph were, McGinnity realized, essential to the proper operation of the Association. She kept the minute books, and she did a great deal of the bookkeeping for David Dow. Rolph Gregg had posted the notice of the meetings, had taken it on himself to remind everyone, and was ever ready to run any errand the directors devised.

The Greggs had an odd compulsion to serve. They sought no reward, not even recognition, for they were both self-effacing. It seemed to be enough to be a part of some form of formal organization. McGinnity was grateful to them. They lifted the burden of scut work. And they looked alike.

Julian Higbee sat at the other end of the line of card tables, at right angles to Gus Garver. He was there by invitation, to impart information and to relay requests.

McGinnity looked at his watch, looked at the audience and tapped the big black gavel on the ebony block, leaned toward the mike and said, "We'll wait another few minutes before starting the meeting. I don't believe we're all here yet." The clamor of voices began again. Rolph Gregg darted up and adjusted the controls on the speaker, then trotted to the open door and looked down the hall toward the elevators. He turned and nodded at McGinnity. More coming.

At twenty minutes of two, sensing his audience was growing restive, Pete McGinnity banged the gavel and said, "I now call this meeting of the Golden Sands Condominium Association to order. As you know from previous meetings, our roll call is a complicated procedure. For any action within the stipulations of the Declaration of Condominium, a simple majority of those present, in person or by proxy, is required. An amendment to the Declaration requires a two-thirds majority of all owners, which in our case means the owners of thirty apartments. In the case of the absentee owners, Mr. Secretary, can you tell us the status of the proxies, please?"

Wasniak said, "With the permission of the Chair, I'd like for Mrs. Gregg to cover that part of it."

McGinnity nodded and Mrs. Gregg cleared her throat and said, "There are eleven apartments where the owners do not reside in the apartments. The owner of Two-E and Two-F, Mr. McKay, is present. We have proxies in hand for the secretary to vote on Two-C, Mr. Horuck; Three-F, Mr. Kubit; Five-E, Mr. Pastorelli; Six-A, Mr. Birnbrode; and Six-B, Mr. Stetman. Our manager, Mr. Higbee, has been authorized to vote in behalf of Investment Equities, Incorporated, for the two apartments they own, Five-A and Six-E. So there are only two proxies missing.

"Now for the remaining thirty-six apartments, I have the master list here and I have been marking off the people I recognize. The first floor would seem to be complete: Gregg, DeLand, Garver, Rastow, Furmond, Taller and Simmins.

"On the second floor, I see Mrs. Santelli . . . and Mr. Quillan. Is Mrs. Neale here? Oh, there you are. Thank you. And there *you* are, Mr. Kelsey. Four present and proxies on three, completing the second floor.

"For the third floor I've marked as present Truitt, Gobbin, Dow, Dawdy and Branhammer. I am missing Mr. and Mrs. Schantz. Are they here? No? One missing from the third floor then.

"On the fourth we are missing a proxy and I have checked off as present Elbright, Ames, Twigg and Prentice. I am missing Mr. Barker."

A voice in the audience said, "He had to take his wife back to the hospital last night. She was pretty bad again."

"Oh, I'm sorry to hear that, Mrs. Twigg. So there's another one absent. And is Peggy Brasser here?" There was a sound of snickering. Somebody faked a loud hiccup. Laughter. Ignoring it, Mrs. Gregg said, "Two absent on four, plus the proxy. On the fifth floor we have the two proxies, and I have marked as present Jeffrey, Winney, Wasniak and Hascoll. I do not see either Mr. or Mrs. Protus."

A voice said, "They're on another cruise."

"Thank you. On the sixth floor, we are missing one of four proxies, and I see that the Clevelands, the Mensenkotts and the Churchbridges are all here. We have just five terrace apartments on the top floor. Mrs. Messenger? Present. And of course Mr. McGinnity and Mr. Forrester, officers of the Association. And Mr. Davenport, present. And the Reverend Doctor Starf?"

"He knew about it. I told him."

"That should complete the roll call, Mr. Secretary," she said and slid her sheet over to where Stanley Wasniak could read it.

He picked it up and cleared his throat. "Mr. Chairman, I'd like to report as follows. Present are members representing forty apartments. Missing are proxies from two absentee owners and five residents, making seven. This is the best attendance we've ever had, and it is enough so according to the Articles of Condominium we can change the Articles if thirty of the forty present vote in favor of the change."

"Thank you, Mr. Secretary. Inasmuch as the minutes of the last meeting were duplicated and distributed to all owners, I will entertain a motion that we dispense with the reading of the minutes of the last meeting at this time."

"So move," said Forrester.

"Second," said Garver.

"In favor? Opposed? Carried. And now we will proceed—"

Frank Branhammer sprang to his feet, red fists clenched, big red face scowling and bulging. "Just one goddam minute here!"

Pete McGinnity banged his gavel. "Please sit down, Mr. Branhammer. You're out of order."

"I want to know what the hell is going on!" he yelled, ignoring his wife, who was tugging at his arm and whispering at him.

"We are dispensing with the reading of the minutes," McGinnity said. "That means we are not spending time having Stanley here read three pages of minutes. That's why we had copies sent to everybody. You got a copy. Now sit down!"

"Does that mean nobody gets any chance to talk about any of the shit you people put in those minutes?"

McGinnity roared at him. "When we get to that part of the agenda, to that part of the list of things we are going to talk about here today, we are going to talk about what's in those minutes, under old business. But maybe you won't be here because if you keep up that garbage mouth of yours, I'll have you put out of the meeting."

After five seconds of fixed glare, Branhammer, mumbling almost inaudibly, sat down.

"What did you call me?" McGinnity demanded.

Branhammer studied him and said distinctly, "I called you an ass hole, you ass hole! I don't trust a one of you overeducated ass holes sitting there in a goddam row."

McGinnity stood up and dropped the gavel on the table, making a thunderous sound over the amplifier. He shook his big head. "I don't have to take this, do I? I don't have to take this at any time from anybody. Have yourselves a nice meeting."

There had been gasps of astonishment and outrage at Branhammer's language. There was a shocked silence as Pete McGinnity strode toward the door. Wasniak and Garver went after him. Gus turned in the doorway and said with the clear and unmistakable ring of authority, "All of you sit quietly until we get back."

Brooks Ames came forward from the back of the room and edged along a row until he was behind Branhammer, who sat with chin on his big chest, fists on his knees, huge belly in his lap. Brooks Ames wore the symbols of his authority, his armband, ID tag, whistle and handgun. He wore his khaki shirt and shorts. He tapped Branhammer on the shoulder and said, "As Sergeant at Arms of this meeting of the Golden Sands Condominium Association, I must request that you leave the meeting."

Branhammer turned slowly and looked up at him. "Eh?"

"You have to leave now, Branhammer."

"Or what?"

"Or . . . I will escort you out."

"Escort me?" Branhammer looked startled and then he smiled, and with reptilian quickness hooked a big finger in the red woven cord around Ames's neck and yanked his head down to within a few inches of Branhammer's red face. "Escort me?"

"Let go! Let go!"

Branhammer released him so suddenly Brooks Ames tilted back and sat on the lap of Mrs. Winney, and jumped back to his feet immediately.

"Go blow your little whistle, captain," Branhammer said. "You wanna get my attention, you better shoot me in the head with that little gun you got there. Go away, huh?"

Branhammer turned back, completely dismissing Ames. Brooks said, in a voice a half octave higher than usual, "You will be permitted to stay in this meeting, Mr. Branhammer, if you will watch your language. There are ladies present. Is that understood?"

Branhammer yawned and sighed.

"You have been warned," said Captain Ames, and sidled back along the row, as twenty different conversations all started up at once. The babble faded away as the three officers came back into the room and took their places at the card tables.

McGinnity said, "I want to apologize to all of you for my display of temper. This is a miserable thankless job, and I would drop it in a minute if anyone else would take it. But I want to make it clear that I will not stand for any vilification. I will not be called names. I will not be treated with suspicion and distrust, as there is no way in the world any of us officers can make one lousy dime out of the hours and hours and hours we put in on this job. Now we will get back to the meeting. I want no interruptions. When I want to open things up to comments from the floor, I will let you know. We will take the committee reports in order as usual, and then we will proceed to old business and then to new business. Now we will hear the treasurer's report."

David Dow reached and pulled the microphone close. In a breathy raspy whisper he said, "As you can plainly hear, I have laryngitis. I have had enough copies of my report made for all. I will wait until Mrs. Gregg has distributed them to all of you."

After the distribution he said, "Total budget is $91,000 per year. You can see the simplified breakdown. We had to make a total assessment of $15,412.50 on June first in order to catch up on back underassessments. The first of this month we dropped back to the regular amount of $7,583.45. Of this total of $22,995.95, we have not yet received approximately $4,000. We will need it in order to make all budgeted payments. Excuse me for whispering."

McGinnity said, "We will skip any report from your president at this time and go directly to old business, which means picking up where we left off at the last meeting: namely, this business of the management contracts and the maintenance service contracts we were stuck with on account of the arrangements were made by the previous officers of the Association, namely, Mr. Liss and his people. Now I am not going to open this up for discussion until your officers have made their comments, so stop waving your arms at me back there and sit quiet and listen. You might learn something. Hadley?"

Forrester pulled the microphone over. "As was recommended, Mr. Dow, Mr. Wasniak and I consulted an attorney about this whole matter, a Mr. Searle Wadkin of Hooper, Wadkin and Lannigan, in the Athens Bank and Trust Company building. We had two sessions with him. I took copious notes, but I see no point in going into detail at this time. He states that constant changes are being made in the law, to protect the condominium dweller, and that though many of these may not stand up in court if tested, most of them will. He said that it would not be possible to do exactly what was done to us, if this project was just starting at this time. But at the time it was done, it was perfectly legal, and it is his opinion we are stuck with it."

He grimaced when he heard the groans from the audience and pushed the mike back to McGinnity.

McGinnity said, "I had some long talks with David Dow, here, before he lost his voice. So I'll report what he was going to report to you. You will remember we noted in passing how nice Mr. Martin Liss was to the four of us when we called on him. (That was one you couldn't make, Gus.) We got class-A treatment in Liss's office, and it puzzled us. In the car on the way back we talked about it, saying he didn't really have to talk to us at all, but he knew we were upset and for some reason he wanted to calm us down.

"Now I have to get into some of the new business in order to say what I have to say, so I guess it will have to be okay with you people. We now know why Martin Liss didn't want any big fuss going on here. He has showed his hand. He is starting one hell of a big project right behind us, a very rich project. And he is taking a big risk starting something in times like these, with empty condominium apartments all over the state, tens of thousands of them. Maybe hundreds of thousands. And so many up for sale by individuals. You can look at the Sunday paper and find page after page. Okay, now let me look at this piece of paper here that David prepared for me. You people look at that ninety-one thousand budget. I asked David to peel it down to what we would actually have to have here in the way of expenses: insurance, maintenance, cleaning and so forth. He came up with a horseback guess of forty thousand dollars. Now we divide that by forty-five apartments, not forty-seven, and we come up with eight eighty-eight a year, or seventy-four a month. No, don't applaud. It isn't a fact, certainly not yet. Of course, using the same pro rata basis, the monthly cost would go from probably fifty a month on the first floor to a hundred on the top floor.

"Well, we sought some more legal advice, and this time I won't tell you the name because he would rather not be quoted. He said the first thing we have to do is catch everybody up to date on the assessment schedule. Then we have to be able to advise Investment Equities and Gulfway Management that we have decided, every single one of us resident here, to stop all payments on the recreation lease and on the management contract—"

"Now just a minute, Mr. McGinnity. You can't—"

"Shut up, Julian. You are here at this table as a guest."

"I just . . ."

Gus Garver reached over and put a powerful hand on Julian's forearm and silenced him with a warning pressure.

McGinnity continued. "The lawyer agreed that it is a ripoff situation, even though it was done legally. We have to stand together, every single resident. We have to try to get every kind of publicity we can. If we can make enough stink we can make this new thing behind us look like a bad bet. And maybe we can give some other condominiums the guts to quit making payments on their lousy contracts too. The lawyer said he thought if we went at it right, that they'd come back to us with some kind of compromise deal. When that happens, provided we all vote to go ahead with it, we can negotiate. The way we are right now, there are people here who just can't keep on paying so much every month. They just can't do it, and it isn't right they should have to. Now I'll open it up for question from the floor. Please, everybody, no speeches."

A hunched little woman in a floral dress stood up. She was wearing a pink hat with a wide brim, and carrying a shiny red purse. Others stood up too, but the pink hat caught McGinnity's eye.

"Yes, Mrs. . . ."

"Taller. Mrs. Boford Taller. What I want to ask is, who was it had the pool party last Tuesday night? I swim early every single morning because I'm allergic to the sun, and I'm telling you, that whole pool area was one nasty mess when I—"

"Mrs. Taller!"

"What I'm wondering, did they even register at the office to have a pool party? People eat like pigs and drop ugly hunks of food in the pool and it lays there and it turns my stomach."

"Mrs. Taller!"

"I want somebody to find out who it was. Maybe it wasn't even people from here. I've said before, we all ought to have special badges and have to wear them, so outsiders won't use our facilities the way they do. I want it investigated. That's all." She sat down, chin high, lips sucked in.

"Anybody else out there who has any comments on anything besides the monthly assessment costs, please save it until later, okay?"

"I want to say something," Julian said.

"Residents first, Higbee."

"I forgot to mention," Mrs. Taller said, hopping up again, "that the pool furniture was moved around every which way, and one of the umbrellas was broken. Just who pays for it, I wouldn't know."

McGinnity sighed into the mike. "Jack Cleveland?"

"Thank you, Mr. Chairman. Grace and me have talked this over. It just isn't fair in a person's retirement to get cheated out of the little extras that make life worth living. Now I would guess that because I had a pretty good success in the building supply business, we've got a little more cushion than most. But I can tell you we have felt it, having the assessment on the first of the month go up by a hundred dollars. That's twenty-five dollars a week that we would be using to eat out more. And I just can't see what we're getting for that extra hundred. Take for example the recreation lease. Neither of us care a darn thing about the pool, not with that wonderful Gulf of Mexico right out there. And tennis is too active, and about all anybody does in this room is have meetings or play cards. I can tell you, I had enough of meetings in my lifetime. I don't need any more, not at this stage in my life. And cards . . . I was going to tell you a joke about that, but the funny part of it has slipped my mind at the moment. I guess what I want to say is that Grace and me, we will go along with whatever the majority says. That's the democratic way of life, as I see it. But if they take legal action against all of us, and it looks as if we could lose the apartment or anything like that—well, I am going to put the difference into a separate savings account, and if it turns out we all have to pay up, I'm not going to fight city hall. I mean, there has to be a stopping place. I'm not going to turn myself into some kind of a martyr just to prove a point. I can tell you this, though. Most of us went along with the developer's suggestion and we set up the mortgage paper on the condominiums with the Athens Bank and Trust Company, and speaking as a director of a bank in Warren, Ohio, I can say that no bank would be very happy about any kind of action that would toss thirty-five mortgages back in its lap all in the same building. God only knows how long the bank would have to pay for all the maintenance and so on before, in these times, they could unload the property. It would seem to me that—"

"Thanks for your valuable advice, Jack. We should probably all put the difference aside in case things go against us, so it won't be too much of a shock to come up with the money. But if we stick together, we'll have a better bargaining position."

Arms were waving. People were calling for recognition. He recognized Phil DeLand from 1-B, a lean, bearded, retired major addicted to wearing tank tops, jeans and beads.

"Pete, will this Wadkin fellow continue to represent us if we go through with this plan?"

"To whatever extent we ask him to."

"Right on," said the major and sat down next to Roxanne, his Indian-looking wife.

He recognized Sally Kelsey from 2-G, a broad tanned woman noted for swimming straight out into the Gulf, out of sight. "Mr. Chairman, if we have a *legal* obligation to pay this additional money, then my husband and I think we have a *moral* obligation to pay it. All over this country we have seen people marching around, burning and destroying, because they didn't like this law or that law. We guessed what might happen at this meeting and we talked it over. We think that the right thing to do is to pay under protest, and at the same time sue the developer for misrepresentation."

There was a chorus of groans and hisses. She glared around at them all. Somebody said, "Those guys are suit-proof, Sally." Another said, "What they're doing to us is legal." Another said, "What about the Boston tea party?"

She continued, angrily, "A lot of people around here talk about law and order all the time, but apparently they don't believe in it. Brian and I will pay our monthly check to the Association as before, in full, and if the Association decides to hold it up and not pay those contracts, then that's between the Association and the people who expect the money. When this matter comes to a vote, we do not intend to vote. We will abstain, and we would hope other people will follow . . ."

Her last words were lost in the shouts of disapproval. McGinnity banged the gavel and said, "We are supposed to be ladies and gentlemen here, and I will expect courtesy and consideration for everyone's point of view. Santelli, you were doing a lot of shouting."

The man stood up, fat, bald and sweaty. "If you are on a courtesy kick, Chairman, how about Mister Santelli for openers."

"Mr. Santelli, do you have a comment to make, or would you rather sit around yelling?"

"Sure, I'll make a comment. The only thing that works in this world is leverage, right? You got some, you use it. If we get nine or ten people not paying, they will pick us apart. Like in the old story about trying to break the bundle of sticks. We got to protect each other in this thing. What we don't need is a lot of people like Mrs. Kelsey, so scared of breaking the law she's about to wet her pants."

"Order!" McGinnity yelled, banging the gavel. "Order! What's the matter with you people. Can't you talk nice?"

Brian Kelsey was trying to get close enough to Santelli to hit him. He was being restrained.

Frank Branhammer was on his feet and working his way toward the door, tugging his wife along, holding her by the wrist.

"Where the hell are you going, Branhammer?"

The big man stopped and glowered at McGinnity. "There's no point in hanging around. You're never going to give me a chance to say a goddam word. Besides, I don't care what the hell you do. I've said all along I bought my place and I agreed to pay eighty-one fifty a month, and I been paying eighty-one fifty a month, and I don't give a shit what you ass holes decide, I keep right on paying eighty-one fifty a month, so fuck off!"

And he was gone, banging the door behind him.

"I demand to be heard!" a woman yelled.

"So be heard, lady," McGinnity said. "Give your name."

"Linda Furmond. Mrs. Gerald Furmond. Apartment One-E." She was tall and very erect, with gaunt cheeks, a forehead peeling from sunburn, and fierce, bulging, blue eyes.

"Go ahead, Mrs. Furmond."

"My husband and I have been saved. We got the message of the Lord loud and clear three years ago next Sunday. We reside in the Lord in eternal love and bliss, and acknowledge his son, Jesus Christ."

"Mrs. Furmond, I don't think this is the time or place . . ."

"Please let me finish. I want you to understand that I do not hate that pathetic creature who just left our midst, dragging his pitiful wife along with him. I do not hate him. I wish only that I could save him from the black depths of hell where he is going to fry in unimaginable torment for all of eternity. So what I am about to say is not revenge for his loosing his foul tongue upon us. You said that the lawyer said that it would be wise for us all to be paid up on the deficit before we make our confrontation. Mr. Furmond and I have paid up our share of the deficit, and I apologize that we were unable to pay the full amount on July first, but had to wait until the fifteenth. How much of the four thousand is owed by that man who left, by that creature who left, for certainly he is less than a man in the eyes of the Lord?"

David Dow found the figure and showed it to Mc-Ginnity, who said, "I guess it's not confidential, not after his final instructions to us. Four hundred and forty dollars and sixty cents."

"Is he the only one who absolutely refuses to pay?"

David Dow nodded. McGinnity said, "Some people are having a lot of trouble with it, but they are going to come around as soon as they can."

Mrs. Furmond said, "Then I move that you take the appropriate legal action against that creature with all possible haste. I move that you file a lien against his apartment, as you have the authority to do, and that you either get the money or have him evicted by the sheriff."

"Second!" said Brooks Ames loudly. "Who needs him as a neighbor?"

"Any discussion?" McGinnity asked. "None? All those in favor raise their right hands and keep them there while Mrs. Gregg counts."

"I make it twenty-four in favor," she said.

"Opposed, same sign."

"Three," she said.

"With thirteen abstaining. Mr. Secretary, will you research the kind of notification we have to deliver to Mr. Branhammer, who has to sign it and so forth, and when you have the dope, we'll get together and do what has to be done at this preliminary stage. I want to make it clear there is going to be no nose-to-nose confrontation between any officer of the Association and Branhammer. I don't want anybody getting hurt or killed, and I think he is capable of it. David tried to explain the situation to him and got nowhere. He left before Branhammer completely lost control. Now as to this vote, I want to point out that when it comes to amending the Declaration of Condominium, we need thirty votes in favor not just twenty-four, and—"

"May I speak to that?" a young man said, standing in the rear of the room.

"Name?"

"McKay. Gregory McKay. I am an attorney-at-law, and I own . . . my wife and I own numbers Two-E and Two-F."

"What did you say you wanted to speak to?"

"I would like to direct your attention to chapter 711 of the Florida statutes, known as the Condominium Act, subchapter ten, paragraph one. 'An amendment of a declaration shall become effective when recorded according to law.' And paragraph two says, 'An amendment shall be evidenced by a certificate executed with formalities of a deed and shall include the recording data identifying the declaration.' Sir, would you attempt to record an amendment stating you will not pay legal contractual obligations?"

"Take it, Hadley," McGinnity said.

Forrester spoke slowly and carefully. "What we have here, Mr. McKay, is an amendment to the Golden Sands Declaration of Condominium. As you know, all declarations are similar, but not exactly alike. Ours has this statement in it, regarding the Association: 'It shall have the power to execute contracts, deeds, mortgages, leases and other instruments by its officers.' I believe that power is as stated in the statutes. We would like to add this sentence, directly following 'its officers': 'The officers of the incorporated Association shall have the right to re-negotiate any contract with any supplier of a commodity or a service, or any lease agreement, for the benefit of the members of the Association whenever in their judgment the cost of the commodity, service or lease is excessive, or the item, service or facility provided is inferior to what could reasonably be expected to be obtained in the open market, and in the process of such renegotiation the officers of the incorporated Association shall be free to exercise their own best judgment as to the steps to be taken to achieve such renegotiation, even to bringing suit to have the matter adjudicated in a court of law.' "

Hadley Forrester put his piece of paper aside and said,

"Of course, when the Articles of Condominium were drawn up by Mr. Traff, Mr. Liss's attorney, who was at that time an officer of the Association, it could have been an oversight that such powers of renegotiation were not clearly put forth. We, your officers, feel we would like to have that power. But before putting it to a vote we thought it only fair to let everyone know how we intend to make use of those powers insofar as the recreation lease and the management contract are concerned. The Declaration forms a part of every deed, and so this amendment will form a part of every deed, provided we can get a two-thirds favorable vote."

As McKay still stood, his expression strained, McGinnity asked him if he had any further comment.

"Just this, sir. If this passes, I am being mousetrapped. I cannot afford to maintain the two apartments I own, and I don't see how I can sell them if they are subject to the litigation your actions will surely bring. Anyone else who wishes to sell will be in the same boat. It isn't fair." He sat down.

"That screwed up the game plan," McGinnity whispered to Forrester.

"Go ahead now, then," Hadley suggested.

McGinnity nodded meaningfully at George Gobbin, sitting placidly, half smiling, in the midst of uproar and turmoil. George hopped up at once and was recognized.

"Mr. Chairman, I have listened carefully to the amendment as proposed by you officers of our Association. I want to say this. You have worked long and hard in our best interests. We all trust you to go on doing so. I do not think it is fair that you should be handicapped by the fact there is a gap in our Declaration where that amendment really and truly belongs. You shouldn't be handcuffed in your attempt to right wrongs. And we are protected by the fact it gives you the authority to renegotiate in only one direction. Down. Let's face it. Marty Liss set us up. We were pigeons. This is our chance to show him we're not that dumb. I move that we consider the amendment as read by Mr. Forrester. And I hope we pass it by a big margin."

"Second the motion," several people shouted.

"Seconded by Ross Twigg," McGinnity told Mrs. Gregg. "All in favor signify by raising their right hands. Remember now, one vote per apartment, except for Higbee and McKay, who are voting two each, and Mr. Wasniak, who'll be voting nine proxies. How many total votes is that, Mrs. Gregg?"

"Uh . . . forty."

"All right. Keep those hands high. No. Let's not do it that way. Everybody in favor, get up and move over by the windows. What? Yes, couples too. Everybody in favor. Except the people at this table. The officers are all in favor and how are you voting the proxies, Stanley? In favor. Right. So that's fifteen yes votes right here at the table, when we include you, Mrs. Gregg. I'd appreciate it if you'd vote one way or the other. You've got the right to abstain, of course. I would just personally appreciate a vote from everybody. Now then, let's see who we've got left. You, Mr. McKay. That's two against. And you, Julian. Two more. Mrs. Kelsey, are you going to . . . Ah, fine. Thank you. Okay, if we have forty, then we have thirty-six in favor, four against."

"Thirty-five. Mr. Branhammer left."

"Right! We count him as abstaining. One abstem . . . The hell with it, we'll count him as absentee, along with the other seven absentees. Thirty-five for, four against, eight absent, totals forty-seven. Your officers really and truly appreciate this from the bottom of our hearts, folks. You make our task easier. Yes, you can go back to your seats. Now I want to report on what we've found out about the project behind us, which isn't too much. . . ."

Thelma Mensenkott stood up slowly. She was in the middle of the front row. She was a quiet woman, big-boned and self-effacing, speaking quite pleasantly when spoken to. Most of them knew she was about thirty years younger than her husband, and that his first wife had died of some kind of cancer. Her mouth worked and no sound came out. Jack Mensenkott tugged at her, whispering. "Thelma, honey. Sit down, honey. It's okay, honey."

She twisted away from his grasp. She stared earnestly

at McGinnity. She had laced her fingers together, holding them so tightly her knuckles whitened. There had been muttered conversations, the sounds of people shifting in the chairs, rustling the papers which had been handed out. Gradually all these sounds stopped as everyone became aware of the tension and strangeness of the woman's silence.

For a time she had seemed to be trying to break her own silence. Now her mouth was still. Her face was emptied of all expression. McGinnity realized she was staring at a spot a couple of feet over his head.

Jack Mensenkott stood up beside her and put his arm around her. "Sit down, honey," he said in a low voice. "Please."

There was no sign she had heard him. He glanced around at everyone and shrugged apologetically and said, "I think . . . . I think we better go. She wanted to say something about . . . everything being cleared off that land. But I guess . . ."

He had to physically turn her. People made room for her to pass. If he kept pushing her along, she walked. If he stopped pushing, she stopped walking. His face was red.

When the door swung shut behind them, there was a concerted sigh. Carlotta Churchbridge, who had been sitting on the other side of her, said, "I think I'll go see what I can do to help. She wanted to speak to this matter. It's important to her. When they cleared that land, something strange happened to her. They're right next to us, you know. She was making a study of that jungle. It was ruthless and wicked, wiping it all out like that. May I be excused?"

"Run along, dear," Mr. Churchbridge said.

Hadley Forrester said, "I think we should have another meeting when we'll have more to report on the construction, Pete. It's almost four o'clock and—"

"Wait! Wait a minute!" Julian Higbee said. "I've got to say something about this thing you're going to do, about not paying Frank West and Sully."

Pete looked at his watch. "We can give you a couple of minutes."

Julian Higbee looked smaller in clothes. He wore a long-sleeved shirt jacket in off-white, with a blue collar and blue pockets. The sleeves covered his big brown meaty arms, and his gray slacks hid the thick powerful legs. His carefully coifed auburn cap which was usually brushed and sprayed across his forehead was in disarray. He had been running his hands through it. He wore a frown of concern.

"I don't know where to start. Look, I know everybody here. What I mean to say is, okay, I got off on the wrong foot around here because the way it was in the beginning, like it still is over at Captiva House next door, was squeeze out the last dime. I mean if I could skip some kind of maintenance, or put in a big bill, or scrimp on parts, anything like that, then I looked better to my boss, Mr. Sullivan. You can see how that is. Gulfway Management has got like thirty-four condos, eleven motels, a couple of car washes. They got a cleaning service, lawn service, linen service, and some franchise distributorships in beer and soft drinks and vending machines and so on. And it is all run the same way, in a good business way, like make the most you can out of everything. It is all on long-term contracts."

"Unless you can get to the point . . ."

"What I'm saying is that Sully, Mr. Sullivan, changed the rules all of a sudden. You people all know the way it is now. I'm following his orders, and his orders to me were to do everything possible to make everybody happy here. I have been busting a gut doing everything like you ask, and you got to admit I've been trying."

"Everybody is happy for the change in your attitude, Higbee, but that is neither here nor there."

"I heard that you were planning to maybe stop paying the management fee, so I phoned Mr. Sullivan and I asked what I should do. What he did was send me a letter to read here to you all if you were deciding to do anything like that."

Julian took the letter out, unfolded it, cleared his

throat and read. He was not a good reader. Though he stumbled over the words, the meaning was clear. " 'Gulf-way Management is one of the subsidiary management companies of the Services Management Group, a Florida corporation based in Miami. The last monthly intra-office report stated that SMG now manages on long-term contracts, through its subsidiaries, one hundred and three condominium complexes, containing a total of eight thousand and eleven residential units. Julian, please tell the directors there at Golden Sands that we would merely report any moratorium on payments to SMG and, because of the implications of such a precedent, I feel quite sure that SMG would defend our legal position with utmost vigor. I do not believe any accommodation could be reached in this matter.''

As he refolded the letter, Julian said, "That's what my point was, Mr. McGinnity. The letter is to me instead of you people, but the easiest way to tell you was to read it and—"

"Thank you, Julian," McGinnity said. There was a different atmosphere in the room. The faces were changed. McGinnity had no doubt but that, had the letter been read before the vote, the vote might have been different. He was glad he had rammed the vote through before Julian took the floor.

Someone said, "Maybe we ought to give it a little more . . ."

"Do I hear a motion for adjournment?" Pete McGinnity asked, leaning toward the microphone.

"So move," said Wasniak.

"Second," Dave Dow whispered.

"In favor? Carried! Meeting adjourned." As he got up he accidentally kicked the card table leg. The table collapsed toward the audience and the microphone slid off and bounced onto the carpeting. Rolph Gregg made a hiss of dismay and snatched it up and spoke into it.

"Testing!" the huge hollow voice said. "Testing. One two three four."

25

THE NEWSROOM WAS on the second floor of the *Athens Times Record* building on Bay Drive, three blocks from the north bridge onto Fiddler Key. During the seven years Mick Rhoades had been on the paper, he had gradually desk-hopped his way back into a badly lighted corner.

He was in his middle thirties and looked younger. He was trim, five eight with his lifts, dark hair, small neat mustache, soft brown eyes which conveyed a false impression of naïveté and gentleness. He was as naïve and gentle as a pit viper. He was always spick-and-span, tailored and barbered and manicured. He affected white: white suits, slacks, shirts, shoes, socks. He had an impressive memory.

On this Saturday morning in late July he was at his desk earlier than usual. He had covered a breakfast meeting of the County Planning and Zoning Board. Local governments were learning to live with the Sunshine Law. The simple answer was to schedule lots of meetings at inconvenient times and places, and send out the proper notifications. Sooner or later there would be a meeting where no press and no public showed up. Then the off-the-record political trades and deals could be made with impunity. He was pleased at the sour hush which had fallen over the small group in a corner of a motel dining area when he had joined them. Nothing of any consequence was said. He had nothing to write. As Holmes had explained to Watson, the significance was that the dog had not howled in the night.

He had a small television set on his desk, the sound off, the screen showing white words appearing on a green background, the local cable channel for news and music. They were repeating a lot of Friday news. It was happening more frequently lately. Automatic equipment. Stay in bed. Let the sucker run. They were turning Saturday into a second Sunday. Pretty soon no mail. Then they'd get to work on Monday morning. And when the bastards did work, when they weren't striking, they had starting blocks screwed to the floor so they could get positioned and be out the door at thirty seconds before five.

He got up and went and got himself coffee out of the machine, with cream and sugar to kill the taste of acid and paper cup. As he went back to his desk a voice directly behind him said, "Your name Rhoades?"

It made him spill coffee on the back of his hand. He looked up at a tall, broad and substantial fellow, browned and weathered by wind and sun, a fellow of khaki, and leather, and metal buttons, with pilot-type shades and a white canvas hat.

"What you are supposed to do, you are supposed to let that lady out there at the desk use her phone and call me."

"There is no lady out there. Not at the moment."

"Oh. What do you want?"

"It'll take a few minutes. My name is Sam Harrison."

"What is it that's going to be worth a few minutes, Sam?"

"Are you the red-hot environmentalist they say you are? Or is that a pose?"

"Come and sit down a minute."

"Thanks."

Mick Rhoades tilted back in his chair, eyes half closed, fingertips touching, and said, "Now don't say anything. Let me guess. You represent some gigantic land-development interest, and what you want to say to me is that there is no way on God's earth we can stop people flooding down here from the frozen North, and so if they are going to be coming down anyway, then the thing we have to do is face the inevitable and do it right. Your company has the money and the know-how. You are an advance man, sticking your toe in the hot water, and you've been told that if Mick Rhoades will buy your story, it might be easier to get started here in Palm County. Okay, what are you laughing at? What's so funny?"

"If I was very very stupid, I would talk about how my vast project would broaden the tax base."

"Bigger is cheaper, sure. That's why property taxes are so much lower in New York City than they are in East Greenbush. Was my guess off?"

"Way way off. How serious are you on the environmental thing?"

Mick Rhoades shrugged. "This paper is owned by a chain. Their policy is, What's good for business is good for the paper. It isn't like the Lindsay papers in Sarasota, where they'll really slug it out with the spoilers. They keep me around because I am sort of the environmental conscience, along with covering the City Council and the County Commission. I get in a good lick now and then. If I start to sting the wrong people too badly, they get me reeled back in. The power structure is very cozy here. Good old boys, all on a first-name basis, all thinking they know what's best. They think bigger is better, progress is wonderful, and so on and so on. They'll keep thumping tubs right up until the day we run out of water completely. They'll make that day happen sooner, and then wonder what happened, and the ones who have made their money out of all the progress will move the hell away and leave the pigeons here to cope. Where do you fit in?"

"I read your article about the Silverthorn tract."

"A half page that got cut down to a filler. Sure. Beautiful!"

"Why?"

"News has to be timely. It took me too long to dig out how those sons of bitches did it."

"Which sons of bitches?"

"I have to know more about you."

"Can it stay off the record for now?"

"If you want it that way."

Sam Harrison unzipped the old leather portfolio he was carrying and put some drawings in front of Mick Rhoades.

Then he picked up his chair and moved it around beside Mick's chair.

"Here we are. I did some digging. It took quite a few days to come up with all this, and some of it is guess-work. Here is the shape of Fiddler Key as far back as I could check it out, about 1875. It turned out I could get pretty good information on about a twenty-five-year interval. Here's 1900, then 1925, and 1950. And this last one is an aerial that's in scale with these others, showing it as it is now."

"It certainly changes!"

"Because the whole damned thing is what you could properly call transient land. Here is how the cycle works, Mick. You have a narrow island off the mainland, and you have a pass at each end of the island. Okay, you have a littoral drift on this coast in this direction. It tends to silt up the passes. As the passes grow shallow, less volume of water goes in and out on each tide. The bays themselves do not become shallower. The heavy load of water is still in there, but it is trapped by the shallowness of the passes. After a time the whole setup gets more and more fragile as it approaches a period of dynamic change. The dynamic change is caused by a hurricane, and by hurricane tides. Waves and tide are wind-driven across the island, filling the bay much higher than normal, creating great pressures for that captive water to escape. A lot of it, of course, is going to go out through the passes. But the greatest escape pressure will occur here, around the midpoint of the island, and given half a chance it will cut across and cut *through* the island. These offshore keys are glorified sandbars. They are subject to dynamic change. Nature changes and renews. This process has been going on for a long long time here. Just think about the names of the passes up and down this coast. New Pass. Midnight Pass. Hurricane Pass. September Pass. And you haven't had a hurricane come in around here in twenty years and more. Look in the aerial how narrow and silted the passes are."

Mick Rhoades bent and studied. He said, "Complaints all the time from the yacht-club types. They can't get in or out except on the high if they draw four feet."

"Getting ready for change," Harrison said.

"Damn! You know, I've known this all my life, without knowing I've known it. I sensed it would happen some day, but I didn't know why it would happen."

"Now here is an overlay for the aerial. Let me get it positioned. It is possible to make a pretty fair guess about where a pass might open up. First I took the three lowest and narrowest points in the mid-key area, along this two-mile stretch here, and marked them with grease pencil. They are possibles, but one of them is my favorite. Right here. Reasons are, first, this area here has been recently stripped of all protective growth. Second, the positioning of these two buildings on the Gulf front—"

"That would be the Azure Breeze and the Surf Club?"

"Right. They would tend to funnel a high incoming tide between them. The water would cross the key along this line here, from this swimming pool area across the road about here, and down this drainage ditch and onto the cleared land. It would gutter the cleared land and the dredged material and run off into the bay."

"Don't they have seawalls and rocks and things in front of Azure Breeze and the Surf Club?"

"I inspected them. They might as well have feather pillows. It's a cheap job. They should have thought in terms of maybe a thousand dollars a linear foot for the revetment with the seawall behind it. First let me explain that the bottom deepens more rapidly off that area than elsewhere. They've got seven- to eight-foot depth about fifty to sixty feet offshore. See how it darkens on the aerial? I won't go into the math, but the revetment isn't thick enough, and it is sloped wrong, and the stones are too small. There isn't enough toe protection. Second, the wall behind it is just as bad. Judging from the height, I think the piling depth is probably too shallow, going down maybe eight or nine feet instead of fifteen. There's evidence of toe failure and some scouring and loss of fill down under the wall already. Wave dynamics are tremendous. Those big beasts will come marching in, smash like freight trains, bust things up, pull them back toward the waterline on the runoff. They'll take the revetment first and then suck away the wall. Ten minutes after the first wave breaks against that wall, it will be chunks of concrete spread wide and slowly being covered by the sand. My third point is that the water depth offshore gives the waves a chance to move farther in before breaking, and also there is the water depth in the bay. The bay is wide there, as you can see, and here is the channel they are quote scouring unquote out to the regular channel. My fourth reason is that this area lacks the protection of that offshore bar that starts farther south down the key."

"Right along there is where the road floods after heavy rains," Rhoades said.

"Low area. Here is the picture. The storm crests will smack and run up the slope after they've finished off the wall. As they run back they'll suck back sand and dirt. When the tide gets higher, the water will spill across the road and it won't run back. The higher the tide, the farther into the key the waves will break. If everything goes right—or wrong—you could have ten to fifteen feet of water across the key and across the bay and into the city. They better have the keys evacuated by then."

"Fat chance."

"They better work on it. When the runoff starts, it will come across the key in the lowest place. At first it will run off across the key everywhere, but as the water level behind the key drops, it will run off where it is gouging the best channel. And that should be right through here. The deeper the channel gets, the more runoff it can accept. And this is where you'll have the new pass."

"How big could it be?"

"The least it will be has to be three hundred feet wide and five to six feet deep. I would guess from here to here, almost straight across." He marked the area.

After a time Mick looked up at him, eyes wide and round. "But Jesus Christ, Harrison, that would wipe out these four condos, wouldn't it?"

"You can bet the family jewels on it."

"Who the hell *are* you? You sell marine insurance?"

Sam grinned and dug into the portfolio. "Here's a copy of my résumé."

Rhoades went over it carefully. He sighed and handed it back. "Mostly ocean stuff? Waves and protection and so on?"

"And mining the ocean deep."

"What's your interest in all this?"

"I was hired to see if it was as bad as my employer thinks it is, and so I could go tell him it is, and he would move away, because he can afford to."

"I would guess that he can afford to move if he can afford you."

"What? Oh, sure. The price is on the second page of that thing. I thought it might be nice if people had some clue as to what might happen to them. I was asking around and your name came up."

"You mean, like . . . warn people?"

"I guess so."

" 'Dear residents of Golden Sands, Captiva House, Azure Breeze and the Surf Club. You bought a bad deal. Your apartments are going to fall into the water.' Come on, Sam. Much as I would like to bring a couple of those big glassy obscenities crashing down . . . my God, what kind of suits would be filed against me and the paper?"

"I can give you a signed report, on the house. With credentials. I can even find some local engineering types in state government to back me up."

"So who would believe it anyway?"

"Don't you?"

"Not quite."

"Come on, Mick. You seem like a reasonable man. If I showed you an empty key, low and flat with no buildings, roads, bridges, or people, and showed you the swash channels silting up, and showed you the history of other sandspits in the same geographical area, you would buy the concept that sooner or later, inevitably, a hurricane would cut the key in two."

"Sooner or later. Okay."

"The more silted the regular channels, the smaller the overtide and excess rainfall necessary to cut the new pass. Buy that?"

"Okay."

"Now does it make any real difference whether this key has people on it or not? No. Does it make any difference whether it happens this year or next or not for ten years? No. The population isn't going to move away. The longer we wait, the more people involved, and the more potential loss of life. Final point. If those fourteen acres had not been cleared, I would have had to nominate one of these other two areas as the most probable."

"So how did it happen? That's what you want to know?"

"If you would like to tell me, I would like to know."

"There's better coffee down the street."

The Place had fresh ground coffee and two hundred kinds of doughnuts. Mick Rhoades and Sam Harrison carried their coffee and doughnuts to a plastic booth in the back. Rhoades kept his voice down.

"We get good county commissions and bad county commissions, and some in between. This one is sort of in between, shading toward bad. Troy Abel and Wally Wing are solid but not too sharp. Jack Dorsey and Steve Corbin are on the make. Justin Denniver is chairman at the moment. They pass it around. We've had trouble getting a good county manager to replace the one we lost three years ago. The present one, Tod Moran, is a fair head, but lazy. He delegates everything to his assistant, Billy Scherbel. Now I had to do some digging for this. I nearly lost my hearing and my sanity going back over those low-fidelity recordings of the commission meetings. I could figure out the approximate date, but I couldn't pin it down. Finally I nailed it. At a meeting in May, Billy Scherbel came in with a lot of things which needed commission approval. Denniver asked him if there were any big deals in that list, anything requiring special discussion, and Scherbel said no. Then he asked if the county manager's office recommended approval, and Scherbel said yes. So Steve Corbin moved that Scherbel read the whole list and they would approve it all in one chunk, and Jack Dorsey seconded it and it passed. The way it was hidden, the request came from the Palm Coast National Bank and the land was referred to by government lot line and marker and so on, and it asked for a one-year extension on a permit to clear the land, and a permit to scour an existing channel to its original depth of five feet at low tide. By the way, the clearing permit included a permit to burn the trees they clear off. That was an old-type permit. You have to have a separate one now. With the way the land was identified, it looked to me as if somebody got to Scherbel. So I braced him, and he got very uneasy and evasive. And he got angry. If I had to make a guess, I would say somebody set Billy up somehow. He's not the type that angles for payoffs. He's too scared of the IRS. He does like young girls. He's always had a taste for them. It wouldn't be too hard to set him up on statutory. It's just a guess, on account of how he overreacted.

"Anyway, I had to check out the ownership on that land. I got Al Borne's side of the story. He's the trust officer at Palm Coast National, handling the Becky Silverthorn estate. He'd sold an option on the property to Marty Liss, head of the Marliss Corporation. Marty sold his option rights to something called the Letra Corporation, which is fronted by Lew Traff, who is an employee of Marliss, and who is Marty Liss's lawyer. Letra picked up on the option, paying in full by certified check to Palm Coast National. Because the actual sale of the land was contingent on its being able to be developed, apparently Lew Traff and the contractor, Cole Kimber, and that group, had worked out the necessary permissions, and they had a contingency approval of a building permit, based on acquisition of the land in question, with all the plans and drawings and specs on file.

"After they got all their ducks in a row, they started the land clearing and the dredging bright and early on a Saturday morning earlier this month. Every conservationist started jumping up and down like a flock of demented hens, but by the time they could get any kind of ear to listen to them it was Monday morning, and too damned late to do anything about anything. You can't save a tree when it has been knocked down, bulldozed into a pile and soaked with old crankcase oil. Nobody even knew who had ordered it done. Let me explain one thing. If all the building trades people were on full time and overtime, like they were up until early last year, maybe a big stink could have been raised. But there is unemployment, and the real estate agents and the real estate lawyers are crying, and the banks are very nervous about a lot of the paper they are holding. Opposing a big new project on one of the keys is not a popular stance in Florida these days."

"Even though that project will go up on very fragile land?"

"If they can get it up and sell it out before the big waves come, that's all they want."

"Do you believe that?"

"I try to believe two or three impossible things every day."

"You can't block water when it wants to go somewhere. All you can do is give it an easier choice, where it won't do as much harm. But in this case there is not one single area in the low and narrow and central part of the key which does not have structures either on it or too close to it. A good job of deepening and widening the passes would help a lot."

"You wouldn't believe how far down the priority list we are on *that* federal function."

"I can guess."

"Sam Harrison, I am still not clear about what the hell it is you want to accomplish by talking to me."

Harrison smiled. "Not too damned sure myself. I'm in the business of building things. And I am a specialist in the ways of protecting structures from the sea. I guess it would be personally offensive to me to have the public at large think that my profession is so inept and unaware that we would build a few hundred million dollars' worth of high-rise living units on a fragile sandspit without knowing what will happen. There are whores in my profession, just as in yours. These structures look so substantial, people are going to be misled. Call it a professional conscience, or something. I would just like them to know they are in such peril that when a hurricane alert is sounded they should get the hell off that key and go well inland."

"And I am to be Henny Penny?" Mick asked.

"A big feature story, with maps, photos and overlay, and a signed report from me to backstop you."

"Let's suppose I could sneak it into the paper. It would need perfect timing. If I try to sneak it in and miss, I get my ass fired out of here. If it does get in, I get my ass fired out of here. Even if it does get in, it could be a one-day wonder, a story that surfaces and disappears and nobody gives a good God damn, like the wire-service stories about predictions of the end of the world. Or it could turn into a sensational story, wire-service pickups, panic on the key, legal action and all that. The developers with unsold apartments will be screaming with fury. Purchasers of the apartments will be suing the developers. People will be backing out of sales contracts. Raw land on the key will fall out of bed. A lot of people will want blood. Mine and yours."

"I am a certified, qualified expert, and I can give expert testimony."

"Want to hear about my house?"

"Your house?"

"It's what you call a ranchette. Four acres eight miles east of Athens, on State Road 757. The land was a wedding present from Patty's daddy six years ago. Three years ago we put up one of those Jim Walter houses on it, finished on the outside, and it took us two years to get the inside finished off. It's fenced. There's a stand of big Georgia pines. Mike is four and Dinah is two. I rented a little bulldozer and in one long weekend I dug a big pond. It's stocked. And we've got some ducks on it."

"Sounds nice."

"I got another raise this year. And they don't mind my doing a little outside work on the side. PR work. Are you married, Sam?"

"Once upon a time. No kids."

"What was it you heard me call myself? The environmental conscience around here? On the other hand, Harrison, why don't you go move people away from the San Andreas fault? Why don't you move them off the slopes of Vesuvius? God damn it, why are you nagging *me*?"

"Don't get yourself in an uproar."

"The thing is, you can't be absolutely *sure*."

"What would you do if I was?"

Mick Rhoades thought it over. "I guess I would do like those owners of those condominiums are going to do, absolutely nothing. Sorry. Very sorry. I told you I get in a good lick now and then. I also kiss ass. Whenever necessary."

"Is it okay if I understand exactly what you mean?"

"I'd almost rather you didn't. Four years ago, sure. Maybe even three, it was possible. But not since then."

"Well . . . I better be going."

"Listen, if I can find any way to get the message across . . ."

"Sure. Thanks. Thanks, Mick. Take care of yourself."

WHEN THE SATURDAY-EVENING SUN had moved low enough to fill the big living room of Apartment 7-A with bright glare, Barbara Messenger had gotten up and gone to the windows and run the long pale draperies across the floor-length windows.

Lee Messenger and Gus Garver had talked it all out with Sam Harrison, had studied the maps and photographs, had checked his assumptions and had decided he was right.

"Unless," as Gus had said, "another area near here becomes more vulnerable and takes the heat off us."

"Becomes narrower and lower?" Messenger said. "Little chance of that. Do either of you men know the law on such matters? Could the Association here send a registered letter to the developers, saying that the land clearing has created a clear and obvious danger to the Golden Sands property?"

"That's what you do when your neighbor has a broken seawall and won't get it fixed. There has to be some action he can take in response, to correct the situation," Sam explained. "Even if he covered those fourteen acres with two feet of concrete, I don't think there would be the same resistance to erosion and guttering as when all those living roots were holding onto the soil. And I do not think you could claim that a hurricane is inevitable, not in any legal sense."

"Can I look at that storm track chart again?" Messenger asked. Sam took it from his portfolio, unfolded it and handed it to the old man. It charted all hurricanes in the Southeast from 1907 on. Prior to the year they began giving them names, the dotted line showing the path of the eye of the storm was identified merely by month and year.

The lines wove a disorderly web entrapping the peninsula. Sam stood behind the old man and pointed at the lines, those few of them which, over the years, had come up through the Straits of Yucatán between Cuba and Mexico, into the Gulf, and had then curved back to a northeasterly direction and intersected the Florida coast, and said, "This chart is misleading because each line should be a broad band, as broad as the range of destructive winds in the particular hurricane being charted. Six of those broad bands would have touched this key in the past thirty years, even though no eye came really close. It makes the residents *think* they were in a hurricane, when actually it missed them. Notice that these three here were not as destructive because the eye came ashore south of here. The great winds move counterclockwise around the eye. When the eye moves ashore from west to east, the winds south of the eye slam the shoreline with the velocity of the winds themselves *plus* the forward movement of the storm. If the winds are gusting at one hundred mph, and the storm is moving at twenty, these winds south of the eye will hit at a hundred and twenty miles an hour. The winds north of the eye will be reduced by two forces, the normal reduction due to moving across land and reduction caused by subtracting the forward movement of the storm. You can have a fifty-mile-an-hour differential between winds ten miles south of the eye and ten miles north of the eye. Of course, the big problem here is the way the water will pile ashore south of the eye. The worst thing that could ever happen to the West Coast of Florida would be to have a major hurricane follow the coastline right from the Ten Thousand Islands up to Cedar Key, with the eye never coming ashore, with the eye staying five or ten miles offshore. It would scour the keys clean, like a big brush. With the state of readiness right now, it would take a month just to count the bodies."

"You serious, Sam?" Gus asked, startled.

"You can believe it."

"I thought that with the search planes and all, they could predict the paths of these things," Messenger said. "What happened here, for God's sake?"

"That one? It went through Cedar Key and flattened it and came on back through it and stomped the ruins, and then went thirty miles and turned and came back through it again. Very rare. The atmospheric conditions were in balance. There was no low-pressure area for the storm to move toward, no high-pressure ridge for it to follow. So it was in equilibrium. The normal pattern in this hemisphere is for a storm to start near the equator, over heated waters, and move due west, lifting a little bit north and adding more northward movement the farther it gets from the equator. It is the rotational effect. The hurricane is spun off. The average track has a boomerang shape, with a tendency to curve back on itself when it gets far enough north, like a plume, like an ostrich feather."

Messenger said, "Can you work out any equations of probability of one hitting here?"

"No, sir. A hurricane has no memory. Like a coin. If a coin comes up heads fifty times, the odds on the next flip are still fifty-fifty, head or tail. But if you flip it ten thousand times, you'll get five thousand heads, plus or minus. Thus the recent banks on this chart are not more or less likely to be hit than the places that have been hit two and three times. But as I was telling you earlier, the damage I am talking about does not require a direct hit. It just requires big enough tides, and that changes the odds. From the wind and tide patterns, I would say it will be within five years. Any of these near misses would do the damage I'm anticipating."

"Freshen these drinks, gentlemen?" Barbara Messenger asked.

They accepted. When she brought fresh drinks to Sam and to Gus, Sam looked up at her. He was pleased to look at her because she was such a handsome healthy creature. She had come in from swimming after they arrived. She wore a slender white floor-length thing that had the look of the islands. She wore her swimsuit under it. It touched at hips and breasts and showed her tan through it. Her hair had been a casual tangle, and she had gone and brushed it but had not changed. He looked up at her, half smiling, because he liked looking upon loveliness in its prime. He looked at her with masculine approval. She was smiling too. Their glance met at precisely the moment her hand touched his, as she gave him his drink. His awareness of her was abruptly increased tenfold. It hollowed his belly and it emptied his heart, and it took a very deep breath indeed to fill his lungs. He knew that exactly the same thing had happened to Barbara, in exactly the same way. In the next instant he was filled with a savage rue. Not this, for God's sake. No more of this stuff ever. Especially not a married one. I can't play these games. I'm not a damned kid anymore. I can find easier solutions to my problems. Quick and easy solutions. Lady, I plain do not want any part of this at any time, now or ever, thank you very much.

He had to work hard to comprehend what Gus was saying. ". . . certainly have some responsibility as a director of that damned Association. The very least I can do is let them know what you've researched. Maybe you could write me a letter."

Messenger said, "I would suspect that a completely professional report would be best. Reduce all these exhibits to eight-and-a-half by eleven size. Include your professional tickets, Harrison. Math, sources, appropriate language, the works. Proper binder. Fifty copies, and then distribute *through* the Association, with a short covering memo from you, Gus."

"That's the best way, Mr. Messenger. But expensive."

"There's no point in my paying for Sam Harrison's services and then not utilizing them properly, is there? We'll get fewer questions and objections by doing it right, and then we need not worry if a copy gets into unfriendly hands."

"But," said Sam, "I have to use so many qualifying phrases, it isn't going to exactly empty out this place overnight."

"How long will the report run?" Messenger asked.

"With exhibits? Fifty pages."

"How much time will you be able to spare us?"

To his own surprise Harrison heard himself saying, "I've decided I might as well stay right where I am, down the beach at the Islander, until the New Zealand thing opens up. It's the dead of winter down there now on that Tasman coast. Can't really start anything there until October." He avoided looking at Gus, knowing Gus could read him too well.

"You said it's a mining operation?" Messenger asked. "Whose?"

"A consortium. Kiwis and Aussies and Mexicans."

"Mexicans!"

"The same group who located about thirty million tons of high-grade phosphate in Baja a couple of months ago."

Messenger said, "It seems as if the world—"

He stopped so abruptly the three of them stared at him. His face was shiny wet and the color of oatmeal, mouth agape, eyes almost closed, hands clutching the arms of his chair. Barbara whirled around and ran out of the room, hurried back with hypodermic and small bottle of clear fluid. She drew a careful amount into the barrel, bared his shrunken arm, popped the shot into the upper arm, outside, near the shoulder.

After she wiped the spot with alcohol and cotton, she

leaned close to him and said quietly, slowly, distinctly, "Hang on, tiger. It will start to work soon. Hang in there."

Sam said in a half whisper, "I think we better be going. . . ."

She snapped her head around and glared at him in an emotion not quite anger. "Stay! It's all right. Stay!"

Sam looked at Gus. Gus shrugged and nodded and sipped his drink. Slowly the tensions went out of the old man, and his color returned. But there was little expression on his face. His eyes looked dull, almost vacuous.

"Come on, dear," she said, and helped her old husband to his feet.

"Can I hel—"

"Please!" she said. "Just *sit* there!"

The old man leaned his tall weight on her strength. In a little while a door clicked shut behind him.

"That was some hell of a pain that hit him," Gus said.

"Heart or cancer?"

"Cancer, I think. Somewhere in the gut."

"He's one sharp old party," Sam said. "Nothing at all wrong with his head. Good with him, isn't she?"

Gus said, "A long time ago I was with the Seabees and we were building a strip on a Pacific island. The marines were supposed to have cleared it a long time before we got there, but they missed one, and he took a long-range shot from the bushes and hit a fat old sergeant right in the belly, from the side. Hit him under the short ribs on the right side and it came out just in front of the hip bone on the left side. When we finally raised somebody on ·the radio, they said the quickest way to get him to the hospital would be if they sent a Norseman from Tinian to pick him up, and could it land, and we said if we worked like hell it could land the next morning. We put gauze pads on the wounds and taped them in place, and we made him comfortable in the shade, under netting, and we loaded him with morphine. Every few hours he would wake up and he would look just like Mr. Messenger looked, and then he would start yelling, and we'd stick another couple of ampules in him and he'd drowse off again. We got the airstrip finished and the airplane came in and took him away."

"Did he recover?"

"God, I don't know. It was a big war. You never got to keep track of anybody unless you were real close. I remembered it because he would break out in sweat the same way, and turn that color, and look way off into the distance just like Mr. Messenger did."

A couple of minutes later Gus made a harsh brief laughing sound, without mirth.

"What's funny?"

"You started me wondering what happened to that sergeant. Hell, he was at least fifteen years older than I was, and that was 1944. So even if he recovered, he's probably dead now anyway. God help me, I don't want to turn into one of these old farts like Brooks Ames, always telling here stories about the goddam war. That war was a lot of wars ago. To some it was the biggest thing in their life, so they talk about it, the way others talk about the big deals they pulled, and some talk about their fraternity days. And . . . I talk about things I built."

Barbara came back so quietly she startled Sam Harrison. She had changed to patchwork jeans and a cotton work shirt. She sat in Lee Messenger's chair and said, "I'm sorry I got snippy. He wouldn't want you to hurry off just because he felt unwell. And he doesn't like anyone to help him except me. When he has one of these, it makes me nervous and I get . . . short."

"No need to apologize. How is he now?"

"Out. He keeps on responding well to Demerol. They told us he'd acquire a tolerance. Mr. Garver, I was listening to the discussion, and I was wondering if you don't have . . . a moral obligation to send the report to those other three condominiums in that vulnerable area on Mr. Harrison's map."

"Planned on doing so. One to each association. We'll need forty-five for Golden Sands. I doubt if they'll pay much attention."

She looked at Sam, and he wondered if he had ever seen

another gaze so direct, searching and thoughtful. "I think it is wicked that there should be . . . a conspiracy against getting this information published."

"Conspiracy is too strong a word. People have not gotten together and decided to suppress. It just isn't in the best interests of the business community to make people unhappy about living out here, about buying and selling land out here, about paying off their mortgages on their houses and apartments out here. And you have to remember that ever since the first house went up on Fiddler Key, I'll bet people have been crying doom. It's an old story along this coast. And too many years since they had a big one come roaring in. Every season the Miami bureau cries wolf and the storm goes elsewhere. If I could take a person out onto the beach and point out toward the horizon and show him a wave fifty feet high out there, moving toward the beach, he would believe it and run like hell."

"But won't your report *prove* that it will happen?"

"It's hard reading. It will prove that it might happen—prove it to other engineers. But I read the other day that thirty percent of all high school graduates are unable to read and comprehend a traffic citation, or fill out a job questionnaire, or write a business letter. So don't be too hopeful."

"Do you have secretarial help?" she asked.

"I thought I'd try an agency."

"Lee suggested I offer my services. I'm a lot better than anybody you could find through an agency. I've got supplies and equipment right here. Would you dictate this?"

"Well . . . I thought I'd write it out longhand."

"When you get ten or so pages done, why don't you bring them here, and we'll talk about spacing and style and so on, okay?"

"If you really want to do this . . ."

"Lee used to keep me very very busy, but lately he's been closing out a lot of the projects he was interested in, and having too much free time makes me restless."

Garver said, "You'll move out of here, won't you?"

"He hasn't said, of course. Hasn't had a chance, but I

would think we'd move out. I hate to leave here. We've had a kind of unexpected privacy here. Because nobody really expects a man like him to live in a place like this, they think it is just a similarity of names. Excuse me, Mr. Garver. I don't mean to . . ."

Gus smiled. "You're not hurting my feelings."

"We wanted everything simplified. And we wanted it to last, but . . . I don't know. He'll decide what's best for us."

The drinks were gone. They excused themselves, and left after telling Barbara Messenger they hoped her husband would be feeling better soon.

They went down to Gus Garver's apartment. Ever since Carolyn's injury and stroke, he had been putting odds and ends into cartons and storing them. Plates on wire hangers. Figurines. Bud vases. Ceramic children and animals. They made him nervous. They had always made him nervous. He did not like the flavor of fragility they imparted to his environment. He was a neat man. He liked clean surfaces, tidy and logical arrangements. He had lived tidily and comfortably and well in many parts of the world, doing for himself, taking a bachelor pleasure in achieving an ultimate simplification of the required chores involved in eating, sleeping and bathing.

Now the apartment was acquiring that look of field-office austerity to which he had become accustomed over the years. It was still her place. He thought of it as her place, even while he was making it his.

Gus opened two beers and brought them into the living room. "What was that bit about the unexpected privacy?" Sam Harrison asked.

Gus grinned at him, wiped his mouth with the back of his hand. "I will tell you some magic names, friend. H. L. Hunt. Getty. Howard Hughes. L. D. Messenger . . ."

Sam stared at him, mouth agape. "*That* one? Him?"

"It finally came to me and I checked it out. Yes. Him, himself."

"What the *hell* is he doing *here*?"

"Achieving unexpected privacy. He's got a couple of private unlisted lines going in there. She's a top executive secretary and a good nurse. Because she doesn't have to run a big house, she can spend more time with him. They have a housekeeper cook, Mrs. Schmidt. And that apartment, you have to admit, is not exactly some kind of slum area. How much room can a person use at one time? Like how many meals can you eat a day, and how many pair of pants can you wear? When they want a car, they call a limo. When they want an airplane ride, they call a limo and a charter jet. But they stay in, mostly. What it is . . . what they want . . . is a nice quiet way for him to die, loved and tended."

"So you brought me in to check out what is bothering you, and between the two of us we've fucked it up. Nice."

"They can move with a lot less pain and suffering than most of the others in the building. So don't worry about them. What you should worry about is finding somebody from an agency to type your report, Sam."

Sam put his empty beer can on the empty coffee table and studied Gus Garver. "That obvious?"

"Obvious? Just because your neck swole up like a hop frog, and your eyes bugged out, and the cords in your neck stuck out, and you breathed all wheezy, and just because she turned nine different colors and her eyes got shiny and she breathed through her mouth, and both of you gave off enough electricity to dim the lights, I wouldn't call it obvious."

"Jesus, Gus!"

"That is one hell of a lot of woman, in all ways, and I think that if you distracted her from the job she has set herself, she would never forgive you."

"I don't *want* anything like that, chief. I have no time or energy left in this lifetime for anything at all real, ever again. Especially do I not want to mess with the pretty young wife of anybody like L. D. Messenger."

"So you'll find some other girl to do the typing?"

"No. It would look weird if I did that."

"Sam, for God's sake."

"I'm fine. I'm fine. Leave me alone, Gus."

27

MONDAY MIDDAY near the end of July. Ninety-three degrees. Humidity, one hundred percent. Thunder rumbled and grumbled, promising afternoon thundershowers as forecast. The people of Palm County scurried from their air-conditioned houses and apartments to their air-conditioned cars, and drove to their air-conditioned shops and offices. The few people on the beaches spent most of their sun time in the water. There was no waiting for tennis courts. Golf carts with bright canvas canopies wandered the rain-green fairways. Stunned birds sat silent in the leaf shade. All over the big shopping plazas the air conditioning roared, sending out waves of heat which raised the ambient temperature of the areas, creating more work for the air conditioning.

Gregory McKay, of Benton, Barkley, Gorvis, Sinder and McKay, was spending a portion of his lunch hour on his back on a beach towel spread upon one of the beds in Apartment 2-F of the Golden Sands Condominium. Loretta Rosen straddled him, kneeling, her torso erect, brown-gold hair spread on her shoulders, sharp breasts and belly gleaming with the mist of perspiration from her prolonged effort.

His hands were clasped loosely around her waist. Her pelvis moved in a strong, slow ellipsis, and she stared past him at the empty wall above the head of the bed, underlip caught behind the white capped teeth. He could hear the huff of the air conditioning, a very faint creaking of the bed, a muted boom of jet or thunder, and an infrequent damp lisping sound of copulation.

"Pretty soon," she said in a small strained voice. "Pretty soon now, huh?"

Her eyes closed. Her mouth twisted into a grimace. She steepened and hastened her effort. A red flush darkened her heavy tan. She snorted, bucked, cried out and collapsed against his broad chest as the spasms slowed and softened.

"Gawd, I didn't think I could again, not so soon anyway. You're beautiful, lover," she said. "You are really beautiful. It's never been like this with anybody before."

"Um," he said.

"I really love you," she said.

"Uh huh."

"Do you love me?"

"Sure."

"Can't you say it?"

"Love you, honey."

"Wow. That's really a lot of enthusiasm there, fellow."

"Sorry."

"Did the poor man get all worn out by Loretta?"

"Uh huh."

She moved away from him and groped and found the hand towel and used it on herself and then on him. She noticed how startlingly dark her thighs were, and thought that it was just like that year with Cole, getting lots of sun so I can look good naked. A good tan forgives a lot of things. It covers the little sags and creases and crepey skin, the busted veins and blemishes. Fish-belly white makes you old. Tan is the color of the young, the color of beaches and vitality and slenderness.

Wasting too much time, she thought glumly. Working on my tan. Working on my face and my hair. Too much time spent screwing, while sales go down the drain and the prospect list looks sicker and sicker. But, oh, Jesus, this feels so good and I love it so much, and I was such an idiot trying to tell myself that I was through with this part of life. It isn't as fantastic as it was with Cole. It was like he could turn me inside out. But this is a nice boy. Sweet. He's nervous about some of the things I want. But he is learning to like it.

Greg stretched and yawned, scratched his chest, sighed loudly and said, "I've *got* to unload these apartments. It keeps getting to me."

"But can't you hang on okay now? The monthly fee for this floor is down to sixty-eight dollars each, isn't it?"

"How long do you think that will last? Those are legal contracts."

"But if everybody sticks together?"

"It may come down some. Not enough to matter. I wish I could just walk away. But Nance and I are on the notes, and we'd lose our house along with the apartments."

"And there's the little problem with Mrs. Neale."

"That wasn't too bright, that letter you didn't answer."

"Don't tell me what's bright, friend. You tend the law and I'll sell your rotten apartments."

"Don't get sore. Okay? I didn't mean anything. Just that maybe she has an outside chance of voiding the contract."

"On account of her fool letter. Right?"

"Please, let's not fuss about it. It isn't only the apartments. We had a meeting of the partners, and there's going to be less to cut up this year. A lot less. I can't seem to get it across to you that I'm really in bad shape. I'm really worried, Loretta honey."

"Then Loretta is going to take your mind off your problems."

"What are you doing?"

"What is it beginning to look like?"

"I've got to be getting back to . . ."

"Hush, dear. Please hush."

It took longer than she expected to get a response from him, and when the response was adequate, she daintily knee-walked sideways, until with her last step she lifted one knee across his head and then settled delicately. In about ten minutes Loretta knew that Greg could come again and she could not, and as she began hastening him, she heard a small sound near the open doorway. She glanced sidelong and saw a young woman in a yellow sun dress standing in the doorway. She had a plump, pretty, childlike face and dark hair. She wore a strange expression.

She said in an apologetic voice, "I just came to get . . . to get . . ."

Gregory roughly and abruptly pushed forward and down on Loretta's hips, collapsing her against his chest. He raised his head until, over the round hillock of a buttock, he could see his wife standing in the doorway.

"Please!" he roared, tumbling Loretta off him. "Please!"

It seemed to him then, and later, a strange entreaty. Please what? Understand? Forgive? Forget?

But Nancy was gone. The corridor door slammed. Gregory bounded up and ran to the door and almost opened it before he realized very little would be achieved through naked pursuit.

When he returned to the bedroom, Loretta was kneeling on the bed, sitting back on her heels, combing her hair back with spread fingers. She wore an expression of sweet concern. "Aw, sweetie, that's too bad. That really is."

He smacked his bare thigh with his fist, so hard that he winced and rubbed the spot. "Oh, Jesus," he moaned.

"Well, she shouldn't have been sneaking around."

"She wasn't! She probably came over here to get something she bought when we furnished the apartments. Probably something we need."

"Whatever she was doing, she shouldn't have been here."

"You didn't fasten the chain on the door!"

"Greg, dear. I got here first. Remember? Whoever gets here last is supposed to fasten it."

"That lousy chain. Two seconds it would have taken. Jesus, all my luck has turned bad."

"*That's* not exactly flattering, dear."

"Well. You know what I mean. What am I going to do?"

"Have you considered the Foreign Legion?"

"This is no time for cheap jokes, damn you!"

She came swarming off the bed and slapped him hard before he could evade the blow. "Watch your mouth, you silly little prick!"

"I just think . . . making jokes isn't going to help."

"Face it. There isn't anything that's going to help. If she

ever did take you back, which isn't likely, she would make you crawl on your belly all the rest of your life. Is that what you want?"

"I just want to explain to her that . . ."

"Explain! What is there to explain, and how would you explain it? We were quite obviously doing exactly what we were doing. About the only constructive thing you can do is come back here and stretch out again."

"You must be out of your mind, Loretta."

"Trust Loretta. Come on, sweetie. Come to Loretta."

"No. I can't, not now."

"Listen very carefully. You come here right now, or there isn't going to be any next time, ever. Either come here, or put your clothes on and get the hell out. That is what is known as an ultimatum."

He stared at her with a look of thoughtful stupidity. All the hours at a desk had begun to give him a pouchy look, and there was a small roll around his middle. He was not as heavily hung as Cole Kimber, she thought. But he was nice.

He sighed audibly and went to the chest at the foot of the bed and took his jockey shorts and stepped into them. He lost his balance and hopped on his left leg a couple of times before regaining it.

"Did you hear what I told you?" she said.

He snapped the elastic waistband. "I heard you."

"I mean it, you know."

"I guess you probably mean it."

He sat on the chest and pulled his socks on. He stepped into his pants, tied his shoes, put on the white guayabera—approved for the summer months at the office.

She watched him, lips tightly compressed. He went into the bathroom and she heard the water running. He came out, still combing his hair with his fingertips.

He stared at her morosely. "Well . . . you take it easy, Loretta. It's been . . . I guess it's been a lot of fun. I don't know. It's been a lot of something."

"Get out of here!"

"Sure," he said, and left.

She sprawled on her face on the beach towel and wept.

She drifted from infrequent sobs into sleep, and when she woke up she was astonished to discover it was after four. She tied her hair out of the way and showered. She brushed her teeth with kitchen salt and a corner of a towel. After she was dressed and had brushed her hair to smoothness, she smiled at herself in the mirror, showing her teeth. She let the smile fade and she studied herself carefully, thinking that it was better without the glasses than with them. Myopia blurred all the tiny wrinkles. They became visible when she moved close to the mirror. She pressed her thumbs against the sides of her face close to the ears and pushed upward. The little puffy places at the corners of her mouth disappeared. The skin under her eyes tightened. The pouch under her chin was gone. Her eyes had an interesting tilt.

Back to the olden days, she thought. P.M. Pre-menopause. Take twenty-five hundred out of capital and get it done. When? Well, right now. Soon as it can be scheduled. Slack time. Summer time. Recession time.

But Greg is going to come crawling back. From the look on her face, the marriage is absolutely stone dead. Hell, he projects a very masculine image, but on the inside he is a weak, scared little man. With no one to hold him and comfort him but me, he'll come back. I won't let him come back too quickly and easily. The little nips and tucks and stitches can wait until I've let him come back, and gotten him finally all trained and housebroken, and then I can get the repairs done, knowing he won't wander while I'm out of circulation. It really comes down to this . . . he has nowhere else he can go.

Jud and Fred Brasser were both prematurely balding men in their early thirties, both too heavy, both florid and authoritative. Jud was a Santa Monica banker, and Fred was a Fort Worth broker.

Dr. Vidal was a sallow young man with metal-rimmed glasses and an oversized black mustache. He wore a white smock. The Brasser brothers had cornered him in a small waiting room at the end of a third-floor corridor of the

Athens Memorial Hospital. Dr. Vidal sat on the shiny plastic cushions of the couch. The brothers had hitched their chairs forward, blocking escape.

"You wouldn't believe that apartment," Jud said. "We had two maids in there cleaning yesterday. They cleaned that place for seven hours. I took down eight of those big plastic bags full of trash. I don't know how come my mother was living like that. My wife, Marie, came here last year in August to look after Mom when she was getting out of the hospital after that jaundice, and the apartment was okay then—"

"As I was saying," Vidal interrupted, "we know very little as yet about the mental effects of severe cirrhosis of the liver."

"She's a carefree person," the broker said, "but not what you'd call sloppy. Not *that* sloppy."

"The needle biopsy we took last year showed typical advanced cirrhosis. Now let me try in layman's terms to give you some indication of what we expect from liver damage. The body's use of protein is impaired so that there is a wasting away of muscle tissue, so that one gets the pipestem arms and legs typical of the advanced case. Also one can expect edema, an accumulation of fluid in the tissues of the face, giving the typical lumpy look of the alcoholic—"

"Now wait just a . . ."

Vidal held up a hand. "Please. Ask your questions when I am finished. As the liver becomes hardened by the accumulation of connective tissue, one sees a kind of back pressure exerted on the venous system, causing varicosities in the places normally expected, but also on the inner wall of the esophagus. At the same time, the liver's function in producing one of the blood-clotting agents ceases, and the blood becomes so thin it can leak through the walls of the varicosed veins in the esophagus, and from there into the stomach. That is why we check alcohol-abuse patients for black stool which would indicate internal bleeding.

"I attempted to tell your mother the seriousness of her situation when she was hospitalized last August. But I could not believe I was reaching her. Let me explain why. The liver is a very complex organ. It does a great many things. In addition to what I have told you, it also regulates the balance of certain key compounds in the bloodstream. It controls the sodium and magnesium and potassium balance. Though the research still has a long way to go, we do know that these substances in proper balance are necessary for adequate brain function. For example, were one to completely upset the sodium balance, the patient would become almost instantaneously unconscious. In fact, that is precisely how one of the spectrum of anesthetics works. It is fair to assume, I think, that when the balance of these substances is altered, brain function is also altered. One could say that the person is semianesthetized, and I do not mean that this is the effect of alcohol directly, when there is a semiparalysis of the cerebral cortex. I am saying that after severe liver damage, even were a person to cease all alcohol intake for several weeks, the fuzziness of the brain function would persist. Yet, after several months of abstinence, if as much as one tenth of the liver were left undamaged, one could expect a very gradual recovery of function. Though the damaged areas cannot regenerate, the undamaged areas can take on a larger share of the total functions than one might expect. At any rate, she could not comprehend or accept the seriousness of my warning. Quite obviously she kept on drinking and, as was her habit, did not eat while or after drinking, so that the liver damage was accelerated. The ... squalid condition of the apartment was due to the semianesthetic effect I have described to you. The electrical impulses in the brain deteriorate. Conversation becomes endlessly repetitive, anecdotal, simplified. They think you are making jokes of some sort.

"She was on the verge of complete liver failure when she was brought in. It was fortunate that she could keep her wits about her enough to call an ambulance."

"It looked more like she was hemorrhaging to death," the banker said. "She threw up in a wastebasket near the bed, and there was so much . . ." He turned slightly gray.

"Less blood than it would look like, actually," Dr. Vidal said. "The thinned blood drained into the stomach and combined with stomach acids to form those large clots you described to me."

"What are you doing for her now, in Intensive Care?" the broker asked.

"A small balloon has been inserted into the esophagus and inflated. This collapses the leaking veins against the wall of the esophagus and encourages clotting and stops the bleeding. She has had transfusions and we have given her clotting agents, and we have tapped the abdominal cavity and drained almost two liters of fluid accumulation. The balloon stopped the bleeding yesterday, but it began again in the night."

Jud, the banker, said, "Doctor, what *can* be done for her?"

"Lay it all out," Fred, the broker, said.

The doctor took his glasses off, sighed, held them to the light, huffed on them, began cleaning them with tissue. "We get quite a few of these cases, people in their fifties. They have had years and years of social drinking, and then it has turned into something else. And finally after ten years of hard drinking, the liver begins to quit. It is difficult for me to separate professional imperatives from moral judgments."

"I think you'd better explain that," said Jud, the banker.

"I hope to try, if you'll let me. If we can't stop the bleeding, the next step would be a procedure called a portal shunt. It means rerouting the whole blood supply system to and from the liver. It is a major operation. It is a very messy operation, because the thinned blood makes a bad field to work in. It takes four or five hours, and a lot of transfusions. If it succeeds, then the patient has another three weeks before going home. Postoperative patients after this particular operation are bad news on the floor. They seldom regain full mental acuity. They are quarrelsome, primitive, demanding and messy. That is not a judgment. That is a fact. If they recover and go home, most of them die within the year of liver failure."

"Why? How come?"

"For the liver to be so bad that a portal shunt is required, it is generally so far gone that the renewed blood supply is not going to hold it steady. Besides, most of them seem to find their way to alcohol as soon as they get strong enough."

Fred said, "You're telling us Mom is dead."

"My professional judgment is that whether or not we stop the bleeding, she will die within the year of liver failure."

"Which . . . which would be easiest for her? Easiest on her?"

"I would think if we could stop the bleeding it would be best all around."

"Do they transplant livers?" the banker asked.

"Not yet," said Doctor Vidal. "At least not at her age in her condition."

After the doctor was gone, the brothers walked down to the parking lot, moving slowly. When they passed a tall metal light standard, Jud Brasser, the banker, stopped and put an arm around it and leaned his forehead against the painted steel. "Oh, Momma," he said in a gravely voice. "Oh, Momma, Jesus, Momma."

Fred Brasser put his hand on Jud's shoulder and patted him. "Come on, kid. Come on."

Jud slapped the metal pole, making it ring. He straightened and pulled out a handkerchief and honked into it. He glowered at Fred, his eyes still brimming, and said, "Don't you hate those little fucks? Those little white-coat fucks with the equipment hanging around their necks? They don't give a shit about anybody."

"I guess this one is pretty much okay, kid. He leveled with us, at least."

"She *wasn't* an alcoholic. I mean she *isn't!*"

"Not the least damn bit when we were growing up. Neither of them were. You know that. Dad liked a few knocks, and he had to do some drinking with the customers in his line of work. And they entertained a lot and wênt out a lot. Hell, they got high, but not drunk. You know. Drunk people belt each other around."

Jud sighed. "You're talking too much to keep from saying what is going to have to be said, sooner or later. Let's get out of the sun."

At the counter in an icy coffee shop in midafternoon, Jud said, looking down at his coffee, "I don't have to remind you how we felt when the old man all of a sudden died from that clot, how all four of us felt, you and Ginny and me and Marie, thinking she would probably be stone broke from the way they always lived, and we were sparring around to see who was going to take her in first."

"But it was——"

"Shut up, big brother. Let's stop the shit, just this one time. So we all gathered up there at the funeral of Newcomb Carlyle Brasser, wives and kids and all, and afterward, when she wanted the advice of her two big-shot sons, we found out, lo and behold, not only did she have a nice little package of utilities stocks, plus the old man's Social Security, but they also had the apartment down here. Now you know exactly what she wanted, Freddy. So did I. She *said* she wanted to get rid of the big house and move down here where she and Dad had wanted to retire, except he didn't make it. We both *knew* she wanted to come out and live with us half the year in Santa Monica and with you the other half in Fort Worth. Didn't you know that?"

"Maybe."

"Maybe, *hell!* Why would Mom want to come down here where she didn't know *anybody?*"

"She never had trouble making friends."

"That's what we told ourselves, Freddy, that she would get along just fine and dandy down here. We said that she ought to do just like all the other old people, go to one of these retirement heavens on earth. We sat there with our sad egg-sucking smiles, and we told that lonesome woman we didn't want her in our lives. We practically told her that her life was over and it was our turn to have our lives, and she would crap up our privacy and our home life and our kids and our entertaining and our vacations and everything else if we had the burden of that old woman!"

"Now, God damn it . . ."

"Shut up." He tapped his fist lightly on the countertop. "We did it. We made the decision. We can't go back now and make a different one. I just think we ought to split this burden of guilt half and half. Hell, we talked to enough of those people in that Golden Sands to know what they thought of her. Peggy Brasser, the drunk. Get out of the road, here comes Peggy Brasser. Some kind of friends she made, hah? You want Peggy, look for her at the Sand Dollar Bar."

"I'm not denying anything," Fred said. "Her letters were always cheerful. She remembered birthdays and anniversaries. How was I to know she was going downhill? I thought it was all working out for her, same as you did."

"If she'd been living with us, or even near one of us, she would have been okay," Jud said.

"You can't be sure of that."

"Maybe not. But I like the odds. And maybe my kids would have had some benefit from it. I have the feeling that the more people there are around kids who are . . . related to them, part of a bigger family around them, the more the kids respond to approval and disapproval."

"Jud?"

"What?"

"It . . . makes me feel ashamed, and then angry for feeling ashamed when I really can't see why I should feel that way."

"It's a start."

"And you are saying that somebody stays here until she can travel west?"

"Which will probably have to be you. I'm in too much of a dog fight with the regulatory people right now over our holding company. I told you about it."

Fred sighed. "Which will probably have to be me. Why not? With these nine-thousand-share days, the office is like a graveyard. If Ginny can get her sister to take the kids, she can come help out."

"Stay in the apartment?"

"I guess so. We'd better wait and see if they stop that bleeding before planning anything."

From the hotel coffee-shop stool, Jud could look left through tinted glass and see the tall caramel towers of the condominiums stretching along the beach of Fiddler Key.

"There's a lot of them," he said softly. "Buildings full of the old folks, under some kind of compulsion to enjoy the hell out of the sunset years. They should be with their blood kin, and deep inside them they know it. Can't admit it. If they admit it, it means admitting their children are selfish, indifferent turds. How the hell did old folks get to be a race apart? For that matter, how did the teenagers become a different tribe? We're all split up into fragments of what it used to be, brother. And it seems to me that no part of it all is having a good time by itself. And the kids don't learn shit about their own family past. All those apartments, Freddy, think of it. What it is, maybe, is a market. The oldsters market. Sell to the senior citizens. Group them and sell to them. If they are scattered all over hell and gone, it costs too much to reach your market. Get them into a herd, and sell one, and he'll sell his neighbors."

Fred said, "I'm going back to the hospital. Coming?"

"No. I'm going to walk to Golden Sands."

"That would be two miles, about. It's hot and we're going to get that rain again today."

"Well . . . drop me off. Phone me there if there's a change."

"Sure. We . . . we did what we thought was best. And she could have gotten sick wherever she was."

"Probably. Probably." His tone was lifeless. The conversation was over. It was the voice he used to bring committee meetings to an early adjournment. He still wanted to walk, but it wasn't worth the argument. And he wanted to cry, but knew he couldn't, not yet.

28

ON A TORRID WEDNESDAY MORNING in early August, Martin Liss took scratch paper and once again computed his net worth after taxes. Four and a quarter mil, figuring it conservatively. The speculation in Swiss francs was doing very very well. With Sherman Grome's crap game listed on the big board at six, he could count a profit thus far of two hundred and twenty-two thousand on his short side of EMMS shares.

And there was no more fun in trying to push the Harbour Pointe project. There was no way he could win and no way he could lose. There wasn't enough money to do it the way he had planned, absolutely first class. The Tropic Towers problem was being solved. What they had done was scare hell out of the few buyers already in residence and gotten them to approve pets and kids. Then they had moved in a dozen families rent-free, into furnished apartments, on a thirty-day or sixty-day basis, families with kids and dogs and cats and so forth. Lots of activity. Young people running around all over the place. And he had cut the average price to $23,995 and taken a couple of full pages, and in spite of the times they had really moved a bunch of them. Take a little loss here and now, but make it up over a period of time in recreation leases and maintenance agreements.

Drusilla Bryne had done an absolutely first-class job at Tropic Towers once she had moved into the penthouse, functioning as manager and sales manager, just as she had in the early days of Golden Sands. Good thing there hadn't been too much to do at the office, giving her more time at the Towers. He rocked back and forth on his elevator shoes and stared frowning at the horizon line and tugged at his goatee, and wondered what sort of bonus he should give her, if any. It could come out of Marliss. Nice cash balance in Marliss since Letra had reimbursed Marliss for all prior costs on the Harbour Pointe project.

He felt edgy and restless. The report on the third Mrs. Liss was a month old and he had not done a thing about it, or wanted to. It didn't seem that important. The investigator had been a second-generation Cuban with a cracker accent. His report was semi-illiterate but crammed with facts, and accompanied by some grainy blowups of black-and-white telephoto shots. Francie Liss was presently getting laid by the assistant tennis pro at the club. It was a matinee arrangement on Mondays and Thursdays, his afternoons off. He shared a frame cottage on a side street a mile from the club with two other gainfully employed jocks. She would drive down a narrow alley and park her gray sun-roof Mercedes between a tin shed and a giant banyan tree and walk through the junk in the yard and go in through the back. They would do most of their screwing on a big blanket-covered mattress on the floor of the so-called Florida room at the rear of the house, and Martinez had gotten his art photos by waiting in the banyan tree one Thursday for her to arrive and staying there until well after she left. The agency had made blowups of the few which showed her face distinctly and left no question as to what she was doing, and no question that it was not with her husband, who was some eight inches shorter, thirty pounds lighter, and far hairier than her muscular lover.

Whenever he needed it, the report was there, documented and notarized. And illustrated. He could not really feel any differently about her than he had before. She was lively and decorative, and sometimes funny, and he had never trusted her and still didn't.

What he ought to do, he thought, was fold up the Marliss Corporation. Liquidate all its assets. The big asset was the stock in Services Management Group of Miami. The quarterly dividends were heavy, but that was, of course, only a part of it. Enough of the income was in cash to permit a skim, nothing like the kind of skim those same boys had arranged out in Las Vegas before Hughes moved in and made a full declaration of all casino income and gave the IRS a basis for comparison. Some of them in Miami had talked about how it used to be in Vegas and Havana. They had some operations over there in Dade County that did not concern Marty Liss, and in which he did not want to get involved, but they kept Services Management Group clean, except for the little skim, because it was a legitimate investment area for some of the money from the other · things. Sometimes somebody passing through would bring his share of the cash over, but usually he would get it when he had to be in Miami. Pocket money. He kept it in the locked drawer of his desk and took some out when he ran low.

He wondered why he felt so down. He wondered if something was wrong with him physically. A lung maybe? No weight loss. How did you feel if you had a cancer you didn't know about? Lung, prostate, throat, liver, bladder, bowel, stomach . . . Jesus! There is no such thing as a good place to have one.

It couldn't be knowing for sure about Francie, because he had felt down before that came out. Would a new woman help? He couldn't feel the slightest stir of interest. It would just be a hell of a chore to go hunt one up and con her onto her back. And once you had her there, she wouldn't be as good as Irish at it anyway. He wondered if he should phone them and have the boat taken out of storage and cleaned up and provisioned. For what? For where? Forget it.

Traffic crossing the north bridge to Fiddler Key was blurred by the heat waves rising from the pavement. He could see little scurries of wind moving across the stillness of the bay. Black storm clouds were low and heavy over the Gulf, and he saw a thick straight orange bolt of lightning appear between sea and cloud.

He looked at the Silverthorn tract, at the fourteen acres scraped clean, and at the curved finger of land protecting the boat basin. The dredge sat in the boat basin, and he knew that if he looked through his binoculars he would see the fill spewing onto the land, and see the cloud of gulls at the end of the fill pipe as they circled and dipped and yapped and snatched up the sea creatures which came hurtling ashore from the bay bottom.

There was no pleasure in the damned place anymore. No risk left. And, if it was built, no pride in it. More junk on the key. Not as bad as that Tropic Towers, but junk nevertheless.

He moved closer to the window and looked down toward the street. He imagined how Jerry Stalbo must have looked, flaming and screaming down through the night toward the hard concrete, and it made him feel sick and dizzy. But at the same time he had a strange soft compulsion to jump. He knew he probably couldn't break through those big tinted windows with a sledge. How long would it last? What would you think about on the way down?

As he backed away, the intercom on his desk spoke with the unfamiliar country accent of the girl filling in for Drusilla.

"Could Mr. Traff come in?"

He said yes and Lew came in, frowning, to sit across the desk from Marty and nibble at the skin at the corner of his thumbnail.

"Something I can't figure out, Marty. You know this revolt we got at Golden Sands, I had told Frank West and Sully that it was my opinion the best thing they could do would be continue to provide everything they had always provided so there wouldn't be any hassle about any discontinuance of services. What they both said, they said it sounded to them like the right thing to do, but they would check it out with the legal guys over at SMG, Miami, on account of they had probably had this kind of thing happen over there and had a policy going on it. I told them I figured they would want to do that, and would they let me know what they say over there. So I didn't hear and I started phoning, and I can't get Frank or Sully on the phone, either one. They won't return calls. It is very strange."

"Some kind of misunderstanding," he said. He called on

his private line, using the unlisted number of the phone in a desk drawer in Miami, remembering the unwritten rule. No names.

"Yeh?"

"I've got something going over here in Athens I don't understand too well."

"Such as?"

"Such as one of my people getting a runaround from both the operations here, like not getting a call back in regard to some payments that weren't made on the first."

"Well, I guess what you are making reference to, we want to cut down on direct contact. Too much of that goes on, it makes confusion all the way around. It's a new management policy."

"What are you trying to tell me?"

"There is a reorganization going on, and you will be contacted in due course when everything is straightened away. And meanwhile, this number won't be operative anymore after today."

"You want I should come over?"

"People are so busy formulating new policy there wouldn't be any time to sit down with you right now."

"What if I want a buy-out?"

"I'll be back to you in twenty minutes with an offer."

Miami had hung up. Martin hung up. He stared at Lew Traff and wondered why it was that he had managed to surround himself with idiots.

"Something is very sour," he said. "Something is going very bad, Lew."

"Such as?"

"My God, I don't know. I don't *know!* What they have over there, they have a good line on what is happening. They've got people pretty well placed here and there. They have to know what's coming up next. You know the feeling I got talking to him? Just from his voice? I'm nothing anymore. I'm worse than nothing. I'm an infection."

"Marty, dammit, that doesn't sound—"

"Shut up." He tapped his plump middle. "I get feelings

in here that I listen to. What is the absolutely worst thing that could happen to me? I mean legally."

Traff was lost in thought for a few minutes. Liss paced. "Okay," said Traff, "here is the worst. The SEC starts building a case against Sherman Grome for draining off the assets of Equity Mortgage Management Shares into his own pocket and the pockets of his friends. Meanwhile the IRS is running a special audit of Marliss and Letra, in addition to the regular audit they have you under personally every year. Okay, the SEC taps brokerage house records to find out who has shorted EMMS, which would be you and me and Benjie, and maybe, for God's sake, Sherman Grome. The IRS guys coordinate with those FBI people, Barber and Grosscup, and some red-hot young U.S. Attorney pulls the whole thing into one big package. So all of a sudden, when they have everything in a row, we are all indicted, and all assets are frozen, the assets of the corporations and personal onnate too. They hit us with huge bail and set us up for legal actions which will take two or three or four years to finish, with maybe big fines plus jail terms at the end of it."

As Martin Liss stared at him aghast, Lew said uncomfortably, "Well, you wanted to know the worst."

"I haven't done anything *that* wrong!"

"You conspired with Grome to make his books look a lot better than they were."

"Fred Hildebert cut off the money. He was the one who suggested Grome!"

"You squeezed that one million out of Grome in return for your taking over Tropic Towers, where Grome was taking a bath."

"Whose side are you on?"

"Yours, Marty. And my own. You asked for the worst. Listen, how long do you think Justin Denniver and Molly would hold out if somebody braced them with the idea you'd been buying services from the commission, and they could have immunity or go down with you?"

"Would you tell somebody where the money went?"

"Marty, I haven't got ten kids."

"Oh. Would he?"

"I don't know. I don't think so, but I don't know. If the worst happens, maybe he would. Just maybe."

"Benjie?"

"Suppose he thinks you're going to make a run for it."

"Run for what?"

"I think you buying Swiss francs has him worried."

"I was just playing the weak dollar against a strong currency. Speculation. That's all."

"Irish studying brochures makes him nervous."

"Just a trip, for God's sake. To the Greek islands. So you've been talking to him about all this. The two of you have been talking it all over!"

"Why wouldn't we? The best thing we could have done back in May was absolutely nothing. That's what we *both* recommended. But you wanted to go ahead with Harbour Pointe."

"So you were *right!* Okay?"

"Don't get sore at me when you want to get sore at yourself."

Marty sat again. "You're right. They heard something in Miami. It is something they can't stop, so what they want to do is—"

The private line rang and he picked the phone up. "Yes?"

"The way things are, it would be twelve a share."

"Twelve!"

"Cash delivered tomorrow and pick up the certificates."

"But twelve is so—"

"Sometime you might want to come back in some way, and what you got is a verbal option it would be the same price. That is the best anybody can do. Okay?"

"I don't think so."

"Included is a buy-out on your personal shares in those two operations over there, fifty on one and seventy-five on the other. For old times' sake, I would urge you take it."

"Not enough."

"By tomorrow maybe it will be."

And that was the end of it. Marty said to Lew, "They want all relationship severed, one way or another. He gave me the feeling they are willing to get pretty hard about it. I've never been on the inner circle over there. I was around, I guess, to make it look better. They want me out, they can push me right out. They would want anybody out who turned into bad news in the paper."

"I could try to see what I could find out, but—"

"Should I run? Don't answer that question. Why should I run? As far as I know, I haven't done anything wrong. Stupid, maybe, but not wrong."

"A lot of times it comes out exactly the same," said Lew.

The country voice said, "Mr. Rittner in Tampa is on the line."

"So what does the broker want? Put him on, please. Good morning, Norm. What's on your mind?"

"Something just came over the wire I thought you should hear, Martin. All trading has been suspended in shares of EMMS. Though they gave no reason, the general feeling around here is that Grome's management put them into too many bad situations and they could be bankrupt. Grome has not been available for comment."

"I never had that happen to me before. What does it mean? Can I close out my short position?"

"No, Martin. You went short sixteen thousand shares. We borrowed those sixteen thousand shares, and to get out of your position you have to replace them, and you can't buy them to replace the loan until trading is permitted."

"Like when?"

"Well, if they are bankrupt, then they would be delisted, and I would imagine somebody would make a market in the shares in the over-the-counter marketplace. Then you could probably pick them up for twenty-five cents or so apiece. That would make your gross short-term profit close to three hundred thousand, eventually."

"Eventually. Great. Al, what I want you should do is take me out of the Swiss francs."

"Hold cash in the account?"

"Send me a check, okay?"

"Of course, Martin. Anything you say."

Liss hung up and said, "Of course, Martin. Anything you say. You can enjoy this with me, Lew. EMMS is delisted and maybe bankrupt, so there's no way to cover a short position."

"Beautiful," Lew said. "Just beautiful."

"Grome isn't available for comment."

"Grome is a crazy person."

"When he was making people rich, he was genius," Marty said. "Back to what you were saying before, when you were telling me the worst that could happen. About freezing personal assets."

"It's done often. Tax cases and fraud cases. Bank accounts and brokerage accounts, lockboxes and so on. And real estate too."

"They can do that?"

"They do it."

"Marliss has a heavy cash position right now."

"I know what you're asking. Yes. It is a closely held corporation."

Martin Liss paced from the desk to the window and back. "This is a crazy day," he said. "I was so bored with my whole life I felt like jumping out the window. Now I'm not bored. I still feel like jumping out the window. How do you fight stuff like this, Lew?"

Traff sighed heavily. "I think you get a better lawyer than the one you got. And you wait for the roof to fall in." He gave a weary laugh. "At least we don't have to worry about Harbour Pointe any more. With EMMS stalled, Fred Hildebert won't release any of that cash. That eight mil will have to go back to Atlanta, a little drop in a big empty bucket."

"I could finish that thing and make money on it."

"Forget it, Marty."

"I could! I know I could. If I could get to Fred to—"

"Marty! Have you gone crazy as Sherman Grome?"

Martin Liss stared at him. In a dead voice he said, "You're right, of course. Get out of here. Try to find out what's going on and let me know."

After Lew left, Martin stood once more at the big windows and looked at the place over on Fiddler Key, beyond the channel. The fill was dark where it spewed out of the pipe. The sun had whitened the fill from prior days as it dried.

He knew he had to stop the dredge. He was mildly surprised to feel a sting of tears in his eyes. He was going to ask the girl to get Cole Kimber for him, but then he punched out the number on his private line. He was glad he caught Cole in. He was hard to reach. He told Cole to stop the dredging and told him why.

Cole sighed audibly. "Okay. Herb's subcontract was finished and paid for, and I got my reimbursement. On Marine Projects it is going to be a little different. Mike has been paid up through last Friday, so we'll owe him two and a half days, plus extra expenses for premature termination. The way the agreement is written up, we are liable for an agreed figure on overhead per day up to a maximum of fifteen days, or until he gets the dredge working on another job. Let me see here. I think it's seventeen hundred . . . right. Seventeen hundred a day. Twenty-five thousand five."

"And I suppose you would take your cost plus on top of that?"

"Shall I read you our agreement, Marty? I mean my agreement with Letra."

"You start to fall and they pick your bones before you hit the fucking ground, Cole."

"I can't afford not to, old buddy. I told you in front that I do not like and did not like the shape and size and color of this whole project. It got way too fancy for me. And I told you that was why I would only deal on an arm's-length basis, strictly by the book, because if I deal in any other way I am part of the package. This is why I can't and won't negotiate any change at all. Understand?"

"I've put a hell of a lot of money into your pocket, Kimber."

"You'll find I've got some termination costs written in there too."

"No doubt."

"I'll bring the final billing over to Benjie just as soon as it can be typed up. I'll ask that the twenty-five five be escrowed along with my percentage of same until we see if Mike can get pumping elsewhere sooner. Frankly I think his chances are zip."

"Great."

"Benjie *does* have enough money?"

"If you hurry, pal. If you hurry on over and get the hell in line, maybe Letra can pay in full. If not, you can sue Letra."

"Now just a goddam min—"

Marty hung up, pressed the bar on the intercom and said, "Get Mr. Wannover in here right away."

That was the day it began. The National Hurricane Center in Miami had not yet named the storm. They had not yet even heard of it because there was nothing yet for the satellite cameras to pick up and relay to the weather stations. The beginning was in a somnolent superheated few hundred square miles of ocean off the west coast of Africa and south-southeast of the Cape Verde Islands. The mechanism of the great engine appears to be deceptively simple. When there is a long period of calm, with no weather fronts to distort the effects of the high temperature of the waters, the heated air will rise. Air on all sides of that upward current will move in to fill the low-pressure area thus created.

Once there is a sufficient volume of air involved in this phenomenon, it can sometimes begin, quite slowly at first, to turn in a counterclockwise direction, an effect of the drag of the earth's rotation, the way a speeding truck will create whirling dust devils along the dry shoulder of a highway.

As the hot air, heavy with moisture, is pulled in, drawn high and whirled out of the heart of the storm, its moisture is condensed by the cold of high altitude and falls in torrential tons ahead of the disturbance. The disturbance begins moving slowly west and slightly northwest. This one's earliest center was at approximately 5 degrees north, 20 degrees west, almost equidistant from Liberia and the Cape Verde Islands. The conditions were ideal for the formation of what could become a mature hurricane, one whose distinctive whirling cloud pattern could fill the entire Gulf of Mexico from rim to rim.

As yet the spinning motion in this disturbance was unpronounced and uncertain. Below it there flowed the constant trade winds of summer, from east to west. Above it, in mid-Atlantic, the clockwise rotation of the winds around the Bermuda high sent a constant wind westerly. The disturbance had begun in the doldrums and only began to move west and begin its turning, hesitant though it was, when a ridge of the trade winds reached up into that area where it was, curling into a trough, into a westerly wave that imparted an initial momentum, along with the spin of the planet. Once the disturbance began moving west, there was nothing in the way all across that broad ocean.

The water temperature was 29 degrees Celsius.

The barometric pressure at its center was dropping.

Altocumulus clouds were beginning to form.

29

ON THURSDAY, in the early afternoon, Fred Brasser telephoned his wife, Ginny, in Fort Worth and said, "Mom died last night, hon."

"Oh, dear. How terrible for you."

"I tried to get Jud but I can't reach him. What if you try, okay? I got a lot of odds and ends to do here."

"Sure. What should I tell him?"

"Tell him that the bleeding never did start again after they got it stopped okay the second time. But yesterday, just before I got there, she went into a coma on account of she had complete liver failure. They put her into intensive care and tried a lot of different stuff, but she just stayed like that until she died about eleven."

"Why didn't you phone me last night?"

"Well, it was pretty late by the time I had a chance to. I was able to see her a couple minutes every hour. That's the rule they got here. She looked dead long before she was really gone. She looked really terrible, hon." His voice broke.

"Poor baby."

"Well, you tell Jud there's no need of him coming here. I'm trying to set up a service on Monday up home, and there's no reason to have any kind of service here. From what I can figure out, nobody would come. We never ought to let her live here. Anyway, she's legally a Florida resident, and I've located a copy of the will she had made down here after Dad died. Tell Jud that the two of us are co-executors, and I've asked the lawyer that made up the will, a fellow named McKay, to take over the tax and estate problems. He seems bright and okay. The way it looks, I ought to be able to fly home Saturday, and then we and the kids can fly up there Sunday or early on Monday, depending."

"Where will you be staying tonight? The apartment again?"

"No. It sort of spooks me. Kind of dumb, I know, but it does."

"I can see how it might."

"I'm staying at a little place here on the key right in Beach Village called the Beach Motel, Room Thirty. Here's the phone number off the key tag: 824-4696."

"Got it. Thanks dear. Anything else?"

"Tell Jud the problem in the estate will be converting the apartment into money. It's almost impossible to sell one of these things right now, and there are other complications I won't go into. I'm meeting the appraiser at the apartment right after I get some lunch."

"No fried food, sweetie."

"Okay, okay. Sorry to drop all this on you."

"I don't mind. You just take care of yourself and hurry home as soon as you can. We all miss you. And I'm terribly sorry about Peggy. She was always wonderful to me and to Marie. Always so generous."

After he hung up he stepped out of the booth and mopped his forehead, and pulled his sports shirt away from his body. He walked across the parking area of the Beach Mall Shopping Plaza. The asphalt felt soft underfoot. He went into the McDonald's on the far side of Beach Drive and got two Big Macs and two Cokes to go. He walked south on the shoulder of the road and turned in past the Beach Motel swimming pool. When he unlocked the door to Room 30, Darleen Moseby came to the bathroom door and looked out at him, smiling. She wore the shirt she had made him buy for himself when he took her out to Woolco last Friday so she could get that kind of lipstick she couldn't get anywhere else. It was a gauze shirt in a kind of gray-white cotton with yellow flowers embroidered all over the shoulders and yoke.

"Sure smells jus' fine, Freddy. I'm rinsing out stuff. You lay it out over there, huh?"

When she came hurrying out to eat with hungry pleasure, he was pleasantly yet uncomfortably aware that all she had on was that shirt. It was long on him, and so it came down to her knees.

He said, "Look, I had to tell her where I am so she can tell my brother. So if the phone rings and I'm not here . . ."

"Hell, no person would phone me here."

"How about Tom Shawn?"

"Well, Tom would know I wouldn't answer the phone anyway. God, I was starving to death!"

"You know, you look like you were about twelve years old."

"Don't sweat it, Freddy. They won't get you on statutory. Honest to God, I'm twenty-three damn years old. Wanna see my driving license?"

"No. I just meant you're small-boned and . . . young looking. How . . . how long have you been—"

"Freddy! I *warned* you!"

"Okay, okay. I'm sorry."

"Why I'm a hooker and how long I've been a hooker and so on, all that is a lot of shit. It doesn't mean anything. The only thing that means anything is I think you're a nice guy, and I'm glad you came along, and as long as you keep on paying, we can both be happy and have some fun, and that's all that counts, isn't it?"

"That's all that counts."

"I'm real sorry about your mother. But I guess she brought it all down on herself."

He finished the last of his Coke and looked at his watch. "I've got to go meet that appraiser. On the furniture and personal stuff."

"Gee, that'll be kind of depressing. You want some cheering up before you go?" She looked blandly at him and ran her tonguetip along her lower lip and winked. Though as flirtation it was obviously habitual and mechanical, he felt such a surge of primal lust that it dazed him. He did not see how he could ever get his fill of this smooth ripe little person.

"When . . . when I come back."

"I'll prolly be out there by the pool again, so you put on your swim trunks we bought you and come out, and bring the oil and I'll cover you good so you won't start to burn again."

As he drove off he could not believe he had been with her only a week. Last Thurday evening he had gone to the Sand Dollar Bar to have some words with whoever had been selling more drinks to a woman than she could obviously handle. The bartender, a skinny red-faced fellow named Lou, said that the owner, Tom Shawn, was usually on afternoons and that was when Peggy Brasser usually came in. Tom Shawn usually stopped by in the evening for a little while and helped out on the bar if he was needed. Lou said he'd heard Mrs. Brasser was sick and he was sorry to hear it. He said he hoped she'd be out of the hospital soon. Meanwhile, have one on the house, sir. Least we can do for the son of a good steady customer.

He sat at the bar and drank, and after a long time he found he was telling some girl all about himself. She looked more elegant than she sounded. She wore too much eye makeup. She listened well. She seemed very interested in him. Then he was somewhere at a table for two, having dinner with that same girl, Darlene Moseby, and buying wine. And without transition they were in a room and he was sitting on the bed and saw her tuck money in her purse and then kneel and unlace his shoes and tug them off, grinning up at him, makeup all scrubbed away, winking up at him and calling him good old Freddy boy.

So he had given her a hundred dollars on Thursday night and, after cashing a check, another hundred on Friday night. Then they had made a deal for a full week, and she had waited until Monday for the five hundred she charged by the week. He had found out a few things about her. She lived with Shawn behind the Sand Dollar in a small frame house. Shawn seldom had need of her. There were four of them, but she was the only one who stayed in the cottage. The other three were Dusty and Louise and Francine. Dusty and Louise lived together. Francine lived with her mother and her kid. Tom took a cut from all the business they pulled, and he kept the freaks off them and kept it quiet in the bar, and gave presents here and there.

If I go home Saturday, he thought, that just about uses up the five hundred. If I go home Saturday I will have to make up a reason to come back.

The appraiser was an old man who breathed loudly. He brought a girl with him who wrote down the items and values on a yellow legal pad. The girl had thick glasses and a sweaty smell. He wouldn't look at the jewelry. He said Mr. Brasser should take that to a jeweler for appraisal. His breathing seemed a sound of constant disdain, as though he were sick unto death of having spent his life tottering around amid the tastelessness of other people's belongings.

When he had finished he sat at the breakfast bar in the kitchen and added up his totals on a pocket computer.

"It looks like eighteen hundred and ten," he said. "You'll get a typed original and three copies, all certified."

"Please give them to Mr. McKay along with your bill."

"Of course. Come, Alicia. Good-bye, sir."

"How do you think I should dispose of these things?"

The old man turned and smiled for the first time. His teeth were large and stained. "Let your fingers do the walking," he said. "People who will make offers advertise in there."

She was prone on the sun cot in her orange string bikini. He went in and changed to swim trunks and oiled the front of himself and all the reachable areas and took the bottle outside. He moved another sun cot close to hers. The scrape of the aluminum legs on concrete woke her and she started up, dazed by heat, sun and sleep.

"Oh, hi. Yeh, gimme the bottle."

She sat up and leaned over him and slathered his back. When she did the backs of his thighs she sneaked her hand under him and gave him a quick tweak and giggled. He lay prone near her for twenty minutes while his need for her got ever sharper. He woke her and they went inside, out of sun heat into coolness, out of bright dazzle into shadows. There was sun heat still in her body, and she was golden and slippery with sun oil.

When they rested she said, "You don't get enough at home, huh?"

"I always thought I did."

"She pretty?"

"What?"

"Hey, your wife. Is she pretty?"

"Sure. She's a good-looking woman."

"Your little girl is how old, did you say?"

"She's ten. Lolly is ten."

"Be nice to her."

"Huh?"

"Always be nice to her, Freddy. No matter what. You're her daddy. What I mean is, I was fourteen, you know? And there was this boy fifteen, we thought we were in love like nobody ever was before. We weren't really going to screw, you know? But we fooled around and we got closer and closer, making each other come and so on, and one night we were too close and he shoved and in it went and we screwed like crazy for a month and then he started going out with my best girl friend. Boy, I was really going to show *him!* And everybody, you know? So I took off with a couple of guys going up to Atlanta. That turned into some weird kind of life-style. I got onto speed and I was down to like eighty pounds there at one point, and I'm still confused about a lot of it. And I picked up a bad dose that played hell to cure it. Don't look nervous, Freddy baby. I'm a healthy girl. When I came up out of nowhere I wanted to come home and I called my daddy collect to ask him to wire money. I'd been gone the best part of a year by then. You see, my ma took off when I was little and he married again and I've got half-brothers and half-sisters. Somebody got him to the phone to ask if he'd take a collect call from Darleen Moseby, his daughter, and I heard him say to the operator, 'Tell that cheap little cunt I never had no daughter name of Darleen.' And I heard him hang up. It broke my heart, Freddy. It really and truly did, you know? That's what I mean about be nice to your little girl no matter what."

"You ever see him again?"

"I sort of wanted to, and then I found out he was dead. He was a construction worker and a piece of steel fell out of a sling, they say, and fell on him. They say if he'd stood still he would be okay, but when everybody yelled to look out, Daddy ran the wrong way. I used to try to hate him. But his old lady, my mother, took off, and I guess he thought I would do the same thing to him, and I did."

He was turned toward her. The windows were behind him. He marveled at the clarity and delicacy and beauty of her features, and ran his fingertips down her cheek.

"You ever think of some other kind of work?"

"Oh, sure. A few times. I learned hair, but there's got to be more to life than standing on your sore feet while some woman yaps about her flower garden and her cock-tail parties and her husband's new Cadillac. I tried to be a model, but they want you to show up so early! I don't know, Freddy. I like clothes and I like to watch the TV and I like to keep my tan going and I like to swim and I like presents and I like being cuddled. I like guys looking at me like you're looking at me right now."

"What about later on?"

"Being old? I've got that figured out. I've decided not to get old. I made up my mind."

"I'm going Saturday, but I'm coming back."

"More legal stuff?"

"Not really. I want to come back and see you."

"For another whole week?"

"Why not?"

"Tell you what. I'll make you a special annual rate, okay? Twenty big ones. Twenty thou."

"Darleen?"

"Now, don't look at me *that* way, okay? Don't get that way with me, Freddy. You're no fun when you get like that."

She flounced back away from his touch and lay on her back, flat, small chin up-pointed, eyes closed. He looked upon her, at the full delicate breasts slightly flattened by the weight of gravity, and banded by the narrow stripe of a paler tan. He studied with care the way the edges of the rib cage on either side of the diaphragm upthrust against the smooth deeper tan. An arm upflung revealed a scattering of dark stubble in the grainy pallor of her armpit. Her belly lifted and fell in the slowed tempo of her breathing. The gingery bush of pubic hair near the juncture of the two round firm thighs was just sparse enough to reveal the plump pale shape of her sex.

Suddenly he saw, juxtaposed upon her fresh young image, the image of his mother in Intensive Care, in almost the same position, but with pipes and tubes and breathing equipment fastened to her in mysterious medical ways. She was shockingly old, her face like those ancient photographs of John D. Rockefeller, all of her slack face and in-sucked lips suspended from the high, hard, narrow bridge of the wasted nose.

And I will be dead too, he thought. The image changed back to the resting warmth of the girl, and all of his response to her and to the thought of his own death was focused in the lengthening, thickening, hardening weight of his erection. He looked down at himself and saw how the rigidity moved slightly to each great thump of his heart. In a despair mixed strangely with a kind of dirty glee, he said to himself, I am lost. I am really and truly lost.

Harlin Barker looked at his wife through the glass that separated him from Connie Mae's cubicle in the cardiac intensive care section. He could see the screen beyond the head of her bed with the little green moving line on it, making a little sharp peak and valley every time her heart beat. He couldn't hear the bleeping sound he knew it was making. Her color, he thought, was terrible. Green-gray, and her hair looked clotted and sweaty.

Just when you think you're getting things worked out, he thought. With Mrs. Twigg coming in to help me look after her. Think she's coming along okay, and then this. Another little coronary and they took her out of Intensive Care after two days, back to the room, and I'm getting ready to take her home again, and now another one. In spite of all their darn medication, she has to go and have another one.

He realized he was feeling angry toward Connie Mae, and he knew that was unjust and unloving. The poor darling couldn't help it.

After he saw her he went to find the woman who had phoned him at Golden Sands. She was in the hospital Accounts Office. Her name was Mrs. Partch. He sat in a small waiting room for twenty minutes leafing through tattered magazines about travel trailers and vans and motor homes, before she came to the door and called his name in a voice loud enough for a banquet hall. She was a tall big woman in a white blouse and a dark skirt, with her hair pulled back into a bun. There was a plastic badge pinned to her blouse: Mrs. A. A. Partch. She took him to a small cubicle and went behind her desk and opened the folder and leafed slowly through the accounts and forms contained therein. She had graceful elegant hands and long red fingernails. They danced on the keys of a mini-computer, and she wrote a figure in pencil on the margin of a buff-colored form.

"I have word from the cardiac section your wife will be able to go back to regular service tomorrow."

"That's great. I was trying to find out up there, but nobody seemed to know anything. That's great."

"We have computed the time she has spent in the hospital for this illness, and I must advise you that six days from now the benefits will run out."

He stared at her. "I don't understand."

"I don't know how I can say it more clearly, Mr. Barker. You will have to arrange for a transfer to a nursing home, or arrange nursing care for her at your home."

"She is a *very* sick woman!"

"Mr. Barker, we must make decisions about very sick people every day of the year."

"Her doctor won't want her to leave so quickly."

"If he wants to make a special presentation to the Care Committee in regards to lengthening her stay here, and if it is then approved, you can, of course, let her remain here, but all costs will be charged to you rather than to Medicare."

"Why?"

"Mr. Barker, I told you why. Your benefits have run out."

"How can they run out? It is supposed to be . . . for medical catastrophes!"

"Agreed. However, in the matter of specific illnesses, we must proceed according to the guidelines which are set up for us. We have no say in the matter. Suppose you came in here with a broken leg, without complications. After three days your benefits would run out."

"Mrs. Barker has had three coronaries."

"The heart condition is considered as a single illness, Mr. Barker. Your benefits will run out on the fourteenth of this month. We try to be cooperative. That is why we let you know in advance. So you can make árrangements."

"But what am I supposed to *do* with her?"

"I cannot help you solve that problem. The hospital has adopted the same schedules as apply to the benefits you receive, with, of course, the doctor's right to appeal to the Care Committee."

"I think he will."

"And I hope he will be successful, for your sake. I should advise you that when a patient's status is changed from Medicare to Self-Pay, a new admissions procedure has to be gone through, and it is hospital policy to require a deposit of three hundred dollars at the time of admitting."

"Who sets up these guidelines?"

"I understand it is mostly done by computer. They have data from all over the country regarding the recommended duration of hospitalization. You realize, of course, you can apply for and receive benefits applicable to a stay in a nursing home after she leaves here."

"But my wife has had three separate coronary occlusions. I can't understand why you people—"

"I have a busy schedule, Mr. Barker, and there are two people out there waiting to see me right now. I wish I could give you more time, but I have the feeling I would merely be repeating what I have already told you. By the way, here is the most recent billing for items not covered by Medicare: $158.50. Would it be convenient for you to pay at the window now? Do you have your checkbook with you?"

"No."

"It is always wise to bring it with you when you come to this office, Mr. Barker. I hope everything works out for you and Mrs. Barker."

"According to the guidelines?"

"I beg your pardon?"

"Never mind."

He went down the corridor and around a corner and leaned against the wall. A woman came along, yanking a small child savagely, squalling at it, beating it across the back of the head with her purse. The child was howling. Harlin Barker envied the kid. It could howl its heart out and stay in character. Old men were not supposed to.

The next step was to locate Dr. Keebler, the heart man, and find out what was going on.

Sam Harrison did forty slow laps in the warm water of the pool at the Islander, climbed out and toweled his head and face and shoulders, then pulled on, over his head, his blue and white Greek shirt to go into the cocktail lounge.

The lounge was completely enclosed with glass, set at unexpected angles. Indoor and outdoor planting areas kept people from walking into it. There was a wide overhang. Reflections were in turn reflected from one big tinted expanse to the next, making all the hot bright world outside quite unreal, with high rises lifting out of the sea, and waves breaking white into the flowers, and people walking across the pool.

Skip, the bartender, made the sour planters' punch with exaggerated, ironic care, but dumping in the rum with that free hand one uses for the heavy tipper.

"To your taste, sir? Your discriminating taste?"

"Today it's merely exquisite."

Skip leaned closer. "The three little ladies out there at the pool? They had their little knock at the bar while you were doing your forty laps. They are three executive secretaries from Birmingham, and I gather they would not be averse to your buying them a drink and going on from there, especially the tall one in the white. A nice laugh and a very nice built, as you can plainly see."

"Skip, you do take good care of me."

"That's what I'm here for. This is a very straight place, you know. No hookers. With all the amateurs we get here, a hooker would starve. Like I am about to starve if the bar doesn't pick up."

"Maybe some other time on that tall one."

"Beach-walking again today, sir?"

"The way you keep track of me is making me nervous."

"I will say this. Whoever it is you do that beach-walking with, she does indeed make the tall one in white look like a vulture's lunch. And that might be she in the misty distance right now. Spill your drink, sir? Let me mop that little bit right up."

Sam looked north up the beach. The reflections disoriented him. Then he saw the figure which might be Barbara Messenger. It looked like her good, swinging stride. White shorts and yellow halter top. A man's ragged old straw hat from the Nassau market.

He left money on the bar and went to meet her. Her smile was vivid with welcome under the shade of her straw brim.

"Hi, Sam! You get all your laps in?"

"Slowly, slowly. That's the way I'm getting back into shape. Very very slowly."

"You look pretty solid."

"Pure deception." He fell into stride with her. They walked barefoot on the damp hard sand. Sandpipers skittered ahead of them, took off, circled wide across the water to land behind them and continue their endless hungry hunting. Her yellow canvas beach bag was slung over a brown shoulder by its drawstring of heavy cotton rope strung through brass grommets. They walked south, past other motels, and into an area of newly killed fish washed up on shore, an area where the faint acridity of red tide tickled their throats. The beach was almost empty of people.

She stopped and bent over to look more closely at a very large mullet, recently arrived, shiny and wet, and very dead. "Not a mark on him," she said.

"Paralysis. The dead bodies of the red tide organism give off a substance that paralyzes the gills."

"It seems like such a waste."

"It could be some kind of a cycle we don't yet understand. A few million tons of fish die along the coast and float in on the tide into the estuaries and get tossed up into the mangrove roots. They lodge there and nourish the mangroves. The mangrove is the basis of the whole marine food chain. Red tide kills the predators in the bays and estuaries so that billions of minnows and bait-fish live to grow up. A few years after a big red tide, fishing is great. And it would be a hell of a lot better if man didn't bulldoze the mangroves out and put in seawalls for the storms to undermine and knock down."

As they walked on she gave him a mocking look. "An engineer talking ecology?"

"I live in the world. I'm a pragmatist. Do this, and that happens. Do that, and this happens. Complex equations and interrelationships. If we were doing things right, the seas wouldn't be turning rancid, and the air would never get to a hundred thousand particles per cubic centimeter."

They walked on until they came to the vacant land with the big fading signs advertising it for sale as an ideal place for a motel complex. There had been a stand of giant Australian pines on the seaward side of the lot, and a storm some years ago had taken a lot of them down. Water and sand and sun had bleached the wood almost white. They sat on a trunk in the shade of the remaining trees, where they had sat before, and she took the folder out of her bag and handed it to him.

"That finishes it?" he asked.

"The final eleven pages," she said, handing him her pen.

He used the folder as a writing surface braced against his thigh. He had learned to concentrate completely in a lot of the noisy places of the world, amid many distractions, but it took a special effort to block her out of his awareness and focus exclusively on the words he had written and which she had typed.

"Didn't I have hydrokinetical here?"

"Let me see. Yes. You are using it as an adjective, and it sounds redundant, so I made it hydrokinetic. I can change it back."

"No. This is fine. I like it better."

He made extensive alterations on two of the pages and minor changes on one other page, all in the interest of clarity. She looked at the changes, then put the folder and the pen back into the beach bag.

"I found a pretty good place," she said. "It's called Insta-Print. They can reduce the charts to eight and a half by eleven, no problem. And they can do the binding too. They showed me samples. Any hang-ups about color?"

"Whatever you choose is fine."

"Do you want to sign every copy?"

"I think it would be best to do it that way."

"Lee thinks so too. Well, if I can get it to Insta-Print before noon Friday, tomorrow, they'll have it all ready by next Tuesday afternoon. That's the . . ."

"Thirteenth."

"And then we can drop it on the world, Sam."

"Just like dropping a piece of lint into a snowbank. Terrific impact."

She had the old hat off. She spun it around her finger and frowned at the marine horizon. She has such a look of lovely vitality in that bright shade, he thought. That strong throat, the good shoulders, the limber tan of midriff, the way that dark blond hair springs from the scalp like fine gold wire.

"They won't listen?"

"Barbara, let's say one person listens—aside from you and your husband and Gus—and that person gets out of Golden Sands in time, when a storm is coming, and gets to safe ground, *only* because Gus got nervous and got Mr. Messenger to finance a study, and Mr. Messenger decided to let the residents know."

"You mean is that enough return on the investment? Come on! You're getting into kid games. If I push this button I get ten thousand dollars and ten thousand Bulgarians die. Do I push it or not? Okay, a life is valuable. Saving a life is a useful thing to do. But dropping lint into the snow doesn't turn me on very much."

"You want a world view, historical perspective and so on?"

"Try me."

"Suppose a hurricane does exactly what I say it can and probably will do. It is still a ripple. A little readjustment of the surface of the earth. Okay? Now try to comprehend what a major adjustment might be. Go to north Florida or to Louisiana, and dig a hole four miles straight down. Four miles! And at the bottom of the hole you might find hydrocarbons, and they would be the result of life forms of the past: forests, animals, marine creatures. Okay? Now try to comprehend the forces involved, the fantastic upheavals plus the length of time involved to put living things *four miles* below what we recognize at this moment as the surface of the earth."

Her gray eyes were wide and she wore a dazed expression. "Good heavens, Sam!" she said faintly.

"Drive down a dirt road squashing frogs, and it is a hell of a serious matter for the frogs. But if they wrote up a report and circulated it, saying that this was a dirt road and cars used it, and regardless of how delicious the mud puddles, they better hop the hell off it, how many would leave?"

She laughed. "You are some variety of strange, sir."

"And you are some variation of lovely."

Her face went blank. "No," she said. She stood up and put the hat on and slung the bag over her shoulder.

He stood up and moved in front of her when she tried to turn away from him. He did not touch her. He said, "You said that the last time. No. Like that. One word. I take one hell of a lot of pleasure in your company. I think you like being with me. I like to watch you laugh. I like looking at you. I go past a certain line one tenth of an inch, and that's what I get. No. Can you embellish that refusal just a little bit?"

She stepped around him and started back. He caught up and walked in stride with her.

"Embellish?" she said. She glanced at him with a brief smile. "My surface has been readjusted, Sam. If you dug down through my crust and went down four miles, you would find no evidence of any past life forms at all. I am a dead lady, floating in space. What there is left of me, Lee rescued. So what there is of me, he owns."

"I don't want to dispute the ownership."

"So keep it impersonal."

"Even though we are both aware that it *is* personal, Barbara?"

"Oh? Are we?"

"Come *on!* Why are you so defensive?"

She touched his arm so that he turned and faced her as she stopped, looking up at him from under the ragged hat. Her eyes were narrow, the pupils small with the brightness of the beach. "No games," she said. "Believe me, no games. I took a little bit more than I could endure, and that was some time ago. It broke me, Sam. I am placing no more bets on the table. I won't talk about it, and I won't explain anything. Think what you like. Imagine what you please. I couldn't give less of a damn, really. What's left of me is totally *totally* committed to the old man who saved me."

"But I told you I don't want to—"

"But I might want to, if I could afford to let go. And I could go crazy too, like I was before. I'll call you when the reports are ready for signature."

She set off at a fast pace. He started to follow her and then slowed down. He strolled along, following her footsteps in the damp sand. She had a high arch, a long slender foot. The tide was moving in again. When he came to the place where her footsteps had been washed away, he looked up and discovered he was almost opposite the Islander.

On Thursday, August eighth, at noon, the tropical disturbance appeared on the satellite photographs as a poorly organized cloud mass with narrow bands of high cirrus clouds radiating toward the west and north. The center of the main cloud body was roughly positioned at 7 degrees north, 25 degrees west. The motor vessel *Mabel Warwick,* Captain R. F. Jackson commanding, en route from Porto Salazar, Angola, to Hartlepool, sent in a radio report of heavy rains and some sharp and significant variations in barometric pressures. These were confirmed later in the day by reports from the steamship *Esso Ulidia,* Captain K. Mackenzie commanding, en route from Ra's Tannurah to Milford Haven, and the steamship *Botany*

Bay, Captain R. A. Wilson commanding, en route Fremantle to Genoa.

At Miami a composite chart was prepared showing the position, track and speed of the vessels involved, along with the pressure readings and wind directions transmitted. From this they were able to say with reasonable certainty that the disturbance was proceeding almost due west at about ten miles per hour, and conditions seemed ideal for intensification from disturbance to tropical storm. Meanwhile, though within range of satellite cameras, it was beyond the reasonable limits of the search planes, those WD-3D Orion aircraft with their tons of electronic hardware aboard.

At six o'clock they received another good picture of it. The overall shape was more circular. It was at 7 degrees north, 27 west. Speed and direction confirmed. Intensification expected. Feeder bands extended out from the storm in long squall lines.

The Bermuda high was positioned well south, which lessened the chance of the storm's curving northward in the Atlantic, if it became a mature hurricane. The Bermuda high would interpose, and it would probably move toward the Caribbean.

If the storm matured it would become that most dreaded of all hurricanes, one of the great Cape Verde hurricanes of August.

30

WHEN LYNN SIMMINS, the Colonel's daughter, answered the door at Apartment 1-G on Friday morning she was surprised to see Julian Higbee standing there.

"Well! We'd given up on you, Julian. Especially since you have reverted to your old self around here."

"Do you want me to look at the problem or don't you?"

"At least your manners are as bad as they used to be," she said. "Come on in." She led the way, suddenly all too conscious of how brief and tight her old maroon leotard was, and how damp she was from the exertion of the strenuous part of her yoga routine.

She led him to the bathroom and stood aside. Julian took two steps into the bathroom and saw it and stopped, in awe. The crack extended the length of the tub, angled up the wall and disappeared into a ceiling corner. At its widest point, along the tub, it was almost a full inch wide.

"*That* is some kind of *crack!*" he said.

"The colonel has often made mention of it."

He looked at her. "You tell your father he shouldn't expect to get anywhere yelling at me." He took a pencil flashlight out of his pocket and leaned over the tub and looked into the crack. It got narrower as it deepened.

"I guess something shifted."

"The colonel seems to think your crummy building is collapsing."

"My building? Anyway, what should be done, this here tile row can come off and a good tile man can run a couple of new rows and cover this up. The other part can be filled and sanded down and repainted."

"When can you get to it?"

"Me? I don't do that kind of work. Your father has to go get somebody to do it. And they make a contract and somebody fixes it and he pays them."

"You're kidding!"

"I'm not kidding. He's been here over a year, right? He and Mrs. Simmins moved in in July last year. There's a year on structure. The year was up last month."

"He'll be absolutely livid."

"That man is always livid. He's always bitching about something or other. Tell him and duck."

She smiled. "The colonel has a short fuse."

"The apartments on this floor are kind of small for three people."

"We manage. They didn't plan on my living here, exactly."

"You going to keep on living here?"

"What business is it of yours?"

"Well, hell, call it a friendly interest, that's all. I mean the building is full of old folks except for some of the renters. You're close to the same age as me and Lorrie. Playing tennis and swimming and all . . . it's nice to have you around."

She suddenly understood. As a physical type he did not appeal to her. And she did not care for his greasy, insinuating smile.

"So you saw them take off, Julian?"

"Huh? Who? What do you mean?"

"The colonel and his lady, with overnight luggage. You had no intention of ever coming up here to look at a crack in the bathroom wall because you had no intention of ever doing anything about it anyway."

"I was just—"

"You were just wondering if I was good for a quick jump. You've been looking at it long enough and hard enough. I'm climbing out of the pool and there you are, goggling and panting. Jesus, Higbee! I finish a long rally and go back to serve and there you are. Now you're trying to stare holes through my leotard. When you get this hard up, why don't you go jack off?"

He balled a big fist and moved closer. "You bitch!"

She realized coldly, without terror, that it would be in character for him to pop her on the side of the jaw, knock her semiconscious, tumble her onto the bed in the nearby bedroom and shuck her out of her single garment. She could see by his expression, by the way he swallowed and licked his lips and slowly shifted his weight, that he was capable of it, and was thinking about it, and soon would be beyond control.

There was always the woman's weapon, too seldom used. Time now to use it. She feinted right, then ducked and streaked left, under his big arm, as he reached for her. She went at top speed down the short hallway and into the living room, hearing him pounding along behind her. She snatched the apartment door open and let out the first of her deafening, throat-ripping, ear-shattering screams. She ran out into the heat of the open walkway over the parking area and screamed again. She turned with her back against the concrete railing and screamed for the third time. "No!" he was yelling. "No! Don't! Please!"

She filled her lungs and smiled at him and let out the best one of all, a scream to stop birds in flight, shatter wineglasses, startle cars into the ditch. The spry gray Greggs, Francine and Rolph, came darting out of 1-A at the far end of the building and came trotting toward the terrible sound. Mrs. Boford Taller popped out of the next-door apartment, swollen with indignation and disapproval.

Gus Garver came out of 1-C and edged past Mrs. Taller. Julian was in stasis, his big hands yearning to grab Lynn Simmins by the pretty throat, and his legs itching to run away from that dreadful sound she was making.

Gus sighed and kicked Julian in the side of the knee. Julian gave a great start and went toward the stairs, in a hobbling run.

"You okay?" he said.

She was annoyed to find out she had damaged her throat. Her speaking voice was very husky. "Never laid a glove on me, Gus."

"Watch out for that one."

"I don't think he'll be back. Anyway, don't worry about me. I haven't been exactly underexposed to freaks."

"Then you should have known enough to keep running."

"I should have. Right. And thanks."

"You going to prefer charges?"

"I don't want to upset my folks. I've upset them enough the last few years."

"Your decision," Gus said, and went back home.

Lynn went back in and locked the door. In a few minutes the phone rang. "Lorrie Higbee speaking, Miss

Simmins. Julian says that you misunderstood what he was trying to do."

"Possibly."

"He said he was trying to be pleasant and you took it the wrong way."

"Well, Mrs. Higbee, we had a difference of opinion. He wanted to screw me and I didn't want him to. So he thought he'd take his shot anyway. He grabbed and missed and I ran and screamed."

"Oh."

"Sorry. I plan to forget the whole thing."

"I'm . . . glad you told me."

"It isn't any of my business. I know that. I don't want to offend you, Lorrie, but if he was my husband, I'd make him go get help somehow. He's got a bad problem."

"I . . . I know."

"Hey, I didn't mean to make you cry."

"It's okay," she said, and hung up.

Lynn took the damp leotard off and took a quick shower and put on a robe. As she rinsed out the leotard she kept remembering the shocked horror on Julian's face as he tried to get her to stop screaming. He could not think of anything except how to turn off that horrible noise. If you are going to scream, girl, stay out of reach while you do so.

After she hung up the leotard and had stretched out on her bed, she giggled from time to time as she thought of Julian's terror. In a little while she was surprised to discover that the muffled snickering had turned into sobs of about the same intensity. Sobbing made her remember that sad funny little old man who had thrown the tennis ball way over her head out of reach and then had started crying when she had been cross with him. Barker? His wife was sick.

She could be grateful to Julian Higbee for one thing. He had stirred her up. She had looked around and looked at herself, and realized it was time to go. What do you do when you are twenty-nine and reasonably attractive, fairly well educated, and know all the social moves, and never lasted more than three months in any job you tried to do? Well, you take things in order. Leaving comes first, and then the job comes out of necessity.

What are you prepared to do, Ms. Simmins? While growing up I lived in Germany, Hawaii, Panama, Japan, Guam and South Korea. After I quit college I roamed around and worked as a dishwasher, fruit picker, receptionist, barmaid, waitress, car rental agent, go-go girl, photographer's model, magician's assistant, swimming teacher, revolutionary, vagabond, part-time junkie, pollster, taxi driver, short-order cook, motel maid, car parker, hitchhiker, smuggler, checkroom girl, cigarette girl, thief, housekeeper and free-lance companion.

In every position I held, dear sir, I left a little piece of that dear girl once known as Lovely Lynn Simmins, and now there is not a hell of a lot of me left. However, on balance, there is a little too much left to permit it to be plundered by that randy son of a bitch of a resident manager, thank you kindly for your attention.

After his long interview with Dr. Dromb about his prognosis for Thelma, Jack Mensenkott went back to Golden Sands, fixed himself a sandwich, changed and drove back to Martin's Marina on Fiddler Key, close to the approach to the north bridge leading over to the city.

Leroy Martin was sitting behind his desk in the small office next to the showroom, wearing his orange baseball cap. Mensenkott had never seen the man without a hat on.

Leroy said, "You better set and have some coffee, Jack. The kid has got three to take off the rack and gas before he gets to yours. Like I keep telling you, all you got to do is phone ahead and we can have her all set for you."

"I wasn't in a rush," Mensenkott said. After he poured his coffee he looked out the big window to where a big redheaded young man was running the fork lift, reaching up to take a boat down out of the third level of the open steel rack of the in-and-out marina.

Leroy Martin pushed the button on the base of the microphone on his desk and said, "Joey?"

The redhead turned and looked toward the office when the amplified voice filled the area.

"After you get them three, get Mr. Mensenkott's *Hustler* off of twelve-two." He raised an eyebrow at Jack. "Gas?" Jack shook his head no. "Just set it in the water, Joey."

Martin leaned back and said, "How's the missus coming along?"

"Not so good. She had a setback and I had to take her in, and Dr. Dromb put her back in the hospital."

"Sorry to hear that."

"I can't see her until tonight, so I thought I might as well go fishing."

"Nothing like it to keep your mind off your troubles. They say this Dromb is pretty good."

"I wish he was more definite."

"I guess with nervous problems they can't get too definite. Like I was telling you before, after the last kid left the nest and my old lady got those spells, every place I took her, they loaded her up with Valium and Librium and so on. She got so she could damn near fall asleep standing up."

"It has something to do with the way they cleared off that Silverthorn property. Now he thinks the reason she has . . . gotten strange again is because she found out they are not going to build anything there anyway. The dredge is gone. All plans are suspended, and so it was all for nothing, all that destruction. That got to her."

Leroy Martin frowned. "Funny it got to mean so much to her. I mean it was just jungly growth there and some mangrove and mud flats. Full of red bugs and mosquitoes."

"The ecologists say that is a very productive kind of waterfront."

Martin laughed. "Hey, you bet your sweet ass it is. Remember, I was born down here, more years ago than I'm going to admit. And when I was a little kid in the summertime, you could swang a quart can and catch you two quarts of mosquitoes." He sighed, and sobered, and said, "Of course back then you could walk across the bay on the backs of the mullets, we had schools of them so thick."

"It does seem a waste to clear it off and then drop the project."

"Me, I wouldn't worry too much about that Marty Liss dropping any kind of project. You can bet he's got something in mind to do himself some good. Chances are he's just squeezing out some kind of weak sister partner, scaring him out. Don't you worry. They'll build something on that land. It won't set empty. Key land is too valuable for that. People thought I was crazy buying that extra land south of here fifteen years ago, and right now I'd give an arm if I'd bought twice what I did. I'd put up more racks in a minute."

Mensenkott looked out the window and saw the fork lift trundling toward the launching area, carrying the *Hustler* between its lowered arms. It was a white Cobia with blue trim, one-fifty stern drive, center pedestal, bait well, canting platform, fighting chair.

"Where would you head today if you were me?" Jack asked.

"I was monitoring Channel Thirteen a while ago, and what looks best to me, you go north up the bay all the way past Seagrape Key and go out Big Crab Pass—after you stop and get some bait at Buster's place. Save you wasting time netting. There's been a big school of blues messing around the pass, and some nice cobia out around the sea buoy. You ought to do just fine today."

Minutes later Mensenkott, standing at the wheel at the center pedestal of the *Hustler*, made a fast white arc and cut through the center span of the north bridge between Fiddler Key and the mainland, trying to clear his mind of Dromb's advice. Thelma, he said, is emotionally unemployed. Nobody depends upon her. Nothing depends upon her. She is in a geriatric community. Sell out, buy her a country place. She can raise vegetables, flowers, dogs, rabbits, children. . . .

Jack Mensenkott glanced up at the bridge as he went under. Two tanned girls sitting on a toolbox in the bed of a pickup truck waved at him and he waved back. He was conscious of how he looked piloting his fast and gleaming boat on this lovely day. Having found paradise, only a fool would move away.

And he had never caught a really good cobia. Not yet.

At six o'clock on Friday, the ninth of August, the decision was made by the Director of the National Hurricane Center at Miami to give tropical storm status to the disturbance in the eastern Atlantic and, because it was now a fair assumption that its winds were in excess of the required thirty-nine miles an hour, to designate it as Ella, the fifth on the list of approved names for this hurricane season.

Though the tropical storm still lacked the total organization seen in the structure of large hurricanes, some significant reports had been relayed from coastal radio stations as received by vessels of the British Volunteer Observing Fleet. There were eight vessels near enough to the tropical storm so that their observations, transmitted in code as required every six hours, permitted the extrapolation of a constant wind speed in the northeast quadrant of Ella of from forty to forty-two nautical miles per hour, and increasing.

By satellite photograph interpretation, personnel at the Center placed the position of Ella at eighteen hundred hours EDST at 10 degrees north, 34 west. She had picked up her great gray skirts and hustled, making the same approximate time as a reasonably fast container ship. The cloud mass covered a larger area. Ella was drawing a line toward the Lesser Antilles, toward the Windward Islands, toward Barbados—toward the frail island barrier between the Atlantic Ocean and the Caribbean Sea.

As the storm moved, gathering mass and tempo, it sent great rollers out ahead, moving across the glassy sea at four times its own speed. These swells had already reached the far islands. Normal cadence of the Atlantic waves breaking on these shores is eight per minute. This change in the constant, unremarkable sound of the sea is the ancient alert for all living things. The oily waves lift high and come racing in, and they turn, tumble, thud against reef and rock and sand like a great slow drum.

The fiddler crabs move inland in small brown torrents, the larger claw held on high. The seabirds circle nervously, crying out, getting ready to head away from the oncoming drop in pressure. Fish turn ravenous, storing food against the tumbled days ahead. Primitive man looks at the streamers in the sky, hears the slow boom of the surf and feels an uneasy dread.

The slow waves thumped against Barbuda, against Saint Kitts, Antigua, Grand Terre, Dominica, Martinique, Saint Lucia, Saint Vincent, Grenada, Tobago. The waves rolled through Guadeloupe Passage, Dominica Channel, Saint Lucia Channel, Saint Vincent Passage. Old men began to work their fishing boats up the inlets, using the high tides to get them as far up as possible, and then making them fast to the old trunks and roots which had lived through all the storms of lifetimes. Small boats were sunk in deep protected coves and filled with even more rocks after they were sunk. Island families began to store water, food, candles. Roofs were fixed. Sheds were tied down. Loose boards were gathered and stowed safely away.

The wind and rain had not yet begun along those barrier islands. The radios had not yet broadcast warnings to them. But people could see the *hurakán* bands in the sky and hear the slow sea, and it quickened pulses, created a bowel flutter of queasy anticipation. The more primitive the island area, the more practiced and practical were the preparations, and the more suitable the structures to the great force oncoming.

The curving chain of islands from South America toward the Bahama reefs is the tips of ancient volcanoes which once erupted along that fault line. Hurricanes have slammed into these islands for thousands of years. Their mountain jungles are impenetrable due to the tangled overgrown blowdowns of previous storms. Few trees have the time and luck to grow tall on the exposed hills. The huge hurricane rains have gullied the slopes of the mountains, washing deep into the limestone and volcanic rock. Where the trees are so well rooted that great winds do not topple them, those same winds of over a hundred miles an hour will peel the bark off the trunks and the trees will die, turning the color of hard dull silver, then rotting and being devoured by the jungle insects.

Uncounted thousands have died on these islands in the great winds and in the flooding surge of the hurricane tides.

Howard D. Elbright, the retired chemist from 4-C, got up before dawn on Saturday without waking Edie, dressed in a long-sleeved shirt and long pants, ate two slightly stale sugar doughnuts, drank some reheated coffee, sprayed repellant on all exposed areas, gathered up his gear and crept out, hoping not to be intercepted this time by one of Brooks Ames's volunteer army. Once one of them had come silently up behind him and yelled *Halt!* and Howard had dropped his tackle box and spilled hooks, lures, leaders and sinkers all over the walk just outside the exit to the parking lot.

By the time the east began to gray, he was standing on the newly formed shoreline of the bay, far out on the curving finger of land the dredge and draglines had created where the oyster bars used to be, and with the skill learned over the past three months, he was casting a brand new lure as far out toward the channel as he could manage. Mosquitoes whined around his ears, looking for an unsprayed place on which to feast.

The lure was six inches long and an inch in diameter, of plastic colored purple, orange, white and vivid green, in broad stripes. There was a transparent scoop on the front of it, three sets of gang hooks dangling underneath and several kinds of rotors and propellers at the bow and in the stern.

The old man at Discount Tackle had said, "This here thang is called an Original Wobblethrasher, and it is guaran-goddam-teed to git you a snook if you use it right. The first thing to do right is larn how to say snook. You see it rhymes with look, not with duke. There's damn fools come down here thinking that to rhyme it with duke makes them sound more like authentical Florida, but it has damn well always been snook like goes with look. What you got to do with this, you got to get out there right about dawn, a little before, and you heave this Original Wobblethrasher way to hell out and you get it to make just as much noise as you can when you bring it back in. Make this sucker bang around out there, then leave it set quiet a few seckints, then smash it around some more. The old he-snook, all that racket gets him irritated, and pretty soon, you do it just right, he'll come on up and he'll try to snap it right in half to shut it up. That comes to three dollar twenty-eight with the tax."

"I'll try it. I guess a Florida cracker should know."

"Cracker? Me? Shit, mister, I come down here from Harrisburg, Indiana, seventeen years ago and I wisht every year I'd stayed home. Lots of luck."

What had sounded plausible in the tackle store seemed absurd in actual practice. Certainly only an idiot fish would bite upon a gaudy piece of mechanical junk like that. He could see and hear the nuisance it was creating out on the dark silence of the bay. Yet he hated to admit that three dollar twenty-eight with the tax had gone for something that now seemed like a laborious practical joke. Whad you say you catch him on, Elbright? Why, I used my Original Wobblethrasher, of course! His wrist was beginning to tire from working the heavy lure. The sky was pink in the east. His doughnuts were not digesting. He kept worrying about money. He missed the protective jungle at his back, and the sense of being isolated from the condominium culture. He kept wondering lately why they had made such a mandatory rule in the corporation about retirement. People doing applied research in chemistry could be all through at forty or at eighty. When your head quit, it was time to quit. If it hadn't quit, you were wasted when they retired you. He kept wondering how some of the unfinished projects were going. Those damned kids were probably messing them up, missing the obvious, goofing off, and—

A silvery something as long as his leg and as big around as his thigh came up under the Original Wobblethrasher and took it up, up and up, silhouetted against the pink light, and came down like a horse falling overboard. And the spinning reel made a whining screaming sound as something went scooting eastward.

"My God," Howard whispered. "My God!"

He knew that the monster was going to take out all his line and keep right on going. He kept the tip up, kept the pressure on. The line stopped going out. He got some of it back in, and the monster then headed south, along the shoreline, and Howard followed it, blundering in and out of the shallows, stumbling and worrying.

By the time all of the rosy sun was above the horizon, gleaming on the banks, hotels and condominiums of waterfront Athens, the big silver fish lay in the shallows at Howard's feet, gills working, tail beating languidly. It had huge flat shiny eyes, a long snout, undershot jaw, concave nose and a narrow line, black against silver, from gills to tail on each side.

He had his little scale in his tackle box. He gently put the blunt hook under the beast's chin and lifted it up. Almost but not quite thirty-two pounds. The terminal gang hook of the Wobblethrasher was in the corner of the fish's mouth. He studied the situation, and then, with his pliers, he cut off the two of the three hooks which were through the flesh of the fish. He could install a new gang hook on the plug. The sunlight was getting bright and hot. He noticed that while maneuvering the fish, he had gotten some sand and shell fragments on the snook's big flat eye. He picked the beast up and took a couple of steps into the water and lowered the fish and swashed its head back and forth to wash the grit off the eye and the silver scales. The fish made a shuddering motion. The big flat tail waved weakly, and the gills worked as the fish gulped.

Howard looked over toward the city, his face pinched into a strange scowl. "Oh, shit," he said. "Oh, shit anyway," he said, and straightened up, looking down at the beast. It rolled onto its side and almost went belly up, but regained stability with a smack of its tail on the water. It turned laboriously, like a newly crippled person working a wheelchair, and moved slowly slowly out toward the deeps, and in moments he could not see it.

Well, that is it with the fishing, he thought. Another bunch of toys for the back closet of my mind. And what am I offered for this Original Wobblethrasher upon which the Honorable Howard E. Elbright, now deceased, caught a great snook on a Saturday morning in an August long long ago? Caught it and then released it, much to his own confusion, because in his heart of hearts, the Honorable Howard D. Elbright wanted to eat that fish. He wanted Edie to stuff it with rice and tomatoes and green peppers and bake it and serve it up.

As he walked back toward Golden Sands, torn sneakers squelching in time to his stride, he realized that if they had not brought in the yellow machines and killed everything on those fourteen acres, he would not have released the snook. He could not properly determine the cause-and-effect equation at work, but knew it was so.

By ten o'clock on Saturday morning, retired Professor Roger Jeffrey had reached the second checkpoint of the Summer Invitational Century. As a member of the Route Committee of the Athens Cycle League he had helped lay out the hundred-mile course which began and ended in the big empty parking lot of Kennedy High School. The kids at the checkpoint had parked the van in the shade. They grinned and waved him on. Jeffrey squinted off into the heat waver on the long flat stretch of county road and could see, at least a mile ahead, the bright clothing of the pack of young people who had started out at much too fast a pace. He had gained a little on them, and as the day wore on he knew he would gain more. A lot of them would never finish, taken out by cramps, exhaustion, or bad falls.

This was the first real test of the machine he had purchased with the check from Mrs. Brasser. He felt a pang of guilt when he remembered how he had extorted eight hundred and twenty-five dollars from the wretched woman. She had been too obviously afraid of his reporting her destruction of the Voyageur. The guilt feeling had lessened with her death, and since the visit from one Frederick Brasser, a vulgar lout who became almost insulting in his demands to know why his mother had written him a check in that amount, the guilt was almost undetectable.

The new machine was lovely. A Panasonic Touring Deluxe in a beautiful deep wine red, with a mirror finish. Shimano Dura-Ace cotterless alloy cranks, alloy quick-release hubs, pedals, and Oro freewheel. A Shimano Crane GS rear derailleur, and Titlist front gear wheel. Alloy micro-adjusting seat post, Dia-Compe brakes, Gran Compe alloy stem with recessed bolt and alloy drop bars. By the time the dealer had altered the basic machine to fit the professor's requirements, the total cost came to six hundred and thirty-five. The only thing old on it was the comfortable leather seat rescued from the shattered Voyageur.

He had begun to sweat heavily in the morning heat. Without breaking his cadence or speed, he took two salt tablets with several swallows of water from his water bottle, took the terrycloth pad from under his Bell helmet, soaked it with water once again and shoved it back under the helmet. Within ten minutes he was less conscious of the heat. Maurine had told him quite a few times that he was an old fool to do a century in Florida in August. He told her he was quite competent to take care of himself. He told her he had been doing it for seventy-one years and planned to keep on indefinitely. He told her she was a tottery baleful old woman married to a spry dirty old man, and she could spend Saturday in the cool gloom watching that tube until her brain turned to fish paste if she chose, but he was going to be on the open road, with the wind in his hair, under the broad blue of God's sky.

"Hey, Prof!"

The loud voice startled him. He had not heard the bike

coming up beside him. "Hello, Rich." Rich coached track at Kennedy and was perhaps the best and most durable bicyclist in the League.

"Aren't you pouring it on a little heavy for this kind of heat?"

"Not so far."

"Don't you push it too much, hear? Hey, you got the padded tape, I see. How's it working?"

"Great. No numb hands."

"The whole machine looks great, Prof. Fits you great. How much you carrying in those gumwalls?"

"Eighty-five."

"Should be about right."

They came upon a young man and woman at the side of the road. He was sitting down, wearing an agonized expression. She was kneading and knuckling the calf muscles of his right leg

"See you later," Rich said and braked and turned off to help the pair.

Cramps would take some of them all the way out, and slow down some of the others. The toes of his right foot felt odd. He reached down and loosened the strap on the leather-covered clip, then pulled the plastic knob and tightened it again, but not as much as before. He wiggled his toes while stroking and in a little while they were normal again.

From time to time he shifted his position on the handlebars. He counted his cadence against the sweep second hand on his watch and found that he was precisely on sixty-five, right where he should be. At this gear ratio, he knew from his memorized chart that he should be making 20.5 miles per hour. His record century time was six hours seven minutes, or 6.116 hours. That translated to an average speed of 16.35 miles per hour. If he *really* wanted to be an old fool, he would try to best his previous time. To best it in this heat would mean riding right through the customary rest stop at the fifty-mile mark.

A small pain appeared in his left knee and began to sharpen with each stroke. He experimented, changing slightly the angle of his foot against the rat-trap pedal. He did not like cleats because they ruled out these small adjustments. The pain diminished and went away, as did his anxiety.

Ahead the pack was closer, more visible. The road went between fenced ranchlands. Lazy cattle, drowsing in the heat, would lift their heads sharply, stare at the lead pack, then wheel and go thundering across the pastureland. He wanted to be the lead machine, the one to startle the cattle. The cattle were used to cars and trucks, took them for granted, were startled out of their bovine wits by quiet gleaming wheels hissing down upon them.

Sweat ran into his left eye and he toweled it away. There were a lot more machines behind him than ahead of him, he knew. One hundred and thirty-one starters. And maybe fifteen ahead of him. All young. Ah, youth, that precious commodity always wasted on the young.

A giant beetle bounced off his lips, stinging him and making his eyes water.

Time? Ten forty. Breathe deeply. The muscles need the oxygen. Suck it in. Just air. No beetles.

The century, he thought. A cheap analogy for life. One of those tiresome comparisons Hawkinson was probably still pulling back there in some classroom. Little pains happen. You adjust. A lot of it is dull stuff indeed, but you make the effort. Man and machine become one organism, stroking away, correcting, favoring, compensating, and trying to enjoy the little moments of magic that come along. At the end of it, you get off the bike, or fall off, or are pushed off, and that is that. Peggy Brasser did not get off, or fall off, or get pushed off. She rode into a wall. Or over a cliff.

Golden Sands was full of people riding their private machines to God knows where. All upset now. Committees and protests and confrontations. Any man who has spent most of his life on a faculty cannot get very concerned about committees and protests and confrontations. You do that when you are young—instructor or assistant professor. In time you learn that if you make the right-sounding excuses at the right time, all the others will be out there in front of you, driving off the wild animals, killing snakes, draining the swamps. Those whose interests are the same as yours will usually do all the work necessary to protect yours as well as their own. Can't help doing so. When their job is done, thank them with great earnestness and sincerity, and that will ready them to go out and do the chores the next time too.

He caught up with the next straggler from the group ahead. A fat girl. One of the little group of housewives who had joined the League. Bright red straining face, mouth agape. She had a heavy machine, an old black Raleigh three-speed. He could hear her breathing.

"Take a break in the shade," he called to her. She seemed not to hear him. A little while later he looked back for her and she was not there. He thought she had sought the shade of one of the infrequent pine trees, and then saw her far back, flattened on the road, the bike down nearby. He missed one stroke as he debated turning back, then realized how soon the others would be along. And in a few more minutes he would be among the pack of leaders. He counted them. Eleven machines. And the professor makes one dozen. Some of them were singing. Good, he thought. Takes a lot of good breath to sing. About six miles to the halfway point, where we turn south. They'll all stop. Get off there and fill the water bottles. Keep moving around. Get back on. Leave as inconspicuously as possible.

Gus Garver headed north along Beach Drive to the north bridge, easing his gray Toyota wagon along in the slow traffic tempo of a summer Saturday. The little wind and rain storm in the night had washed away a lot of the dead fish, covered others with sand, moved the floaters south. The air was fresh and clean, and the summer season people thronged the beaches, along with the inland locals.

The traffic clotted and stopped, and Gus, by force of long habit, went into his stomach exercise, putting the tough heels of his hands on his thighs, pushing down hard, holding the tension until arms, thighs and belly muscles fluttered. A little family threaded their way between the cars, heading for the beach: a tall stringy knuckly young man with a vacuous adenoidal expression, face and neck and arms to above the elbow deep brown from outdoor labor, the rest of his upper torso fish-belly white turning pink with the first blush of sunburn; a two-hundred-pound young woman in a flowered cotton beach robe, all of a soft spilling and joggling and wobbling of self-indulgent flesh with each step, her features tiny and delicate in the middle of her great moon face, her mouth a righteous little possessive red rosebud as she clutched the arm of her husband with her baby-fat hand; four kids of indeterminate sex, all towheads from three to seven, the smallest smeared with food, the eldest belting a smaller one, another one yelling with the desolation of heartbreak. They carried their food and their toys and their private conviction that things could have been a lot better, with a little more luck.

Traffic began moving again, and thinned out abruptly after he crossed the bridge to the mainland. At the Crestwood Nursing Home he found an empty slot in the herringbone parking area and went in and up the stairs to be certain Carolyn was all right. She was clean and fresh and napping, so he went down to the offices and let himself into Oscar Castor's private office with the key Oscar had given him.

There was nothing of great interest in the "in" basket containing items for his attention. One note from Castor, clipped to inventory sheets, was gratifying. It said, "Gus, I couldn't really believe this could happen. But you were right. Incoming shipments of supplies are consistently short count or short weight by ten to fifteen percent. It has been double checked. That would be ten to twelve thousand a year down the drain. I'm putting in claim forms for the current shipments, but there's no way to recover what was lost before last month."

Gus sighed. In forty or fifty more years he might turn Oscar Castor into an administrator. The man was a fussbudget who consistently fussed about the wrong things. He would diddle around with ten minutes of low-pay overtime, trying to save a dime here and a dime there, while dollars ran out of the stock-room door.

He studied the bids which had come in on interior painting. They were grotesque. Probably the way to go was see if the Palm County Retirement Home had any old men painters in there who needed therapy. Get Maintenance to do the ladder work, and the old men could paint the low places. Make them feel useful and needed.

Suddenly he laughed out loud at himself. Just like I'm making myself feel useful and needed around here. Old fart. Old hoss getting restless in the barn.

He scrawled a few notes to Castor and knew he'd have a chance on Monday to go over them with the man. Castor had been very edgy and reluctant at first, until Gus had saved the man a few dollars on his budget. That was the big problem. Work inside the budget and still provide better care and attention.

He went back up to Carolyn's room. She looked at him, and the good side of her face lifted in her half smile, and she made the gluey sound of her welcome to him and tried to tell him something about the television. He looked at it and saw that the picture was rolling. He adjusted the vertical hold and it made her happy. It was a Japanese movie. People in pajamas were sucking air between their teeth and swinging two-handed swords.

He sat beside her and watched the movie and held her left hand. When he had been with her a half hour or so, she drifted into sleep again. It was strange to him to look at her sleeping and see her familiar face, the face of the wife of the long marriage, and know that the Carrie he loved and who loved him was no longer inside that familiar skull. This was a simpler and more primitive organism. It was aware of heat, cold, hunger, discomfort. It could think only on those terms, communicate only on those terms. He had attempted many ways of trying to communicate with her on some more complicated level, codes and slates and objects, but had not been able to arouse any stir of interest. So accept this stranger, and this obligation.

A very old woman maneuvered her wheelchair into her room. Seventy pounds of wrinkles and blemishes, some tufts of thin white hair and two small bright blue eyes. She wore a stained pink robe and carried a Raggedy Ann doll on her lap.

"Sleeping her life away," the old woman said.

"How are you doing, Mrs. Dibble?"

"I'm just great. You should be calling me Ruthie like everybody."

"Ruthie, then."

"Mr. Groder finally had a visitor this morning."

"Great!"

"It was a lawyer with a paper his granddaughter-in-law wanted for him to sign."

"You wouldn't know who steals personal things from the patients, would you?"

"Sure I would."

"Who, Ruthie?"

"That would be telling."

"Aw, come on, Ruthie."

She wheeled closer, lowered her voice. "Don't you dare tell anybody I told you. It's the members of the poor woman's fambly."

"Huh?"

"They're all fighting each other about who gets what, you know what I mean, so what they do, they come prowling and sneaking in here and they take stuff to make sure it's theirs instead of it going to somebody else. I seen them get the silver bowls and the little enamel boxes my daddy brought back from China and the jade dragon and all those gold watches. That's what it is, all right. Her fambly. Don't you tell."

"Okay. I won't tell."

She laughed a very small silvery laugh, startlingly like a child's laughter. "I fooled my fambly," she said. "They were all waiting on me to pass away. Waiting and waiting, and now every friggin' one of them is in the ground. Joke's on them, you bet." She backed the chair into the doorway and said sadly, "Sleeping her life away. Rudy, damn your soul, don't you tell anybody I told you the secret. 'Bye now, Rudy."

He got up and turned the dial until he found a golf match. Carolyn slept on. He adjusted the sound until it was barely audible to him, and sat back and once again took her hand.

The lithe young men in their bright clothing struck the ball high and far, the camera following it against the blue sky, watching it come down and bounce and roll onto the green carpet. ". . . and now, here on the par-five sixteenth, he has closed the gap to just two strokes, and he has a chance to catch Nicklaus . . ."

The hand of the sleeping woman squeezed his hand twice. He wondered what images moved through the empty rooms of her mind.

". . . if he can hold second place through tomorrow's play here, he will pick up the second-place check for twenty-two thousand five hundred dollars. Al, what do you have on the fifteenth now?" "Jimmy, we've got Super-Mex studying a very difficult punch shot he'll have to make from the far right rough and under the limbs of one of those big old trees, and put it on the green, or he stands a good chance of losing a stroke to par right here. . . ."

He looked at her and wondered how it would be if she woke up and smiled and said, "Hi, honey. How long have I been asleep anyway?"

At three o'clock on Saturday afternoon, August tenth, tropical storm Ella was centered approximately at 12 degrees north, 41 degrees west, still holding course and speed, with winds approaching fifty knots. This put the storm roughly eleven hundred miles east-southeast of Barbados, or fifty-five hours away, and twenty-four hundred miles southeast of Miami, or five days away, assuming, of course, that it did not slow down or alter direction.

Warnings were sent out to all weather stations and all ships in those areas. All incoming reports were given most careful analysis at the National Hurricane Center at Miami. Long-range forecasts were made of probable high-pressure and low-pressure profiles in the path of the storm in order to estimate how any ridges or wind patterns might alter the storm track.

Toward nightfall the skies darkened over Puerto Rico and the first heavy patches of rain began to move across the islands. Throughout the Greater and Lesser Antilles, the West Indies and the Bahamas, the small boats of summertime were heading for harbor.

ON SUNDAY AFTER CHURCH Benjamin Wannover went
back to the Palm County Courthouse and was let in the
back door by one of the security people, and climbed the
rear stairs to the borrowed office on the third floor.

Mr. H. D. C. Franklin, the young assistant U.S. Attorney from Washington, was there with Wise from Tampa
and Howe from Atlanta, sitting at the long oak table
strewn with documents, talking in low voices.

Franklin said, "Hello, Mr. Wannover. Have a seat.
You'll want to wait for your attorney, I believe, your
Mr. Sender."

"Sinder. With an 'i.' Yeah, I'd rather wait." Benjie
smiled sadly and shook his head. "All this makes me feel
pretty shitty, you guys can understand that."

"Sure," said Wise.

"And there are things I'd rather see you going after."

"What does that mean?" Howe asked belligerently.

"Like this, for example. We had trouble on a good-sized
apartment in Azure Breeze. That's a Marliss Corporation
condo, out on the beach side from Golden Sands. What
happened was these people, this old couple, they had
two hundred thousand in time deposits, bringing in like
thirteen thousand a year. They had been reading the ads
in the paper about how these east coast outfits would pay
fourteen percent and put up good first mortgages on land
as security. The couple didn't have Social Security, retirement, nothing. So twenty-eight thousand looked very
damned good, and when the time deposits matured they
shifted them over, and they got two quarterly payments

and then zip. Those merciless bastards over in Hallandale were putting fifty cents' worth of land behind every fifty dollars they borrowed, and using the old Ponzi system of paying the old suckers with money from new suckers. There's a good half dozen of those outfits operating over there, stealing money from old folks directly. Shouldn't you guys be working on that kind of thing first?"

"We'll get around to it in due time," H. D. C. Franklin said. "The state has to move first on that one."

"That couple is indigent. Totally broke."

Franklin looked at his watch. "Is Sender likely to be much later than this?"

"Sinder. Morris Sinder. He should be here."

Franklin was dark and handsome, with high coloring. Rosy cheeks, red lips, and blue beard shadow. A lock of dark hair curled across his forehead. He picked up a sheaf of papers and leaned back and began to scan each sheet quickly, laying it face down as he finished.

Sinder came hurrying in. "Sorry. The damned bridge was stuck again. Hope I haven't—"

"Let's get started," Wise said.

Sinder sat down beside Benjie, saying, "I want to point out to you that my client is really not in trouble so serious that you can—"

"And I will point out to you again, Mr. Sender, that I can read these statutes and compare the law with the information we piled up *before* Mr. Wannover chose to cooperate, and I can assure you that we had every chance of tucking his ass into jail for five years and taking fifteen to twenty thousand dollars out of his pocket in fines, to say nothing of the expense of his defense in court. Now let's get to it again." He punched the forward and record keys of the tape recorder. "Mr. Wannover, have you had a chance to study the expenses incurred by the Marliss Corporation over the past six years?"

"Yes, sir."

"Have you been able to identify those payments supposedly made to County Commissioner Denniver, Justin Denniver?"

"Pretty close, sir. I wouldn't say I'm a hundred percent accurate. I would say—"

"Wait for the question," Morris Sinder said. He was a very tall man with a shaved head and a youthful face.

"We're not in front of a jury," Wise said.

"I want him to be in practice in case you people put him in front of a jury."

"Do you have a total amount and total number of payments?"

"Eight payments totaling thirty-eight thousand."

"Does that include the payment of May last?"

"Yes, sir. It includes the ten thousand dollars in May."

"What special treatment did Mr. Liss expect to receive for this money?"

"The usual thing. We put up four condos on Fiddler Key and one on Seagrape. If you crossed every i and dotted every t, you'd never get anything built. So what we were after was favorable consideration on zoning requirements, permits, setbacks, buffer strips, number of parking slots per apartment and so on. The payment was bigger for Harbour Pointe because it was going to be the biggest project we'd done, and we had to get into some no-no areas, like land clearing and dredge and fill. Let me interject, this isn't exactly a one-way street, you know. Those guys aren't dummies that sit on that commission. If they decide to get hungry there can be a lot of roadblocks in your way. It is cheaper to pay off in front so that things will run smoothly, and that's what we did."

"Who knew about this system?"

"Marty, of course. And me and Lew Traff and Cole Kimber. And probably Dru Bryne, Marty's secretary. And on the other end of it, Justin Denniver, and his wife, Molly. I wouldn't know if they told anybody. But the impression I get was that Denniver paid off two of the other commissioners. Oh, and Billy Scherbel knew. He's assistant to the county manager."

"And the county manager?" H. D. C. Franklin asked.

"Tod Moran? No. He doesn't know anything about what's going on."

"How was the money transferred?"

"A check would be made out and Lew would go downstairs to the bank and cash it, and then he would take the cash out to Denniver's house and give it to his wife. I asked him once. He said she always put it in a safe in a closet wall, a barrel job. The house is in a very private spot. Lots of plantings. A car parked there, you can't see it from the street. It's been a good safe way to do it."

"You seem to be on the verge of telling us something else about the arrangement."

"No, sir. That's all."

"Now would you identify these Xerox copies, please?"

"Uh . . . sure. These are copies of my account at Stone and Brewster, of my monthly statements for . . . the past six months."

"Is this your only account with a brokerage firm?"

"Yes, sir."

"There are some transactions here showing that you went short on Equity Mortgage Management Shares in May. You covered at various times and covered the last two hundred shares in June. Would you accept the figure of $13,126.88 as your total short-term profit on EMMS?"

"That sounds just about right. I report every source of—"

"Some of the short sale was consummated a few days before the first agreement between Mr. Grome and the Letra Corporation was signed. But you shorted more shares *after* you had knowledge of the deal Grome made with Liss, for the loan and the kickback and the imminent failure and default on Tropic Towers. That constitutes inside knowledge."

"Are you asking a question?" Sinder asked.

"I want to say something," Benjie said. "You can ask Steve Millard. When I placed the first order, I told him to keep on trying to short more. Until I said whoa."

"Do you know a floor broker named Dean Hart?"

"I think so. But some other house, isn't he?"

"Lannon Daniel and Company. Did you know that Miss Bryne has a margin account there?"

"No, I didn't know that!"

"Did you know she was shorting EMMS at the same time you were?"

"No shit! You're kidding."

"Now let's go back to ground we've covered before, if you don't mind. Let's go back to the conversations you had with Martin Liss when Lew Traff was present, regarding his report of his conversations with Sherman Grome, and what Grome had promised him."

"Repetitive?" Sinder asked.

"We have some blanks which still need filling," H. D. C. Franklin said. He turned the machine off. "We'll take a short break here while I reorganize my notes."

Benjie Wannover said, "I feel so rotten about all this."

"Then you shouldn't have started cutting corners," said Wise.

Wannover stared steadily at him for a moment. "Don't give me all this moral rectitude shit, Wise. I don't need to hear it from somebody squatting up to his belly button in the public trough."

"Hey now!" Franklin said. "Hey there."

"Just keep that jerk off me," Benjie said, pointing toward Wise with his thumb. "Sure, I fudged some records. I put my thumb on the scales sometimes. I did as I was told because if I didn't, I would be out on the street. If that jerk had my job and my ten kids he would have been twice as far into—"

Franklin said quickly, "I want to remind everyone that we are here to take a deposition from Mr. Wannover, not to pass judgment on his actions. Understood?"

Wise nodded gloomily, lit a cigarette and went over to stand and stare out of the window down at the parking lot.

"Has Mr. Grome been located?" Sinder asked.

"Not yet. We'll find him."

"His decisions seem . . . irrational," Sinder said.

Howe, from Atlanta, laughed. "Very very crazy even? What if Sherm decided a year ago, based on the evidence, that he had made a bad move, taking the job as head of that real estate investment trust, and no matter how hard he tried to rescue it, it was still going to go down the drain and he was going to look terrible. So what he did with Mr. Liss, and with a lot of other suckers, was use them to buy time. And he used the time to carefully cash every chip he could put his hands on. If the auditors can ever untangle all those records, we might find eight or ten million missing. He could have been cashing the chips and at the same time building an identity in some nice place, like maybe São Paulo, with the money in a nice number account in Brussels. Sherm may be very very strange, but he isn't dumb. All the guys like Liss will serve time. And Grome will be by some pool with some great broad, smiling and smiling and smiling."

"Serve time?" Sinder asked politely.

"The best shot is for tax evasion, for taking a million-dollar payoff for taking over Tropic Towers and setting it up as a capital gain. It was straight income. He was cheating the IRS out of a quarter mil," Howe said.

"Tax evasion before he even files?" Wannover asked blankly.

"He runs his personal taxes on a fiscal year ending June thirty. He filed."

"Oh, shit, I forgot that," Benjie said.

"Gentlemen!" said H. D. C. Franklin, snapping his head to toss the black curl back from his forehead. "Shall we continue."

Martin Liss stood naked, looking north through the sliding glass doors of Penthouse A of Tropic Towers, across the low one- and two-story buildings of Beach Village, toward the curving pattern of the high rises marching into the misty heat of the August Sunday afternoon. He stood with bare feet in deep orange shag, a hairy man of small stature, the black mat of thickly curled hair covering his chest, growing more sparsely on shoulders and back and protruding belly, thickening again into the forest of the groin, where the flaccid tube of sex lay dead against the heavy asymmetric dangle of balls. He stood with his arms crossed under his plump hairy breasts, elbows in his palms. He looked out at the penthouse deck where Drusilla had nursed the dying plants back to luxuriant life.

"It wasn't out off that wall Jerry jumped?" he asked.

"Stop thinking about it, love."

"Probably around from the back. Sure. From where he hit."

"Yes, it was around from the back," she said. "Darlin', stop worrying your head."

She was supine upon a low deep couch fashioned of a three-quarter mattress on a low frame, covered with the dynel skins of imaginary animals, with a rainbow of pastel pillows in large sizes and strange shapes. Nearly all the draperies were drawn, leaving the big room in shadow.

She lay propped on pillows, ankles crossed, one arm across her stomach, the other behind her head. Her hair was tousled. He walked back across the shag and plucked his brief mesh shorts from a chair and pulled them on, hopping for balance. Buttercup mesh. Swedish. Imported. Fourteen bucks a pair. He had a dozen pair in assorted colors.

He looked at her and said, "Hey, when I was a kid I had a postage stamp looked just like you there, same position, everything."

"A postage stamp!"

"Spanish. Let me see if I can remember. Sure. Goya's portrait of the Duchess of Alba. The word was that he was getting a little on the side, so he made two paintings of her, one with clothes and one without. Among my group it was a very hot number. You're not as heavy as she was."

"Thank you so much!"

"Think nothing of it. You look better, even. And you are better. The way it's all coming down, I would have bet forty to one nobody could have got me in the mood."

"I should have wagered. Darlin', you have to have some relaxation, you know."

"Who can relax? The way my head is, I think I'm falling out of my tree. It's very weird. I don't know. I am going along like always, and then I get a sudden feeling as if something slipped inside my head. A gear comes loose and the motor races. I go right back into last week or last month or last year, with memories so strong and bright they are as if they were happening all over again. Like in a dream, but I'm not asleep. Things happen to me and I know how they come out, but I want them to be different the second time around, and I am standing over at the side, sort of gnawing my hands and saying, Don't happen! But it does, just like before."

She said, "But he told you what it was. Simple anxiety. Just take your Valium, Martin."

He sat at the foot of the couch. She braced a slender bare foot against his thigh. He scowled into space. "I don't know exactly how they are coming after me, or how much blood they are going to want. But I'm not going to be able to sidestep it."

"You haven't done anything so terrible!"

"I know. I know. Look, the times are wrong. I guessed exactly right a lot of times, and this time I figured it all wrong. People are hurting. They are taking big lumps. So it has to be somebody's fault. I'm all of a sudden a leper. My connections close me out, even. They buy me out for discount rates, and there's nothing I can do. I should have packed up and left back in April or May. I thought about it. I could have written off everything I put into the Harbour Pointe project and walked away rich. I think of how close I came to doing just that, and I ache all over. No, I couldn't walk away. Not Martin Liss, the high roller. Know something? Benjie is going to fink out. I know it. How can I blame the little guy? Ten kids. Never hire anybody with ten kids. If he finks, so will Lew. They'll load it all onto Marty. Immunity. You'll see."

"Aw, they wouldn't be doing that to you now!"

"I don't want to think about it, even, but I can't think of anything else. The thing is, Irish, I gave the folks a fair shake. Mostly, what they paid for, they got. You know? You got to watch Cole because he cuts those corners. And so I always watched him, and so he never got away with too much. You want to know something I know that chills my blood?"

"Should I want to know?"

"There is one condominium on Fiddler Key that was put up maybe five years ago. I could take you to the courthouse and we could find the plans and drawings in the file. All approved. We could find the inspection reports and the approval reports for every phase of construction. It called for pilings, so many, so deep, with lab tests and so on and so on. Safety factors, et cetera et cetera. And you know something? There isn't one goddam piling under that sucker. Not . . . one . . . single . . . piling! It sits on the fucking ground like a big fucking box, like some package that fell off a truck!"

"You are joking!"

"I am absolutely dead serious. Think of how many people had to be paid off! Compared to the bastards who put that one up, I'm a charitable foundation."

"Martin, maybe nothing at all will happen. Maybe it will blow over."

"There's too many agencies involved by now. Too many people got hurt in this Grome thing. All of the REITs have come tumbling down like stones. People invested for income. Hell, Dru, I was just out there playing in the traffic when the truck came along. These agencies, they try to out-tough each other. It gets political. Nobody can afford to ease off."

"Shouldn't you be doing something? Shouldn't you be making some contact with a very good attorney?"

"I know what I should be doing. But what I am doing is spending Sunday here with you. You know, everything looks different." He took hold of her ankle. "Like feet."

"Feet!"

"I don't know how to say this. I am looking at your foot as if I never saw a foot before. These toes are like funny little fingers. Once upon a time they could grab ahold of branches. Now these little fingers that don't work so great anymore are shoved into little leather boxes and we walk on them, on pavement."

"My darlin', you are quite mad, aren't you?"

"I keep thinking I should go home. She was sleeping when I left, and she doesn't know where I am."

"Maybe she's having a special tennis lesson?"

"I guess I shouldn't have showed you those pictures."

"I wouldn't have wanted to miss them. She looks so terribly intense, you know?"

"What have I got, really? Adding up my life is one of the things I've been doing." She reached and tugged at him and he slid up to lie beside her against the pillows. "Take my two kids, for instance. They say Sue's got a hostility problem. What it means is she won't look at me or speak to me or have a goddam thing to do with me except spend the money I send her. She lives on that California beach, pops pills, screws musicians and cracks up automobiles. Marty Junior lives in the goddam desert with that fat Indian wife of his that had the three kids when he married her, and they make that junk jewelry and sell it and he paints pictures of cactuses and gets bombed on peyote most of the time and can't carry on a logical conversation. I tried. Jesus, how I tried. And one day I said to myself, why are you trying so hard? Give up! So I gave up, and you don't know how really relaxing and wonderful it was to say, after all those years, I just don't like those kids. I not only don't love them, I don't even like them! Shall I continue? I take three good shots at marriage, and on the third try I get Francie. Hell, I can't hate her. She watches the soaps. If her life isn't fucked up emotionally, she doesn't feel as if she is living. That's the secret to her and that tennis guy. She doesn't really enjoy getting laid like that. She feels she owes it to herself as a person. If I throw her out now, who sends me gift packages in the slam? It will really turn her on if I go to jail. The plot thickens. Will Frances Liss divorce her jailbird husband to marry her tennis pro, or will terminal hangnail end her dramatic life first?"

"Martin, Martin, Martin."

"No, I'm mostly laughing. Don't be concerned. Now we come to my friends and associates, Benjamin Wannover and Lewis Traff. The way it works, once they make their deal with the Feds, they will have to hate me. It's the way they rationalize it. It's how people tick. They can dump me because I lost my leverage. Which brings us to you, Irish."

She turned and hooked a long leg across his thighs. "The loyal and diligent Miss Bryne?"

He looked into her shadowed eyes, six inches from his. "What I think, kid, is that maybe it's time for you to get out of the line of fire. You could get felled by a random shot."

"I couldn't possibly—"

"Let's have some honesty, okay? I have listened to enough bullshit lately."

"Well . . . I *have* thought of it, love."

"That guy still waiting?"

"Of course."

"And you've got the money to take back by now?"

"Well . . . rather more than in the . . . game plan. Quite a bit more, in fact. Thanks to little suggestions you gave me. Little speculations. And I am quite close about money, you know."

He stroked her in an absentminded manner. "You let him know you've got more than you planned on?"

"No."

"Why not?"

"Because Peter would tell me to come home and be married."

"What would be wrong with that?"

"Nothing, I guess. The garage is doing well. We'd live in the cottage where his grandfather was born. It's of stone, very snug. We'd be but fifteen miles from the sea, and have a small sailboat. I should go back. I'm getting a bit long in the tooth to be starting a family, you know. But I think of it, and there is no flutter. No rush of warmth. I just think of it and it seems a nice thing to do. But it should be more than that, Martin."

"Am I what got in the way?"

"Oh, no. Not really. This was a decision I made at a time when I really did not like you. It seemed . . . a safe solution. It's certainly nothing Peter need ever know, but he certainly has every right to suspect. It would make little or no difference between us. We're adults, you know. Then, in time, I came to like you, Martin. You can be very nasty and overbearing and egotistical. But I like you."

"Thank you."

"You are a very good lover, Martin."

"Two ex-wives would give you an argument there. Anyway, I am not any kind of lover at the moment."

She got up and clambered over him and stood smiling down at him. "I'll scramble some eggs with roe?"

"Fine."

"Make us a drink if you'd like one. About my going back, I don't know if I will, ever. I just don't know. And I will take my chances on that stray shot you mentioned." She started away and picked up her short robe and turned back as she shouldered into it. "Oh, by the way, I have this apartment sold, I think."

"Beautiful."

"Don't sound so impressed!"

"Look. You've done a nice job. You are doing a nice job. Every dime over expenses goes right onto the loans. I can't even give you a bonus for selling this one. You've made it look great. Where'll you go from here?"

"One floor down. Empties are getting scarce. And that will be the last furnished empty one. The furniture is hideous, even worse than this one was."

"Who's buying this one?"

"A jeweler from Memphis."

She went to the kitchen. Before she started the eggs she came back to ask Martin if he was going to fix a drink. He had fallen asleep. She sighed and covered him with a bright yellow afghan, bent and put an imperceptible kiss upon the bald front half of his tanned tired head. She sat at the kitchen bar and had bread and tea, and thought about Martin and about Peter. The next place, she thought, might be Dallas. Joyce's last letter said there would be no trouble finding a lovely position, in spite of the way everyone was talking about hard times coming, about the new great depression. Joyce said that handsome Irish girls were in short supply and high demand. Joyce now worked for the senior partner in a large advertising agency. She decided that if Martin was still asleep by six o'clock, she would have to wake him.

At six o'clock EDST on Sunday, August eleventh, analysis of the satellite photographs established Ella at roughly 14 degrees north, 48 degrees west. This placed the center at about one thousand statute miles due north of Belém, Brazil, and seven hundred and twenty miles due east of Barbados.

Mick Rhoades phoned an old friend on the *Miami Herald,* who said he had been over at the National Hurricane Center earlier in the day.

"I tell you, that is one bi-i-i-g mother out there, so big those experts are laughing and punching each other on the arm and generally carrying on, like somebody lands a record marlin."

"Any predictions on it, Harry?"

"Except for predicting that it will turn into a hurricane in the next twenty-four hours, which is something you already got over the wire, they won't say much. The thing which seems to turn them on is the way it moves right on course and at the same speed. Conditions are ideal for it to grow bigger and nastier. They'll probably be flying into it tomorrow. We had those funny-looking clouds radiating out of the southeast all afternoon today. They've got big surf in the islands, and very heavy rains starting there. If she continues coming a little north of west, she could move up far enough to put this town right in the way of the worst quadrant of the winds four days from now. Anyway, if she doesn't slow, she'll bang into the Lesser Antilles tomorrow, with the eye getting there like about midnight tomorrow to three in the morning. Then we'll know how rough that mother is."

"We don't need one like that over here, Harry."

"Bet your ass you don't. Not with all those condos sitting on those sandspits. You are a disaster waiting to happen over there."

"Everybody says the same thing, but they still issue building permits."

"Not any more, they don't."

"That's economics, not weather forecasting."

"It hits, you run for high ground, Mick."

"Great! Twenty miles inland we got some high ground, I think. Thirty or forty feet above sea level."

"How are things with you anyway? You getting any?"

"A little here, a little there. How's Myra?"

"Due to pop."

"Again?"

"Fourth and last, fella. Fourth and last. We took an oath."

After he hung up, Mick went across the city room to the big wall map of the Gulf and the Caribbean. Somebody had moved the little hurricane symbol to its most recent position. The little doughnut looked tiny in the vastness of the sea.

WHEN THE BIG DREDGE had been grinding and grunting away in the bay behind Golden Sands, George and Elda Gobbin had taken to closing the bedroom windows and sleeping in the cool hush of the air conditioning. When the dredge stopped they tried to go back to the previous system, but it seemed too sticky and uncomfortable. They told each other that they did seem to sleep better under a light blanket, with the thermostat set at seventy. She said she hated to have her hair get sweaty.

It was full bright daylight when George awoke on Monday morning, August twelfth. He had slept so soundly, he did not know where he was. His first thought was that he was late, that he had overslept, that he would have to call the office. Next he realized that he was not at home, that he was in a strange hotel somewhere. He looked over at the neighbor bed and saw a strange blond head and a brown shoulder, and he erupted with panic and guilt. Suddenly it all fell back into place.

He was retired and living at Golden Sands and he could get up when he felt like it. Elda had finally found something which enabled her to tan rather than turn dark red. And her hairdresser was doing something to her hair lately.

As his panicked heart slowed, he yawned and wondered why he was feeling so disoriented lately. And why he was having so many horrible dreams. One in the night about Vicky Antonelli had awakened him, all cold and sweaty. He dreamed they were back in that cabin they used to go to, twenty years ago, on the land her father leased, and she was standing and holding her arms out to him and crying silently. Her breasts were shaped like big firm white drops of melting wax, greatly magnified. They ran down her and down the fronts of her thighs and shins and onto the old grass rug, and she would step away from them as others slowly grew and grew, breaking loose when they were the right size. She wanted him to do something to help her. She could not tell him what. She could only cry and hold her arms out. There had been other dreams too, but he could not remember any of them. He had the sense that they were horrible too.

He got up without awakening Elda and went into his bathroom and quietly closed the door before snapping the light on. After he urinated, he leaned on the sink and studied his face in the mirror, and took his brush and adjusted his dark hair to the new way he had discovered. If he brushed it forward and then across, and sprayed it into place, it did make him look younger. Elda agreed that it did, much to his surprise. He thought she would tell him it looked silly.

George got out the tape and measured his belly bulge. Forty-one inches. Down from forty-three already. And it was going to go down a lot farther. It was going to go down to thirty-six, he had decided, even if it did mean taking in a lot of his clothing and giving away a lot more.

Funny how, down here, they had become so much more conscious of appearance. Elda was serious about finding out how much a face lift would cost. With her tan, and her new-found figure, and her always youthful clear green eyes, she could create a magical change by merely putting her thumbs by her temples and pushing the loose skin upward. She had done it several times for him, and it made him feel odd to see an Elda from many years ago. Staring into his mirror, he pushed up on his own face in exactly the same way and saw young George peer out at him, the folds and tucks around the mouth disappearing.

"Maybe," he whispered. "Maybe we will."

They would never have thought of this rejuvenation program back in Iowa. Hell, everybody knew them and knew just how old they were, and the kidding would have been without mercy.

Maybe the reason here was because they were living in the middle of a gigantic throng of old old old old people. Once you started noticing, you couldn't stop. A billion living tons of wrinkles and tremors and totterings. Of gray locks and swollen knuckles and shuffling foot-steps. Of broken veins and naked skulls and grave marks. Of dentures and staleness and trifocals.

What it did was make you damned conscious of the same attrition going on in yourself.

But we are nowhere near as old as most of these retired people. I'm seven years away from Social Security, and Elda is nine away. No reason to hurry to catch up. The thing to do is go as far as you can in the opposite direction. Toward youthfulness.

When he came out in his white tennis shorts, his Mexican sandals and his white T-shirt, still puffing slightly from his exertions with that tangle of plastic rope and pulleys which was melting his stomach down, Elda, in her terry robe, was fixing breakfast.

He gave her a good-morning kiss on the temple and a good-morning pat on the rear and said, "Looks like a hot one."

"Paper says it'll be ninety again. Who are you playing with?"

"Lynn and me against Stan and Honey."

"Lynn again?"

"Why do you say it like that?"

"I didn't say it like anything. I just said, Lynn again?"

"If you would learn to play . . ."

"I have no intention of chasing a fuzzy ball around in this heat. I'll be in the pool, thank you. And don't get too exhausted. The Kelseys are coming here for bridge, remember?"

"How did we get trapped into that?"

"*You* asked them. That's how."

"You are really in some great mood today, aren't you?"

She looked at him in genteel astonishment. "Me? I am in a *perfectly* good mood, in spite of not getting very much sleep."

"Why not?"

"Oh, nothing in particular."

"You couldn't sleep on account of nothing?"

"You were thrashing and muttering and moaning most of the night."

"I seem to be dreaming a lot lately."

"Of Lynn Simmins?"

"Jesus Christ!"

"What's the matter? Too close to the mark?"

"Lynn is the thirty-year-old daughter of two of the reasonably pleasant friends we've made down here, Mark and Edie Simmins. Colonel Simmins picked up bursitis in his right shoulder a couple of weeks ago. When he gets over it, he will partner his daughter. Until he gets over it, I will. She is pleasant to play tennis with."

"Anyone can see that. Anyone can see you really enjoy it."

"You got any butter for this?"

"It's off our list. There isn't a drop of butter in the house."

"Okay. Well, I better get going."

"Don't keep her waiting, for heaven's sake. It's okay if I sit here alone and eat. But don't keep her waiting one single second."

He turned on the kitchen television. Barbara was asking a bald impatient guest one of her strangely lengthy questions. He fixed the color tones for Elda, got his sunglasses and his tennis hat and went down to claim the court.

Loretta phoned Greg McKay at ten on Monday morning.

"Are you in your office?" he asked. "Okay, let me call back."

She waited, fidgeting, fixing her mouth, clicking her lighter, chewing an end of her gleaming hair, scratching her thigh. When the phone rang and she was certain it was Greg, she said, "Where are you calling from?"

"The private line in Mo Sinder's office. He's in Atlanta."

"Greg, it has been one hell of a long time."

"At one o'clock it will be fourteen days."

"I know."

"You made it pretty clear, Loretta. You made an ultimatum."

"I guess I did."

"I've been through hell."

"I can guess. All is forgiven?"

"No. No way. Never. There was a pretty wild scene. It went on practically without a break for three days and nights. It went on right to the point of total physical and emotional exhaustion. She's not very strong, you know. She has all kinds of allergies, et cetera. We just fought and fought and fought, until there was no fight left. We came right down to the bitter end of it when she sat in our living room and I sat beside her and she looked fifty years old. She looked at me and she said she was sorry but there was no way she could ever understand or forget or forgive what she saw. She said she had no love left for me. She said I was a stranger and would always be a stranger, so I better move out, or she would. So I moved out."

"Where are you living?"

"Where do you think?"

"In our apartment? Hey!"

"I'm not in any mood to be cheery or funny or anything like that. I'm really down, Loretta. I really loved her. And she said that if I didn't stop trying to put my arms around her, she was going to vomit."

"She's a dreary little prude, honey."

"She's a lovely sensitive woman."

The tone of his voice made the little warning sign flash in the back of Loretta's brain: Mistake—Mistake—Mistake.

"I really didn't mean what I said, Greg. I . . . I guess I struck out at her and called her a prude because I feel, you know, kind of self-conscious about what she walked in on. That's because I guess with us it has always been pretty much my idea, not yours. Any expression of love is totally okay in my book, no matter what it is, as long as it gives pleasure instead of pain, right?"

"Well, I—"

"I *certainly* will accept your analysis of Nancy as being a lovely, sensitive woman. And not at all aggressive. Okay?"

"I guess so."

"Darling, regardless of how sensitive she is, you just can't afford to let her hang-ups cheapen our relationship. You can't start seeing us through her eyes, or she will have spoiled what we have together."

"What we *have?*"

"I didn't mean to make it sound like an ultimatum. I was frightened. I was confused. When I get like that, I come on too rough and say things I don't mean."

"I parked by your office the other day trying to get up the nerve to come in. Then you came out, laughing away, talking with a couple of people, smiling. You looked pretty happy."

"That's my act. I sell things. I've been desolate."

"Me too."

"I want to see you, Greg, because I need your advice. Two men came to see me about buying out my business. I named a very fat price and they went away and thought it over and came back with some earnest money. They want the name and the goodwill, and they want me to agree not to go into the same line of work anywhere in Palm County. I need your advice, and if we agree I should sell, then I'll need your help drawing up a contract of sale."

"I'd be glad to . . ."

"Where can I bring the papers and things?"

He said ruefully, "It's pretty easy nowadays, with me living at Golden Sands, Two-F. F for frolic, as you always say. It's been pretty grim. I've been there . . . ten days. Don't come by until maybe eight o'clock, Loretta. The place is a mess."

"Okay," she said. "I'm so happy, darling."

"That's nice."

"See you," she said and hung up and leaned back and smiled up at her office ceiling. She looked at her watch. If she could get to the apartment by four o'clock, she should have it very very tidy by the time he came home from the office. Drinks all made, dinner ready for the oven, wine on ice. She had a mental image of herself bounding on all fours into the living room, carpet slippers in her teeth, and she laughed aloud.

Carlotta Churchbridge was in the pool by eleven in the morning, and when Henry went down to see how she was coming along, she was still churning slowly from end to end, doing what she had called in the early days of her English lessons, "the dog puddle."

When she saw him she came over to the ladder. She took his hand and he helped her out. She came out nimbly, and he was pleased with her small tidy brown body, her mid-sixties agilities.

"They are too damn bloody far away!" she said, toweling herself.

"What? Oh. Sure. Anchorage and Melbourne and Guadalajara. A scattering of grandbabies."

"I want to be hugging them. Ready to walk now?"

"Okay," he said. It seemed pleasant to be able to cross Beach Drive without that long delay for season traffic. There was not as much glare as usual. There were very high clouds hazing the sunlight. He tied the laces of his sneakers together and hung them over his shoulder so he could walk with her in the wash of the small waves.

"Strange day," she said. "The weather smells funny."

"Hurricane Ella."

"Now it's a hurricane?"

"According to the radio news at eleven. Sustained winds of eighty miles an hour, gusts to a hundred and ten."

She looked up at her tall husband sidelong, mockery in her dark eyes and in the expression on her weathered brown face. "Something worth being afraid of, eh?"

"The real menace versus the imaginary menace."

"Where on earth does the man get those trousers?"

"Eh? Oh, you mean C. Noble Winney. They are the trousers that go with his suit, of course."

He knew what she meant. Though broad and vast and flabby, Winney had gray trousers with a slight overall sheen which fit him so abundantly he wore the belt taut above the most prominent bulge of the belly, so that the belly made a rounded convexity of the fly area. They sagged in folds in the rear, and flapped about his legs as he walked. With the trousers went white shirts, dark ties, and suit coats always a little too small across the chest, but of the same silvery gray fabric.

"I was too sleepy to listen last night," she said. "Your friendship has ended?"

"Our acquaintanceship. He wouldn't let me back away without any explanation. He had to keep worrying at it. Why should a retired diplomat be afraid of the truth? Because one retires, that does not mean one should turn one's brain off forever. I should be thinking of how much I could contribute to his study groups and work sessions, not how I could avoid them."

"Oh, boy."

"Yes indeed. Oh, boy. He wore such an earnest face. As you talk to him, his mouth makes little motions, trying to help you along. And he nods and nods as you talk. Somehow like an old nun. Like an old Mother Superior. Yes, that's what it is. A kind of ecclesiastical fervor. The true believer. Nothing can shake his faith. I realized that just as I was about to hit him with logic. Logic would have been as effective as throwing marshmallows at a tank. So I said that I had studied his materials and I had given his discoveries and insights a great deal of thought. I said I had decided that when I had been in the Department, I had been asked to assume a certain amount of risk. I had to live up to my oath, and besides I was paid to do a job. But now, in my retirement, I did not feel that I wished to assume the risks he was asking me to assume."

"Oh, boy."

"I said that as his influence spread, inevitably word of his activities would reach the ear of somebody who would feel it necessary to do something about him and his associates. I said it would be done cleverly and painlessly, of course. It would look like heart attacks and strokes and so on, so as not to create any publicity. Or any martyrs. I said that, from my experience, I thought it too great a risk to take, as I would prefer to live out my years in peace."

"You *bastard,* Enrique! You utter horrid *bastard.* You've terrified the poor hulk."

"Terrified him? My goodness, no! He couldn't have been more delighted. I have reinforced his paranoia. I have verified his most foul suspicions. I have given him a credible object for his fears. I launched that idiot into euphoria. He held my hand in his large damp cold hands and shook it slowly for a long time as he kept telling me that he understood, that he would not press me further, that I had already given enough of my life to my country and on and on. He would respect my wishes and I would hear nothing more from him on these matters, ever."

She pounced upon a shell, examined it, found it flawed and threw it into the sea. She turned to look up at him. "It makes me wonder just how many times you have manipulated me?"

"Physically? Let me make an estimate . . ."

"No! You are an old sex fiend."

"Retired with honors," he said. "I do not believe I have ever successfully conned you into anything since the day I conned you into marrying me."

"In frightful Spanish."

"The best of Berlitz."

"Now I am going to con you, Henry *Iglesia-puente.* Next month I will get the next payment from that estate of my dear dead sister's father-in-law, and with it I wish to be taken to Guadalajara and to Melbourne and to Anchorage—in any order you choose."

"I swear upon the great gray stomach of C. Noble Winney that I shall arrange the trip and we shall go."

"And first you will finish your paper? Swear on the stomach."

"It doesn't go all that well. It doesn't march."

"What I've read marches dandy. Swear on the stomach."

"I do so swear."

"We're past our marker, dear. More than a mile. We can turn around."

After David Dow, the treasurer of the Condominium Association, left the manager's office at Golden Sands, Julian Higbee said angrily to Lorrie, "It doesn't *mean* anything! An absolute minimum we can get along on? Work for the Association? Forget it, baby. I don't want Gulfway Management sore at me for any reason."

"Mr. Dow is only working up—what did he call it?—a bare-bones budget. He was asking what *if* we'd work for them, what would we have to make. That's all. They haven't asked us yet."

"You didn't have to answer any of those questions about what we make."

"What do we make anyway? Thursday is the fifteenth. You think a check will come? Mr. Sullivan, the girl said, is no longer with Gulfway. Mr. Gellroy is in charge. Mr. Gellroy is busy. Three calls and he won't call back. Mr. Frank West is no longer at Investment Equities. The man in charge is a Mr. Milremo. And he doesn't call back either. I don't even know if we've got jobs and I can't find out, and you don't want me to even answer questions." She stared at him. "Jesus Christ, Julian, the thing about you is you are so thick-head, stubborn, damned dumb, sometimes I . . ." She shrugged hopelessly and started toward the office door to unlock it and take off the CLOSED sign.

Julian caught her by the shoulders and pulled her back and turned her around. "Honey, it's a big organization and they pay us good money, and if things go bad here, they'll put us someplace else, some other condo, maybe over on the East Coast. We don't want to rock any boats, right?"

"Oh, shut up. Maybe they've gone broke like everybody else."

"You need cheering up," he said, and pulled her close and began caressing her. In a little while he realized she was standing slack and unresponsive. He held her away and looked at her. "What's *with* you?"

She shook her hair away from her face and said, "You want to rape somebody, go find somebody that'll put up a fight."

"Who said anything about rape?"

"Who said it was ever anything else with you?"

He pushed her away, made a mindless, wordless, howling sound of rage and frustration and went storming out.

Because he happened to have on him a key to 5-E, the unit owned by Pastorelli and ready for furnished rental, and empty now for four months, he went there and turned the color set to a game show and stretched out on the couch.

It took anger a long time to fade. The worst mistake he had ever made, he realized, was setting up Bobbie Fish. How was he to have known in advance that Bobbie would become Lorrie's best friend? They'd gotten very close. Lorrie had always wished she'd finished her nurse training. She liked to talk to Bobbie about nursing. And Bobbie acted as if Lorrie had saved her life, getting her off the sauce.

The trouble was that with Bobbie hanging around the office and hanging around their apartment all the time, it was a constant reminder to Lorrie of his infidelity. Actually she didn't seem as sore about the cheating as she was about how he had taken advantage of Roberta. She bought that crap about his forcing Roberta into it, and she was willing to believe that all the times Bobbie phoned trying to locate him, it was because she had been drinking.

They had wept together and hugged and had somehow become best friends—a big dark-haired woman and a little one. He had tried to explain to Lorrie that Bobbie hadn't really been forced, that she had only tried to make herself believe she had been forced in order to save her own face, that she had been so ready she had come in about a minute and a half after he got in, but Lorrie didn't want to hear one word of criticism of her new best friend.

It made him feel strange the way they would both look at him when he walked in and interrupted one of their long conversations. They would stop talking and giggling and both stare at him. Identical looks, cold and full of hate. No, not hate. Contempt. As if he had messed on the rug. They closed him out. Each one of them was down on him for what she thought he had done to the other one. Disliking him was part of their friendship. There was no possible way now for him to get a piece of ass from either one of them, and it was beginning to make him very jumpy. He wouldn't have gotten into that situation with Lynn Simmins if it hadn't been for Lorrie and Bobbie freezing him out.

What did they expect him to do, anyway? Go up to the Sand Dollar Bar and buy it from one of Tom Shawn's hookers? But that Darleen Moseby would certainly be worth the price from the look of her. Very choice. The only one he knew of at Golden Sands who ever got any of that was the Reverend Doctor Harmon Starf. Once a month Mary Starf had to fly up to Chicago for a meeting of the family corporation which was supposed to own lots and lots of coal and pipe lines, and one of the two nights she was gone, the Moseby girl would make a house call.

Thinking of money made the bottom fall out of his stomach, and made him feel sick and dizzy. There was a good chance no check would come on the fifteenth. And that increased the chance of Lorrie's finding out sooner, instead of later, that the joint savings account was about three thousand smaller than she thought.

He wished he could die, or disappear. Rub the magic lamp and disappear. Maybe the thing to do was clean out the account and go. Twenty-five hundred left. Go out to Oregon. Pick a new name. Make a new life. If Lorrie didn't stop going dead every time he touched her, it would serve the bitch right. What did she expect a man to do? Go without? Forever?

Maybe by now she was feeling sorry for the way she had acted when he had tried to show some affection. He went over to the phone and dialed the office number. No answer. The office phone extension rang in their apartment, so she wasn't in either place. He sighed. She had probably made another trip up to Nurse Roberta's place to tell her all her terrible problems and have another little session of tears and hugging.

He drifted off to sleep and wakened with a start an hour later, with a bad taste in his mouth. He creaked big shoulders as he stretched, and then he tried the office number again.

With equal measure of apprehension and indignation, he hurried down to the office. As he got there, he saw Lorrie unlocking the office door. Roberta Fish stood close behind her. They were laughing. When Lorrie turned as she pushed the door open, he saw that merry, rosy, dancing look on her face, a look he had not seen in several years. He knew exactly what it meant, and in his moment of realization, he knew that he had really known about it for some time, somewhere in the back of his head, hidden, inadmissible.

That look was gone in an instant, and Lorrie said something in a quiet tone to Bobbie. They both looked at him in that way they had. Bobbie kissed Lorrie lightly on the cheek and patted her shoulder and then turned and swept by Julian on her way to the elevators. Julian came to within a fractional part of an impulse to club the nape of her neck with his big clenched fist, with all the strength he could muster. He knew the blow would have killed her. It shook him to have come so close. He leaned against the corridor wall, weak and sweaty, hands trembling, and in a little while he felt well enough to face Lorrie. He could hear her typewriter.

He went into the office. She looked at him blandly enough and he said, "I know what's been going on."

"So?"

"Aren't you going to even deny it, Lor?"

"I happen to be sort of happy. In spite of you. I'm even kind of grateful to you. In a weird sort of way."

"What's going to happen to us? What's going to happen to *me*?"

"Julian, for God's sake, go fix a faucet washer. Go clean the pool. Go haul trash. There is absolutely nothing you can do about us, ever."

Ella was a life force of immeasurable strength. Her vitality was fueled by the heat of the summer sea beneath her. She sucked up the warm moist air from near the surface, whirled it high into towering clouds. Rain squalls radiated in all directions, billions of tons of rain, falling with a smashing awesome weight. From the clouds she spewed forth, tornadoes dipped down, spinning, ripping, smashing. She moved, advanced, threatened. She was a personage, reaching her deadly maturity, destined to die many many days in the future, much farther west, much farther above the equator.

By Monday evening at six o'clock Ella's approximated center was at 15 degrees north, 55 degrees west, approximately three hundred miles due east of Martinique. But so vast was the basic cloud-shape in its distinctive oval pattern, the leading edge of the main body of cloud was already blotting out Antigua and Guadeloupe. The aircraft had flown in and out of it. The instruments had been read, the data fed into the National Hurricane Center computers. Ella was a major hurricane, well-organized, of large size, with sustained winds of almost one hundred miles an hour, with an increase possible. One gust of a hundred and fifteen had already been measured at Saint Johns, Antigua, coming right after ten inches of rain had fallen in five hours.

After the NOAA researchers aboard a 41-C four-engine turbo-prop had measured, within the eye and adjacent to it, water droplets, ice crystals, pressure gradients, wind speed and direction at various altitudes, with the stationary camera taking pictures of the changing values on the instrument panel, the track of the hurricane was plotted on the on-board computer and the results radioed to Miami for use in preparing the next advisory.

Classified as a five on the Saffir-Simpson scale, Ella was confirmed as a major hurricane, one of the same size and intensity which in 1944 took a toll of seven hundred and ninety men, one hundred and forty-six aircraft and three ships of the U.S. Third Fleet in the Pacific. Ella was as dangerous as the one in 1789 in India which left twenty survivors out of a coastal population of twenty thousand where she came ashore, as impressive as the 1881 hurricane which killed three hundred thousand people in China and the one that drowned three hundred thousand more in Bangladesh in 1970. Ella was sister to Beulah, Celia, Carla, Hilda, Camille and Betsy, who had all come slamming into the upper Gulf Coast in the 1960s.

The hurricane's anatomy was powerful and complex. Heavy rain clouds rushed inward to be caught at the perimeter of the eye and there whirled upward in spiral pattern. As the clouds rose they became cooler, and as the water condensed as rain, it created and released heat. This heat made the air mass rise more rapidly, just as in a fire storm. This rapid elevation reduced the pressure and thus increased the size and scope and velocity of the input of the moisture-heavy cloud masses.

Ella's energy was the reverse of the energy of the sun. The sun had heated the tropic seas along the Intertropical Convergence Zone. It had expended great energy in the form of heat to turn the water of the sea into vapor. One part of volatile fuel such as gasoline will turn twenty parts of water into vapor by boiling it. Ella was now condensing twenty billion tons of water a day out of the cloud pattern. And so the energy released each day was equal to a billion tons of fuel. Air descending inside the eye—which was thirty-five miles wide and forty thousand feet deep—was cooler and dry. At the top of the cloud wall the air, after having shed all its contained moisture, was pumped away in anticyclonic pattern. Ella fed on an apparently endless supply of warm moist air from the vastness of the Atlantic, sending belts of heavy rain ever farther out in front of her, and to either side of her path.

SAM HARRISON was at a shady metal table by the pool at the Islander at nine on Tuesday morning. He had finished the tall chilled glass of fresh orange juice, and the scrambled eggs, sausage and grits, and Kitty had brought him his second pot of coffee. The table was in the shade of a giant sea grape, and his chair was positioned so that the Gulf breeze kept the small biting insects away. He wore brief turquoise swim pants and large, very dark sunglasses. He had taken a lot of sun in the past few days, putting such a deep burn atop his permanent tan that he was a heavy brown-red, with the body hair on his arms and legs bleached to a dynel white against the startling hue.

As he turned back in the *Athens Times Record* to read once more the detailed report on Hurricane Ella, Kitty arrived with the plug-in phone. "At your service," she said. "I wouldn't want any guest to have to stand up and walk twenty feet, would I?"

She plugged it into the receptacle in a post behind the table, lifted the receiver and handed it to him with an ironic little curtsy.

"Sam Harrison," he said.

"Hi. Good morning!"

"Morning, Barbara."

"They had to hunt you down, so I guess I didn't get you up."

"I'm still about four time zones away from here. I can't seem to get back on the track."

"I went down to Insta-Print yesterday at about four and checked to see if we'd get those reports today as they promised. They had a little trouble reducing the graphics to the right size, but they'll be out this afternoon. I saw the covers. It should look very . . . authentic."

"And it now looks as if people might have a little more interest in reading that stuff."

"I know. I know. Did you hear any news this morning?"

"The *Today Show* at seven. It sounds as if Ella is really chewing up the islands down there."

"Sam, if she comes here, comes ashore here, I'll feel as if we sort of caused it. Isn't that silly?"

"She wants to prove my point, you mean?"

"Something like that. I don't like to impose, but I try not to go out when Mrs. Schmidt isn't here. Could you drive down and pick those fifty copies up at four o'clock today and bring them back here?"

"No trouble at all."

"Payment is all arranged. They'll be expecting you. You can sign them here and Gus can sign his cover memo, and we should be able to start distributing them."

"Okay. I'll see you about four thirty, then."

As Kitty came to take the telephone away, the tall executive secretary from Birmingham moved in and sat at the table. Kitty glanced at her with thin-lipped disapproval. The executive secretary had rotated back to the white swimsuit. "Aren't we important, though?" the girl said. "People darting about, bringing you telephones. Good morning, Sam darling."

"Good morning, Liz."

"About last night, I decided to forgive you. Isn't that nice of me?"

"What did I do to warrant the dispensation?"

"Listen to him! I thought we were getting along beautifully last night. I thought we were both absolutely enchanting. And suddenly I looked around and you were gone. Men's room, I thought. And waited and waited and waited. Maybe he got tight and went walking on the beach, I said to myself. I waited some more. I went looking for you. I called your place on the house phone. Nothing. You walked out on me, pal."

"Did I? I thought I said good night. Sorry."

She studied him. "You know, when I was seventeen and I became Miss Fork Lift, I didn't think I'd ever have this kind of trouble."

"Trouble? I'm sorry. I felt restless. I went for a long walk down the beach. By the time I got back the bar was closed and all the people had gone to bed."

"All seven or nine of us. I forget the size of the group. I would have walked on the beach if that's what you wanted."

"If I was rude, I'm sorry. I apologize."

She sighed. "Okay, fella. I win a lot, so I have to lose one here and there. Something went wrong with the chemistry."

"There's nothing wrong with you, Liz."

She got up, smiling. "Nothing a good cry won't cure. See you around, engineer."

She was good to look at as she walked away from him, and she was graceful as she ran three steps and took a flat racing dive into the pool. Sorry, lady, he thought, but I seem to have picked up a little something you might call emotional impotence. It seems that if it ain't Mrs. Messenger, I don't want it at all. She is even interfering with my normal healthy appetite, and she keeps waking me up now and then in the middle of the night. I don't have a thing that your average pimpled wistful schoolboy isn't familiar with. I am that round-headed kid, Charlie Brown, dreaming about the little redheaded girl. The trees keep eating my kites. I can't pitch a strike to save my soul. If Barbara told me to go jump off a building, I would ask her which one.

Snap out of it, Harrison, he told himself. You are heading into your middle years. You tried marriage once and it didn't work out. Hell, you can't even keep track of friends, much less a wife. And she is already married, and she is very rich. And lovely.

Dr. Dewey Dromb made his morning rounds at his usual late hour at Athens Memorial. He had only three patients in the psychiatric wing as of that Tuesday morning. He had Mo Sinder's teenage daughter, Kathy, who had gobbled down so many strange compounds and combinations she had scrambled her head and was just beginning to be able to separate hallucination from reality. He had the father of Fred Hildebert, the president of the Athens Bank and Trust Company, and he was beginning to be quite certain that the old man's trouble was an irreversible senile dementia requiring permanent custodial care. The old man had been quite weak and feeble when his brain was functioning reasonably well, but now that he was (Freud forgive me) crazy as a bedbug, he had become very spry, agile and disconcertingly strong. After he had tried to assassinate the United Parcel Service delivery man, failing only because he had pulled both triggers simultaneously on his son's shotgun, with the effect of blowing a hole in the porch roof and knocking himself down the steps into the shrubbery, he had trotted for six blocks before they could catch him. He told Dromb he'd overheard the nurses plotting to slip a cobra into his bed some night, and he wanted to be issued a snake bite kit, and he wanted a night lock for the inside of the door.

Dewey Dromb saved Thelma Mensenkott for last, knowing she would be more rewarding this morning than his other two.

Thelma was wearing a simple blue dress and sitting in a straight gray chair which was bolted through the rug to the steel floor, near the window. She had an open book in her lap, and when he came in she got up and closed the book and put it on the windowsill.

"Sit down, Thelma. You look better today."

"I feel better, I think."

He sat on the foot of the bed and smiled at her. "Did you think about what I asked you to?"

"Yes. I tried lots of different things. And . . . well . . . I've come up with an analogy that isn't really exact, but I think it is as close as I'm going to be able to get."

"Tell me."

"Once when I was little I was running in the house when I wasn't supposed to and I struck a table and a dish fell off and broke. It was a white dish with raised purple flowers on it. English pottery, in the family a long time. I wanted to hide the fact I'd broken it. I could hear them talking. They hadn't heard the dish break. It landed on the rug and cracked in half. I took the two pieces to my room. I had some airplane glue and I thought I could mend it perfectly so that nobody would notice, at least not for a long time. But when I tried to stick it together I found that some little pieces were missing. It would not fit together well enough so that the joint would be inconspicuous. But I tried anyway, and that was stupid. It would have been better not to try at all, because they found the evidence of my trying to glue it, and that was deceit. So . . . that is the analogy."

"How does it relate to you?"

"Can't you see how it does?"

"I think so. But I want to see how you feel about it."

"I . . . I am broken. I broke in half. I can mend myself, I think, but there will be little bits forever missing and people will see what a clumsy mending job it is."

"What if you were never broken at all? What if you were always in two pieces, and what happened was that you had your attention called to that fact?"

"Oh?" She tilted her head slightly and frowned at the wall. He thought to himself that she was quite a handsome woman in repose. "I guess I've never felt whole . . . in the way that other people seem to be entities. Jack is such an integrated person. I've never been entirely sure of who I am, I guess."

"You do love your husband?"

"Oh, yes! Very much. He is a very kind man."

"What would you most like to do with your life?"

"Have children, but I can't."

"Other than that."

"I think I would like to go back to school and study living things. Mammals. Botany. Marine creatures."

"Why don't you, then?"

"Oh, I guess because Jack would probably think it a silly thing to do."

"Can you notice any physical changes since Friday that you think might be due to the medication?"

"I get a kind of . . . excited anticipation, a joyous kind of breathlessness which comes and goes away very quickly. And there isn't any reason at all for me to feel like that."

"Do you find it unpleasant?"

"Not really. I feel flushed and my heart pounds, but not really."

"How did you sleep last night?"

"Like death. I think I awoke in exactly the same position I went to sleep in. I don't think I moved. Is there any reason why I can't be home, taking these things?"

"I want you to have time alone to think about yourself. I do not believe you have thought about yourself enough. You are dismayed by the thought you might be neurotic, self-involved. We are all self-involved, Thelma. Each of us is the only person we have any chance of ever getting to know, and if we avoid the self-knowledge, then we can become rather odd."

"Like me?"

"I think you are complicated, but not odd. Not odd at all. I don't want to send you home again just now because I think your husband takes up just a little bit too much of your time and attention when you are home."

Her face darkened suddenly, and her eyes narrowed. She hit her fist on the arm of the gray chair and said, "Sometimes I *hate* that arrogant little old shit! He makes me keep—" She stopped suddenly and put her fingertips across her mouth, eyes wide.

"Say the rest of it, Thelma."

"Oh, no. My God. Where did *that* come from?"

"From the other half of the broken dish?"

"But I love him. I love him with all my heart."

"But you feel humiliated by him."

"Never!"

"Thelma!"

"I guess that . . . sometimes I sort of resent him."

"Because he wants both of you to live *his* life, as *he* has planned it?"

"I hate that fucking building!"

"Because . . . ?"

"It's a place for dying! It's a place to come to die!"

"And you aren't ready."

"Where did all that come from? My God, my mouth opens and I don't know what is going to come out. You're right, Doctor. I shouldn't go home yet. I shouldn't go home ever, maybe."

"You'll go home pretty soon. I'll see you tomorrow. I'm changing your medication just a little bit, okay? Meanwhile, as another favor for me, I want you to work up another analogy for what has happened inside your head, Thelma. Will you?"

"I'll try, but I don't know if—"

"This time try to make it something living instead of just a dish."

"Living? Well, okay. You trimmed your mustache."

She blushed brightly. He laughed and said, "Just a little on the ends. Thanks for noticing."

After Lew Traff rang the doorbell of the Denniver home on Fiddler Key the second time, he heard the faraway, irritable response. "Coming! Coming!" Molly Denniver cried.

Bees were working a big bush by the doorway. A mockingbird was developing a new routine. Some summer teens roared down the quiet street and out again, their motorbikes ripping the air with flatulence.

"It's you!" she said, surprised. "Whyn't you phone up?" She wore pale blue denim shorts and a white denim work shirt, both spattered with yellow paint that matched a dappling on her jaw and cheek and on her work gloves.

"Is Justin home?"

"If the son of a bitch was ever home, he could do some of the painting I kept asking him to do until finally I got so tired of asking I'm doing it myself. But I'm almost through."

"I tried the store and I tried the courthouse."

"He's thinking of trading boats. Kingsley's got him out somewhere on what is supposed to be a good used Bertram. Come on in." He followed her through the living room and out to the kitchen. Three freshly painted barstools stood on newspaper and the fourth was half done. "Make yourself comfortable while I finish this, huh? Hey, get me a beer out of the box there, and one for you, of course. I shouldn't drink it. I'm getting a beer belly. I've told Jus a dozen times that the Mako out there is all we need. If we get something too big for the davits, then we got all that scraping-the-bottom business twice a year, and it costs, you know? And even with the Mako, the channel coming in here is getting so shallow you have to be real careful taking it in or out at low tide. But you know how he is. He decides he wants something and he has to have it right now." She reached and took the opened can of beer. "Thanks, hon. Hope you're not in a hurry or anything. Maybe we could have a little swim. It won't be too refreshing because that pool water is what I mean hot, but it will help some." She shoved her hair back with the back of her wrist and looked at him. "Something wrong?" There was a ghost of anxiety behind her round green eyes.

"Pretty much wrong, I guess. Big wrong. Bad wrong."

She finished the last brush stroke and put the stool with the others, then stripped her gloves off again. "What do you mean?"

"Marty is jammed up. Harbour Pointe is dead. The financing collapsed."

"I heard about that. It doesn't have to be so bad it makes you look like that, does it?"

"It's all going to come before a federal grand jury in Tampa. A lot of charges. Conspiracy to defraud. Fraudulent certifications on loans. Misuse of insider information."

"They're after you too?" she asked.

"Let me tell you how this goes. This is exactly what Benjie Wannover told me. They came to him and wanted to take a preliminary deposition. He said no way. They said they would subpoena him and haul him before the grand jury. He said to them, Okay, lots of luck. They said the grand jury, on the instruction of the Assistant U.S. Attorney, would offer him immunity in return for complete testimony, and Benjie said he would not testify. Okay, they said, if you refuse to testify after being granted immunity, that is contempt, and the penalty is eighteen months in jail. He said, Hey, I've got ten kids. They said, Tough. He said, I only did what I was told to do. They said, Tough. He said, I got to have a lawyer. They said, Okay, but he can't appear with you before the grand jury. He said, That isn't the way the American system works. They said, Where have you been, Mr. Wannover. It's been working that way a long long time. So Benjie came and talked to me and he went back to them and said, Okay on the immunity. What do you want to know?"

"Can they really do that?"

"They really can. And they can do it to me too."

"What are you trying to tell me?"

"In the FBI investigation of the books of Marliss and Letra, they came across thirty-six thousand dollars over the past several years without enough documentation. The checks were cashed downstairs at the bank, usually by me, and Benjie will say it is his understanding the cash was given to you by me. It is hearsay, but there isn't a hell of a lot of reliance on the rules of evidence at a grand jury hearing."

Her plump little mouth sagged open. Her eyes looked stunned. She sat in the breakfast booth and looked up at him. "Oh, Jesus, Lew. Oh, Jesus."

"I know. And the IRS is standing in the wings. You and Justin file joint returns, I suppose."

"Sure. Why not?"

"Look, I'm going to get immunity too. I don't think I could live through eighteen months in jail. I'm not in that great physical shape. It's been tentatively offered and I'm grabbing it, and I am going to tell all, Molly, even to where that safe is and what it looks like."

"Not *all!* Not really *all!*"

"What? Oh, no. Not that part. No need."

"Oh, God, what am I going to do?"

"I'm sorry, but I think you are down the tube, you and Justin. I don't know exactly how it will happen. All I know is that things will never again be as good for you two as they have been."

"Will I go to jail?"

"I doubt it. Justin might, but I doubt that too. Big fine, big tax delinquency, probation, resign his office, and so forth and so on. Odds are you'll lose this house."

Tears ran down through the dotting of yellow paint on her cheek. "*Why* did we ever get into anything like this?"

"Pure, simple greed, I guess."

"Don't be such a bastard, Lew. The children. All my friends. Everybody at the club. Oh, God, I'm going to be ashamed to show my face." She clenched her jaw. "The son of a bitch responsible is Marty Liss. My husband would have been *glad* to do him little favors, just out of friendship, just to see progress in the community. But that slimy little son of a bitch had to send money."

"And Justin didn't send it back."

"We got used to it. We began to think we deserved it. We even tried for more, remember? Now . . . wait a minute! Just a minute. How did I know that you were bringing money here?"

"I gave it to you."

"In an envelope. I never opened the envelope, did I?"

"Molly, every time I—"

"I never opened it. I just took it and put it in the safe like Justin told me to do. I thought it was business papers. You're a lawyer. How could I know your only client is Martin Liss? Let me tell you something, Lew. No matter what happens, Justin will swear on fifty Bibles that he never told me what you were bringing, and that when he went to the safe the envelopes were always sealed. If he says anything other than that, he is going to be the sorriest human spectacle in west Florida, and unless you play it that way too, you are going to be as sorry as he is."

"What do threats like that mean anyway?"

"Try me and find out later. I am protecting myself and my home and my children and my reputation, and if you lie about me and tell anybody I knew about the money, I will personally shoot you stone dead!"

Lew stared at her with a new awareness. "By gee, I think you would!"

"Did you tell Benjie I knew about the money?"

"I don't think so, not in so many words."

"Well, in so many words, you tell him I didn't know and don't know now and never knew. I am never going to mention it again."

"Molly, that's a very nice move. It might work and it might not work, but it is worth a try at least."

"Justin isn't here right now. I expect him back about five."

"Okay."

"Were you leaving off an envelope for him?"

"Uh . . . not this time."

"Shall I tell him to phone you?"

"I always knew you're the smart one in the family."

"Shut up, Lew. Go away. I have a lot of thinking to do."

Pete McGinnity, president of the Golden Sands Condominium Association, sat with a leaden lethargy in his tilt-back leather chair in penthouse apartment 7-B at three o'clock on Tuesday afternoon. The draperies were partially drawn, darkening the small "television room." He had a Pay-Vision movie on the small screen. He had seen it one evening, an English movie about spies, and had guessed that he had not understood the plot because he had the two cocktails before dinner, a glass of wine with dinner, and the tall brandy afterward. Now, in sobriety, he realized glumly that he had not understood the plot because it was not consistent, coherent or understandable. It was an overacted mess.

Irene, sitting in the corner of the couch doing needlepoint, was competing with the sound track. He hesitated with his thumb and finger on the dial of the remote control, wondering whether to turn the volume up or down, and decided on down.

". . . it is a disgraceful thing," she said. "He's such a strange kind of spooky man, don't you think? And Mary

Starf seems like such a *nice* little person. That girl that comes up here is young enough to be his granddaughter. She's pretty, but you can see at a glance she's hard as nails. Grace Cleveland says the girl hangs around the Sand Dollar Bar a lot. There's a very rough crowd hangs out there, they say."

"I had the chance," Pete McGinnity said. "There I was. I had walked out of that goddam meeting. I was mad. All I had to do was keep walking. But no. I had to let them con me into coming back. So I'm still stuck in the middle of everything."

"This is a decent place with decent people in it, and I just cannot understand the Reverend Doctor Starf sending out for a prostitute to come and visit him. Grace says we should get Brooks Ames to . . . what do they call it? . . . stake out this floor the next time Mary Starf goes to Chicago, and then he can stop that little slut and ask her what her business is."

"How the hell can you renegotiate fees with people who won't even return a call? Gulfway Management, Investment Equities—you'd think they didn't give a damn whether we pay or not. But I know better. Those people are going to come down on us like a ton of bricks, and the worst of it is that there are some people living here who just can't pay the full amount. What about them? What are they supposed to do? Sell? Ha!"

"Then again I suppose she would say that she was visiting Reverend Starf, and what could Brooks do about that? Nothing. The other day Grace said in that deadpan way of hers that maybe the girl was giving Dr. Starf some kind of therapy, and it got Honey Wasniak laughing so hard I thought she'd have hysterics."

"What I've got out of retirement, I've got more on my mind than I had when I wasn't retired. I'm getting more indigestion, even. I thought I could get Jack Cleveland into my slot, but he's too smart for that. He'd rather stay on the outside and complain. Everybody would rather complain than do anything. I say we ought to expand the Board and put Jack Cleveland and Colonel Mark Simmins on it. Spread the load a little."

"I'd like to know if that minister has been in trouble before. I'll bet you he lost his church on account of something like this."

"You going to have any more iced tea?"

"And if I am, you want some?" She smiled and got up and left the room. Pete stared gloomily at the screen. A marksman shot a girl off her water skis, and she tumbled dead in a sprawl of long white legs as the marksman jumped into a small car and was driven furiously away.

Sam Harrison found Insta-Print on the north side of Athens, on the truck route, in one of a scattering of small shopping areas and service areas. He and the girl who came to the counter had to speak up to be heard above the clattering roar of equipment in the back room, and something that made an inaudible thudding which shook the floor. They had prepacked the report in two cartons, heavier than he expected, and he signed the receipt, put them in the car and drove on out to Golden Sands.

Mr. Messenger was up and dressed, with better color and looking more vital than the last time Sam had seen him. Barbara was astonished that Sam had waited until he was at their apartment to take a look at one of the copies of the report. Gus Garver was already there, anxious to get at the chore of signing his cover memoranda. Barbara and her husband and Sam sat and leafed through copies of the report as Gus signed the others.

It was bound in dark blue with a light blue card glued to the front cover with the title they had agreed upon: *Possible Topographic Alterations in Fiddler Key Due to Storm Surge* by S. D. Harrison, C.E.

"Looks pretty good," Sam told Barbara.

She smiled her pleasure. "I think so too."

He turned to Gus's introductory memorandum and then looked with mock astonishment at Gus. "If I'd known you thought that much of me . . ."

"You'd have wanted more money. Read on."

Gus had named the four vulnerable condominiums—Golden Sands, Captiva House, Azure Breeze and the Surf Club—stating that they stood upon the narrowest and most frangible and vulnerable portions of the middle segment of Fiddler Key.

He backed Sam's conclusions, mentioned the major hurricane now damaging the Antilles, called attention to the official policy of trying to give residents twelve hours of daylight before a storm to evacuate the keys, and finished with the warning, "I feel it would be the height of folly to try to ride out a hurricane in any one of these badly situated condominiums and, in fact, on any part of Fiddler Key or Seagrape Key."

"Strong," Sam said. "Points it up nicely."

"Joint effort," Gus said. "Mr. Messenger made it sound better than the way I had it first."

Lee Messenger said, "I wish I'd had you two working for me a few years ago. I like the way your minds work."

"What kind of work?" Sam asked.

"Hydraulic mining. Campeche."

"Wasn't that Tech-Mex?" Sam asked. Lee nodded. Sam said, "They struck out, didn't they?"

"Yes, it was a bad bruise, but my interest was through Far West Resources, and because our deal with Tech-Mex was turnkey, we didn't get hurt badly. If it had gone well, it would have been a bonanza. Well, the sooner those are signed, the sooner Dow and Forrester can start the distribution."

At six o'clock Ella was centered approximately at 16 degrees north and 62 degrees west. The eye, approximately thirty-five miles in diameter, had just finally cleared the town of Basse-Terre on the island of Basse-Terre, the southern island of Guadeloupe. Screaming winds of a hundred and fifteen to a hundred and twenty miles an hour were tearing at Antigua, Montserrat, Saint Kitts, Saint Croix, the Virgins and Hispaniola. The great winds circled and came down out of the north across the Caribbean Sea sending heavy breakers against the shore of the La Guaira peninsula of Colombia, against the sheer rock cliffs of Aruba and against the beaches of Curaçao and Bonaire.

The hurricane had great reach and scope and power, blowing down walls and trees and power lines. It smashed the people and drowned them and washed them into treetops. It turned rivulets to roaring streams and turned brooks to rivers. The pressure inside the eye was measured at 27.33 inches. Nearly all communications with the exposed islands were severed. Satellite pictures were taken and distributed every thirty minutes until nightfall. Ella was too huge for radar to be of much use except to reveal the onmoving areas of the most intense rainfall, much of it coming down at a four-inches-an-hour rate.

Meanwhile, scientists were attempting to predict the effect on water levels in those areas of the continental United States where Ella might make landfall. There were too many variables as yet to make any sort of precise prediction. In addition to the timing in respect to the tides, and the prediction of direction, there were the constant forces in the area which would affect the final computation. For example, the Gulf Stream moves through the Straits of Florida, between Key West and Cuba, at a speed of 3.5 nautical miles per hour, at a volume of thirty sverdrups. A sverdrup equals one million cubic meters per second. The volume can be appreciated by comparing that flow with the total flow of all the rivers of the world, combined. The total flow of all the rivers of the world is two sverdrups.

Another factor is the effect on water depth of the spinning of the earth. This spin moves water northward from the equator in the Northern Hemisphere with a constant force. The sea level off Cat Cay and Bimini is ten inches higher than the water off Miami.

There is another imbalance in water levels to take into account. The southeast trades normally push water into the Gulf of Mexico, establishing a level generally four inches higher than the water in the Atlantic Ocean. This forms a hydraulic impetus for that portion of the Gulf Stream which flows from there, going to join the eventual seventy sverdrups off the Carolinas.

There are minor considerations, a deep cold fast current which runs northward into the Gulf along the Mexican coast, and a weak southerly current, an underflow, along the Florida coast running counter to the Gulf Stream.

It was necessary to begin the predictions, to feed in the data on existing weather patterns, upper and lower currents in the atmosphere, the seasonal intensity of the tide patterns, the estimated effect of rainfall, the velocity and direction of the storm itself, and its effect on all the other factors affecting ocean levels. Input could be revised hour by hour as the hurricane moved closer, with the hoped-for result that when it finally came ashore, if indeed it *did* come ashore, whether in Palm Beach, Galveston, Pensacola or the Keys, the hurricane advisories could give the anticipated number of feet above high-tide level which could be expected, and a close approximation of the time of maximum water.

The occasional heavy rains had reached the eastern end of Cuba. The Rio Salado and Rio Cauto had already overflowed their banks in their headlong rush into the Gulf of Guacanayabo. There was flooding already in Santa Cruz del Sur from the Rio Najasa. Hurricane Center bulletins were picked up by Radio Havana and broadcast over all stations on the emergency warning service. The land was sodden, with the heaviest rains yet to come.

35

ON WEDNESDAY MORNING Audrey Ames listened to the weather news on Channel 13 on the kitchen television set. She looked at the charts and the pictures, and then went to her bulletin board and put a magnetic marker at Ella's coordinates on the metal chart which included the entire area, from the coast of Africa to Texas.

When Brooks Ames came out of the bathroom he

went over and studied her chart. "She's sure been moving straight and steady," he remarked.

"And quite fast, they say."

"She ought to smack right into Yucatán."

"If she doesn't turn north."

"There's no sign that she will."

"Except that most of them do."

"Because most of them do doesn't necessarily mean that Ella will."

"You are becoming an expert on practically everything."

"What's that supposed to mean?"

"Lately you contradict everything I say, no matter what I say. Have you noticed that at all?"

"Come on, now."

"You do, Brooks. You really do."

"I don't."

"See?"

"See what?"

"You contradicted me."

"What kind of a game is this, Audrey? I reserve the right to disagree with you when I know you are wrong."

"But most hurricanes *do* turn north."

"I agree."

"Then why did you contradict me?"

"I didn't. I said that because most of them turn north, it's no reason to say that Ella will."

"Why won't she? What's to keep her from turning north?"

"Nothing. I was being logical. You can't say she *will* turn north. That is not accurate. You have to say that the odds are in favor of her turning north."

She sat down and stared at him blankly. "My God! What's the matter with you? That's what I said. I said she might turn north because most of them do."

"If you had really said that, I would have agreed with you."

"Word games! Word games! You want to play these damn irritating games with me all the time. I am *not* one of your volunteer guards in your private army, Brooks."

"Thank God. You'd destroy all discipline."

"Please don't be so snotty. I only work here."

"And you argue a lot."

"And I get contradicted a lot."

He poured himself coffee, sat and said, "You read that thing Gus arranged to have sent to us?"

"I skipped a lot, but I got the sense of it."

"Think it could happen?"

"Brooks, I don't *want* to think about it."

"I *have* to think about it. It comes under security. Security is part of my job." He took a piece of paper from his shirt pocket and looked at his notes. "I'm going to get a list of emergency shelters from the Red Cross or Civil Defense and figure out which ones will be handiest for people coming off the key and make a list of those and distribute the list to everybody. I'm going to make a list of emergency phone numbers in Palm County and distribute that too. All my men have CB radios in the cars now, and that will help. I've been working out a hurricane checklist, as the third item to distribute. Lay in a portable supply of food that needs no cooking or refrigeration. Gallon thermos of water. Water purification tablets. Everybody gases up their cars ahead of time. Emergency flashlights. Battery radios. Candles. Matches. First-aid kits. I am going to ask every resident and every renter to contact me when the family unit is ready for inspection and then I will inspect or have one of my men inspect, and we will give them the okay if they have everything they need. I'll be checking the approved units off the master checklist. And then—"

She threw her head back and yelled, "Jeeee*zuss!*"

"What's the matter with you, Audrey?"

"Honestly, you are so . . . so picky and self-important and you bustle about so. You turn everything into checklists."

"Your life would be a lot more orderly if you would do the same, woman."

"I prefer disorder, thank you."

"Obviously. What I was about to say was that you will go on ahead to a place of safety and I shall remain behind with Jim Prentice and Ross Twigg, my best men, and see that the building is empty as requested by who-ever orders the key evacuated. Clear?"

"Maybe if you give me a little close-order drill every-thing will suddenly be revealed to me."

"You are as bad as that goddam George Gobbin. What neither of you understand is that I am in the busi-ness of protecting life and property, and that is just what I am going to keep on doing. Clear?"

"Yessir, Captain, sir."

He leaned and stuck his face close to hers. "Sarcasm is cheap!" he shouted. "Very very cheap!"

With a look of dismay she said, "Brooks, I really wonder if you are losing your mind. I really wonder."

At breakfast Henry Churchbridge was rereading por-tions of the Harrison report. Carlotta was reading the morning paper, glancing at her husband from time to time, trying to guess from his expression his reaction to the report.

When she particularly wanted his attention she would revert to the kind of English she had spoken when first they met. "Wot you theenk of eet, Yawnkee?"

"Hah? What? Oh, hell, there's no arguing with it. The man is competent. He is right, and the building they've been doing along this coast is insane, and we were crazy to buy this place."

"I am not really so red hot about this place, my dear. It is just a little bit too institutional. I really would rather have a house."

"Lot of work."

"Not so bad. What I can do, there are so many poor branches of my family, I can invite nieces and grand-nieces to visit. They are very well brought up, and very pretty, and they would all like to help me, one or two at a time, of course. And I have the money for a nice little house. Maybe not so little."

"What would I have done without a rich wife?"

"You would not have lived as nicely. That is all. Darling, what we should do is move all our treasures out of here, put them in a nice, insured, air-conditioned storage warehouse, and then go visit our children as you promised we could, and then we will think about a house somewhere. Possibly nearer one of them?"

"And just when do we start this epic program?"

"In the night when I couldn't sleep, I got up and I got two empty boxes and filled them with things, and made a list. You know, to be orderly. You could tie them up and put them in the car and go find the warehouse this morning, while I fill more boxes."

"Just like that!"

"Just like what? Look at the paper here. They are counting dead people, from drowning in the rivers and from buildings being blown down upon them and from trying to save their little boats. Twenty-two so far in Puerto Rico. Seven on Guadeloupe. They think maybe fifty or more in the Dominican Republic. And you are reading that thing that scared me last evening. There are enough messages, Enrique. I do not think this is a time for dallydilly."

"Dillydally."

"Whatever."

He sighed and looked around the bright and pleasant apartment as if already bidding it farewell. "Okay. More coffee, please, and then I'll start on the Yellow Pages."

"Good!"

"Most probably nothing at all will happen here, but at the very first warning we are getting out right away."

"Good!" she said.

"It isn't very macho, I guess, to run like a rabbit."

"On the way to the mainland I will pass rabbits. I will leave them behind me, panting their little lungs out."

"I have always liked your images."

"And my coffee."

Jack Cleveland stood in the pool Wednesday morning in water up to his neck, chatting with Frank Santelli from 2-A, who was holding onto the gutter and slowly exercising his bad leg. An inflammation of the sciatic nerve had created atrophy of certain muscles of the lower leg, ankle and foot, leaving him with a condition known as drop foot. Exercise was conditioning other muscles to take over for the ones no longer usable, and he had recently been able to give up the special shoe he had worn for six months.

Jack Cleveland said, "Back in Ohio in the lumber business and in banking and so on, I had to deal with these engineer types with their computer models and their systems analysis and their goddam gobbledygook talk. I'm telling you, Frank, when you deal with computer technology you have to remember GIGO. Always remember GIGO."

"What the hell is this geego?"

"They are the initials that stand for Garbage In—Garbage Out. Gee Eye Gee Oh. You see, what you got to remember, the computer can't think. It isn't a holy object. It is just a goddam dumb machine. And men put the information in one end and those same men take it out the other end after the computer gets through screwing around with it."

"Hey, that's pretty good! I like that. Garbage in, garbage out. Sure. What you're saying, Jack, that report we all got from Gus Garver, that's all garbage?"

"No, I *didn't* say that. I am saying that a guy can put in perfectly good and valid information into the input. But if he gives the wrong weight and importance to some things, and if he happens to leave out some stuff, or if he puts in stuff that really doesn't form part of the problem he's solving, then his answer is going to be skewed."

"Screwed?"

"Skewed. It means twisted, warped, that sort of thing. I read a dozen pages carefully and then I knew I could just scan the rest of it and toss it aside."

"Marie read it and she's scared shitless. She wants to leave now, for God's sake, and that hurricane is like maybe a thousand miles away from here and it could go anywhere. She *knows* it's coming right here, right at her, personal. I'm going to tell her you say it's a lot of crap. And she is going to say, How do you know?"

Jack thoughtfully scratched his haunch. "Look at it this way, Frank. Look down there, south, along the beach. Look at those places. Do you really think that the county and the state and the federal government would let that construction go on, let all those hundreds of millions of dollars be spent, if they thought there was any chance of all that being washed away? I know the construction game. You can count on that. And I know that all these big high-rise buildings are anchored right down to solid rock. They don't float for God's sake. And you got so many millions of tons, you can't put them on any kind of mushy base. You think the banks would loan money the way they have on these structures if they thought they could get washed away? For Chrissake, Santelli, look around you and tell me what you see!"

"So don't get sore!"

"I'm not sore. I'm telling you what to tell your wife."

"Did Grace get all upset when she read it?"

"She wouldn't have the patience to go through dull stuff like that. I think she got past about two pages and then gave up and said she'd take my word about what to do."

"What *are* you going to do?"

"Lay in a good supply of drinking water and food that doesn't need cooking or refrigeration. That is, of course, if the storm comes anywhere near us. I've got friends who live down here, been here in Athens for twenty years, and they say that every season they try to scare everybody about hurricanes and nothing much happens. It's kind of a local joke. People have hurricane parties. But it doesn't hurt to take *reasonable* precautions. I've got a gasoline lantern I'll make sure is working okay. We'll get candles and batteries for the portable radio, and I've got a portable TV that'll work on batteries too. When the winds start blowing, we'll pour a nice big drink and wait it out."

"That Brooks Ames says we all have to get out."

"Who the hell is Brooks Ames? This is my home, Frank, and if I want to leave, I leave. If I want to stay, I stay. Brooks wants to boss people around. He's a Nazi at heart, that guy. I fought a war to keep guys like Ames from taking over the world."

"He said he'd use force if need be."

"Let him try. Just let him try *that* on me."

"Maybe it wouldn't hurt to go to a shelter."

"If you want to spend three days and nights in some damn gymnasium full of squalling kids, sitting on the floor and sleeping on the floor and eating doughnuts, go ahead. Enjoy. Grace and me, we'll be here enjoying the view and sleeping in good beds."

The six o'clock evening news located Ella at 16 degrees north, 62 west. At about five o'clock a gust of a hundred and thirty knots had been registered at Santo Domingo, and shortly thereafter the wind-velocity recording device was destroyed by the winds. The hurricane was said to be intensifying. Communications with the badly damaged islands in its wake were slowly being reestablished. There were appeals for food and medical supplies. Estimates of total fatalities and total damages were fragmentary. Ella still moved at a steady pace, moving almost due west, covering an ever greater area in the satellite photographs.

ON THURSDAY MORNING Fred Hildebert, president of the Athens Bank and Trust Company phoned Marty Liss to see if he was free and then rode up to the twelfth floor of the bank building to see him. Fred bustled into the office, obviously upset. His eyes seemed to goggle larger than usual behind the heavy lenses. His bald head was dewed with sweat and there was a faint sharp odor of nervous anxiety about him.

"What are you *doing,* Marty?"

"I am taking things out of these drawers and I am putting them in this box."

"Why?"

"Jesus Christ, Fred! Why don't you keep better track? Wannover is gone because he is getting immunity for giving testimony against me. Lew Traff is gone because there is nothing here for him to do anymore. The Irishman is gone because she is doing better selling apartments for me than running a desk. I let the other two girls go because—maybe you noticed—the Marliss accounts downstairs are frozen and so are the Letra accounts. So I can't afford the rent here. And don't tell me I have a lease, pal. Marliss had a lease until you froze the funds."

"Me? You know better than that!"

"Sit down. You're making me nervous. I know it was the Feds that froze the account balances. Money can come in. Nothing goes out. Great. Wish I could always do business that way. Want to buy a nice desk? Look at it. Real slate and teak and pewter, pal. Beautiful. Thirty-four hundred bucks it cost. You can have it for one thousand cash."

"Marty, I came up to talk to you about *this!*" He held out a bound report.

"What have you got there? Oh, the big report on how we're going to have two keys out there instead of one. Where'd you get it?"

"Mr. and Mrs. Davenport brought it in. A very nice old couple. They're in Seven-C in Golden Sands. This upset them terribly. And me too. What's it all about?"

"Didn't you read it?"

"Of course I read it. It says that a hurricane will cut the key in two and wash away Golden Sands, Captiva House, Azure Breeze and the Surf Club, right? *If* it hits here at the right time and the right angle. I mean, Marty, what is it *about?* Why this? *If* lightning strikes me on top of the head, I will probably fall over dead. *If* your aunt had balls, she'd be your uncle. Do you know how much paper we've got on those apartments out there in those four condos you built?"

"Lots and lots."

"Do you know how much we're already writing off anyway?"

"Lots more."

"What I do not need is some jackass engineer predicting those buildings are going to be washed away. How can you let stuff like this get distributed to your customers, Martin?"

"*My* customers? I'm out of all four of those. I wheeled and dealed and sweat blood to buy that Franciscus tract nine years ago on credit, Fred, and what I thought I had left out of it was some money, a good reputation, and a nice feeling of pride whenever I drove by and looked at those honest buildings. I did that. Me. Martin Liss, who twelve or thirteen years ago didn't have enough income to warrant an audit. Thirteen years ago I was still partners with Jerry Stalbo and we were scramblers, believe me. You know what? I think that if that hurricane comes anywhere near close to here, those four buildings are going to go, just like the man said."

"Don't *say* that, Marty. Don't even *think* it. I'm in enough trouble with my board and the examiners already. Just a little bit more bad luck, and we are going to be so weak we are going to get shoved under the wing of some bank holding company strong enough to pick up our losses and bail us out. And where am I going to be if that happens? Oh-you-tee, out. In the street. And I've put a lot of my life into that bank."

Marty sat in his big black judge's chair and put his sandals on the slate desk, ankles crossed. He thumbed the wiry hair of his goatee and smiled up at Fred Hildebert. "Fred, I'm crying for you. See? I'm all cracked up over your terrible problem. You, you son of a bitch, set me up with that Sherman Grome, and he fixed me good. I still have your letter guaranteeing me a line of credit. Eleven million. Your honor, I present this letter in evidence. Mr. Hildebert told me he could not honor it, and he sent me to Mr. Grome, assuring me that Mr. Grome could loan me what I needed. I thought that Mr. Grome was okay because my own banker advised me to do business with him."

"Hey!" Fred said. "Hey, no!"

"But that is exactly how it was, friend. Exactly."

"No. You leave out how I told you that it was a very very bad time to get into anything that big. But you wouldn't listen. You wanted to go ahead with it. And at that time, as far as anyone knew, Grome was substantial and reliable."

"If I get indicted and have to go to trial, Fred, will you appear for me and testify that you put me in touch with Sherman Grome? Because if you don't I can make it sound a lot worse."

Fred took out a big white handkerchief and mopped his mouth and his bald head. "It's the least I can do for an old and good customer."

"Can't you lay off that paper on the apartments somehow? Can't you discount it with somebody?"

"I don't know. We took . . . just the class-A risks out there."

"How good are they if the buildings fall down?"

Fred went to the window wall and looked out toward the key. "It's all crap. They won't fall down. I could discount those mortgages and peddle them. Sure. Then I have to explain it at the next board meeting when the hurricane has long since hit the Texas coast and died in New England. It would be like giving away money. 'What are you, Hildebert, some kind of hysteric?' What do I do, read them this Harrison report? Put it in the minute book as an exhibit?"

"How much paper do you have? Approximately."

Hildebert pulled a short length of machine tape out of his pants pocket. "We've got a hundred and twenty-one total at an average present payoff of twenty-eight thousands three hundred, or three point four million."

"Of which a certain amount would be collectible even if the buildings blew away."

"A certain amount, sure, with a lot of legal diddling around and a lot of insurance adjustor finagling, and a lot of it would be a plain dead loss because some of those people, a lot of them, in fact, have an okay income to live on but no cushion at all. And on the other hand, of course, over a certain age we make it a stipulation they have to pay diminishing term insurance on the outstanding face amount."

"So it would be fine if they got washed away with the people in them, huh, Fred?"

"It would be nice to be able to carry on a civilized conversation with you, Martin."

"You came to the wrong place at the wrong time. Get out of here, Fred. Don't forget your disaster report. I've got a copy. I feel good about one thing. I've had to suck up to you for years, and now that I don't, it feels good. I never liked you, Fred. I tried to, but I never could."

"You're a slippery little bastard, Liss. I never trusted you. Not for a minute."

"You loaned me a hell of a lot of money over the years."

"You'll never be back in business in this town."

"Don't bet on it."

Mick Rhoades of the *Athens Times Record* sauntered casually into the private office of Billy Scherbel, the assistant to the Palm County manager. Mick wore white slacks, white shoes, a short-sleeved white shirt and the kind of white cap one sees in old newsreels of gentlemen golfers. His gentle brown eyes peered placidly out from under the down-tilted brim of the cap. His face and arms were very brown from outdoor labor on the grounds around his new house.

Billy looked up sharply when Mick closed the door.

"I said I wasn't to be interrupted!"

Scherbel was middle-sized, soft, petulant, with thinning blond hair and glasses with thick black rims. Mick didn't answer until he had lowered himself into an armchair and shoved his cap back. "It's sure God humid out there, Billy."

"How'd you get *in* here?"

"Me? You saw me walk in. I walked in here. I hung around until Helen had to go to the can. That girl has a very small bladder."

"You can leave, Rhoades. Right now."

"Don't you want to know how I happen to know that the whole thing is going to blow?"

"What whole thing?"

"Denniver. Marty Liss. Payoffs. Harbour Pointe."

"I know all about it. Don't you read your own paper?"

"And it's going to blow you up too, Billy."

The door was flung open. Helen said, whining, "I didn't let him come in here, Mr. Scherbel. Honest, he just——"

"It's okay," Billy said. "Shut the door."

Helen glowered at Mick and pulled the door shut. Mick said, "You still balling her, Billy?"

"Never! I'm a happily married——"

"Forget it. We're wasting time."

"You're wasting my time."

"When we had a little conference about this whole thing, I told the guys that it was my opinion that you were not in on any payoffs. And I really don't think you were. Traff was the bag man for thirty-six thousand, minimum, that got passed along to Jus Denniver. It's obvious that Denniver, as the ramrod, kept the biggest part of it. He would pass some along to Steve Corbin and Jack Dorsey. They said you probably got a share and I stood up for you. I said you were honest, in a certain limited sense of the word."

Scherbel was staring at him with horrified fascination. "Who were you talking to?"

"Just a little group of people who'd like to have a cleaner city. I told them your trouble is that you're always horny, in town or out of town, and if somebody wanted leverage on you, all they'd need do is set you up with jailbait and document it. I said you'd be in too much of a hurry to worry if the lady was thirteen or thirty-nine."

"This is an outrage!" Billy Scherbel said too loudly.

"For a puffy, balding, myopic-type guy, I must confess that you certainly seem to get your share, Scherbel. You do pretty well."

"What are you trying to *do* to me?"

"I'm worried about you, Billy. Aside from doing too many favors for that son of a bitch, Justin Denniver, you are a pretty fair bureaucrat. You are a hell of a lot more effective than your boss, Tod Moran, himself."

"Why should you worr——"

"You've seen the Harrison report on Fiddler Key?"

"It's nothing official. I heard about it. I did a little check-ing. It doesn't come from any official governmental source, Mick. It's just another one of these so-called scientific studies of doom from another one of the ecology freaks."

"Let me tell you something that's in that report. It says that if the Silverthorn tract had never been cleared of all its natural growth, and if a great deal of dredging and draglining had not gone on, then the key would have been in a lot less danger of a new pass occurring at that point. The report is out. There are lots of copies. A lot of people have read it. Now you're a pretty fair practical politician, Billy. Let's say that Ella, or the storm that follows her, or the one after that, comes ashore out of the Gulf near here. And let us say that the engineer, Sam Harrison, who, by the way, is a very impressive and competent guy, is right, and the pass does cut through, and ten million dollars' worth of buildings fall down, with a considerable loss of life, and a special grand jury is appointed to look into the whole mess. They are going to come across that little arti-cle I wrote about how the land clearing and burning per-mit and the permit for some minor work, scouring a channel, were slipped into a long list of dull stuff you read to the commission. They are going to be made aware of the payoffs over several years from Marty Liss to Justin Denniver and company. Would you say it is a fair guess that they are going to haul your ass in front of that grand jury and they are going to tag you with some of those funny words like misfeasance, malfeasance, misprision and plain old common corruption?"

"But the report is nonsense!" Scherbel said in a high thin voice.

Mick Rhoades leveled a finger at him and said slowly, "I believe every single word of it. Every single word. And even if it wasn't as persuasive as it is, are you in a position to take a chance on standing on the tracks when that kind of a train might be coming? Suppose even one person is killed if the condos fall down? Suppose twenty die? Liss and Traff and Wannover and Denniver and Corbin and Dorsey will be straining in every direction to find some dumb jerk they can nail it on. Could be you. It might fit, pal. It could be you."

Scherbel shoved the folders aside and took off his glasses and patted his eyes with a Kleenex. He said, "You think you can come in here and . . ." His voice was listless. "Oh, shit, I don't know. This goddam job. Neither of those permits should have been granted. I slipped them in. You know that. If they had been considered on their merits, Troy Abel or Wally Wing would have started jumping up and down, and there would have been so much fuss, Jack Dorsey would probably have broken away and gone with Abel and Wing and killed it."

"Why did you do it?"

"Not for money."

"That was my guess."

"You guess pretty good. I went to a conference in Orlando in January, and they set me up with a girl at the bar I thought I was picking up. Cindy Martinez or Fernandez. One of those names. They got an affidavit how I took her to room so-and-so at the Tropic Winds Motel and laid her, and they've got a copy of her birth certificate. Everything is notarized. She was fifteen. Hell, I've got a daughter seventeen. And my wife, Bets, would leave me if she knew. I couldn't ever get through life without Bets. I guess I wasn't flexible enough. So they needed a better handle on me, so they set it up. I didn't know about it until the first time I wouldn't go along with what Denniver wanted. That was the permit for scouring an existing channel, when I knew they were going to build a whole yacht basin. So I dragged my feet and they set the hook and gave a good yank, and I went along. I shouldn't be telling you this."

"Expect to read it on the front page tomorrow?"

"No. You've always been pretty straight with me. I want to be able to . . . find some way out of all this if the roof does fall in."

"With my help?"

"If you're willing, when the time comes."

"I think I might be."

"Thanks."

"But don't count on much, Billy. I don't think there's

any way in the world you can sidestep all hell, if a new channel cuts through where Harrison says it will. No way."

"If I'd only had more guts . . ."

"Exactly what I keep saying to myself. Every day."

"You? What are you afraid of?"

"Look at your own laundry list. It's the same as mine. See you around. I'm fearless, all right. I did a story on the condominium dwellers' revolt at Golden Sands and the resident creep killed it. I did one on Harrison's report yesterday. Same fate. Now I'm going back and write one about how difficult it might be to get off the key in a hurricane if you wait too long, and they will probably kill that one too. Bad for the condo trade. Don't make people edgy. Don't rock the boat. Don't irritate the advertisers. Don't criticize the sheriff. Instead, go write a fearless feature on the new plantings being put in by the downtown merchants."

Cole Kimber sat on the near corner of Loretta Rosen's desk in her small office in the rear of her small building. He wore a white straw ranch hat, a thin gray shirt of Western cut with pearl snaps, custom slacks, custom boots. He smiled down at her. "Tell you again, pretty lady. I got rid of every son-of-a-bitching thing I had left. Sent all my old customers a letter they should get in touch with A to Z Construction and Maintenance, anything they want done. Took a loss on a termination agreement with Letra, on account of their accounts were frozen there at Athens Bank and Trust. Emptied out the apartment, even. Sold stuff, gave it away. Pretty lady, my ex-employees are on the unemployment insurance, and I gave them a nice bonus to tuck away, every one. Went out to Roger Gandey's place and made him a cash offer on that custom motor home he took out to California and back last year. It's in first-class shape. Generator, air conditioning, electric galley, rugs this thick. Runs smooth as a new Greyhound bus."

"Are you trying to sell me a bus ride, for God's sake?"

"You closed on selling this real estate office yet?"

"Tomorrow, the sixteenth. Noon. They take over then. I hope your advice was good, Cole."

"It was perfect. If you made a cash deal."

"I made a cash deal. I discounted a little to make it cash. Certified check for the balance."

"You're something, Loretta."

"Cole, the answer is no!"

"We'd just drift on down around the Gulf Coast to Brownsville, and get the tourist cards and papers for Mexico there. No big hurry. Take all the time we want. Get all the way down to Guatemala, spend some time, then come back up to Yucatán and pick up the ferry service to bring the motor home on back to Miami. Make it last a year and then come on back here and see how things are going for everybody. To tell the plain truth, I got a little too close to Marty Liss and Lew and Benjie and Jus Denniver and those boys, and I think it would be a nice year for traveling."

"Good bye. Have a nice trip."

"You remember why I used to have to take you way out in the wide bay or the Gulf somewhere in the old cruiser? Or why I had to take you way off into the piney woods to that hunting shack?"

"Shut up, Cole!"

"On account of when I'd get you going good, you were by God the noisiest piece of ass south of Atlanta."

"God *damn* you!"

"Now here you are messing around with that kid lawyer, that pretty boy, that Gregory McKay. Little young for you, ain't he?"

"You are a bastard."

"Does he ever get you going to where you howl like a hound in the moonlight? Lord God, I've tried quite a few since you busted us up so you could go back to making money and keeping your mind on it, and they came on very stale ladies."

"Cole, Cole, Cole."

"I could make sure I always park the motor home way off in the boonies somewhere so you won't scare all the Mexicans, honey. *Look* at you, by God. You're getting all pointy just at the thought of it."

"Go *away*, Cole."

"And another thing. How many apartments did *you* sell in those four buildings? If they fall down, like the man says, those people are going to come right to this office with fire in their eye, and those new owners are going to send them right to you. But it could be hard to find you, the places I want us to go."

"You are a persistent man."

"You're old enough to know exactly what you want, and I know just how to give you what you want, and you've held onto your build better than any woman your age I ever saw anywhere. You shouldn't be messing around with some kid lawyer. You are forty-six damn years old, pretty lady, and I am forty-eight, and right now we are both free as birds and we can leave Saturday or Sunday, whichever you say. And here is a pretty I got for you, to give you when you decided to say yes, but here, take it anyway."

She opened the box and gasped at the lovely ring. It was an oval cabochon of opal, big enough to reach almost from knuckle to knuckle, a milky white with a shifting glimmering fire of orange, red, green, blue, aqua. "You idiot," she said in a low voice. She exhaled. "Sunday."

"Hah?"

"Sunday. I can't leave until Sunday sometime. I have to store my stuff. I have to pack. I have to put the house up for lease."

He stared at her. "I never thought you'd say yes."

"You didn't give that impression. You acted certain."

"Well, hell. Turn that kid back to his old lady, and we'll have us a vacation you wouldn't believe."

The photograph taken at six o'clock located Ella at approximately 17 degrees north, 75 degrees west. That placed the center a hundred miles southeast of Morant Point, the easternmost tip of Jamaica, and about two hundred and fifty miles due south of Guantanamo. In the photograph the great spirals of rain cloud curved in toward the tiny visible eye. They were counting the dead in Santo Domingo, and estimating the dead in Port-au-Prince. It was raining very heavily and steadily in Havana, and heavily but intermittently in the Keys. The flow of data into the National Hurricane Center was very heavy. From the pilot program of the Integrated Global Ocean Stations System, supervised jointly by the Intergovernmental Oceanographic Commission and the World Meteorological Organization, oceanographic data was being transmitted through the World Weather Watch along with the usual atmospheric observations. Prediction of probable direction was becoming ever more critical as Ella neared major land masses. Wind currents in the upper atmosphere and the hemispheric patterns of highs and lows indicated that Ella would probably turn northward in the next forty-eight hours. If it was an angled turn, the hurricane could carry on up into the pocket of the Gulf of Mexico. If it waited long before turning it could be in large measure subdued by the hills and jungles of Yucatán. Were it to turn sharply and abruptly, it would smash across Cuba into the lower Keys. As with a person walking down a long hallway lined with doors, each stride reduced the number of choices remaining.

37

A HEAVY RAIN FELL across the lower half of the Florida peninsula during the dawn hours on Friday, August sixteenth. Sarasota, Venice, Athens, Boca Grande, Fort Myers and Naples all received about two inches, and almost three inches fell at Key West, Matecumbe and Islamorada. Havana reported seven inches in the previous twenty-four hours, with winds gusting to seventy.

A bright blue bolt of lightning and instantaneous slam of thunder snatched Francie Liss up out of another of those dreams about Troy Mallory. In the dream he had been giving her another tennis lesson, but the court was soft and yielding, as if they were playing on a gigantic mattress. She kept falling, and when she fell she would lose the racket, and while she looked for it, Troy would yell angrily at her. When she found the racket and did hit the ball, she could not make it go fast. It seemed to float over the net toward him, and she wondered why he was not wearing anything at all as he played. As she looked down at herself, the lightning and thunder woke her.

In a few moments the torrential rain began again and she relaxed, having heard and believed that the lightning travels in front of the rain and there is no danger once the downpour begins.

She got out of bed and in her short nightgown she padded over to the sliding doors onto the terrace that overlooked the bay, looking west toward Fiddler Key. She held the Mexican draperies aside and looked out at the silvery bounce of rain from the terrace stones and felt such a great surge of romantic love for Troy Mallory that she felt unable to take a deep enough breath. Yesterday afternoon had been the very best yet. It just seemed to get more and more fantastic for them every time they met. And everything had become so dear to her. That narrow little alley and the big old banyan tree, and the walk through the overgrown little back yard to the funny cottage, where he would be waiting to open the door and take her in his arms, all of it had become magical. He was so tender and so strong, and he had such a wonderful crinkly smile. He was a perfect age for a man, twenty-four, and by wonderful coincidence just one day older than she.

She went back to her queen-size bed, separated from Marty's identical bed by the shared night table with its controls for the sliding doors, the draperies, the electric blankets, the rheostat for the lights, the dials for the sound system, the thermostat control for room temperature.

Francie lay on her back with her hands up under her

nightgown, fingers laced across her flat stomach, thinking about Troy and listening to Marty make that goddam popping sound with his lips every time he exhaled. If he wasn't snoring, he was making that incredible popping noise. Really a creepy little person to be married to. So hairy. Troy wasn't hairy all over like that. And where he did have hair it wasn't all that black curly hair with white hairs in it. Troy was so damn beautiful in every way, in every part of him, perfect. She thought that after four years married to Marty, it was as if she had earned the right to Troy. Why not? She was getting older and older, every day. Marty would make a person old before their time. Lately he was worse than ever. Mean and nasty. Business problems of some kind. Worried about money. What would he do if she ran away with Troy Mallory? What would the people at the club say? What would her goddam mother say? Poor Troy. Doesn't have a dime. Was seeded way up there before his knee went out on him. Now he can't cover enough court to play the big money game. Look at that snitty little girl over there on the East Coast. Thousands and thousands. It isn't fair. And Marty making me sign that agreement before we got married. Jesus, that was dumb of me. Troy is so sweet. Could I live the way I'd have to live? Waitress or something? Gee, I don't know. Maybe. Maybe I could, because this is true love, and it means for better and for worse and so on. Richer or poorer. Sickness and in health. My God, Troy is certainly healthy.

She got up and went over and put the heel of her hand against Marty's shoulder and gave him a hard push.

"Whassawarra!" he said.

"You're doing that popping thing!"

"Poppythin?"

"Stop popping your mouth!"

"Time sit?"

"Twenny past six."

"Jesus, Francie! Go to sleep!"

"I *want* to go to sleep. You are popping your mouth and I can't!"

"Gess room," he muttered and rolled over. In thirty seconds he was popping again.

She grabbed up her pillow and her light cotton blanket and left, banging the door. She went down the hall to the bigger guest room and lay atop the spread, cocooned in the yellow blanket.

"Troy," she said aloud in a sweet little voice. "Troy, darling, I love you so. I love you. I love you. I love you."

Maybe he is awake, listening to the rain pour down and remembering how much fun we had yesterday afternoon, and maybe he is saying he loves me too.

Lee Messenger had awakened with a white crackling hissing pain at six on Friday morning, a pain that devoured all will and resistance, and he had awakened her at once to give him a shot. He fell into the Demerol sleep and was summoned out of it by the same merciless force a little after ten o'clock.

When it increased beyond his capacity to endure it, he yelled and hurt his throat, and then said, "Sorry, sorry, sorry. I just . . . can't . . . "

She gave him the second shot, and when he was finally at rest she phoned the doctor. She said, "I really haven't seen my husband like this before. It's like a new dimension. It's frightening."

"Well . . . normally I would say let's wait a bit and see. But I've heard that Ella is turning north and we might have confusions going on here that would make it difficult to get him off the island and into the hospital later if I decided that's where he should be."

"We'll want that suite arrangement, one of those suites, at Physicians and Surgeons Hospital that I looked at before, if one is available. Otherwise, two private adjoining rooms, Dr. Wadkin."

"I'll arrange an ambulance, and by the time you arrive with him, they'll know where to put you, Mrs. Messenger."

She checked the sleeping old man, then phoned down to the office and said that an ambulance was coming to take Mr. Messenger to the hospital. She packed a bag for him, tears blurring her eyes as she wondered if he would wear these clothes and come home in them. She packed her own bag, then took the emergency money from the wall safe Lee had arranged to have installed before they had moved in.

She wrote a note to Mrs. Schmidt, who was due to arrive at eleven, telling her to go ahead and do the cleaning, but there would be no one at the apartment to cook lunch or dinner for.

As she waited for the ambulance, she remembered that Sam Harrison had said he would stop by in the afternoon. She phoned his room at the Islander and he answered immediately.

"Sam? Barbara. Lee is pretty bad this morning, and with the storm coming, Dr. Wadkin thinks he might be safer and more comfortable in the hospital, so we're going over there as soon as the ambulance gets here."

"I'm sorry to hear that. What can I do?"

"Nothing I can think of. He's asleep now. We'll both be staying at Physicians and Surgeons. It's a private hospital."

"Both of you?"

"I always stay with him when he has to be in. He frets if I'm not nearby. He thinks of business problems and what should be happening and he has no one to order about if I'm not there. And I've turned into a pretty fair practical nurse."

"I'm glad you're both getting off the key and staying off. It's beginning to look more and more possible the lady might come here for a visit."

"Oh, dear."

"If I were you—"

"I have to hang up. The ambulance is here. Talk to you later."

"We interrupt our regular programming to bring you, as a public service, a message from the Palm County sheriff, Sheriff Alton Lowe."

"Ladies and gentlemen, I am your sheriff, and I want to thank the management of WATH-TV for giving me time on the air to give you this message. All of you who heard the six o'clock news and weather know that Hurricane Ella is now approximately three hundred miles almost due south of Key West and she's on a heading now of a little bit west of north, which should take her right up into the Gulf. It looks like she'll cross Cuba in the Isle of Pines Havana area, which is too narrow a land area to do more than slow her a tiny bit for a little while. She has just about lashed the Cayman Islands to bits and she is giving Cuba hell, excuse me, right now.

"It looks like we could be in for it, but if we all do our part and follow instructions, we can minimize the damage she might do to our area. We've got a couple of daylight hours left, and I want you to know that the odds are very strongly in favor of an evacuation of the offshore keys, right from the Ten Thousand Islands up to Tarpon Springs, a mandatory evacuation to start first thing tomorrow morning. Those of you that are elderly and infirm, or have little kids, and who want to stay in motels on the mainland, I'd truly suggest that it might be best to make your arrangments now and pack and get off tonight. We'll get rain so heavy traffic might have problems moving tomorrow morning.

"I hope most of you have gone through the hurricane checklist in the paper and gotten what you need to get. I want you to remember this. We could be without electric or drinking water for two or three days, and we're in the heat of August, so guide yourselves accordingly. We've been lucky on hurricanes so long, we're due for a big one. And if you're a little scared and nervous about it, and anxious to do everything right and avoid harm and damage, that's a good healthy attitude to have. Remember to pull the main switches when you leave your homes, and turn off all pilot lights, and turn off any bottled gas or underground tanks at the main valve. Keep your radios, if we lose power, turned on at all times for bulletins. Pick up all loose stuff around yards and in carports and on porches. Take in potted plants and hanging baskets and so on.

"Ella accelerated and made a big curve up toward the north and she has now slowed a little in forward direction but she hasn't lost a thing in intensity. I want to point out that even if she misses us clean and goes on past us up the Gulf, we are still going to get a lot of very dangerous winds and a lot of very high water and waves pushed by that wind.

"I want to thank the station for having me on, and I wish everybody good luck in this emergency, and we'll be all right if you follow orders and keep in touch."

The Eastern 727 came down at dusk through rain so thick Fred Brasser couldn't see the runway lights from his window seat until moments before the wheels touched.

When they had taxied close to the terminal he un-clicked his belt and leaned close to the glass, but he could not see her among the small group of people waiting in the bright lights under the deep overhang of the terminal building.

In fact he did not see Darleen Moseby until she danced up beside him as he was walking through the terminal and caught his arm and said, "Hey, you made it, you made it! You got loose!"

He stopped and kissed her, and as he walked along with her, smiling his pleasure, he saw a stern middle-aged woman looking at him with curiosity and amused disapproval, and for an instant he saw Darleen through her eyes, but only for an instant.

She had borrowed an old Chevy van to come out to the airport and get him. Lurid desert sunsets were painted on the side panels, and the interior was entirely carpeted—floor, walls and roof—in electric-blue shag. She wouldn't let her Freddy get wet. She scampered through the dwindling rainsquall and brought the van around to the terminal and picked him up.

"Whose is it?"

"Some guy named Dave that hangs around the beach."

"Have you . . . been busy?"

"No. Things are real slow. How long can you be here, hon?"

"A week. I've got the money. You want it now? Here."

"Sure. I guess so. Thanks. But you know Tom isn't really into this kind of thing."

"What do you mean?"

"You know. Like a steady person. What he worries about, you'll make me some kind of a deal, I'll run out on him and go to Fort Worth or some weird place. He's afraid if any of us get any kind of regular thing going with a mark."

"I'm a mark?"

"Honey, you're not really like a mark-type person to me. You are Freddy, and I really like you a lot. You're more like a boyfriend, sort of. Okay?"

"Okay, Darleen."

"Louise was going to take off with a guy she really liked one time. But Tom found out about it somehow and she finally admitted it to him, and so he broke her thumb."

"He what?"

"Wow! Did you feel the wind then? It nearly blew us into the ditch, hon. Wow, I love storms. I really do. What? Oh, sure, he broke her thumb, reached out and grabbed it and twisted and zap, it broke, and she screamed bloody murder. It was in a cast for weeks. I'll tell you one thing. She doesn't make any plans about going away."

"I don't like you staying with that mean son of a bitch."

"Oh, Tom is okay. He really is. Not to worry."

"Would you think maybe about coming to Fort Worth?"

"Don't get like that, Freddy. Don't spoil things. I got us the same room again by the pool."

"That's fine."

"It's in your name like before. We'll have us a ball, sweetie. Hey! Feel that wind? It'll be cozy in bed listening to the rain and the wind. You know something? I'm starving. I know a good take-out place for Chinese. It isn't much out of the way. How about we get some? Good! The shrimp flied lice is fantastic. Dig me out five bucks, hon."

He sat in the dark van outside the Chinese restaurant on Route 41 in the hot Florida night. Big trucks groaned by, their furies fading down through a minor scale as they drove south. Gusts of wind rocked the van, making a small motion he could feel. He remembered the two small dark moles on her lower belly, off center to the left, perhaps an inch above the curled, springy tuft of auburn brown. His erection was uncomfortably constricted by the entrapment of his jockey shorts, and he shifted in the seat to ease it, his heart bumping and his hands sweaty. He could see her in there through steamy glass, while a man packed the order. She stood erect, feet apart, hands shoved in the slash pockets of her tie-dye jeans, barefoot, wearing a yellow sweat shirt three sizes too big for her— a small jaunty figure whose life seemed almost entirely focused upon her own considerable appetites. He wondered how all this had happened to him, and why he did not give a damn where it was all heading.

38

BROOKS AMES HAD COFFEE in 4-D at seven o'clock on Saturday morning, with his two most trusted lieutenants, Jim Prentice and Ross Twigg.

"Okay, this is it," Brooks said. "Audrey phoned and said that she and Doris have got a good corner for the six of us at the Sports Center shelter. Hardly anybody else has arrived there yet off the keys. They drew six cots and got them unfolded and set up, and while Audrey was phoning, Doris was blowing up the air mattresses with that foot pedal pump you bought, Jim. Good idea, by the way. Helen hadn't got there yet, but remember she was going to stop and get more canned stuff on the way. We're thirty-three feet above sea level there and we should be okay. When our work is done here, you'll drive the three of us to the Center, Jim. Any questions?"

Ross Twigg, an adenoidal-looking man with the ghost

of a cured stammer, said, "It doesn't look like any storm coming."

"Now here is my master list, men. I have weeded out the vacant ones and the ones I know have left. I'm going to take them right from the bottom and work up. When I give a name I'll pause, and if any of you know anything, you just speak up. Anything about their attitudes, even. Okay. Starting way at the bottom here we have the Higbees, Julian and Lorrie."

Jim Prentice said, "I saw her late yesterday afternoon and she was madder than hell at him. He took off early yesterday morning and she didn't know where he was and hadn't seen him."

"He take their car?"

"Apparently."

"Then we'll get her a ride with somebody. She'll be sensible about getting off the island."

The faint music of the small radio stopped and there was the long high-pitched note to warn of a bulletin. Brooks held up a hand for silence and turned the volume up.

"The eye of Hurricane Ella has just crossed Cuba west of Havana and is back over open water, about a hundred and twenty miles southwest of Key West. Winds of over a hundred miles an hour are savaging Key West at this moment, and the waterfront is being punished by huge, wind-driven seas rolling in out of the Straits of Florida. The course of this great hurricane remains north-northwest on a path which, if continued, will bring the eye within seventy miles of Fort Myers. Wind-driven tides are expected to be six to eight feet above normal by this evening from Fort Myers to Tampa Bay, and all exposed locations in the area should be evacuated without delay. Please keep tuned to WANS Radio, fourteen-ten on your dial. Further bulletins will be broadcast as they are received." When the music began again, Brooks turned it down.

"Looks worse and worse," he said. "I am putting a T beside Lorrie Higbee's name, Ross. That means you are the one finally responsible for remembering to get her evacuated. Okay, now for the first-floor apartments. Francine and Rolph Gregg? I don't see any problem there. Major Phil DeLand and his wife, Roxy?"

Prentice said, "They should be gone by now. Phil said he would never fool with these things. He's been in a couple in the Pacific."

"Good man. Gus Garver. I talked to him yesterday. He picked up a sleeping bag and a batch of stuff on the checklist and he is leaving, or has left, to go over and stay at that Crestwood Nursing Home with Mrs. Garver. He said he was afraid those nits over there would run for cover and leave her alone if it got bad. The Rastows?"

"Ready to go as soon as the orders came through," Ross Twigg said.

"Mrs. Boford Taller?"

"She doesn't drive. She's going, or has gone, with Major DeLand and his wife."

"The Shumlus family. Mark, Edith and daughter Lynn."

"I spoke to him yesterday," Jim said. "He pulled rank. He said that he was accustomed to making command decisions and he said he had made life-and-death decisions before, and he was experienced in weather patterns, and he would keep track of the storm through the bulletins and decide whether or not they would leave the key. He's one bullheaded old bastard."

"I'll go have a talk with him myself. Second floor. Frank and Marie Santelli?"

"They think this is the safest place they can possibly be," Twigg said. "They've got a hurricane party all cooked up. Them and the people next door to them, the Quillans, and Jack and Grace Cleveland from up on six. They don't any of them believe the Harrison report, and they've got friends who've lived down here a long time and who tell them not to worry, it never amounts to anything."

"We'll come back to that situation. Mr. and Mrs. Fish?"

Prentice said, "She's an emergency-room nurse at Athens Memorial, and they've moved the emergency-room staff right into the hospital to be available for twenty-four-hour duty. He's in the school system and is helping operate the shelter in the high school."

"Fine. Mrs. Neale. Ah, I remember, she moved out. Something about misrepresentation. She's suing the realtor. Mr. and Mrs. Kelsey?"

Twigg said, "They told me they were ready to leave as soon as the word was passed that it was time. So they're gone by now."

"Good. On the third floor we have the Truitts. They're all set; I checked their emergency list. Schantz. They're all set. Jim, did you learn what that goddam George Gobbin is going to do? He wouldn't tell me a thing or let me check his stuff against the list. He kept giving me that Hitler salute business."

"Oh, he's leaving. I talked to Elda. Sensible woman. She said George likes to bug you, Brooks. You shouldn't let him get to you."

"Get to me! He doesn't *get* to me, dammit."

Twigg said, "It sure looks like a nice day. No clouds except that real high misty stuff, and the wind coming from the east now, Brooks. Are they *sure* it's going to—"

"That wind is a little bit south of east, Ross. Face into it."

"Hah?"

"Face into the wind, dammit, into the direction it's coming from."

"Okay. Sure. I'm facing, Brooks."

"Now point your right arm straight out from your side. Point with your finger. Okay. You are pointing right at the center of that hurricane. South-southwest of here, and coming north."

"But it looks nice. No rain."

"Ross, it won't look all this nice by tonight. Believe me, it won't." He stood at the windows with Twigg and looked at the coconut palms which had been planted north of Golden Sands, in front of Captiva House. "Look at the fronds on those palms, men. That's a stiff, gusty little breeze there. . . . Where were we? You confirmed the Gobbins are getting off the key. We don't have to worry about any of the directors and officers of the Association. They understand they have to set an example. So David Dow and his wife will be leaving this morning. I can vouch for Fred and Rose Dawdy getting off. Did you check Branhammer, Ross?"

"I sure did. He o-o-o-o-o-o-o—"

"Hold it! Take a deep breath, Ross. Then try it again. Take your time."

"He o-opened the door and left the chain hooked and when I tried to tell him everybody had to leave, he said that it was a trick to get him and his wife out of their apartment, and once they left we were going to move his stuff out and change the locks. He said he wasn't that dumb and he said that *nobody* was getting him out of there. He slammed the door. He used pretty bad language on me."

"Forget him," said Brooks Ames. "Let the son of a bitch drown. Fourth floor. The Brasser apartment is empty. So is Four-B, since Sapphiere moved out. Howard and Edith Elbright will evacuate as advised. Then there are us three in a row. Then Harlin Barker."

"Mrs. Barker is bad off, they say," Prentice said. "He's going to stay in a shelter they got at the Legion Hall that's only a block and a half from the hospital."

"On the fifth floor," Brooks continued, "we've three empties. Five-A is for sale, Five-E is an empty rental and the Protuses in Five-G are still on that cruise. How about Mr. Jeffrey, Ross. You covered that floor."

"Which one is he?"

"The skinny old professor on the bicycle."

"Oh, sure. He said he'd probably leave."

"Probably?"

"He said it really wasn't any of my business because we guards had sort of appointed ourselves and he had no part in it, no voice in it, which made it undemocratic. Because of that he said he did not have to give me a specific answer about his personal plans. Then he gave me a long talk about personal privacy and so on."

"We'll check him again. How about Mr. and Mrs. Winney?"

"He just kept smiling and shaking his head no and saying that he and Mrs. Winney would be quite all right. He said they'd made all the preparations to wait it out right here."

"I'll give it a try later. Let's see. The Wasniaks are leaving. Ben and Alice Hascoll are leaving—have left, in fact. I saw their Olds go out last night, loaded. They were terrified. They were heading for the hills."

"Hills?" Prentice asked.

"It's just an expression. Okay, the sixth floor. Three empty rentals and one for sale. So there's only three occupied on six. We know that the Clevelands are staying and going to the Santellis' hurricane party in Two-A with the Quillans. Has anybody checked with Jack Mensenkott about staying on the mainland? His wife is in the hospital, you know."

"I tried knocking on his door three times," Jim Prentice said. "And I've phoned him a couple of times. I haven't reached him."

"Keep trying. Henry Churchbridge and his wife are getting off the key. That takes care of the sixth floor. Now for the penthouses. The Messengers are gone already. She's staying at the hospital with him. The McGinnitys and the Davenports and the Forresters are evacuating. How about the Starfs, Jim?"

"The Reverend Doctor Harmon Starf listened to me, and when I told my story he stared at me for, I guess, five seconds, and then he slammed the door. I mean he is one big man and he really slammed it."

Brooks Ames nodded and said, "That's another neighbor I can do without. Okay, let's recap the master list, men. Here are the ones we know are staying, no matter what we do: Santelli in Two-A; Quillan in Two-B; Branhammer in Three-G; Winney in Five-C. Cleveland in Six-C; Starf in Seven-E."

"I don't know if Starf is going or staying," Prentice said.

"There's nothing we can do anyway. The ones we have to make another contact with are Colonel Simmins in One-G, Professor Jeffrey in Five-B, Jack Mensenkott in Six-F . . . wasn't there somebody else?"

"Lorrie Higbee on the ground floor."

Ames studied his list. "Dammit, it doesn't add up. I've got forty-six apartments accounted for. I'm missing . . ."

"Hey," Ross Twigg said. "We left out the Furmonds."

"Who?"

"You know. On the first floor. She's that tall woman with the sunburn and the bulgy eyes that found Jesus and stood up at the meeting after Branhammer popped off."

Ames checked his list. "Right! They're in One-E."

Ross continued, "I remembered because I saw her out in the parking lot yesterday and asked her to leave pretty early to avoid the rush. She said that she and her husband, they were putting their fate in the hands of the Lord, and if they were meant to die in this hurricane, running off to the mainland wouldn't change a thing. She said everybody would be better off praying than running around with candles and lanterns and first-aid kits."

"Damn!" said Brooks Ames. "That makes seven staying, if we count Starf. I'd hoped we'd do better than that."

"You know," Jim Prentice said, "we're doing one hell of a lot better than the people in Azure Breeze and the Surf Club and Captiva House. I've got a friend from Azure Breeze I talk to on the beach. He does a lot of surf casting. He told me yesterday afternoon that he didn't think even a third of their people would leave. He said they got the revetment and the seawall and pilings way down deep, and most of them think that building is the safest place they can be."

"Not according to the Harrison report."

"He'd heard something about that, but he hadn't seen it. He said everybody tries to scare you these days, and the hell with it. He talked it over with his wife, and they're staying."

"Well, men, let's split up and check these people out as best we can, and then ride on over to the Sports Center shelter and see how much help we can be getting the people settled in over there."

"Helen still thinks we should have all gone to a motel," Ross said.

"I think it's better to go where we can be of service. We all know first aid. We all know the rules. We can be a big help."

Justin Denniver was eating glazed doughnuts and watching the little color set in the kitchen when Molly Denniver came wandering out of the bedroom in her old pink robe. Her face looked puffy and her eyes looked small and red. Her dark red curls were matted and her little plump mouth was pallid.

"What's new about the storm?" she asked.

"Shut up," he said, taking another bite of doughnut.

He had Channel 13 out of Tampa. They were on the cable. Roy Leep, the chief meteorologist, was explaining the radarscope picture of Hurricane Ella and had moved over to the satellite photograph.

Molly said, "You know, I don't ever really believe anything about the weather unless I hear Roy Leep say it's true."

"Shut up," said Justin.

Roy Leep was saying, "You will notice that the cloud mass of this major hurricane reaches all the way from mid-Cuba, to Merida in Yucatán, to Tampa. And right here we can see the well-defined eye, which in this picture, which has a half-mile definition, is approximately forty miles in diameter. It has now changed direction again and is moving due north, at approximately fifteen miles an hour. If it continues on this course, it is going to do enormous damage to the entire West Coast of Florida, particularly the offshore islands and keys.

"All hospitals, law enforcement agencies, fire and rescue organizations and civil defense groups from Naples to Apalachicola have been placed on an emergency basis, and those of you who might be watching this station from any of the exposed keys are urged to evacuate as soon as possible. Very strong winds are reported at Key West. Heavy rains and high tides may block access roads to the keys before a complete evacuation can take place, so those of you in the Fort Myers, Athens and Sarasota areas are advised strongly to leave now."

"Are we getting off the key, Jus, honey?"

"Shut up!"

"The strong winds from the south are pushing the water levels very high in the Gulf, and the residents of the coast can expect that as the eye of the hurricane passes their location, as it moves northward up the Gulf, the winds will shift to a westerly direction, piling the water against the coast. The actual direction of Hurricane Ella has now become less stable and more unpredictable. She may move in toward shore and cross the shoreline at any time late today or during the night. If this should happen, there will be very strong winds just south of the eye, perhaps a hundred and fifty miles an hour and more, from the west, plus a storm surge of possibly ten to twenty feet.

"I repeat, this is a very strong and dangerous hurricane and all residents of the West Coast of Florida should take all precautions suggested by the advisory services."

A man in a hairpiece the color of a red setter began extolling the car deals he was willing to make. Justin Denniver punched the set off and Molly sat down across from him with her glass of juice and said, "I think this time maybe we ought to get off the key."

Denniver stared at her. He was a big man who seemed to be fashioned of mismated parts. He had an oblong face of an unhealthy yellow-gray cast, short heavy arms, a barrel chest, a pumpkin belly, long slender legs. He wore his gray hair in a high-bristling brush cut and dyed his mustache black. He had a hollow clanging voice, as if he were speaking down into an oil drum. He said, "All my life I've been here. Born during the hurricane of '28. I built this house hurricane-proof. I've got respect for those mothers. I laid in all the supplies we need for a week. We couldn't be no better place than right here."

"But you heard what Roy Leep—"

"Shut up. Go fix yourself, for God's sake. Why do you come out here before you even wash your face or brush your hair? You turn my stomach sometimes, Molly, you really do."

"I think maybe I'll let you sit this one out here."

"I thought you might."

"What does that mean? Why are you looking at me like that?"

"I've got my tail in a crack. You know it and I know it. You made it all clear what I'm supposed to do. No, sir, Your Honor, my innocent little ol' lady, she never once opened them envelopes Lawyer Traff was leaving here for me. She thought they were some kind of legal stuff is all. She put them in the bedroom safe like I told her to."

"So?"

"So I'm going to be the loser and you're going to come out winner. You sure do like to win anything you play, Molly."

"What's this all about?"

"What if I tell you that Lawyer Traff's car was here a lot more times than Lawyer Traff was leaving off them envelopes?"

"I'd say you were absolutely correct. Why?"

"He was here?"

"Of *course* he came here! Quite a few times. Mostly to tell me his troubles. Maybe I'm a mother figure. How should I know? I'd offer him a swim and a drink and a sandwich, and it would shape him up. I think I told you about that more than once."

"The hell you did!"

"Justin, honey, you seldom listen to *anything* I say. You nod and grunt, and that's it. I might as well talk to the wall."

"I would have heard you say that."

"Who would bother to tell you a nothing thing like that?"

"Somebody that figured I shouldn't be such a damn fool."

"About what?"

"About you getting screwed by Lew Traff is what!"

"Oh, Christ, Jus, your troubles are clouding your mind. If I really wanted to get laid by somebody other than you, I would probably pick that kid over at the club, the assistant pro, Troy Mallory. But they say he's already got his hands full with Francie Liss. Maybe he could fit me in somehow. I could make an appointment. What do you think?"

He looked at her in a puzzled way. "What do *I* think?"

She laughed with delight. "Oh, God, you look so funny and sweet, Justin. If I'd brushed my teeth yet, I'd have to kiss you. Honey, if we're going to stay here, are you going to put up the shutters? You'll need help, right?"

"I'll get them out now."

"Nothing ever happened with Lew. Nothing ever could, honey."

"Okay, I'm sorry, I'm nervous lately."

"I know, I know. Poor honey. Be with you in a couple minutes." On the way out of the kitchen she stopped and turned, frowning, and said, "What's that!"

They both listened. The roar came from a long way off and then arrived, a rain as heavy as they had ever seen. It enclosed the house in a silver curtain, so impenetrable they could not see the dock and the Mako on its davits. The roar was so loud she moved closer to him and raised her voice. "I think we better hurry!"

"Take your time," he shouted. "There's plenty of time yet."

In five minutes the rain slackened as the squall moved northwest.

LeGrande Messenger and his wife were in Suite B on the fifth floor, the top floor of the Dickinson Wing of the Physicians and Surgeons Hospital, four miles east of downtown Athens. Sam Harrison anticipated a lot of arguments about the two heavy suitcases he carried in through the driving rain from the parking lot, but his look of confidence and his seeming awareness of exactly where he was going took him past the momentarily thoughtful gaze of the desk people.

The foyer door and the inner door were open. Barbara was sitting beside the sleeping man. She got up quickly and came out into the hall and said, "You're drowned!"

He pulled his shirt away from his chest. "Drip-dry."

"What on earth have you got there?"

"Emergency stuff. Lots of water, food, candles, flashlights, batteries, radio and so on. All that kind of stuff."

"For us? But this is a *hospital!*"

"With a limited capacity on the emergency generators, and they'll save those for emergency-room work. And your odds against getting food and water by using a telephone that won't work either are not good."

"Are you trying to scare me, Sam?"

"I was making the assumption you're an adult. Precautions are the cheapest thing you can invest in."

"I'm sorry. You're right, of course. And it is very kind of you. Thank you. Where are you going?"

"Not sure. I've got some stuff down in the car."

"Were you going back to Golden Sands for anything?"

"Why?"

"I left something there I shouldn't have. I've been wondering what to do."

"No problem. I can go back. What is it?"

"Here are my keys. Sam, it's a bronze bull about this long, six or seven inches. It dates back to twenty-five hundred B.C. It's Chinese."

"Valuable?"

"Lee bought him at a London auction ten years ago and bid him in for ninety thousand dollars. I think he'd be worth three times that now. But it really isn't the money. Lee loves the style and the elegance of that beast, the way he holds his head. I brought a couple of the other pieces that are special favorites and forgot him, and I so want Lee to know that I was . . . very competent about leaving and packing and so on. The bull is in a glass case on the bedroom wall."

"I will see that you keep your reputation."

"It's pouring again."

"It comes and goes. The wind is stiffening. Coming a little more from the south. How's everything here?"

"Lee is not doing very well. They can't seem to find anything that will dull the pain. They have to keep knocking him out. He hates that. He'd so much rather be alert. Come on in."

He carried the heavy suitcases in and she had him put them down in an alcove between the two rooms. She said she would unpack the items later, hoping they wouldn't need them. In hushed voice of explanation she showed him the suite. The hospital room was large, and had its own bath, with grab rails by the tub, shower and toilet. The other portion of the suite, of similar size, was divided into a small bedroom and bath, and a sitting room with a small kitchen alcove. There was an intercom in her bedroom and in the sitting room which picked up any sound from the hospital room. She turned it on and he could hear, amplified, the guttural breathing of the unconscious old man.

"Anything else you want from the apartment?"

"Nothing else, thank you. I can't believe there could be a real danger of . . . everything going."

"You don't believe the report?"

"With one part of my mind, yes. With another . . . I just don't know."

"There certainly isn't any great flood of people coming off the key."

"Do be careful, Sam. If things look rough, don't bother with the damned bronze. Okay?"

"Okay." He wanted to kiss her on the cheek. He reached to put a hand on her shoulder, leaning toward her as he did so, and then stopped. It was an awkward moment for both of them. She gave him a flat and meaningless smile which did not reach her eyes, and he left.

It was 11 A.M. when he reached the north bridge onto Fiddler Key. Police in yellow rain capes were checking the cars going out to the key, turning some of them back.

Sam remembered he had forgotten to turn in his key to his room at the Islander when he paid his bill. His single carry-on bag was in the trunk of the rental car. He fished for the key and held it up when it was his turn. "Going to get my stuff and check out, Officer."

"Well . . . okay. But don't hang around out there to see the sights, friend. Anybody you see at the motel, tell them the time to get off is now."

"I'll do that. I saw you turning cars back."

"People wanting to go out there and gawp, for God's sake. Sightseers. And would you believe a van with four kids and four surfboards? Okay, move it along."

As he went over the crown of the bridge a sudden hard gust of wind wrenched at the car, pushing him over toward the curbing at the right. There were fast-moving clouds going by, very low. The whole day was in shades of gray and silver, all the leaves in tumult, car lights and street lights on. A half mile south of the north bridge, where Beach Drive curved slightly toward the beach, he got his first good look at the Gulf, and it startled him. Great humps of green-gray murky water were gliding in, lifting higher, curling and smashing against revetments, seawalls, pilings, groins, and sending solid water and spray high into the air. The spray was being wind-driven across the drive. Even in the slow-moving car he believed he could feel the repetitive thud as each line of combers broke hard against Fiddler Key.

For perhaps half a minute a watery sunlight shone down through an opening in the fast-moving cloud cover, making rainbows above the beach, and then the rain came, slowing the light traffic to a crawl. A sheriff's car appeared behind him, speaking with its huge electronic voice. "Leave the key! All residents are ordered off Fiddler Key. Leave the key! This is an order! Everybody has to get off the key at once. Now!" It would stop and the siren would whoop for thirty seconds and the voice would begin again. But the rain dimmed it, and the wind whipped the words away, tearing them to ragged shreds.

There were several inches of water across the road at the entrance to Golden Sands, and he made the turn carefully, leaning close to the windshield to see. He parked as close to the rear entrance as he could get. There were three or four cars in the lot in the rear, and apparently quite a few parked under the building. He punched the elevator button, then realized that if the power went out while he was between floors, that would be where he would wait out the hurricane.

He did not see anyone as he went up the seven flights. The Messenger apartment was cool, and it was nice to be out of the worst of the wind and rain noise for a little while. He found the bronze bull in the glass wall case in the master bedroom, along with some small bottles which seemed to be fashioned of jade. He told the bull that he did not look like a quarter of a million dollars. But then, an object is worth what a willing buyer will pay for it. And the bull, as Barbara had pointed out, had class. He had a valiant stance. He looked alert.

He put the jade bottles in his pocket, and he wrapped the bull in a hand towel from the nearest bathroom. Then he prowled, very aware that She had lived here. This was the cave of the She, touched with all her scents and fancies, imprinted with her dreams and doubts, marked by her oblique passions and mysterious purposes. Riddles to unravel. Fractionate her life scents in the cracking tower of your heart, and give it all a name. Intimate lace, a sleekness of nylon, two gentle hairs caught in a brush, a dignity of shoes, a crackle of silk, a smudge of lips.

He went to stand at the sliding doors and look out at the sea, visible once again between rains, feeling as faintingly enamored as any schoolboy, summoning up erotic images of the She.

Car lights crawled north along Beach Drive. In the dark of the oncoming noon he saw that many apartments in Azure Breeze and the Surf Club were lighted. Packing to go, my friends? Or celebrating the staying. Wind drummed the big glass doors. He turned off the lights and picked up the towel-wrapped Chinese bull and left.

Between outside door and car door, wind caught him and took him two hurried steps before he braced himself against the car. He drove through a couple of inches of water in the parking lot and out through the deeper water on Beach Drive. A few hundred yards north, traffic stopped. Rain hammered down. It bounced a foot high off the hood of his car as the wind whipped it off toward the northeast. He turned the car radio up to compensate for the rain noise.

". . . repeat, the drawbridge at the north bridge to Fiddler Key is stuck in the open position. It opened a half hour ago to let a vessel through and the heavy winds damaged the mechanism so that the bridge tender cannot close it. All traffic waiting at the north end of Fiddler Key should turn around and go down to the south bridge. Repeat, the drawbridge at the north bridge to Fiddler Key is stuck in . . ."

A fat man, his face warped by anxieties, slapped at the window at Sam's left. Sam turned the radio down and opened the window.

"The bridge is stuck open."

"I just heard it," Sam shouted. "I thought they weren't supposed to open the bridges after evacuation starts."

The man shrugged. "They aren't. Some kind of foul-up. Maybe they were letting a Coast Guard boat through. Makes no difference."

"What?"

"Makes no difference. There's a palm tree down across a couple cars up ahead anyway. And some people hurt with trash flying through the air."

Sam saw the Civil Defense insignia on the man's jacket. "What do you want me to do?"

"Don't try to turn around unless you can turn into a driveway. There's a lot of them in the ditch up ahead, no way to get them out, blocking traffic up there. I get these cars behind you to back up, you can all turn around there in front of the Seven-Eleven."

"Nice of you!"

"I can't get out until you get out, buddy. Two-lane and deep ditches along this part of the key."

About six miles to the south bridge. Two miles to Beach Villa and four more to the bridge. And, he thought, I will be passing the Islander once again.

But once he was opposite the entrance to Golden Sands, he came upon a group of stalled-out cars, three heading south, two heading north, all up over the hubs. Before all momentum was gone, he pulled the shift into low, roared the engine and tried to make it around the stalled cars by riding the shoulder. The right side of the car tipped down into the ditch, and he crunched into a driveway culvert and stalled out. End of car. He got out, steadying himself against the wind. He could look out at the wild seascape between the Azure Breeze and the Surf Club. Wind was blowing the crests off the big waves, whipping the sea to a white foam which blended with the sky very close offshore. He opened the trunk, unzipped his suitcase and put the bull and the jade inside, zipped it and slung the strap over his shoulder.

Old couples with staring eyes and white fearful faces peered at him through smeared windshields and side windows. He waded to each car on the downwind side and yelled through car windows, cautiously opened a few inches, that if they stayed there they would drown. He told them the water would get deeper. He pointed and told them to head for that tall condominium on the bay shore south of Golden Sands. He told them to crawl if they had to, but make it there and go in and go to the top floors and see if anybody would take them in. He could not tell if they were going to do it. They seemed frozen in some strange apathy of terror. Their automobiles were familiar. They did not want to step out into the soaking gray hell of rain and wind, into kneedeep water covering invisible hazards. He stopped cars coming from the north and told them the same. The road was blocked. He moved to where he could hail any car coming from the south and direct it to where it could turn around and, hopefully, cadge a ride. Finally a car came along, a brown young man with big wrists driving a battered old Land Rover.

He shouted to Sam, "Any chance of getting through?"

"None. Bridge is stuck open anyway."

"I know. Hoped it was fixed. Road's washed out south of the village, just beyond the Islander there. Jesus! Got any ideas, mister?"

"No good ones."

"I was afraid of that. The thing to do is get something that'll float and cross the bay on it. That's what I'm going looking for. Get in, if you want."

Sam climbed aboard and the young man turned the Land Rover and went back to the village, throwing water high on either side. They turned left in the middle of the village, heading for the bay shore. They passed old frame houses, old trees. He turned right and left again, and stopped at an old small-boat marina. It seemed abandoned. It was a little quieter this far away from the Gulf, but it was still roaring like distant freight trains.

"I'm Jud."

"Sam."

"Sam, they tooken the boats off yesterday, moved them way up Woodruff Creek, but you see here, they got some little stuff rolled over and tied. So let's bust into that shed there."

They found an old Johnson 25 with a dented housing chained to a stand. Sam spotted the big cutters and chopped through the chain. Jud put the outboard into a drum after checking the gas. It coughed and died, coughed and died. He cursed it and took the housing off and began tinkering with the carburetor.

Sam noticed a faded red-white-and-blue pay phone booth in the lee of the marina building. He shut himself into it, out of the wind roar, and found to his surprise that it was working. He looked at the shreds of a phone book and found the *Athens Times Record*. After three busy signals, he got through to Mick Rhoades.

"Who?" Mick asked. "Who?"

"Harrison. Sam Harrison. The engineer."

"Looks like I should have taken a chance and run your report."

"Too late now. Listen. I'm on Fiddler Key."

"They said the phones are out."

"This one isn't."

"We've got two reporters over there somewhere. What's going on? What are you doing over there anyway?"

"Shut up, Mick. There's no way to get off the entire northern two and a half miles of the key except by boat. People are trapped between a busted bridge and a washout. I'm at a small marina behind the village and we're trying to get an outboard working so we can cross the bay by boat. There are a lot of old people trapped in their cars near the approach to the north bridge. The water is coming up fast. A lot of the cars are abandoned."

"But Ella is still way south of here!"

"Just listen. Okay? Get hold of the authorities. Maybe if the Coast Guard or Coast Guard Auxiliary could get some heavy-duty boats running a ferry service near the north bridge they could get some of those people off before the wind gets too bad."

"Communications are terrible, Sam. All we're getting on the citizens' band channels is a lot of roaring, people stepping on each other's broadcasts. You keep fading."

"Did you hear me about the boats?"

"Yes. Yes."

"See what you can do? Mick? Mick?"

The connection was dead. He tried the operator. The second time he tried he could not even get a dial tone.

The wind pulled at him as he ran over to the drum where Jud had mounted the outboard. Jud was fastening the housing back on, and gave him a tight grin and glanced skyward as if in prayer. He gave a hard pull on the starter rope and the outboard caught. As it sputtered he adjusted it to run smoothly. Jud turned it off, patted it and loosened the transom clamps.

They decided on a sixteen-foot skiff that looked as if it would have enough freeboard to take a lot of rough water. They cut the lines to the stakes holding it down, rolled it over, and were about to clumsy it down the slope to the muddy beach when Sam caught hold of Jud and forced him down just as a big four-by-eight sheet of some sort of wallboard went sailing by, close overhead.

Sam had seen the pile beside a fence, with tarpaper held down by cement blocks sheltering the pile from the rain. Wind had gotten under the tarpaper and rolled the blocks off and whipped the tarpaper away. Now the wind was lifting the sheets, one at a time, and sailing them off into the gray murk over the bay.

They crouched by the skiff until the last sheet was gone, and then launched the boat. They loaded Sam's suitcase, Jud's backpack, a pair of oars and a manual bilge pump. Sam stood in water up to his knees, holding the boat steady while Jud mounted the outboard on the transom. Sam could see all the white water out in the bay.

He hoped Jud knew that with that kind of following wind and following chop, if he tried to turn the skiff, she would broach in moments. He hoped the bilge pump had good capacity. He hoped there were no more piles of wallboard or lumber being flipped out there from the key to the bay.

The motor caught. He leaped in, whacking his kneecap painfully against the gunwhale, crouched, snatched up the bilge pump and was ready when the top of a white wave came sloshing in over the side as the wind eddied and tilted the skiff.

AT TWO O'CLOCK on Saturday afternoon, Darleen Moseby shook Fred Brasser awake in Room 30 of the Beach Motel. He came reluctantly up out of sleep, conscious first of being very hot and sweaty, then of a very loud whistling roaring sound as if an airplane were dive-bombing the motel, and finally aware of her narrow angry eyes.

"Chrissake, Freddy! Damn you anyway! I've been shaking you and shaking you until my arm is nearly wore out. You sleep like some kind of dumb pig."

"What's happening?"

"What's happening is the wind and the surf are so loud nobody can hear himself think hardly, and the electric has gone and I'm like melting away, all over sweat. It's like I can't breathe. And it keeps raining oftener and oftener as if the sky broke. I'm getting scared. You look out that window, hear? Just look out there."

He went to the window and looked out. The entire swimming pool area was covered with water. Wind was riffling it and rain was dappling it. The chairs were all gone. The metal tables were bolted down. Their tops were a foot above the level of the water.

"My God!" he said.

"Look at that damn lightning. Just wait a sec and you'll see some. It's *blue*. It's some crazy blue color, and you can't hear the thunder even. On the TV, before the electric went out, they were saying everybody get off the key. What I want to do, hon, get dressed and we'll wade over to the Sand Dollar, because they're having a hurricane party, and if I'm with a lot of friends I won't be as scared as I was here with you out like a light."

He came back to bed and caught her as she got up and pulled her back, trying to roll her onto her back. "No!" she said loudly, over the storm roar. "Let go, huh? Please?"

When he began rubbing her breasts, she hit him with her fists, pulled free and ran into the bathroom. He tasted blood between his teeth. When she came out of the bathroom he was dressed too. He thought of the depth of the water and thought of leaving his shoes, then wondered what sharp things might be under the water and decided to keep them on.

"I'm sorry I had to pop you, Freddy," she said, and kissed him lightly. "You're beginning to puff up." She laughed. "That was a pretty good shot, huh?"

"We'll be okay here, Darleen."

"In a rat's ass, we will. I want my friends around me. Come on. You'll have a good time. I promise. They're wonderful people, a lot of them. It's a real hurricane party."

They went down the corridor toward the front of the motel, splashing through five or six inches of water inside. Once outside, they were not in the grip of the wind until they got out to where the curb and the street began. The

411

wind caught them from behind and on the right side, shoving them faster than they could wade. They both went down and scrambled up, spluttering, and held each other and walked bent over and well braced, feet wide apart.

She poked at him and gestured, wide eyed. He looked, and saw a yellow VW floating across the street at an angle, coming to rest against the shuttered front of a dress shop.

The Sand Dollar was shuttered too, and after knocking and getting no response, Darleen led him down the side alley and around to the rear and in through the rear door. About twenty people yelled their greetings above the sound of the storm. There was a foot of water inside the bar-lounge. Lou and Tom Shawn were tending bar. Several gasoline lanterns cast their hard shadows and white glare. Darleen led him around and introduced everybody, but in all the noise and confusion he did not catch very many of the names.

By the time Jack Cleveland had decided they ought to merge the two hurricane parties he knew about—the Santellis' party which was, after all, only the six of them, and the Leffingwell party over there on the beach, on the eleventh floor of Azure Breeze, which was at least twenty people, if old Deke Leffingwell had his way—the phone had gone out. The wind was whistling and moaning and roaring and the rain was being driven in flat gray sheets against the windows.

Good old Deke had been in the class ahead of him at Ohio State. Done damn well too, if that apartment was any clue. It had to go at at least a hundred eighty-five, maybe two hundred thou. And any fool could tell Marcia had used an expensive decorator.

Jack felt slightly numb around the mouth and decided he would slow down on the drinks for a time. This little party was turning into a drag. Grace was getting scared of the wind and weather, and it was affecting Marie Santelli. It wasn't bothering Tammy Quillan a bit. The damn woman was so tight you couldn't understand a word even when she came up and yelled in your ear, as she kept doing more and more often the last hour.

He wished he could get over there and see good old Deke and see how that party was coming along. Well, why the hell not?

He went over to Grace and leaned toward her ear and said, "I left some good wine in the car trunk. I'm going down and get it out."

"You can't go down there now!"

"Why not? Take it easy! Be right back."

He walked out before she could catch him, and moved quickly to the staircase and went down and was startled to find that, at ground level, the water came six inches above his knees. He looked into the parking area and was appalled to see that the cars parked nearest the front of the building, that part that faced the Gulf, had been moved by the water, had been jammed back into pillars and the cement block walls of the divided areas for utilities and laundry, and had been shoved back into each other. There weren't many of them. The wind was whistling and howling through the parking area. He waded to where he could see over toward the Surf Club and Azure Breeze. It was like dusk, even though only about three o'clock on an August Saturday afternoon.

There was solid water between him and the condominiums on the beach side of Beach Drive. Plantings were gone. The hard wind was rolling small white waves all the way across to Golden Sands. He could see drowned cars on Beach Drive, perhaps a dozen of them, with water up to the door handles. The wind drove brackish water into his face, stinging his eyes. He tasted the salt on his lips.

Thrusting against the wind, he waded to his car, a lime green Chrysler New Yorker with a white vinyl top, white vinyl upholstery. The Churchbridge Buick which was usually parked next to him was gone and someone had put a red Datsun in that private slot, a car he remembered seeing out in the open lot behind the building. His Chrysler was flush against a pillar, and the Datsun was rocking and grinding against the left rear panels and fender. The wind and water had brought loose junk and trash floating in. A lot of it was caught in the angle between the front of the Datsun and the front half of the Chrysler. A big palm bole, broken off, was nudging and thudding at the front left fender of the Chrysler, surrounded by pieces of crates and pieces of redwood deck furniture, all afloat and bobbing in green torn leaves and green beach grasses, pieces of paper and plastic.

He could not endure that thing gouging at his fender. He always kept his cars nice, washed and waxed, with polished chrome and blazing whitewalls. He saw that if he could work that tree trunk free, it would either go all the way on into the bay or would hang up and start bumping at something else. He clung to the Datsun as he worked his way around it, feeling it lift and rock as it was shoved against his car. He got hold of the palm trunk and tried to pull it back. It seemed to be stuck somehow. There was some kind of bright yellow thing under it. He reached into the murk of the water and got hold of the yellow thing and pulled it out from under the weight of the palm bole. It came to the surface and rolled and he saw in the flash of blue lightning that it was a life jacket strapped to a middle-aged woman. She rolled to float face up, her hair spread wide in the litter of grass and leaves and paper, dead eyes half open, and continued the slow roll to float once again face down, to move toward his car, to start to thud the top of her head high against his fender, lightly and persistently.

When finally he was far enough up the first flight of stairs to be above the water, he stopped and leaned against the wall, gasping and gagging, eyes closed, holding his clenched fists against his big chest. Finally he was able to climb slowly to the second floor and walk down the open-air walkway to the Santellis' apartment, holding the concrete safety rail with an unsteady hand.

When they saw him come in, they all came to him, their faces open with their concern. He sat down and began to cry. As he cried he was furious with himself. He could not call it grief. He did not even know the damned old woman. He could not say he was crying for his car.

That was idiotic. He did not tell them he was crying from fear, because he was not even sure that was it, until suddenly the first spasm of painful diarrhea cramped his bowels and he got to the bathroom in the nick of time.

At three that afternoon, with the wind coming in ever more from the west, moving up the compass points as steady as a great clock, and increasing its velocity, the waves that marched against the shore became broader and higher and more muscular. One cubic yard of water weighs three quarters of a ton. The waves were breaking against Fiddler Key opposite Athens, and Seagrape Key to the north of the city, moving in at a speed of fifty miles an hour.

A wave lifts, topples, smashes forward as the runoff from the previous wave is sucked back into it and lifted to add its mass to the new wave. Whatever a wave smashes, detaches and pries loose is brought back and lifted to become a part of the smashing force of the ensuing wave.

By three o'clock the waves had hammered away a portion of the seawall in front of the Islander. Oncoming waves sucked the backfill out through the gap and out under the wall and pulled big slabs of smashed concrete down toward the Gulf, where the waves busily buried them. The sea will bury what it cannot lift, when the shore is sandy. The fine white-sugar sand of Fiddler Key moved easily. As the water coming back down the slope moved around each slab of concrete, it pulled the sand away from the sides; when it was sufficiently exposed, the water pulled the sand from under it, and it settled. Then the process was repeated. At last the slab was buried, and new waves jammed sand up the beach and washed it back, leaving a little more than before.

The glass-enclosed lounge and restaurant began twenty-five feet back of where the seawall had been. The glass was tempered, and when a wave broke one panel it fell in hundreds of chunks no larger than bottle caps. The shrieking wind burst into the big room and blew away the doors at the east end beyond the bar and tumbled tables and chairs and service stands into a windrow that jammed the opening, in a wild circling of tablecloths, napkins and menus.

Waves smashed the rest of the glass and reached in and gathered up every movable object. A wave would fill the room, almost to the ceiling, run through and thud against the east wall, and slide back, pulling everything with it. The next wave would lift those objects up its steep concave slope and hurl them at whatever had not yet been displaced. The bar was overturned, rolled, smashed. The back bar came down with all its mirrors and bottles glinting in the roaring murk. The supports tilted, the walls and ceiling came down. Big slabs of roofing and siding tumbled, slid, were hurled forward again. From the time the seawall was broached, the total destruction of the restaurant-lounge and adjacent kitchens took less than six minutes. The only objects protruding from the smooth slope of sand were the corner of a big color television set, one side of the largest kitchen range and one edge of the custom walnut bar. The destruction of the rest of the complex was proceeding as rapidly. Earlier the waves had washed out Beach Drive south of the Islander.

As the sea gnawed the complex back, there were nine people who took refuge, first in the reception area and then above it in the resident manager's apartment. They had not left soon enough. All of them had intended leaving. There was Harry, who had been on the desk, Skip the bartender, Pete, a restaurant supply salesman, Kitty, the waitress, a touring couple from Denver, and Liz, the tall executive secretary from Birmingham, and her two friends.

The wind sound was constant, a whining roar, and the crash of waves was continuous thunder. They had to yell at each other, lips close to ear, to be heard. They heard breaking sounds from below. They saw the few cars in the wide lot being rolled over. They wept and screamed, unheard, and clung to one another as the building was pulled down. Not one lived one minute past that terrible moment when they were lifted up and up and up toward the toppling crest of the next wave.

By then the sea was rolling all the way across the key in a half-dozen places. The small-boat rescues had retrieved nearly forty people from the key before the increasing strength of the wind made the bay far too dangerous. One launch, bringing ten back, broached and foundered near the wind-damaged bridge with, as was later determined, two survivors.

At the National Hurricane Center, occupying the top two floors of the Computer Building on the University of Miami campus, a current reading of the pressure at the center of Ella was received, and it was a shocking nine hundred and thirty millibars. By using the tide forecast system devised by Conner and Kraft, this gave an estimated maximum tide of approximately fourteen feet. In addition, as confirmed by radar, the hurricane was still changing direction and was now moving to the east of north, and if it continued on that course, the eye would cross the Florida beaches somewhere between Tampa Bay and Athens at 10 P.M. The appropriate warnings were sent out, with the knowledge that there was really very little remaining that anyone could do.

Two tired graduate students took a break and walked out into the sultry late afternoon. There was hazy sunlight. It was very hot and humid, with a sticky and fitful breeze from the south.

They sat on a bench in the shade. She slapped a mosquito off her wrist and said, "It's like some kind of huge irony, you know?"

"Not exactly."

"My parents live on Siesta Key in Sarasota."

"I know."

"Since I've gotten into meteorology, when I've been home I've *told* them to get off the key if the authorities order it. They say yes, yes, sure, honey. But they don't . . . they *didn't* believe. You can tell by their eyes. I told them how once there was fifteen feet of salt water in what is now downtown Tampa, and how it destroyed a whole fort there, and they say yes, yes, sure, honey. So, dammit, I *wished* there would be one that would come in and shake them up. I *wished* for this, Dave!"

"Hey. Don't cry, Sue."

"I'm sorry. But with this thing, even if they did go to the mainland, it could still get them. Figure the water levels yourself, my friend. Fourteen-foot tide. *Plus* the coordinating high tide. *Plus* all the rainfall and runoff. And what if the eye comes ashore north of them? Add on the storm surge *and* the seiche effect, and it's all the way off the scale! You saw it up there. You saw those printouts. All they can say is twenty feet plus."

"They'll be okay. On the mainland you have a lot of stuff in front of you to break the force of the waves. The water level will creep up. People will have a chance to move to a safer place."

"Oh, sure. So they are in a one-story motel, and like we heard, the Tamiami Trail is broken in forty places already, so all they do is climb up on the roof somehow and try to stay there in a wind blowing a hundred and fifty miles an hour, hard enough to blow bark off the damn trees!"

"Sue, honey."

"I'm sorry. I'm okay. I just have to bitch to somebody. I wanted them to have a nice *little* hurricane, so they would have more respect. And we have to get this great big monstrous killer."

He patted her clumsily and kissed her beside the eye, and said, "We better get back up there."

The waves had plucked away the riprap, revetments, seawalls and backfill in front of Azure Breeze and the Surf Club. It was thudding against the very heavy reinforced wall that was a part of the seaward foundations of the Surf Club. At Azure Breeze the waves dug into the spaces between the support pilings. They smashed the thick slab between the pilings once they had undermined it. They pulled out pieces of the slab, and once they had reached far enough back under the building, they began the same process on the pilings that was used to bury the heaviest pieces of slab. The water, rushing back out, scoured sand away from the sides of the pilings, making deeper and deeper furrows which extended farther and farther down the beach slope.

Loretta lay sweaty in the bed at Golden Sands, in the dishwater light of a dying day, listening to the awesome tumult of the great storm. Rain was crackling against the windows like hail. She could feel the building shake. There was an actual mist in the air of the bedroom, of rain pinched and driven through the tiniest openings by the monstrous gale. In the brightness of lightning preceding the unheard thunder, she could see the moist highlights on her breasts and belly and her upraised thighs. Interwoven in the frightening and deafening roar she could make out unknown thumpings, crashing, creakings.

Damn fools not to get off in time, but no great harm done, she thought. Yesterday she had told him about leaving with Cole on Sunday. Wouldn't make it now, of course. There would be three or four days of utter confusion. She'd told poor dear Gregory that it was really all in his best interest. If he persisted, his sweet little wife, with all her allergies, would take him back. She might make him eat a whole generation of crow, but she would take him back. Loretta was glad she had brought her two big suitcases up to the apartment. Had she left them in the trunk of the car she was going to put in storage, they might have been damaged, the way it looked out there when she had glanced at the world a couple of hours ago.

She had become ever more convinced that taking off with Cole was the right thing to do. She had not realized how bored she had been running the office, manipulating people, maneuvering them. Nobody manipulates Mr. Cole Kimber. A mean bastard with a quick temper. Not at all acquiescent like Greg. Poor Greg. Poor sweet Greg, so very anxious to please her and win her favor. He had actually wept real tears when she told him she was leaving for a year. She had kissed his eyes and tasted the salt of his tears.

It had become an excitement to her to think of leaving with Cole. It was an anticipatory fluttering, not unlike the onset, the first hint, of orgasm. It was like being a little kid in Ohio again, and putting your ear against the rail to hear the faraway funny droning whisper of the oncoming train. When it got so loud it was frightening you sprang back to safety and in a little while the great engine would come surging around the curve, unstoppable, all big wheels and pistons and black roaring energy, giving the first great *hoohaw* for the valley crossing ahead, steamy and rackety. Then there would be the long rhythmic clatter of the trucks over the expansion gaps in the rails. Finally it would go away, the crummy rocking on the roadbed, the sound fading into summer silence. Then you would go try to find the flattened penny you had left on the rail, find it among the rank grasses and the broken ballast stone.

She turned and looked at Greg, asleep with his mouth agape. Poor boy, so worn out with loving he could sleep through hurricanes. She got up and stretched and yawned and walked to stare through the sliding glass door. She stared, first in confusion and then in growing consternation. Through the horizontal rain, it seemed to be all water down there, and it seemed to come to a very unlikely height, certainly high enough to be up to the roof of her car. She could not see through the rain as far as Beach Drive. She turned and yelled to Greg to come look, but saw that he could not even hear her, much less understand her. The sliding glass door seemed to be vibrating in some strange way, almost humming in its track.

As she reached to put her fingertips against it, the plate glass blew inward. The sliding door tracks in the whole building were just a fraction wider than they should have been. Cole and Marty had jollied the young architect representing the large busy firm which had styled the building. Cole Kimber had used the minimum specification for plate glass allowed under the Southern Building Code. Some of the doors were substandard. This was one of them. The County Building Inspector's personnel had been less than thorough. Golden Sands had gone up during the last of the big condo boom. They were busy.

The sliding glass door was seven feet high and three feet wide. It is reasonable to assume that the wind gusted up to one hundred and fifty miles an hour when the door ruptured. Wind at this velocity exerts a force on an exposed surface of one hundred and twelve pounds per square foot. Winds had long since blown down or broken the anemometers in Palm County. The total force against the door was thus three hundred and fifty pounds in excess of one ton. The explosion of wind and shards of glass blew her back across the room, smashing her lower spine against the dressing table. When she fell, spraying blood from a dozen slashes, it pushed her half under the dressing table. When Greg McKay sprang from the bed, the wind knocked him down. He crawled to her and she looked up at him in a mildly puzzled way before her eyes hazed over and she was gone, all her cleverness and tricks, all her tics and habits, all her sales charm and her hungers, gone like a candle puffed out by a casual giant. Rain drove all the way across the room, washing and diluting the blood. Wind roared through the apartment and out the service door by the kitchen, hurrying across the bay toward the dark city. He crawled, clutching his clothing, to a sheltered alcove between bedroom and living room, and was able to stand up and dress. His hands were shaking, and though he could not hear his own voice except as a vibration in his throat, he suddenly realized he was saying, "Momma! Momma!"

At 88 Bayview Terrace the only way Justin Denniver could hear his portable radio was to shut himself in a sturdy closet in the hall and turn the volume high and hold it against his ear. Then, over the continual roaring, he could hear the tiny insect voices of the excited men yelping about disaster.

". . . latest information . . . five and six feet of water over the keys . . . expect possible fifteen feet . . ."

"Fifteen feet!" he said. In pitch blackness he held the radio out in front of him in both hands and shook it, as though to rid it of such nonsense. He was already standing in water above his ankles, and if there was nine more feet coming, there wouldn't be much room in any one-story house. He listened again.

". . . extensive wind and water damage. It is no longer possible to stand up outside. Do not try to leave from wherever you are. Nothing is moving in all of Palm County. The flow of the injured and dying to the emergency rooms of the hospitals has ceased. . . . Hurricane Ella will cross the coastline—" It stopped. He shook it. He wondered if the batteries were dead. He held it against his ear and turned the tuning dial and soon brought in music from a strong distant station. Music! He wanted to drop it at his feet and jump on it.

He went out and got Molly and yelled into her ear. He saw from her expression she wasn't getting it. He took her by the wrist and hauled her to the closet and shut them in. She screamed into his ear, "My rugs! All my new rugs!"

He turned her head around and yelled, "The water is going to get nine feet higher! Higher than this! Nine feet!"

He had one hand on her shoulder, one on the back of her head. He felt her grow rigid.

"What do we do?" she shouted.

"We got to get out of here."

"How? Where?"

The world, he thought, always finds a way to screw you good. Build a house like a fort, anchor it deep so it will take anything that comes along, and they send you a flood higher than the house.

"Maybe get across the bay in the boat."

They hurried to the windows that looked out onto the pool terrace, for a glimpse of the boat at the dock, on the davits, at the end of the lawn. At first they could not see through the rain. Then in a bright flash of lightning they saw the trees and bushes stripped of all leaves and small branches, tossing wildly, and they could see the davits stripped of any trace of a boat.

They trotted back into the closet and closed the door. The heavy shutters were holding.

"Maybe it won't get that high," she shouted.

"Where's that Winslow raft, that blowup thing?"

"Garage rafters."

He could get through the kitchen into the garage. He brought back the raft and two life jackets. He had to take her back into the closet to tell her his plan.

"We wait as long as we can. Inflate the raft, lie in the bottom of it, let the wind carry us as far up onto the mainland as it can. Find some shelter there. Okay?"

Her response was to kiss him. Her lips felt uncharacteristically thin and cold. A few moments after they left the hall closet, the whole roof blew off the house. A shrieking gust got under the broad handsome overhang and lifted it up and hurled it out over the bay in one windmilling piece, tile and all. The wind felled them both. The walls started to go. He crawled to the raft and popped the inflators and it swelled, all plump and orange and reassuring. He fell into it as it started to float away from him. She managed to get to her feet and came running, wind-driven, to dive in beside him, her forehead smacking him just under the left eye, stunning him for a moment. She was trying to yell into his ear but he couldn't understand her as they were out in the full shrieking roaring whistling fury of it, beginning to lift and fall on the chop as soon as they were fifty feet past the davits.

Molly Denniver looked back toward the house, a stunted thing, half seen, being devoured by the wind, and the rain stung her face as she looked. She felt as if her life were being devoured too, all her impacts and purposes, her tastes and decisions being ripped and raveled, torn free and blown away beyond memory. She stuffed her face into a corner of the bounding raft, into a smell of rubber and plastic, and tried to weep.

ALL THE DRINKS were on the house at the Sand Dollar Bar hurricane party. Freddy Brasser marveled at the way he seemed to oscillate between very drunk and icy sober. Everybody smiled and nodded at everybody. Sometimes, between wind bellowings, you could hear a thin thread of music from Tom Shawn's complicated radio. People talked in sign language, hoisted their glasses in frequent toast, hollered a word or two into often uncomprehending ears.

Fred was astonished at the incredible noise of a hurricane. It seemed to fill the whole scale from supersonic to subsonic. It was like living inside a giant pipe organ, with a giant holding all the keys down at once, never letting up.

He was overjoyed to finally recognize someone he had seen before, the manager at Golden Sands who had helped him get into his mother's apartment after she was in the hospital, get the bags of trash hauled away and get the women to clean it all up. After the name was yelled in his ear three times, he went and got a pad and pencil and gave it to the man, and he printed his name in block letters: JULIAN HIGBEE.

Fred beamed at him and printed his own name right underneath. Julian studied it and frowned and nodded. He seemed quite drunk. He stood in water, swaying, his arm around a tall woman with an oddly long neck and narrow sloping shoulders. She wrote her name on the pad in schoolgirl script. Francine Hryka. The name rang a bell. Darleen Moseby had said that the night waitress who had the little daughter and who took afternoon tricks was Francine Reeka. So this is how you spell Reeka.

He printed a question. "Where are Dusty and Louise?"

Francine worked her way out of Julian's grasp and took him over to where two women sat on a table in a corner, their feet on the chairs. He could tell from the Hryka woman's mouth movements which one was which. The little one was Dusty. They looked at him with a questioning hostility until the Hryka woman held out the pad with her thumbnail under FRED BRASSER. Then they both beamed and nodded and Louise pointed over toward Darleen and Dusty held out her small paw to be shaken.

They all toasted each other and made gestures about the strength of the storm, and the water height in the room. Everybody looked strange in that white glare of the gasoline mantles. Darleen came sloshing over and hugged his arm and the four of them all laughed for no particular reason. He laughed because Darleen was better looking than any of the other three who worked out of the Sand Dollar. The others there seemed to be regulars. People from the Beach Village area. Clerks from the shops. An electrician. A female pharmacist. He tried to count them but he kept getting a different count. He decided it was about twenty-two.

The waves began consuming Beach Village after they had disposed of the fifteen or twenty small wooden beach cottages between the village and the beach, the oldest structures on the key. The light materials were whipped away by the wind. Heavier pieces were ground into splinters and kindling. Refrigerators, window air-conditioning units, television sets and dishwashers were buried in the sand. All the palm trees were broken off ten to fifteen feet above the ground. All the Australian pines fell eastward, and the firehose rain quickly hammered all soil off the roots as the wind broke away the larger roots and sailed them toward the bay.

The middle of Beach Village was somewhat higher than the average height of the key, so it was not until after darkness fell that the sea began shattering the backs of the buildings which fronted on Beach Drive, facing toward the Sand Dollar Bar. The combination of wind pressure and wave impact took down cement block walls easily, and when they were gone, the waves began pulling out the contents of the big Walgreen's, of McDonald's, of Kathy's Boutique, and the Self-Serv Amoco Station.

Waves and wind mingled a broken sodden madness of magazine racks, sunglasses, Big Mac boxes, deodorants, Navajo bracelets, All-Weather Oil cans, charge slips, greeting cards, oil filters, laxatives, lighting fixtures, ceiling panels, kitchen plastics, pantyhose, windshield wipers, hair nets, car batteries, light bulbs, paper bags, serving trays, napkin holders, suntan lotion, seashell earrings, wading ponds, cash registers, tomato sauce, candy bars, Instamatics, razors, sandals, raw meat, seat covers and denture adhesive.

There was a rhythm to each attack. The defenses would be penetrated. The bewildering array of odd-ments would be pulled out on momentary display, and with each ensuing wave there would be less of the display remaining. And then the side walls would begin to come down.

With flashlight in hand, Roberta Fish, R.N., led Lorrie Higbee down a hospital corridor to a small treatment room. As it had no outside windows, and the heavy door fitted closely and well, once the door was shut, they could hear each other if they spoke loudly.

Bobbie Fish put the flashlight on a stand with the beam pointing at the white ceiling, reflecting back to fill the room with a soft radiance. Lorrie backed up to a treatment table, braced the heels of her hands on it and hopped up, sighing her weariness.

"That uniform seems to fit okay," Bobbie said.

"It's okay."

"Tired?"

"Pooped."

"You're doing great, Lorrie. Really great."

"Not the way that son of a bitch was yelling at me."

"Don't mind him. He's okay. He's a good doctor. I explained to him you weren't trained. Just a volunteer. Don't try to do anything you don't understand. Okay?"

"That kid nearly got me. You know the one?"

"I know. I don't know what was keeping him alive."

"Everything went all black and buzzy and I nearly went down. God, I didn't know it could be like that. You know, you think of being a nurse, you don't think about things like that happening. No wonder you got on the sauce, Bobbie."

"That part of my life is over now."

"A lot of things are over."

"How did you get here? Julian bring you?"

Lorrie looked bleakly amused. "I don't know where he is. Fat chance of him bringing me here. Things haven't been exactly great since he found out about us. No, I came over with Colonel Simmins and his wife and daughter and we must have gotten over the bridge minutes before they opened it and couldn't close it. We went to the shelter at the Legion Hall, you know, a couple of blocks from here. So I came here. Because I couldn't *not* come here. You understand that?"

"Sure."

"I had to crawl. I had to hold onto buildings and fences and trees. I got knocked down. What happens? You put me to work."

"You came in looking like a kitten somebody'd tried to drown."

"Alley cat."

"There's side rails on that table. Here. You pull up like this. There should be a pillow here someplace. Right. Here it is. Lorrie, dear, take a nap. Get some sleep. I'll leave the door open so it won't be this stuffy."

"What do you do about sleep?"

"I'm used to going a lot of hours straight. I pace myself. If I can rest, I will. Because when things start moving again, when the ambulances can make pickups again and people can move on the streets, it's going to make what you've seen already look like play school. We'll work until we're sleepwalking."

"Okay," Lorrie said. "Okay." She yawned.

Roberta picked up the flashlight, and in her hunger to look more closely at Lorrie, she turned the beam on her. Lorrie stared calmly up, above the beam, toward Bobbie's eyes. Lorrie's hair was fastened back with a twist of wire from a hospital bouquet. Her face was not pretty, not even distinctive. Her eyes were too small and set too close to the thin bridge of the long nose. Her whole face was too narrow, the mouth small, chin ineffectual. Her eyebrows were dark and smooth and gentle. Her skin was flawless and pallid. There were smudges of weariness under the small dark eyes. Roberta looked upon her and felt her heart turn over.

"You look about eighteen," she said.

"I wish I was eighteen again, for you. I was a lot prettier when I was eighteen. I really was."

"You look exactly the way I want you to look."

Lorrie bit at her lips and then said, "What is happening to us? In the middle of all the damned wind and in the middle of all those people yelling and moaning and bleeding, I think about you."

"Go to sleep. Get some rest."

"I don't even know who I am anymore, Bobbie. I don't even know." With an air of petulance, Lorrie yanked up the other side rail, thumped the pillow with her fist, swung her legs up and stretched out. Bobbie kissed her lightly on the forehead, went out and braced the door back, and walked down the corridor toward the glow of the standby light circuits in the emergency areas.

She thought of Gil, over there running his shelter area at the high school with his gentle and understanding competence. She thought of herself standing by her sink on a rainy morning, drinking the glass of tepid vodka so fast she threw it back up immediately into the sink, but kept the next glass down. She thought of wanting Julian in her so intensely she would phone down to the office and get the icy, hostile voice of little Mrs. Higbee. All four of them were people she had known in some other life she had once lived, and would soon entirely forget. She and Lorrie were the new people. She could work anywhere, and help Lorrie get her cap. And they could have their own place forever.

Ella, nearing the coast, spun off small tornadoes. They were not as big or destructive as the ones of the midwest plains. Where they touched ground they were but twenty to fifty yards in diameter, with the winds around the center seldom exceeding two hundred and fifty miles an hour. The pressure differential between the center of the tornadoes and the area just outside them was at times a full pound of pressure. They were spun off the right front quadrant of the advancing eye.

One of them moved directly across the Groves Mobile Home Estates three miles up Woodruff Creek from Fiddler Bay. By that time there had been considerable storm damage in the park. All the big longleaf pines were down, some of them squashing mobile homes and their occupants. The big live oaks on the banks of the creek had lost their leaves, and then their small branches and then their large branches, but most of them still stood, blunt broad shattered trunks, unlikely to survive. The creek had had a reverse flow ever since Saturday morning, salt water and rainwater moving east, inundating an ever-expanding area of the sloughs and ranchlands beyond the park.

It was an old park, and most of the residents were there year round and saw no need to leave their homes for dubious shelter elsewhere. Their mobile homes had porches and Florida rooms and carports, along with extensive plantings. All the mobile homes had tie-downs in conformity with state and local ordinances. In preparation for the storm the residents had brought in everything they thought the wind might blow away. Water began coming into the units nearest the creek at about seven o'clock. By the time the trees were going down, the wind was too strong for anyone to venture out to help those who had been injured but not killed. The wind was plucking away at the mobile homes, looking for loose edges, for anything which could be peeled back and ripped away. Sometimes when the wind came at precisely the right angle and force it would create over the aluminum roof of a trailer that same negative force which provides lift to an airplane wing. It shifted some of them on their foundations and snatched the tops off others, immediately whipping everything out of the trailer which could be lifted and hurled.

When the tornado moved diagonally across this deteriorating area, it created explosive forces. If one imagines a mobile home thirty feet long, twelve feet wide and eight feet high, and if one takes into account only the sides, ends and top, there are nearly one hundred and fifty thousand square inches of area. If outside pressure suddenly drops one pound per square inch, there is an abrupt outward push in all directions of seventy-five tons. Great shredded sheets of aluminum and fragments of paneling and insulation burst outward and were spun up into the dizzy debris of tornado.

Twenty-one mobile homes disappeared as though

demolition charges had been planted in them. A dozen others were rolled about. The wind smothered the groans of the wounded and the cries of the dying.

It was later established that two tornadoes crossed the Athens Airport, one demolishing the hangar used by Execu-Craft along with the aircraft sheltered therein. That meant that only those private airplanes which had been flown out of the area before the storm survived. All those tied down were flipped over and blown away. The second tornado wrecked a security area, crossed the airport, picked up the engineless hulk of an abandoned DC-3, carried it across the Tamiami Trail in a westerly direction, against hurricane winds, and dropped it through the roof of a supermarket.

Noble Winney owned a very good all-band receiver which he used to monitor foreign propaganda broadcasts, taping them off the air if he found them particularly significant. It worked on a line cord as well as on batteries, and in preparing for the long outage of power which might occur, he had purchased three fresh sets of batteries. The set had a headphone jack which he found necessary in order to hear anything over the incredible tumult of the storm.

When he looked at the strained, pinched, wild-eyed expression on the face of his wife, Sarah, he was glad that she was unable to hear the hurricane bulletins which came over the air.

The damage already in Key West, Everglades City, Fort Myers, Punta Gorda, Boca Grande, Athens, Venice, Sarasota, Bradenton, Anna Maria and the whole of Tampa Bay was so extensive, it was being called the hurricane of the century. They now believed the eye would cross the coast of Venice, possibly as early as nine o'clock. Winds were now coming out of the east in the Sarasota—Bradenton—Tampa Bay area with such force it was said that the bays were almost completely emptied. The worst damage was believed to be south of Venice. There had been no communication at all from the Athens area since about four forty-five, not even from ham operators. A hurricane surge was expected just before the eye crossed the coastline, or at the same time as it crossed. The Red Cross and all other relief agencies were planning a massive aid effort to take effect as soon as the first cargo planes could get in. It was expected that the Athens area, as well as other areas along the West Coast, would be inaccessible by road except over some of the small secondary and tertiary highways leading toward the middle of the state. The huge rains plus the wind had caused the culverts under Route 41, the Tamiami Trail, to be blocked by fallen trees and debris from houses destroyed by the winds. "The water, piling up behind these obstructions, has washed away the highway in dozens of places. There is no electrical power and no phone service to the area. It is believed that the high percentage of elderly and infirm in the coastal population will increase the number of fatalities over what could be normally expected."

He reluctantly handed Sarah the earphones after she tugged at him again and gave him another imploring look. He picked up a flashlight and went into his workroom. Usually he was able to find comfort in the long rows of giant scrapbooks, in the look of work well done, orderly and cross-indexed. Now it all had a silent and lonely look. He could not identify the impression they made upon him until he remembered the incised tablets he had seen one time in a museum, a message carefully carved into stone which no living man could read.

His records suddenly had an artifact look. Dead records, compiled by a forgotten man. At that moment he could recall no sudden insight, no discovered link, no shock of recognition in all that work. He felt bleak and deserted. The air inside the apartment was close, moist and sticky. His truss was uncomfortable. He had heartburn. His head itched. Maybe it was all meaningless, every single part of it. . . .

Suddenly he remembered what Henry Churchbridge had said, and why Henry had refused to become involved. The work was of surpassing importance. Henry knew that. Henry had represented his government all over the world, and he was too aware of the dangers involved to even join a study and discussion group.

In fact, if They had found out about his research over the years and what it proved, They might well have planted something in the apartment or near it which would send out some kind of microwave radiation to give him this sensation of hopelessness and defeat. It was clear They had tried a ruse with that engineer's report. They would know he had too much material now to move it off the key if he let himself be frightened into leaving. Leaving would have been an open invitation for Them to come in and destroy the most damning parts of it, or all of it.

He had a sudden suspicion, and he hurried out to look at the storm track they had printed in the paper. In the somewhat meager light of the battery lantern, Sarah sat with the earphones on, her fist against her lips, her eyes closed, and tears wet on her cheeks. Scared to death, he thought, and walked past her to pick up the paper. He put the flashlight beam on it and then took it into his workroom and spread it out. He got a felt marker and traced the long line right from the west coast of Africa right up into the Gulf and then north, then northeast, and now east. Right at him! Right from the west coast of Africa, direct and deadly, aimed right at Noble Winney and all his collected evidence.

Sarah startled him by clutching at him, trying to be taken into his arms. He was very cross. She wasn't even supposed to come into the workroom. She knew better than this. And he did not like hugging people. It was awkward and made him feel ridiculous.

"I'm busy!" he yelled at her. "I'm very busy! Can't you see that?"

As she slowly shuffled out he opened his master index and began looking for the references under Climate comma Control Thereof.

The hurricane party on the eleventh floor of the Azure Breeze, on the beach opposite Golden Sands, was not very successful, Marcia Leffingwell decided. It surprised her to discover that she was giving anything less than a perfect party. No party can be great, she thought, if the hostess is bored and irritated. And I am bored with the interminable roaring and whistling of that damned wind, bored with my guests, bored with drinking, bored with having to holler a lot of chitchat at the top of my lungs and not being able to understand a tenth of what they shout back at me. I am irritated with watching drinks get slopped onto my lovely new rug in my lovely new apartment, and I am irritated at watching these idiots stomp the snacks into the pretty shag, and I am irritated by the harsh light of those stupid lanterns, and by the stink they make, and I am terribly tired of being pinched and goosed by Johnny Rogers. I am ready to scream and I might as well, because nobody will hear me at all.

She glanced over at her husband, Deke, the poor dear, and saw that he looked almost as bored and distressed as she felt. As she moved toward the fake fireplace intending to put her drink on the mantel, she noticed a small ripe olive on the faun-colored shag. It was almost the last straw. We shouldn't have tried to give a party under these conditions, she thought. The way you handle a hurricane party is go to somebody else's. We could have gone over to that much smaller party at that tacky little Golden Sands on the bay side. Jack and Grace Cleveland begged us to come over there. The party was in the apartment of somebody we don't know, though. Some guinea name. At least if we'd gone there, people would be stomping their fucking olives into somebody else's fucking shag rug.

She picked it up between thumb and middle finger and put it on the mantel. It promptly rolled to the left and kept rolling and fell off the end of the mantel, and bounced under a love seat. Oh, great, she thought as she knelt and found it. Oh, dandy. My new fireplace is crooked too. When she stood up to look for an ashtray to put the olive in, she felt strangely dizzy. She had to take a quick step to catch her balance. She noticed everybody else. Even in all that constant horrid screaming and roaring which had been going on practically forever, she had the odd impression there was some kind of silence in the room. Nobody was laughing. Or moving. Or looking at anybody else. They had their heads a little bit tilted as though they were listening for some sound buried in the wind.

They were all in a picture where the camera was held at a small careless angle. A woman staggered back against the wall. The model car, an MG, with wheels that turned and a workable steering wheel, the model car that was a lighter if you pushed the button that snapped the trunk lid up, the little car rolled off the glass-topped table. A man ran for the door, knocking a woman down. They had all broken out of that trance of listening. They staggered for balance. Their mouths and eyes were round and they made hooing sounds heard but faintly in the thunder of wind. They tried to claw and crawl and struggle away from the dreadful window wall, away from the terrors outside. But the furniture toppled and slid, and the people tumbled and rolled to the base of the window wall, there entangled with one another in utter darkness, and with the furniture and hot parts of lanterns, and the breaking glasses, grabbing at the shag, trying to climb the terrible slope, their faces wet chalk.

She felt the slowness of it. Feet crushed her back against the glass. Realization came more than once. It kept exploding in her brain over and over, erased each time by her disbelief, as the tall building, its seaward supports exposed, undermined and crumbling, leaned past that point of equilibrium and crashed, unheard, into the black and white turbulence of the huge hurricane waves and was there slowly broken apart and dispersed over the floor of the Gulf and the sugary beach.

Mr. Harlin Barker hurried from Connie's two-bed hospital room down to the nurses' station in the middle of that third-floor wing. There was only one person there, a woman in a blue uniform, writing on five-by-eight file cards under the light of a very dim bulb.

"Come quick!" he shouted. "My wife. Mrs. Barker. Quick!"

"You need a nurse?"

"She's bad, I think."

"I'm not a nurse. I keep these here records, mister."

"Call a nurse, please."

"Nobody can call anybody, mister. Nothing works. All the wires got wet. We got a hundred leaks in the crummy building."

"Where are the nurses? Where are the doctors?"

"A nurse went by going that way a little while ago."

He hurried down the hall in the direction she had pointed. He looked in a room and saw a flashlight moving about. "Nurse," he yelled. "Nurse!"

A broad-bodied elderly nurse came out and glowered at him and tried to walk by him. He grabbed her arm. She wrested away. He grabbed her again and she hit him across the bridge of the nose with her flashlight. She put her mouth near his ear and yelled, "Get back in bed!"

"I'm not a patient!"

"Then go home! No visiting hours!"

"My wife is dying!"

"What?"

"Dying! Dying!" She suffered being led at a half trot all the way back to Connie Mae's bedside. She shone the light on Connie Mae's face. She took her pulse.

"Fibrillating!" she yelled at Harlin Barker.

"She did that before."

"Cardiac section. She should be in the cardiac section."

"Put her there. Okay? Put her there!"

"No use. Nothing works over there. No electric."

"Do something!"

"Who's the doctor?"

"Keebler."

"Keeler? Don't know him."

"Keebler! Keebler!"

"Go to Emergency."

"What?"

"Go get any doctor from Emergency downstairs."

"Help her!"

To his consternation the hefty nurse raised her fist high and thumped it down onto Connie's frail chest. She took her pulse, and raised her fist to do it again, as Harlin Barker fled. It took him a long time to find the Emergency area in the darkened confusing corridors of the hospital. Patients grabbed at him, thinking him a doctor. Nurses tried to intercept him.

When he found the emergency room he was astonished and relieved to find Nurse Roberta Fish at a desk sipping a plastic cup of coffee.

He leaned toward her ear and yelled, "My wife is fibrillating!"

"Whoa, Mr. Barker. Slow."

"She got out of Intensive Care, Cardiac Section, on the ninth and they said she had to get out of the hospital in six days. Dr. Keebler got them to let her stay. She's had three heart attacks already and this is the fourth. . . . "

She motioned to him to stay put, and in moments she was back with a doctor in a stained smock, rubbing his eyes and carrying a medicine case. Harlin told her the room number, and then he followed them. They made very good time. It was difficult for Mr. Barker to keep up with them. He was smiling and weeping as he ran along behind them. Everything was under control. As he rounded the last corner, he hit a wet patch, his feet flew up. He landed on his hip. The pain was excruciating. He tried to get up and tried to call out, but the blackness came welling up from behind his eyes.

When he woke up he felt strangely groggy. He was in a small cubicle with walls of white canvas. The storm roar was still going on. Nurse Fish came in and leaned over him and smiled with her eyes and leaned close and told him to go to sleep. He asked about Connie. She patted his cheek and told him to go to sleep. He motioned her close and shouted weakly, "She's dead? Dead?"

Nurse Fish nodded and left, after patting him again. He exhaled all the air out of his lungs and tried to keep himself from ever inhaling again. But pretty soon he did, with self-disgust for his weakness, and soon he slept.

41

PROFESSOR ROGER JEFFREY and his wife, Maurine, had made themselves at home in the tenth-floor apartment of Professor Alden Maitland, in the Bay Terrace Condominium, a large complex on the bay shore of Fiddler Key a half mile from the north bridge.

Alden and Peggy Maitland had made the apartment as safe and as snug as possible in preparation for the storm. Their apartment overlooked the bay and the city beyond. Even with all the windows closed, a condition they could not endure for long, and even though they had no window facing west, the only place where it was possible to carry on any kind of conversation was the windowless storage and utility room, half of which Alden had converted into a darkroom.

"Couldn't go forward after the bridge jammed. Couldn't turn around. Couldn't go backward. And poor old Maurine wouldn't have lasted long trying to walk back to Golden Sands in that wind, would she now? She gets no exercise at all. Stay there and we'd have drowned like rats. Damn good thing I remembered you good people lived right here, what? Even so, it was all poor old Maurine could do to make it, even with me bundling her along like a sack of old potatoes. Had her in one arm and my machine in the other. We'll be forever grateful to you two, won't we, dear? We'll go on very short rations because the little we had, we had to leave in the automobile. A borrowed car. Too bad. Water coming up fast. Of course, it would have had the same fate if we left it at Golden Sands. Belongs to a chap named

Mensenkott. To his wife, actually. She's a loonie. They put her away. Mensenkott is one of those network types. Very macho and very dull. Now if I could spread newspaper out in your living room, dears, I have to take my trusty Panasonic Touring Deluxe apart. I am afraid she got some salty water in her innards, and she is too exquisite a machine to let rust out."

A long time later Peggy Maitland maneuvered her husband back into the darkroom, knowing that with the door closed, no word they shouted at each other could be heard outside the room.

"We hardly *know* these terrible people!"

"I know, dear."

"She's no problem. She keeps her nose in that book. She doesn't know or care where she is. But he is so goddam . . . jolly! Did you see him glom onto those sandwiches? Short rations! Did you see him down our beer?"

"What were we supposed to do when we opened the door to them? Close it in their faces?"

"The stink of that stuff he uses on that bicycle makes me feel sick to my stomach."

"He'll be finished soon."

"Soon? He's got a lot of little bearings and things rolling around on the floor loose. I don't think he'll ever get it back together."

"Peggy, honey, Roger Jeffrey and I were in the same line of work. We were in different schools together. We were on one national committee together. Okay? They called on us when we moved in. We never returned the call or invited them back."

"Invite them *out!* They are eating our food, drinking our drink, and breathing up all our air."

"I give you permission to go right ahead and do it yourself."

She hugged him. "Okay. I can't. Neither can you. We'll have to just live through it."

"Cheer up. The building might blow away."

"Please don't make that sort of joke, not when it sounds like it does. It's getting worse. You know that? It isn't possible, but it *is* getting worse. I swear it."

"We'll be okay."

"We should have gotten off."

"And left your mother here?"

"I know. I know. I'm sorry."

"It isn't your fault she's with us and she's bedridden, Peg. And it isn't your fault I made fifteen phone calls without finding one damned hospital or nursing home that would take her in. We can't take her to a motel or a shelter. What are we supposed to do, for God's sake? Put her to sleep like an elderly hamster?"

"I better go look at her again. All the noise is scaring her. And me. But not those damned Jeffreys of yours."

"Of mine?"

"There isn't enough air to breathe anywhere, is there?"

After the level of the water in the bay had risen to where short steep waves were rolling in across his big terrace and slapping the side of his house, Marty Liss began to pay a lot more attention to Hurricane Ella. As a developer he knew the elevation of his own property. He had arranged an exception to the stipulation as to the height of the floor level above mean high tide. On a broad part of the bay front, on the mainland, he was supposed to be eleven feet above mean high tide. He had obtained permission to build eight feet above mean high tide. Water was about eighteen inches deep in the long living room. Okay, so there was nine and a half feet of water everywhere. It awed him to think of what it must be like out on Fiddler Key and Seagrape Key. Not only would they have the water out there, but it would be rolling in, big waves a lot higher than the water level. Way down under the deep hard roaring of the big wind he thought he could hear the heavier thunder of the surf out there, smashing up the key.

Those damned doom merchants could have been right, all along. All that weeping and wailing and wringing of hands about how criminally dangerous it was to build out there on those beautiful damned keys. They called it transient land. Hell, a lot of Fiddler Key had the same contour it had back in the thirties. The market factors all the risks in any situation. When you have to pay up to twenty-five hundred a foot for beach-front land zoned high rise, you have to know the risk is very small. If the risk was big, the price would be dirt. Everybody knows that. It made for a wonderful lifestyle out there. Turn the key in the door and go on a nice little cruise, no need to worry. No noisy kids racing around. No dogs crapping in the grass. No cats stinking up the corridors. Little tennis and swimming to keep in shape. Get a small boat and keep it right at your own dock, and ride out there into the Gulf and hook into those great silver kings.

The waves and wind had broken the French doors into the dining room, and the water came in there. Standing in the living room he could see the current that flowed through the arched doorway from the dining room. This place was going to be a mess when the water went down. Wouldn't be any plantings left at all. The pumps, air conditioning, intercoms, wiring—everything would be shot.

He felt almost amused. Everything else is shot. Why not the house too? Martin Liss, the fall guy. Blame him for the hurricane too, while you're at it. Stick his ass in the slam, and let him rot there. All those red hots need a victim. Here's Marty. He'll do fine. Everything he has touched his whole life has ultimately turned to shit. Marriages, kids, home, business. Marty the high roller. Now the dice come up craps every time. Snake eyes. Snake-bit.

Suddenly Francie grabbed his arm from behind and yanked him around to face her. She stood yelling at him, face and posture ugly, slacks, shirt and hair water-pasted flat against her, makeup gone. She was pointing behind her, and making fists, and stomping her foot in the living-room water. He felt very oppressed by her and irritated by her. He could not understand one word she was saying. Whatever she thought he was supposed to do, he had no interest in doing.

In a languid manner designed to infuriate her, he gave her the finger. Without hesitation, she tried to kick him in the groin, and perhaps would have succeeded had not the water slowed the beginning of the furious attack. He turned just in time and her foot thumped his thigh. There were pictures in the back of his head, of her and the young tennis pro, and they lent additional force to his open-handed blow. The heel of his hand caught her on the angle of the jaw and she dropped face down into the water.

She made a few vague movements and he thought how very easy it would be to place his foot, in its nonslip boat shoe, on the nape of her neck and keep her down. It gave him a rush of pleasure, an almost sexual feeling, to think about doing it. If he waited, he might not have to do anything.

At that instant an object came through the heavy glass of the picture window that faced the bay. It bombed through the glass at a flat angle and struck close behind him, as the wind thrust the rest of the glass out of the frame and ran shrieking around the room, blowing paintings off the walls and objects off the tables. He braced himself against the wind and picked Francie out of the water. She came up gagging and coughing, but he could not hear the sounds she was making. Arm around her, he helped her toward the stairs. He looked behind him and saw that the object which had come through the window was a dead great blue heron. It looked too frail to have broken the glass. It looked as if it was made of sticks and string, like a model of a bird. The sticks were crumpled. He remembered something about how you can shoot a candle through a pine board if you have enough velocity.

It truly shocked him to see the dead bird. He had not thought about the birds being in any danger. They could fly away, couldn't they? But they didn't. They were as dumb and helpless as people, and evidently the storm was killing them too. Halfway up the stairs Francie pulled away from him, clutched the railing, bent over and spewed water from her mouth and nose.

He realized she was just a kid. A dumb young little wife with no sense at all. Soap opera addict. Terrible bridge player. Dangerous on the highways. Stinking temper. Built pretty good. Okay in the sack. Just a kid.

You get what you go looking for. You want a kid, you get a kid. It isn't so much marriage as it is a sort of rental deal. Make a premarital agreement. When it busts up, if you've kept careful track, you can even figure out what each piece of ass cost you, on the average.

He patted her and she looked at him and tried to smile. They went on up the stairs together. It was probably okay not to be able to talk because of all the roaring going on. Maybe if they'd both been mutes, he thought, it would have been a better marriage all around.

The great surge had built up in the Gulf, built by the greatest winds working on the water as the shoreline shallowed. It was like a broad bulge moving toward shore. It had been enhanced in size by the seiche effect, which can occur when the pressure in any area is so low that the water is actually sucked up to a greater level, as though a gigantic soda straw had been put to use. The surge was not in itself a wave. The hurricane waves remained, moving at the same rate or a little faster than the surge. It was a black blister a few miles in diameter, swollen to fifteeen feet above the already high level of the hurricane tides.

A surge like this, though not as large or as high, had drowned almost four hundred people in Louisiana in 1957. Other surges had sent fifteen feet of water over Bimini in 1935 and drowned four hundred in the Florida Keys in that same year. In November of 1932 a hurricane surge drowned twenty-five hundred people in Santa Cruz del Sur, Cuba. On Semptember 8, 1900, a hurricane tide and storm surge killed six thousand people in Galveston, Texas.

The surge moved just ahead of the eye and a little south of it.

The moving light awakened Sam Harrison. Incredible torrents of storm sound assaulted his ears and he marveled that he had slept through any of it. He was in her bed in Suite B. He thought it might be a nurse and then saw that it was Barbara. When the light came near his face he smiled up at her.

She sat on the edge of the bed and showed him the thermometer in the light of the small flashlight, shook it down, looked at the reading and then put it under his tongue as he opened his mouth to receive it. She fumbled for his good wrist and found his pulse.

He wanted to laugh and cry and beat his head on the wall. Some tower of strength he had become. Big help to the Messenger family.

He would tell her some day about that two-mile ride across the broad part of Palm Bay. It hadn't taken long, because every time Jud tried to slow down they began to wallow dangerously in the following sea. Each time Jud tried to turn, they shipped water. So it had been a straight shot across the bay, wide open, bailing, peering ahead through the gray-silver curtain of windblown rain, looking for one of those little bay islands that might be in the way, looking for floating junk which could rip them open. Then something loomed up ahead of him and he yelled and they zoomed through thick plantings which stung their flesh, and slid to a stop on a green lawn a few feet from a pool enclosure.

He wished he could tell her of his idiot journey to her side, the four-mile trek in the thrusting gloom of great winds and driving rain, all the way from that bay-front house to the P&S Hospital. No traffic. Nobody on the streets. Junk whirring and hurtling by. Stinging rain, so thick you could drink it. Rivers in the streets, with waves on them. One day he could tell her about it. Sense said seek shelter. Crawl into a hole. Keep your head down. Something else said to get to Barbara and stay with her. Be with her. Know she was okay.

Nearly made it. Got within two hundred feet of the place when that limb came along, God knows from where, from how far away. Big around as his thigh. Fifteen feet long. Had that last open space to cross. Some instinct made him turn as he scurried, the wind pushing him. Turned and threw his arm up to ward off the vague shape. Like getting hit by a falling truck. Broken wrist, broken shoulder, probably broken ribs. Head lacerations. Stayed right there, flat out in the rain, sick and hurting. Finally able to try to crawl. Gathered up the bag of belongings. Crawled a hundred miles and finally came to a door on the lee side and kicked it until it opened and they pulled him in.

Emergency generator service dead. Everything dead. Lanterns and candles and flashlights. Splinted his arm. Taped his shoulder and ribs. Immobilized the arm. Stitched the scalp lacerations. Put dressings on them, like a turban. Got it across to him there were no rooms left and they would stow him in the hall. Couldn't get his message across to them until he tricked a little nurse into coming close enough so he could grab the nape of her neck with his good hand and then yell into her ear. She went and got Barbara Messenger. An orderly wheeled him up and they put him in Barbara's bed, and he had dropped out of the world at once.

After she read the temperature, he beckoned her down and felt a lot of resistance in her as he brought her ear close to his lips.

"Lee?" he yelled.

Her lips touched his ear as she shouted, "Same!"

"Sorry got hurt!" he yelled.

"Glad you're here!" she responded.

And on that he felt himself in that faint dizziness of pre-sleep and said to himself, No! It can't be. Not in the middle of . . .

But it was and he was gone again.

There was a place at one of the front windows of the Sand Dollar Bar where the shutter had warped or shrunk, leaving a half-inch gap where one could look out through the wet window at the swarmy night. Fred Brasser kept going back there and looking out every once in a while. Once he tried to report that McDonald's Golden Arches were gone, and even though he wrote it down, he could not get anybody very interested in that phenomenon.

Now that the ice had run out, he had started drinking white wine. It was still cool. He carried a bottle around by the neck, taking a stingy little sip every once in a while, guarding against getting too drunk. It was dangerous to get drunk. The water inside was up to his crotch, and there was a scum floating around on it made of ashes and cigarette paper, Sand Dollar cocktail napkins and what seemed to be sawdust. If a person got too drunk, he thought, or too tired, they could drown in here. In a sense, he thought, my mother drowned in here. And that is a pretty profound observation there, Freddy old buddy. Keep your cool, Freddy, because that gas-jockey type over there is certainly doing a lot of handling of your five-hundred-dollar-a-week merchandise. And from the forearms on that kid, if you object, and he objects to your objection, there is a third way you could get to drown yourself in here.

He roamed back to the window and put the wine bottle inside his shirt, with the cork back in it, so he could use both hands cupped against the window to see out. He saw that it wasn't raining at the moment. Good! And then, in a vivid play of lightning, he saw a dark gleaming wall that stood higher than the fronts of the shops across the street. When lightning came again, the storefronts were gone and the wall was crossing the street toward him. He knew then what it was, deadly, incredible, inexorable, coming to gobble him up because of his dreadful dirty lust, and his selfishness, and his rotten little soul.

The front of the frame building crashed in, and all the members of the party were borne upward, as the water smashed the hot lanterns. They were borne upward between the beams, and past the glass floats and fishnets, up to the high peak of the roof above the beams, where there was a small window with wooden louvers for ventilation. Tom Shawn was jammed through the window by the pressure of the water, even though he was larger than the opening. Several others followed him through as the rear wall went over and the boiling surge continued on, smashing the cottage behind the bar, carrying the debris, including all of Darleen Moseby's stuffed animals, including all the party people, out across the streets and small houses behind the village and out into the bay, the bodies suspended in the depths of the surge, wrenched and tugged this way and that by the currents, bounced against the mud and shell bay bottom and rolled along with the other debris from Fiddler Key.

When the surge hit the lower floors of the Tropic Towers Condominium, Drusilla Bryne was cautiously padding her way back to the deep pillowed couch in the living room from the kitchen, bearing two tall vodka tonics with the last of the ice, using the lightning to help her find her way, and hoping the rather nice man could see well enough without his glasses to appreciate how she must look coming toward him, naked in the quick bright flashes, as with those strobe lights that time.

In the impact of the untold tons of force, the top of the building snapped like a slow brutal whip. It snapped Drusilla off her feet and she fell painfully on hip and elbow, to remain terrified and motionless, waiting for the building to come down. But it did not. Cursing to herself she felt for the shrunken ice cubes, put them back into the glasses and headed back to the kitchen to try again, wondering how Marty Liss was doing over on the mainland.

Earlier, after his car had been rolled into the bay and the marina building had started to go, Jack Mensenkott had crawled and clawed and plunged his way to the nearest segment of the in-and-out marina, a structure of open structural steel fifteen boat-spaces long and four high. He had looked around for Martin and the clerk, but had not seen them again. With water swirling to midthigh he had climbed up out of it to the second level and there had carefully worked his way over to where his own boat, the *Hustler,* lay in the padded rack.

The sea cocks had been pulled on all the boats to let the rain run out. He stretched out in the *Hustler,* below the grasp of the wind. The noise made it difficult to think clearly. From time to time unknown objects would thud against the steelwork, and he could feel rather than hear the impact.

When he got up at last to make an inspection he saw, to his dismay, that not only had a lot of the boats been washed out of the bottom level and washed away, but that some had been blown out of the top tiers. Gusts rocked the *Hustler*.

He debated using the spare dock lines aboard to lash the *Hustler* to the steelwork, and decided it would be advisable. As he began, using every handhold, he looked west and suddenly saw the front slope of the storm surge approaching. There were roofs in it. There were cars in it with their lights on. He took a deep breath and hugged the steel beam in front of him, locking his arms around it. He took a very deep breath. All he could think about was how the hell the television news services could possibly show forty million living rooms what a thing like this was really like.

Too late, he realized the weight of the surge was turning the rectangle of tiers into a parallelogram, bearing him back and down and slowly crushing him from groin to hairpiece, yards under the black salt water.

When the surge struck Golden Sands, it was moving in just a little bit south of west, spray whipping off the top of it.

After the shattered parts of Azure Breeze had broken up, the storm waves on the elevated hurricane tides came rolling across the key unimpeded and threw the stalled cars aside. The average depth of the water on Beach Drive was over nine feet, with the waves breaking there and rolling in white tumult across the tennis courts and pool and landscaped lawns, to smash against the so-called first floor, above the submerged parking and utilities and manager's apartment. When the front windows had started to go, the Furmonds, Linda and Gerald, had fled up the stairs.

There, on the fifth floor, Gerald Furmond, praying to God to forgive him, broke into 5-E, a furnished apartment which had not been rented for some time. They were thirsty and hungry. Gerald took fresh water from a toilet tank and Linda found a tin of potato chips in a kitchen cupboard. The kitchen seemed, in a relative sense, the quietest place. They brought in cushions from the couch and sat on the floor, side by side, leaning back against cupboard doors. The big flashlight was on the countertop above them, broad beam aimed down. Each had a Bible. They thumbed through them, looking for words about tempests and disasters, pointing out passages which seemed useful and heartening. They had been saved in one sense, and were totally confident their lives would be spared, because they had not yet had enough chance to spread the Word. They rejoiced in being so selected. Until they had been saved, three years before, their marriage had been unrewarding. Gerald had been a fornicator, sinning with women in his office and women at the country club, and even with some of her friends. She had stayed with him for the sake of the children, for the sake of that last daughter to graduate, three years ago in June. She had sought her own comfort in the wrong places, in strong drink and in gambling at the bridge table every afternoon.

It was an out-of-doors graduation at the State University, and when the sudden rain came, the students ran for shelter under the old trees. The lightning that struck one tree stunned a half dozen of them, but Patricia Furmond was the only one it killed.

It was a sign, of course. It had to be accepted as a sign. They had to take from it the message sent by the Lord. At first they could not understand. They could not accept. The world was without sense or purpose. But they knelt and prayed together and fasted together and wept together and knelt together until after the nightmare weeks they were saved, were taken into the bosom of the Lord, and learned the ecstasy of His mighty presence. Every part of their relationship had been enriched beyond measure. To each of them, in the hungers of the flesh, the other was an instrument of the divine rites of holy marriage. They were closer than they had ever been before. Their past lives meant nothing.

When the surge smashed into the structure, they felt it and could not understand what had happened. It shook them. A high cupboard opened and dishes streamed out, smashing unheard on the vinyl floor. They looked into each other's eyes, waiting for it to happen again, but it did not. She smiled and nodded and he touched her cheek, and they turned back to the Scriptures.

The surge emptied out most of the apartments on the second floor. It broke through the front windows, rolled through the apartments, broke through the rear walls and windows, smashed the concrete railing off the rear walkway and continued on, velocity undiminished. The surge and the wind cleaned the apartments out, right back to that stage in the construction of the building when basic appliances were being installed. The continuing surge filled the second floor to the ceiling, with the water force pulling away the carpeting, the padding under the carpeting, the paneling, the wall sockets, eating each apartment down to the basic structure of reinforced concrete, column and beam and slab.

Long before it hit, Jack Cleveland had recovered from his weeping. By now the others were as terrified as he had been. Grace Cleveland and Marie Santelli sat in a deep couch, their arms around each other. Tammy Quillan had passed out on the floor and her husband had rolled her out of the way and seemed to be trying to join her as soon as possible. Frank Santelli had held up well until he had discovered, when the rain slackened for a few minutes, that Azure Breeze was gone. The others looked too. The Surf Club was there. You could see a few feeble lights in some of the windows. You could see other condominiums farther down the beach. But Azure Breeze was gone, as completely gone as a front tooth. And that had panicked Frank. He decided they had to get off the key right now. But he came back after ten minutes, sopping wet, bruised and trembling.

Jack Cleveland was in the rear bedroom when the storm surge hit and cleaned out the second floor of Golden Sands. His first startled impression was that there had been some kind of explosion. He found himself underwater, in strong conflicting currents, with unknown objects bumping against him. He had played water polo for several years when he was young. He had good lung capacity. He worked his way upward and burst out into black night, stinging wind, long enough to take a breath before he was rolled under again. He managed the same feat several times, noticing that the water was becoming less turbulent. Waves weren't bashing him under. He came to the surface and in a stutter of lightning he saw a building at his right, perhaps a hundred feet away, and he was astonished at his own velocity as he was carried by it. Something caught at his feet, and he kicked free. He was slammed into some upright flat surface with a force that drove the wind out of him. A little later his feet touched and he tried to stand and was hurled forward. He stood in shallower water and ran thrashing out of it and was wind-driven into a thick tree trunk, flattening his nose as he hit it. Hugging the tree, he moved around behind it, knowing if he let go, the wind would blow him away.

Sobbing for breath, gagging over the blood that ran into his throat from his mashed nose, he peered with slitted eyes around the side of the tree into the wind, trying to make out where he was. A chain of lightning cooperated. He was so disoriented that at first he could not comprehend. He had to interpret the afterimage as he pulled his face back into shelter and leaned his cheek against the rough wet bark. The cluster of buildings off to the right of him and ahead of him, that had to be downtown. So he was inland, on the mainland, maybe a mile inland. And way out there, straight ahead, was Fiddler Key. Or whatever was left of it. "Son of a bitch!" he said softly, and the wind blew into his mouth and puffed his cheeks out.

Frank Branhammer had given up trying to communicate with Annabelle in any way. She stayed right there on the bed, curled up in a damn ball, knees hiked up to her chest and her arms wrapped around her fool head. Goddam fool woman. Work every day of my life and try to make up to her for us losing all three of the kids, get a nice place like this, and she acts like somebody kicked her. Walks around snuffling, looking tragic. Told her and told her, if a man works his ass off all his life he's got a *right* to live as good as anybody, as good as these smirking little educated pricks that want to steal the place away from you after you bought it. Fucking woman isn't happy unless she's crying her eyes out, over a dog, or the kids, or not having some place where she can have an orange tree.

He roamed around restlessly, admitting to himself that he wished he was still working, so he could get out of this place eight or nine hours a day, stop off after work, have a few beers, come home and damn well expect supper on the table and get it.

He was listening to the sound of the wind and the roar of the surf, waiting for the storm to begin to let up. It had to. It couldn't get any worse than this. It had been getting worse than he thought possible for hour after hour, but this had to be the absolute top.

The storm surge threw solid water up over his windows when it thudded against the story below and cleaned it out of everything movable. He knew he was actually on the fourth floor, if the idiots had counted the floors right the way they should have. There was just the one wash of solid water, seen in the flashlight beam, and then it was gone. But to reach these windows, it had to be one hell of a wave. He went close to the windows and angled the flashlight beam, but could not make out the water level in the boiling spray and wind-whipped scud. That big wave had made one heavy thudding sensation. He felt sick. All his life he had wanted to live beside the ocean. He had never counted on its being like this. It was like something that wanted to grab you. It had a personal interest. It came after you.

He knew the car was gone. Paid for and gone. Probably washed right off the lot into the bay. Have to file a claim. Comprehensive coverage. So some snot could file it away, wait three months and send you a check for half what it was worth, with no chance of ever finding anybody who'd give you a fair shake. It's the rules, Mr. Branhammer. That's the law, Mr. Branhammer. It's the regulations, Mr. Branhammer. Sign here, please.

He was filled once again with that terrible anger. He wanted to smash the whole world with his hands. He wanted to kill something. Nothing ever turned out the way you wanted it to turn out. Nothing. Never. Anywhere.

The hurricane surge shouldered into Martin Liss's house, burst through the upstairs windows and washed them out the bedroom door and down the hall past the guest rooms and out onto the frame deck which overlooked the curved driveway and the entrance. Martin managed to lunge to one side and catch a rung of the metal ladder fastened to the side of the house, the ladder that led up to the widow's walk above, an architect's fancy, a bit of seaside kitsch. He had Francie by the wrist and for a moment he did not think he could hold her against the pull of the water. It felt as if his shoulders were being pulled loose. Yet he managed. He got her closer and boosted her up the ladder ahead of him. He urged her up until he could climb free of the water. He could feel a slight and ominous shifting and movement as he clung to the ladder. He was certain his house had been nudged off its foundations, and he realized that if it started to go, it could very easily roll on them.

Francie sagged down and he realized she could not stick her head up over the edge of the roof without the wind trying to blow it off. They could not get their heads close enough together to communicate by yelling or sign language, and the ladder was too narrow, the wind too fierce even in semi-shelter for him to crawl up beside her. The ladder was so straight, up and down, clinging to it put too much strain on the hands and arms. When she sagged again, he moved his head to one side, edged his right shoulder up under her soft rump and took some of her weight.

So, he thought, I can do this much. A fat, half bald, very short man can do at least this much. What else? If the house goes, it goes. What you do about it, you do what you can.

The house shifted again. All this water running in, he

thought, is going to run out sometime. It is going to leave in a bigger and bigger hurry. And the house won't take that. Not weakened and shifting. So we got to make a move or ride it out into the bay later and drown. She put too much weight on him. He gave her a sharp pinch in the butt and slapped his hand back onto the rung. She took a lot of the weight off fast and did not put as much back. He felt a smile stretch his lips and he thought, Are you crazy, Marty Liss? Grome used you for a pigeon. He ruined you. You're going to jail. You got a young wife taking the wrong kind of tennis lessons. Your house is breaking up. You can't think of a thing to keep yourself from drowning, and you got a cramp in your leg, and she's sitting too heavy on your shoulder again, and you're smiling? What at?

After Cole Kimber had given up trying to drive the secondhand custom motor home out of the way of the oncoming storm, he gave careful thought to finding a safe place to park, where water wouldn't rise high enough to drown it, where no buildings would fall on it, and where no flying debris would scar the glossy vanilla-white-with-red-trim surface of his new pet. He was anxious to have Loretta see it, but by the time he got nervous about her being out on the key, the phones were all out and the bridge was jammed open. It began to look as if they wouldn't be leaving Sunday. It might take three days before the area got straightened out and the roads were cleared.

He decided the best place was around in back of Gandey and Mason's warehouse on School Road. It was an L-shaped structure with the point of the L facing west. Bug Mason had once had a warehouse blow down in a storm years ago, and when he had given Cole the contract on this one, he had made certain this one wasn't ever going to blow down. The building was high enough to shelter the vehicle from anything that might come blowing on the wind. It was dangerous but not impossible driving when he tucked the vehicle into the protected corner, backed it in snugly, turned the motor off. The little Onan generator was mounted in a cargo compartment that opened from the rear, but it started from the inside and was husky enough to run the small air-conditioning unit, the inside lights, and one burner on the tabletop range, as well as the small water pump. He drew the heavy curtains and made himself comfortable. The screaming and roaring of the wind around the corners of the warehouse muffled all sound from the generator. Eddies and whirlpools of wind rocked the big camper in a gentle and almost continuous motion. He tried to listen to the CB, but had to turn the volume so high that the speaker diaphragm broke down into a meaningless clatter of sound.

He stretched out on the wide bed and read road maps and travel brochures. He napped, woke up and scrambled some eggs and made a tall bourbon and water, then cleaned up and napped again. Each time he woke up the storm sounded worse.

He was napping again when the storm surge reached the School Road area, bringing in eight to ten feet of water which came curling around the corners of the warehouse to meet in whirling turmoil in the corner where he had parked. There was enough buoyancy in the buttoned-up body to enable the water to lift it and skid it around so that it faced the building before tipping it over. When the generator was killed, he was plunged into darkness. When it went over, a side window was shattered against the edge of the curbing of the parking area, and the water rushing in ended the meager flotation effect. He was completely disoriented, thrashing about in darkness, water rising swiftly around him. He knew he had to find a door and open it and get out. He could not see. Nothing around him was familiar. Surfaces, edges, drawer pulls. He felt exasperated, put-upon. Planned everything so beautifully, and now this. Where the *hell* is the door? He felt glass overhead. He got up onto some solid object. He did not know what it was. He braced himself and got his shoulders against the glass. The last of the air was going fast. He took a couple of deep breaths and held his breath and pushed against the glass. When he made a final mighty effort, instead of the glass giving way, the front of the storage locker he was standing on collapsed. His feet went down into it. He could not yank his right leg loose. He bent down to try to free it and moved slowly, as in a dream. It doesn't make any difference, he thought. Not any at all. He was breathing. His lungs pumped the water in and out. He saw lights behind his eyes. He slid down without panic or urgency, telling himself he would take another little nap and rest up and then try again.

The McGinnitys, Davenports and Forresters had three pleasant adjoining units at the Travel Motor Lodge, just south of the Athens City limits on Route 41 and a mile north of where Woodruff Creek had backed up and washed out the highway.

They had all made a special effort to bring things which would make their stay as pleasant as possible. They had imagined drinking wine and playing cards by candlelight, safe from the storm outside. But water blew in at dozens of little places, sopping the rug and steaming the air. When they tried to get some ventilation, the candles blew out. They could not hear the radio, and they could not play bridge except by writing down the bids and holding them up. Mr. Davenport began having severe attacks of angina, and Mrs. Davenport kept loading him up with nitro, and everybody pretended he was not going to get any worse, because there was absolutely nothing they could do if he did. The constant hard whining whistling roar frazzled their nerves. The women wandered about, picking up the wet towels from the doorsills, wringing them out in the toilets and replacing them. Pete McGinnity drank too much wine. They all fretted about what might be happening to their homes and possessions out on the key.

At about eight thirty Hadley Forrester discovered, with their strongest flashlight, that there was about a foot of water outside, and that was why it was coming under the doors so insistently. The others could not believe it. They had to look too.

When, a little while later, the storm surge swept in over Route 41, the smashing tonnage of water broke down the doors and broke all the windows in the entire length of the motel, and covered it to a depth which left the top of the motel sign out of water and put the long flat roof about three feet under.

It was later estimated that the great surge moved in at a relatively constant depth for about six or seven minutes, was held in stasis there for a few minutes by the seas pounding behind it, and by the velocity of the wind, and then began to move out, slowly at first, then more rapidly than it came in, scouring and guttering, sluicing its way back into the bays and the Gulf. Where the coastal plain had the least elevation, the surge had moved a considerable distance inland, generally up to the contour level of thirty feet above mean high tide. It had come slopping right up to the very doorway of the most secure shelters, and brought two and three feet of water into many others less favorably located.

The runoff quickly exposed all the places it had smashed and covered, tugging movable objects along with it, carrying them for varying distances as it receded.

It left Pete McGinnity wedged under his Cadillac, his mouth packed with mud.

In a small and handsome house five blocks from the bay in the northern part of the city of Athens, Nancy McKay had been spreading newspapers in the hall to soak up the rain spray being blown in around the door when the storm surge reached her home. The house faced west. The wall of water had dwindled to a depth of about three feet above her floor level.

It burst the door from the hinges and knocked her down and floated her backwards into the living room on the muddy crest. She struggled up and was knocked down again by wind and water. She grabbed a chair and got to her feet. Everything was floating and blowing. Everything was mud and stench, leaves, sand, dirt, papers and oily water. Soon it receded, carrying magazines, sofa cushions, throw rugs, books and wastebaskets out the front door, leaving them on the steps, on the lawn and in the driveway.

It took all her strength to shut the doors opening onto the front hall and thus close out the worst of the wind. She trudged through the rain to her bedroom. Dirty puddles were draining down into the spread. All his shoes had drifted out of the closet and lay in random pattern on the carpeting they had selected together.

She sat on the wet bed, hunched, elbows cupped in her palms. She knew that Greg was dead and the house was spoiled, so she reached down into herself for tears and found she had none left.

42

THE STORM SURGE BROUGHT WATER up onto the long porch of the Crestwood Nursing Home and into the ground floor, up to a depth of two feet in the rooms of the patients.

Gus felt the thud when it struck the frame structure. He got up quickly and went down the hall and down the stairs, carrying the big camp lantern with the adjustable one-mile beam set for its widest pattern.

The surge had knocked the front door open, and the huge incoming wind was adding to the panic. Heavy old nurses were galloping and stumbling around the main hallway like the buffalo he had seen once in Africa, spooked by lions. He went to work on the door, and one of the quicker-witted women, half again his size, came to help him, motioning to the others. They managed to brace it shut with a steel chair from the office waiting room.

A big nurse grabbed at him and yelled something he

couldn't understand. His engineer's mind had been at work on the problem of the volume of water and the contour of the land. Water could not get this deep on anything but the most temporary basis, merely because it had such a vast land area beyond the city which it could spread out and cover. This had to be some kind of tidal wave. Clamping the flashlight in his armpit, he tapped his wristwatch, then held up five fingers, then held both hands out, palm down, and made a lowering motion. She nodded and some of the anxiety went out of her face and she sloshed off to tend her patients. The water came halfway up to the fourth step on the staircase. That was his mark. He looked at it from time to time, and when he saw that the dirty water had begun to recede, he went back to Carolyn's room just in time to intercept an old old man in the act of stealing the food. In the bright light of the gasoline lantern, he was stuffing it into a pillowcase. When Gus put the light on him the old man stood motionless and then began to take the stuff back out of the bag and put it back on the bureau. When he was finished he stood with his underlip protruding, tears running down his face, and his right hand held rigidly out, palm up. Gus finally realized what the old fellow was waiting for, so he gave the hand a hearty whack with his own, and the old man fled, head down.

Gus sat back in his chair beside the bed. Carolyn put her hand out and he took it. He looked at her eyes. There was no particular recognition, no fright, no tension. Her face was slack and the eyes looked out of it, bland as wet polished agate. He was glad she was peaceful. She had been irritable for hours, and he had guessed that it was because the television set had not worked since the power went off. She missed the meaningless movement and sound.

He clicked the camp light off, pumped up the pressure in the lantern and sat down to work out a rough estimate of elevations. There was a lot of guesswork involved. This was very flat country. The problem was to get a reasonable estimate of how high that crest had been out on Fiddler Key. He finally found a minimum he could accept. Twenty feet. He could remember no observation of terrain which could cut this estimate. If Apartment 1-C was still standing, it was sluiced pretty clean. Good thing Carrie would never know that. She had loved the place. He had removed all the small stuff of value, relying on Sam Harrison's analysis of where a new pass would cut through the key. But now, of course, Harrison's model was inoperative. Harrison had been computing forces almost in balance—the trapped water trying to escape the barricades of the land itself and the silted passes. With this incalculable tonnage of water inland of the key, the forces were far out of balance, so the sea could cut through at will, in one, three or nine places, gouging torrential channels, guided more by the volume of upland runoff and bay bottom contour than by the width or height of the alternate portions of the narrow key.

Another factor, he remembered, would be the sand shoved up by the hurricane tides and waves. Huge bars would be pulled apart and shoved ashore, millions of cubic yards of sand and shell, and the random dispersal of the new dunes on the key would affect the location of the new passes the sea would cut through it.

No computer model of a storm of this magnitude could be set up in such a way that the contours of the keys could be predicted in advance. One could only say that they would be changed in major ways. Carrie's hand made small twitching motions, and he knew she was asleep. He wondered what dream possessed her, what shape pursued her through the tilted hallways of her damaged brain. The great forces of the world we live in, he decided are wind, water, fire and time. They change all they touch. He gently disengaged her hand and stood up, head to one side, listening to all the deafening tumult, and then went out of the room to hunt up the old nurses and see if there was anything else he could do to help them through the night.

When the storm surge began to run off at increasing velocity, the turbulence reached down through the high level of the hurricane tides and ripped at the surface of the key, setting up whirlpools around major obstructions, guttering the sand and marl and shell. By then the eye of the hurricane was crossing the coastline. At its forward speed of fifteen miles per hour, it took two hours to cross the small city of Venice, one hour to cross Sarasota, fifteen minutes to cross Boca Grande. Winds in the eye dropped to twenty miles an hour. The surf thundered unabated. The sky was clear overhead, and in starlight the huge strange side walls of the cylindrical eye were visible. When the hurricane winds resumed after the eye passed, they came out of the north and, hour by hour, began diminishing.

North of the eye, as the winds changed from east to northeast, the Gulf came tumbling back into the wind-depleted bays. South of the eye, in Palm County, the final great runoff began at one in the morning on Sunday, August eighteenth. All the water, backed up at places such as the headwaters of Woodruff Creek for as much as ten miles from the Gulf, added all its volume to the increasing speed of the dropping levels of bay and Gulf.

For a time the waters flowed across all portions of Fiddler Key and Seagrape Key, turning the hurricane waves back into an erratic and very steep chop, with the wind blowing the spray from the wave crests toward the south.

As the water level dropped, portions of the keys emerged, and the runoff was restricted to narrower and narrower areas. Finally there were but three, and they were scoured deeply into the substance of the keys. They bit more deeply as the level dropped. One pass was formed a mile north of the southern tip of Seagrape Key. Two new passes ate through Fiddler Key. One was just to the north of the south bridge, so close that it took the bridge supports out on the key end and dropped the structure into the bay.

Broad Pass, between Fiddler and Seagrape, was completely accreted with sand brought in by Hurricane Ella. A dune crossed from key to key where the channel had been. The second pass crossed from the Silverthorn tract to the Gulf, and in the hours before dawn it had eaten under Golden Sands, Captiva House and the Surf Club and collapsed them into its awesome current. For a time, each structure, in turn, had obstructed the flow, so that spray leaped high from the places where the current impacted against concrete corners and uptilted slabs and columns piled like jackstraws. But the tireless current worked around and under the jumbles, shifting them, turning them, breaking them up, burying them, sucking the contents out of the little concrete boxes, like a fox at the hen's nest, and spewing the soft fragments out to sea.

On Sunday morning there was a milky, hazy sunrise, and the winds were down to twenty miles an hour. Ella, her mortal balance upset, her fury fading without fuel, was grinding and churning her slow way past Orlando, heading for the Atlantic and her probable rejuvenation.

There were early overflights by the Coast Guard, Red Cross teams, state officials, newspaper and television reporters. They reported the anticipated damages at Fort Myers and Naples and Key West, at Venice and Sarasota and the Tampa Bay area. Heavy wind damage. Wave damage along the waterfront.

But the Red Cross observer radioed back a different message about Athens. "It looks like we've got a full-scale disaster here. Roads in and out of town are gone. I'd estimate heavy loss of life, and hundreds of millions of property damage. Incredible desolation on the keys. Bridges out. Buildings gone. We're going to put down now near the terminal building and see if there's any men and equipment here to get a major runway cleared. We can't raise the tower. I will say right now that what we are going to need here is body bags, food, medicine, mobile kitchens, maybe an air evac hospital unit. It looks to me as if this whole damned place was underwater for a time. Water purification units will be needed. Portable generators. This one is a bitch. A real bitch."

The injured and dying had started to flood the hospitals before dawn, when the wind had gone down enough so people could venture out. With limited power, supplies, treatment was primitive. After the sun was up, people left the Sports Center shelter to go check on their homes. They were shocked by the naked look of the city. The leaves had been blown off the trees, shedded, mixed with muck, echoes plastered against anything which had withstood the winds. The muddy paste steamed and stank and dried pale in the early sunlight.

Few of the cars in the Sports Center parking lot were operable. The ones which started were driven until the owners became convinced there was no clear street they could find which would lead them to their homes. The destruction sickened them. They drove back to the shelter. There was nowhere else to go.

The dying of the sound of the wind had awakened Carlotta Churchbridge just before dawn, and she had awakened Henry. They had found shelter on the second floor of the old Holiday Inn in downtown Athens, two blocks east of the Athens Bank and Trust Company building. The wind was fading rapidly, and by the time the sun came up it was but a stiff breeze from the north. The phone was dead. Carlotta had said their first obligation was to find a way to get word to the kids they were all right. Henry, with the wisdom of other disasters, when he had been flown in to help with the details of embassy administration in times of crisis, suggested she wear shoes she could do a lot of walking in, and slacks. Their window faced the inner courtyard of the inn. All the pool furniture seemed to be stacked in a corner, in a tangle ten feet high, mixed with limbs and pieces of roofing. The once green lawn was mud. The pool was more than full.

He wore a shirt with two breast pockets, and put the little Zeiss binoculars in one, the small Rollei in the other. They ate two of their apples and drank some of their water before they left the room.

There was a hot dank smell in the stairwell, and they found that water had come up to the sixth step above lobby level. The still-wet steps were slimy, and she slipped and caught his arm for support.

There was a bald man in a white shirt and dirty white

pants behind the desk. He was carefully laying out sodden documents on the counter like someone setting up a game of solitaire.

Henry said, "Excuse me, do you know where I could find a working telephone?"

The man said, "This goddam mess! You ever see such a goddam mess? It'll never get straightened out."

"Telephone?"

"They won't come in to work this morning. They're supposed to be here, but they won't come in. I'm the one they'll hold responsible."

"Telephone?" Henry insisted. Carlotta touched his arm and drew him away.

"He can't hear you," she said. "He's in shock. He doesn't really know what he's doing."

They found their car. Carlotta gave a cry of dismay. They had parked it in a slot beside a camper. The camper had toppled onto it, crushing the roof down to dashboard level. Windblown trash was caught in the narrow wedge-shaped gap between the side of the camper and the crushed roof of the car. She was desolate. She loved the car. She talked to it when she drove it, patted it to encourage it to start, always parked it with careful precision.

Holding his arm she kept up her complaint about the smashed car until they came upon the first body. Henry had hoped they could walk by it without her seeing it. But when she stopped and her hands clamped hard on his biceps, he moved her along quickly. It was the body of a young girl in her early teens. She had been pierced clear through, impaled upon a piece of two-by-four which had gone through her chest cavity from side to side. She had been washed into the twisted tangle of the ornamental iron fence which had encircled an old downtown building's shallow grounds, and there the timber had wedged fast, holding her, face up, a foot off the mud.

"Ah, *Enrique, pobrecita . . . pobrecita . . .*"

He saw the tears on her face and stopped and said, "I think I better leave you back at the room."

"No! No! I have to be with you. I must be with you. I'll be all right."

They saw other people moving about slowly, stunned, trying to comprehend the extent of disaster. When they reached the bank corner, he saw that a small car had been wind-rolled right into the bank lobby through the armored glass. A single small weak alarm bell was still ringing, and he guessed that it was on standby battery and probably had been ringing ever since the car had rolled in, across soaked rugs, to come to rest in a welter of crushed executive desks. A fat uniformed guard sat in an office chair just inside the gap in the bank windows, a shotgun across his lap, nodding and then coming awake with a start, nodding again.

The streets at that important corner were impassable, blocked with downed trees, dead automobiles, drifts and windrows of broken junk and an astonishing number of bashed and shattered boats, ranging up to a good-sized ketch which lay across the street at an angle, sticks gone, hull crushed, the hood, grill and front bumper of a small red car peering out from under the weight that had crushed it.

From the strength of Carlotta's fingers he knew she had seen something else which dismayed her. He looked and saw, trapped in the angle of a wall, a heap of dirty white rags. Then he realized that it was a pile of a few dozen seabirds, gulls and terns mostly, and near them, drying in the early sunlight, were three large fish, their eyes popped from their heads and their flotation sacs bulging from their open mouths with the effects of the abrupt pressure change which had killed them. A little meeting of predators, grotesquely far from the sea and the beaches.

He went into the lobby of the office section of the bank building and found the fire door unlocked.

"I'd rather you wait for me here," he said. "I just want to go up where I can see the key and the bridges."

"No. I'll come along."

The air was close, damp and hot in the stairwell. As

they climbed slowly, Henry could feel his shirt beginning to cling to his back. Sweat ran into his eyes, stinging until he had to stop and mop it away. He lost track of the flights. He tried a door and it would not open. They climbed to the next floor. Locked. By peering up the center of the stairwell he could see they only had a few more to climb. If they were all locked it was going to be a discouraging waste of time.

At last one opened, and they went into the wide corridor. From the office numbers he saw they were on the twelfth floor. He led his wife to the west side of the building. There was a window at the end of the corridor. As they approached it they could see the morning Gulf out there, a dancing blue with tufts of white where the wind spilled the waves over.

They reached the window and stood side by side. The window was slightly bleary. Salt had blown against it and dried.

He put his arm around her waist and said, "Oh, dear God!"

"But where *is* it?"

"Orient yourself by the bridge. Jesus, look at the bridge! The whole lift part of it is gone, and the causeway at this end is gone. Out there, where it looks like a great big beach, that's where Broad Pass was. It's filled in. And one new pass is right where that Harrison report said it would be. See that condominium, dear, the tall one that's sort of pale orange? That's the one that was just toward the village from Azure Breeze."

"It's really *gone!*" she said in a strange voice.

"Four of them are gone. And maybe more too, further south. And certainly a couple are gone from the south end of Seagrape. There, you see what looks like some kind of ancient ruined fort on Seagrape? That's the bottom of a condominium. That's what's left."

He remembered his binoculars and took them out, dried the lenses, adjusted them and focused them. He saw two helicopters hovering and dipping over Fiddler Key like slow questing insects. One hovered and moved slowly down until he could not see it any longer. He leaned close to the glass and found the south bridge had fallen, and saw the evidence of the brand new pass from bay to Gulf just this side of the ruined structure.

He said, still searching the scene through the binoculars, "Actually, Fiddler lost its south end, below the south bridge, and picked up a mile of Seagrape. With Broad Pass filled in, it's as if we've got four new keys, the south end of Fiddler, the middle of Fiddler, then the north end of Fiddler joined to Seagrape, and then the north end of Seagrape. Good Lord, dear, you should see the way the sand drifted across both keys. You know, I think Beach Village is just about entirely gone!"

He lowered the binoculars. She was leaning against the corridor wall, tears running down her face. She tried to smile at him and couldn't. "All those people," she said. "All those people who wouldn't leave."

"Not crying over the loss of all your pretties?" he said, trying to make small and gentle jokes, to break her mood of despair.

"Foo. Things are things, no more than that."

"Easy for any rich Guatemalan person to say."

She sobbed and dived against his chest and he held her. "The sons will worry," she said in a smothered voice.

"Okay, we'll go phone them," he said cheerfully.

As they plodded down the stairs he knew that there would be no phoning for quite some time. He had wanted to find other windows and look at the rest of the city and the shoreline, but he did not want to disturb her any more than he could help. Right now this whole area was in that strange hiatus that follows catastrophe, when all the complicated procedures of administration and communication have been shattered. Key people are missing. Nothing is in operating condition. The imperatives are food, water and medical attention, and the identification and disposal of the dead. At the moment no one would know who was responsible for what. Small men would run about blowing whistles and giving orders no one could obey. People would shuffle through the broken trash and wreckage, looking for family and friends. The probable resolution would be the declaration of a condition of emergency, the arrival of some kind of military command—to establish a command headquarters, appraise the situation, clear the airfield, make the streets passable, fly in the generators and the field hospitals and the Red Cross and the food and the water treatment plants and the medical supplies and the network news teams—and, as the situation began to improve, every busybody with any ghost of a reason for coming here to Athens.

When they came out onto the street, a military jeep came along, threadings its way between hazards. It had a tripod-mounted bullhorn and an officer passenger with a microphone held close to his lips. A huge resonated brass bellow was saying, "If you have food and water and shelter, stay where you are. Stay where you are. If medical treatment is needed, hang a white sheet or towel from a window or doorway where it can be seen from the street. An aid station will be set up for this area. You will be advised. If you have food and water and shelter, stay where you are. Stay where you are. Stay where you are."

Henry guessed they had opened the airport and flown these people in. More would be coming. There would be some very bad days ahead. He decided to take Carlotta back to the Holiday Inn and then go find where they were setting up and offer his services.

They walked on the far side of the street from the dead girl-child. As they neared the Holiday Inn they saw a couple coming toward them. They looked vaguely familiar.

"Who are they! Who are they!" Carlotta demanded.

"They're on the fourth floor. That's all I know."

As the two couples approached each other, they all wore uncertain smiles. The man put his hand out. "I'm Howard Elbright. My wife, Edie. Aren't you. . . ?"

"Churchbridge. Henry, and my wife, Carlotta. Six-G."

Edith Elbright said, "My God, wasn't it horrible! I never imagined! We're in the Holiday Inn. The salt water came right into the room."

"We're there too. It was a very rough night," Henry said.

"We were wondering whether we should get off the key in case of a hurricane, and then that report about what might happen . . . that decided us, didn't it, dear?"

"We can't get anything on the little radio. The batteries are dead. We were going to walk down and look across at the key and see if we could see—"

"*Se fué,*" Carlotta said. "Excuse me. It's gone. Gone."

"Gone!" Edith said blankly. "Gone?" Her face began to crumple. She reached out unsteadily to grasp her husband's arm. "All our things. All our good things."

"Along with quite a few people," Howard Elbright said with a note of reprimand.

"Of course. I'm sorry. It's just . . ."

"The bridges are down," Henry Churchbridge said. "And the four condos Harrison predicted would go down. There is a new pass where he said one might appear, and another near the south bridge. Broad Pass is completely out of water. If you could get over there, you could walk to Seagrape Key. But then you couldn't get off Seagrape because there's another new pass through Seagrape. And most of the one-and two-story buildings on Fiddler Key seem to be smashed or gone."

"What are we going to do?" Edith wailed.

Carlotta patted her on the shoulder. "Come on, now. We'll go back to our room. Second floor. The radio works. They don't want us on the street. There's a dead girl over there by that fence. Very sad. You don't want to look at that. Come on, dear."

They turned back. Carlotta and Edie walked ahead. Henry and Howard strolled along behind them. "You were in government?" Howard asked politely.

"State Department."

"I was a chemist. But it looks as if I might be going back to work."

"The legal tangle is going to be beyond belief," Henry said, and tried not to feel too smug about not having to go to work again himself. There was not exactly a broad market for his talents.

43

ON THE LAST FRIDAY in September, Sam Harrison and Barbara Messenger picnicked on that truncated section of Fiddler Key between the two new passes—Saturday Pass, down near the remnants of the south bridge, and Harrison Pass, where the four condominiums built by Marty Liss had stood.

They came out through Harrison Pass on an outgoing tide in the little catamaran Sam had salvaged from the mangrove islands and repaired. Once clear, they beached the cat south of the pass and pulled it up onto the beach before off-loading the towels, beer cooler, food basket, blanket and big yellow umbrella.

It was a perfect tropical day. Breeze riffled the flat blue calm of the sea. Sandpipers ran along the wet sand, legs twinkling, as they stabbed for food. Gulls, on their way by, wheeled close to check them for edibles.

They were on a broad, featureless beach. A quarter mile south there were more picnickers, men surf casting, children throwing Frisbees and running in and out of the warm water.

In the early afternoon Sam saw Mick Rhoades approaching, walking down the gentle slant of beach past the tall, silent, moldering high rise which had been called Fiddler Shores Condominium. Mick wore white slacks and a white straw hat. He carried his white shirt over his arm. His torso was very brown and trim.

Sam opened the cooler and took out a can of beer and held it up. Mick broke into a parody of exhausted running, grabbed the can and dropped into the shade of the umbrella.

"Aren't you supposed to be wearing the sling?" he asked.

Barbara said, "He can have it out for an hour or so every day, to retain muscle tone. But he cheats."

Mick smiled at her. "How is Mr. M coming along?"

"Very mean. As he improves, he gets meaner. He'll be walking again by the end of the week. He ordered me on this picnic, a reward for enduring a lot of mean remarks. If you're through for the day, why don't you wait and sail back in with us?"

"Wish I could. The hearing adjourned early, but I have to go back in and write it up. I'll walk back across that pontoon bridge, and that same jackass will make me show my press pass again."

"Don't you think he looks like a looter?" Sam asked Barbara.

She tilted her head. "Sort of. It's the mustache, I think. It's a shifty mustache."

"I *am* shifty, but not looterwise. Today they took a little more testimony from me, even. The same old bullshit. They thrash around looking for somebody to blame a hurricane on. I didn't handle it as well as you handled your appearance, Sam. You were great. Nobody budged you an inch. Ella did what you said she would do. And more. Now they are wondering why I didn't give your story more early coverage and scare more people off the keys, which would have cut down the body count."

"Any additions?" Barbara asked.

Mick made a face. "A few. One especially nasty one. Some kids were fooling around late yesterday in the new dunes south of Saturday Pass, using a metal detector. They located a big hunk and dug down to it and found themselves a whole Ford Fairlane with what turned out to be a family of five people in it. Male, female and three littlies."

"God," Barbara breathed. "How long can it go on?"

"Quite a while," Mick replied. "Aside from the four hundred and sixty-one bodies, about thirty not identified, we don't know exactly how many are missing. When a vacationing family is wiped out, it doesn't get reported for a while. But they keep crosschecking the power company customer lists and the phone company lists, tax rolls, bank records, vital statistics, vehicle regisistration, Social Security, Veterans Administration and so on. Move people from the probably missing lists to the known missing, and finally to known dead. The body count is maybe a little bit on the inflated side because they include people like Fred Hildebert who died of a heart attack at the height of the storm. If he hadn't then, he would have later, once he found out what a whipping the Athens Bank and Trust is taking on their real estate loans on the keys. Then, of course, there was the trouble with the looters. Those two women who were raped and strangled were put on the list, and so were the three looters shot and killed."

"Why make the list even bigger?" Barbara asked.

"Political," Mick said. "At first the city and county fathers wanted to minimize the extent of damage and the death toll. You know, for the sake of the tourist industry and the retirement market and so on. Then, when they began to realize the dimensions of this whole disaster, they swung the other way. Now, the more they inflate the damage, the more help they can demand from the state and the federal government."

"This will fascinate Lee," she said.

"Also," Mick said, "there is another way the figures get warped. I will venture to say that the known-missing—presumed-dead figure is screwed up by people who saw this one dandy chance to walk out on a lot of responsibilities they had gotten very tired of. People who were in big jams."

"Like you were saying about Commissioner Denniver and his wife?"

"Okay, so I was wrong. Look, Sam, they were ripe for running. Justin was nailed to the wall. So they found them in the mangroves, wrapped around each other, drowned and dead. Funny. She was a strong swimmer. She was a jock, that lady was. Probably Justin started drowning and grabbed her and she couldn't get loose. But I don't think I'm wrong about Marty Liss."

"Even with his wife's statement?"

"Francie said Marty used his belt to fasten her to that ladder they were hanging onto. Then when that wall of the house tilted over toward the bay, he was washed away because he was lower on the ladder than she was. Washed away to where? Brazil? A lot of money has been washed away too. They can't find it. You watch. She'll hang around for six months and then go on a long trip. They cooked it up. I'll tell you, Lew Traff and Benjie Wannover are happy men. With Denniver and Liss and Molly Denniver gone, and nobody able to find Sherman Grome, and a lot of the records missing in the storm, they're home free, both of them. Tell you another one. Young lawyer named Greg McKay. He wasn't getting along with his old lady, and he was having fun and games with a realtor name of Loretta Rosen. She sold out her business and got the money up front, and nobody is going to find *those* bodies either."

Barbara said, "I suppose it does give people a chance to go and try to become somebody else, somewhere else. But wherever you go, you take yourself along, and that self is the same old person who got you jammed up in the first place."

"Nobody ever thinks so, though," Mick said. He had finished his beer. He began pawing out a deep hole to put the empty can in. He dug down and suddenly frowned and looked down into the hole and began digging with both hands.

"What you got?" Sam asked.

"Don't know yet."

They watched as Mick enlarged the hole and plucked out an oblong object with wet sand clotted to it. He got up and took it down to the water and washed the sand off it and brought it back, swinging it by the short length of broken line cord. He smiled in an odd way and said, "Anyone want a perfectly good digital clock-radio?"

"Heavens!" Barbara said.

"I ought to be able to think of something very compelling and significant to say about finding a clock buried in the sands of time, and so forth. But all I can think of is that all this sand, these millions of tons we've got we didn't have before, they are covering up the damnedest collection of plastic and trash and gadgets and kitsch and junk anybody could possibly imagine. Ella was one hell of a housekeeper. She swept everything under the rug."

After a thoughtful silence Sam asked, "Any closer to a decision today?"

"Hell, they've reached a decision, all of them. They just won't say it out loud. That terrible jackass, Tod Moran, he gets the floor and he talks about how with a little help from the state and the federal government, the good citizens of this area will put their shoulders to the wheel and demonstrate the spirit of pioneer America or something, and put everything back just the way it was before.

"Then the Department of Transportation fellow gets up and points out that they have cooperated on an emergency basis with a crash program to put the Tamiami Trail back in passable condition from Venice to Fort Myers, so that people who want to come to this area, or leave it, won't have to head over into the middle of the state first. Then he points out that replacing the bridges would be a minimal four-year program, with an estimated cost of twenty million dollars, allowing for anticipated inflation, and that amount is not in any present or projected budget.

"Next the Corps of Engineers spokesman says that even if they had the technology to change the passes back to their old locations, they couldn't start on it for two years even if they had the funds, which they don't. Then the representative of all the condominium associations gets up, and in that big boomy voice of his he demands that electricity and sewage disposal and water supply be provided to the keys so that the people he represents can move back into their homes. The man from Florida Power and Light then gets the floor and says that in view of the heavy expenses they have undergone to begin to restore full power on the mainland, and in view

473

of the fact that the entire power grid was destroyed on Fiddler Key and the southern half of Seagrape Key, and in view of the fact that no one is in residence out here and no businesses are functioning out here, they have no plans to supply power.

"You've heard it all, Sam. The Fiddler Key Utilities Authority rep says their only option is to default on their bonds and get out of business. Their water mains are gone, their sewage treatment plant is gone, their water purification plant is gone, and they have no funds for replacement. It built up slowly out here. It started slowly. Little wooden bridges. Beach cottages. Sand and shell roads. Water wells and septic tanks. Old Florida. There were fishermen's shacks before the bridges came over. It had to slowly pay its way. The power came when there were enough customers. Funny thing. It can't ever start that way again."

"Why not?" Barbara asked, puzzled.

"My God, the property rights on this island are going to be tied in knots for a hundred years. If a man has a building lot on the bay and the house is still sort of standing, and he survived the storm, okay, it is his. But he can't live in it because all certificates of occupancy have been rescinded on health grounds until there is sewage disposal and water supply and so forth. And there won't be, because there won't be any bridges. Once the Waterway is redredged to depth, they can open it again and the pontoon bridge will have to be dismantled. But take that condo there, behind us. Maybe a hundred units. Okay, a hundred different people own that five acres, right? Some of them died in the hurricane, so those rights are now in estate litigation. What do they do with those rights? What happens? No sale is possible. How about the property rights in Beach Village? They will have to resurvey to even find the property lines. And who is going to pay for a survey? Some will, some won't, and some aren't here anymore. Do the heirs of the people who died in Azure Breeze and the Surf Club own a proportionate share of the land on the bottom of—excuse the expression—Harrison Pass? No, we built the whole thing up to its ultimate, creaky, freaky complexity and it all fell down, and it would cost twice as much to build it up again, so there's no chance."

"I see," Barbara said. "But doesn't something have to happen to it?"

"Every problem has a resolution?" Mick said. He stood up again. "Got to get back, people. Thanks for the beer. On my little dead radio clock here it says half past afternoon. When you see your old buddy Gus, Sam, tell him a lot of people think he's doing a great job."

He went off, dangling the little blue clock-radio by the end of the frayed cord, swinging it back and forth.

"Is that true," Barbara asked, "what he said about it being too far gone to ever build up again?"

"He's right. You can buy all the parts to a six-thousand-dollar Pontiac for thirty thousand dollars."

"What has that got to do with anything?"

"If you damage one fifth of the parts in an accident, and four fifths are okay, you have still totaled your car. Look at all the high rises still standing. Millions and millions of dollars. But the millions Athens will get will go to fixing up all the essential services and roads on the mainland. This place is as dead as Corinth, and after a while all the rest of the survivors will accept that and move their stuff out of the units. Who is going to spend the fifty or so millions to fix the roads, bridges, water supply, phones, electricity, sewage disposal and so forth to put a hundred and fifty million dollars' worth of condominium apartments and a few thousand people back in functioning order on this sandspit? Some of the units have no damage at all. But they are finished. Monuments to some kind of ultimate assininity."

"What did he mean about Gus?" Barbara asked.

"Oh, maybe I didn't tell you. They combined the city and county Public Works Department about two weeks ago and gave him the county too. They got pretty fond of him at the nursing home during the hurricane, so he knows Carolyn is getting a lot of care and attention. Now he's putting in an incredible workday and he's happy as a clam. Gus was always a make-do guy, a very practical engineer. He found some idle equipment in an old county barn last Monday and found a couple of old retired machinists who could turn out some parts for those trucks and loaders, and he's got some of the units rolling already."

"I like him."

"He is one very solid type. What's funny? Why the laughing?"

"That's exactly what Gus said to my husband about you."

"I probably am. I guess I am. It means I know what I am doing, and I get it done."

She looked at him, close range, with an expression he could not read and then got up and walked away, up the beach. He opened another beer, drank half of it and then followed her. She stood near where Harrison Pass had eaten into the sand at high tide, leaving a three-foot drop down to the water. The tide was almost on slack and would soon start coming in.

"Penny," he said.

She turned and smiled. "I don't know. Thinking of people *owning* land. Like the bottom of your pass. People don't really own anything, ever."

"They like to think so."

"They borrow something for a little while. That's all. What will happen to all this, really?"

"I can make a guess. In time, after everybody gives up, maybe a slow process of condemnation, a lawyer's permanent festival, and then turn it into a park. A wilderness park. A marine park. In time they will come around to Lee Messenger for a signature and he can sign away a chunk of the empty air . . . let me see, right about in that direction . . . seventy to eighty feet in the air, the exact size and shape of the apartment you once had. Along, of course, with one forty-seventh of the land at the bottom of the pass."

"I see. And there is a bird flying through it. See? Does it know it is trespassing? A wilderness park might be nice, you know. But they should have somebody here to keep people from leaving the beach looking grubby."

She looked down the length of the key, squinting in bright sun. "Will they have to tear down the buildings? There's dozens and dozens of them still standing."

"I would imagine they'd fence them and put up warning signs so as not to be sued. Conspicuous nuisance problems."

"Look, there is a sort of green fuzz beginning to show above the high-water line, Sam. Things are beginning to grow again. It will be nice here, you know? I wish there would be huge lush vines growing up these condominium towers some day, like some giant kind of ivy, so that it would all be like those old Mexican ruins in Yucatán. A park can be a memorial to . . . I can't say greed and stupidity, really. There was something else, wasn't there? A kind of autohypnosis."

"And human optimism and strange tax advantages. And too much time between hurricanes."

They went back to their portable shade. She sat in grace, looking down, drawing patterns in the sand. He felt as if he dared not draw a deep breath for fear of alarming her in some way. She had a bewildering vitality about her. She was all his magic for all time, but there were no moves he could make. He could not conceive of ever being without her.

She looked at him suddenly, a quick glance which slanted through his heart. He saw the tears in her eyes.

"Barbara," he said in the rustiest of voices.

"No. Just something I want to say. Something I'm learning. I'm only a little way along. It's hard for me to learn. I'm going to need some time."

She stabbed her spread fingers into the sand, picked up a handful, let it trickle out of her fist.

Looking down she said, "What you do is either take no risks or you take them all. I took a risk with you without knowing it, sending you after that fool bull. I can knock on the tin roof of that Ford Fairlane and holler down to those people in there. I can ask them things. Are you sorry you had love? Are you sorry you birthed these three dead kids? My God, when does being a tragic figure turn into a pose? How much bleakness can I stand in my life?" She tried to smile at him then. "What I guess I am trying to say is keep in touch, Sam. Keep in touch. Now please, please, go for about a fifteen-minute hike down the beach."

He walked. His arm was beginning to tire again, so he put it in the sling. When he looked back she was sitting in Buddha fashion, back straight, a distant bright-haired woman looking out at the innocent and harmless sea.

There was a great rush of baitfish a hundred feet off-shore, as something predatory came up under them. Seven pelicans went by, with slow beat and then long glide, close to the water. A gray crab ran sidelong down the beach and popped into its hole. He stopped and looked at a place just above the high-tide mark where a tendril had poked its way out of the sand, unfurling three small pale-green leaves. From that point he could see the city and its tall white bank buildings. Thunder grumbled far away, and he turned and saw that it had become dark in the north, and the breeze was now coming from that direction. He headed back to the woman, lengthening his stride as he saw, in the distance, that she had collapsed the umbrella and was stowing it on the catamaran.